MAGE EMERGENCE

Christopher George

Mage Emergence 1st Edition

This novel is entirely a work of fiction. Any resemblance to actual persons living or dead, is entirely coincidental.

Cover design by Christopher George
Cover photography by Ian Harding Photography
Cover artwork by Megan Owenson
Typesetting by Odyssey Books

ISBN: 648578420
ISBN-13: 978-0-6485784-2-0

DEDICATION

This book is dedicated to my nephew Harrison.

We often write the stories we would have liked to have read as children. You're a little young right now for these stories, but one day I hope you'll come up to me and say 'Cool story, Uncle Chris.'

Stranger things have happened. With much love as always, your uncle.

ACKNOWLEDGMENTS

This book is the final in Devon's story and represents about eight years of work, during which I had to learn how to make myself into the writer that I have become. My high school English teacher would be very surprised at my persistence.

I couldn't have done that without the help of some very important people in my life. As always, Rebecca and Imogen for being patient with me and understanding while I spent untold hours in front of my computer.

To my friends who dragged themselves through my unedited thoughts and story as I sought to bring some clarity to my ideas. You no doubt have a much greater understanding of the insanity that lurks just below my psyche. Thank you, Rebecca Truong, Jane Sandham, Nic Van Arkadie and Don Cameron. I cannot thank you enough.

And lastly, I'd once again like to recognise the efforts of Ian Harding and Megan Owenson. You have been with me since the first book and I cannot imagine that the success I've had with these books would have been possible without your efforts.

Emergence

/ ɪˈməːdʒ(ə)ns/

- the process of becoming visible after being concealed.

- the process of coming into existence or prominence.

PROLOGUE

And so we come to the end. It is fitting that my ending takes place where I began. It is also perhaps fitting that I am surrounded by the ruins of the city in which I was born. This is my legacy. I leave behind me only waste and desolation. Those who come after me will not remember my name fondly. Any friends and family who still remain behind will not even know I have passed. There will be no one to mourn my name when I am gone. Yet, I am content. This is as it should be.

My name is Devon Wills and I am going to die very soon. I can feel it in my bones. I can taste it in the very air around me. With each passing moment I become more certain that I will not survive the night. Even as I kill more of those sent to end me, I know it is simply a matter of time. I have already dispatched three teams of soldiers who sought to kill me, but it will not be such as those that will be my downfall—it will be my former master. I glance down at my watch uncertainly. It's past time. He is late.

My former master is Victor Whittlesea and he is never unintentionally late.

I grip the mobile phone in my pocket nervously as I

glance across the city. I'm not looking at the city as it is now, with its fallen towers and burning streets. I'm not seeing the scavengers hiding in bolt holes and sewers. Their fates don't interest me. I look past the gangs and marauders who have taken control of the streets since all order had fallen. No, I'm looking at the city as it had once been.

God knows it hasn't been perfect—we've had homelessness and graffiti, vandalism and muggings in the past—but it was better than this. It had worked. It deserves better than this. I remember shopping with my father at a small supermarket that was now a pile of rubble. I had eaten at a restaurant that has since been gutted and opened to the elements. I had probably ridden the exact tram car that was now smashed and lying abandoned in the middle of the street.

I don't care to see the people on the street below now, as they fight and kill each other. I know in my heart that many are just victims of circumstance and they aren't truly responsible for their actions, but it doesn't really make much difference at the end of the day. A starving man killing another for tinned fruit is still just as damaged as a psychopath who kills for pleasure. The damage is still done and there is no coming back. I know all too well the damage done by being forced to commit murder. I have killed many times and I will kill again, once more at least.

I still see those who have fallen before me when I close my eyes. I hear their death screams and I remember the light as it left their eyes. Yes, there is truly no coming back from inflicting death. I am broken, but I am not unusual in that. Everyone in the city below me is broken in one way or another. I wonder how many new damaged souls have been created as our 'war' intensifies across the globe. It had begun so simply and has spiralled out of control so quickly.

Our kind spread like wildfire across the globe as we turned upon each other in righteous fury. We fought each other in an attempt to prove our dominance over one another and we had dragged the rest of the world along with us.

I had chosen to stand against my kind. I saw them as nothing more than a cancer on the face of world that needed purging. We were the evil. We were the ones who had started all this. Our quest for power had brought the old world down. I knew the hypocrisy of my statement, as amongst my peers I was the most responsible, but that just meant I had to be the one to do something. Many of my kind had fallen to me, but there were always more. As the war expanded across Europe and then into the United States I realised I could no longer work alone. The collateral damage was too much. This war needed to end.

What had started as a conventional war had twisted into something new, something more dangerous—a mage war. In a conventional war, the winner is usually determined by who has the better tech. A mage war winner is determined by one simple factor—power. Whichever side has the more powerful mages wins.

That didn't matter to me though. With every fallen mage on both sides, my objectives would be furthered. The death of my kind would relieve the shackles held around the world's throat. This war would pass, and people would recover, and the countries and economies would regrow. Soon the world would return to the old ways and it would be as if our kind never existed. I was a fool. It had taken me far too long to see this simple truth: the old world was gone. In the end I was forced to come to the same conclusion as everyone else. There simply wasn't enough left to save. Our war had changed everything.

Only one true relic remains from the old world: my former master. And I am going to remedy that tonight.

Victor is here; he has been for some time now. He isn't hiding from me. He is far too sure of himself for that. So why does he delay? I am here, alone and unarmed. Well, at least as unarmed as our kind can be. Why hasn't he struck me down yet? I'm sure it's not through a lack of motivation. He's already tried to kill me before.

He had almost been successful, too, on several occasions. Instead he had left me crippled and broken. Only my magic prevented my injuries from seriously handicapping me. I had used Mana to make myself powerful once again. I had used it to keep myself mobile. I had used it because I had no other choice. Without my powers I was as feeble as a child, barely able to walk or hold myself upright, but with them I was unstoppable.

Victor and I are probably the last two most powerful

practitioners of our art left. Once he deals with me he will have free reign and stand supreme. His domination will be complete and he will rule over the remains of our planet with a tyrannical fist. The problem is, should I survive, my rule won't be any less brutal. I've already proved I am capable of acts no less savage than his. My evil is just as pronounced as his. It doesn't really matter who wins—our future is fucked either way.

I don't much like my chances of survival, but I am going to fight anyway. Why? Because I have no choice— this conflict needs to end. I know it and so does Victor. All he has to do is come and finish me off. And here I am, standing on a building rooftop in plain sight. Surely this opportunity is too much to pass up? So why isn't he here? I check my watch again.

"Victor!" I call out, using my Mana to amplify my voice. "Come out and finish this. It is time!"

My voice would have been heard across every inch of this city. He would have heard me, but more so he would have felt the Mana surge across the city as I amplified my voice. I can still see the shockwave caused by my Mana passing over the smouldering rubble of once-familiar buildings and across the beloved landmarks of my childhood now falling into ruins.

The loud explosion of sound that usually precedes a teleport spell brings me spinning around to face my old master. It is time. I steadied my nerves as I gripped my fingers into fists. I casually clip the loose battery on my mobile phone into place and close the lid. I carefully flick the phone on, never once taking my eyes from my adversary. The familiar electronic jingle notifies me that it has finished loading and then I drop it into the rubble beneath me as I step forward and look at my upcoming death squarely in the eyes. I will not flinch in the face of it. I am ready.

This is how it ends. It is fitting. Let me now tell you how this begins.

CHAPTER ONE

My eyes flared as the sound of rockets firing overhead blocked out all other noise. I shuddered involuntarily as debris of dust and ash washed over me like a wave of seawater on a beach. I gritted the dirt beneath my fists as I pulled myself back onto my feet and drew upon my powers. The sound of gunfire echoed across my shield as I made my way across the battlefield. I vaguely heard the screams of the dying as I waded through the rubble, but I ignored them. I didn't turn to look at them, I didn't need to see them. I knew they were there and there were too many to count. They either fell because I was unable to protect them or they fell because they chose to stand against me. Either way, they meant nothing to me now.

I burst into the abandoned building at the other end of the field. The bullets on my shield were nothing more than a steady stream of noise. With a wave of my hand I brought the doors barring my entrance to the ground, their fall echoing through the remains of the gutted building. The building shuddered as the doors hit the marbled floor and dust fell from its ancient ceiling. The building at some point must have been a church; it had the look of a place of sacred worship, but now it was nothing more than a barricade to those who would stop me.

I ignored the terrified shouts and further volleys of rifle fire that ricocheted off my shield. I was way past the point where conventional weapons could harm me. Only one thing gave me pause, and that was the figure on the far side of the church crouched behind the over-turned altar.

With a snarl I tore the pews from the floor and sent them smashing out towards the back of the church. The wooden benches did nothing to those huddled behind the altar, but they ended the others who weren't so lucky to be behind solid cover. A vortex of splintered wood and furniture cascaded out in every direction as my Mana tore the place apart.

The Mana signature of the figure on the other side of the church flared in response to my assault. From the look of the flare, the figure was a powerful member of my former order. I couldn't see the figure properly through the shadow and the dust in the room, but the shield surrounding it was impressive. It wasn't a problem though; I'd broken through stronger shields.

I didn't give the mage a chance to strike first. I reached out with both hands and tore the altar from the ground. It was heavy marble; only another mage could have turned it on its side. With a contemptuous flick of my wrists I sent the altar flying backwards, slamming into the crowd it was supposed to be protecting.

They didn't stand a chance. The soldiers using the

altar as firing cover were immediately killed as the several hundred tonne table tore through them. The loud explosion of air and flash of Mana indicated that the weight had been sufficient to bring my opponent's shield down.

The altar had smashed into pieces by the impact and covered a wide area of the church floor. Two large chunks of marble lay over the body of the fallen mage, but I had to be sure. I couldn't leave anyone behind—I'd made that mistake before. It was better to be sure, better to make certain they were dead. I needed to see the Mana fade from their body as their life left them.

I hurled the crumbling marble away as I surveyed my handiwork. The body of the mage lay crumpled on his stomach. No, that wasn't right, my opponent wasn't a man. She was a woman—but the gender of my enemy made little difference. In Mana potential, women were just as powerful as men. I couldn't make out any more details as dust and rubble covered most of the slender woman.

I gazed down on her body. She was obviously dead; her Mana had long since faded. There was no need to look at her face, but morbid curiosity got the better of me. With shaking hands I pulled her over onto her back. I gritted my teeth as I noticed her hair was reddish brown. My breath caught in my throat as her face rolled over into view.

Renee.

My scream echoed throughout my skull and I awoke in a fit of panic and sweat. I had had the dream again. I rubbed layers of grime and sweat from my face as I surveyed my surroundings. It took me longer than it should have to realise where I was. The room around me was utilitarian and bleak. I was in an underground bunker. This room was designed to sleep twelve soldiers, but due to my privilege I was currently its only occupant.

I was grateful for this small mercy. I wouldn't have wanted any to witness my sleep. As far as the others were concerned, I didn't need sleep, I didn't need air—hell, I didn't even need food. I needed this illusion to be maintained. If they learned I was just as clueless and directionless as they were, they would turn on me in an instant.

I pulled myself up from my bed, using my arms to support my weight. I cursed the numbness in my legs that meant this was a necessity, but there was nothing I could do about that. I glanced briefly at the clock. It's flashing digits told me that it was 3:00am. It was too early to get up. It didn't matter much though, I had no intention to returning to sleep. I pulled my feet from the bed and gently rested them on the floor.

I grimaced slightly at the painful sensation of setting my feet on the solid concrete. It was a bittersweet pain. It meant I wasn't totally paralysed, but I wasn't getting any better either. I grunted as I activated the Mana that would restore my motility. Using my Mana to support my actions had once been a huge drain, but I had quickly learned to compensate. I would never be an athlete or be able to move spryly, but I could move around without being dependent upon others, and that was all that really mattered.

I sighed as I used my powers to pull myself to my feet and willed my legs to make me walk. The walking was an unnecessary affectation. I didn't need to make myself walk; I could have simply glided across the floor like a ghost, but I didn't want that. I didn't want anything that would make me seem weak. I could walk, I wasn't crippled. I was strong. No one could say otherwise. I wouldn't allow anyone to see otherwise.

I pushed the door to the bathroom open and blinked as the lights flickered on. This bathroom was again meant to serve a dozen soldiers; again it served only me. I moved over to one of the sinks and ran some water over my face. I gazed into the mirror with disdain. I needed a haircut and shave, but again these civilities didn't really matter much in this time either. Most of my soldiers sported similar growth. No, it was my scars that bore my attention. My face was calloused and cracked, sporting ugly scars that ran the length of my features. My skull had been fractured and broken in my final fight with my former master and I bore the marks of this defeat for all to see. I ran my fingers across the length of one scar. It wasn't such cosmetic damage such as these scars that worried me; it was the internal—the psychological. The dreams were happening more regularly.

It wasn't always the same dream, but it always ended the same way. I pulled my enemy over and it was Renee. It was always Renee. The thought sent shivers down my spine. Every time I was called into action I wondered if this would be the time that it happened for real, that this would be the time I would be forced to stand against her.

I had fought in over forty battles with my kind, and the thought I would have to face Renee terrified me every time. I hadn't seen her for six years, since I had left her in Paris to rescue my sister. Looking back, I wonder if she had seen the future, if she had somehow known what fate awaited us. She had claimed she was going off the grid, hiding out from our kind as much as the real world. I hoped she had managed to hide herself deep. I hoped she was well enough hidden that I would never find her. God I hoped she was safe. I was aware of the hypocrisy of my philosophy, and it tore me apart. Our kind must die. I knew this for a fact, but not Renee. Dear god, not Renee. I couldn't do that.

I scowled as I looked at my haggard figure. The fear in my eyes was almost tangible in my reflection. I clenched my fists into the metal frame of the washbasin. I hated the fear reflected in my features. I loathed the fact that I should feel this way. I was more powerful than I had ever been, and yet my fear hadn't subsided. I could perform feats that even two years ago would have humbled all but the most accomplished of my kind, and still I feared. This wasn't the way it was supposed to be. How strong would I need to be before the fear left me? How many would I need to bend to my will before I finally conquered my own demons? What did I have to do to defeat this fear?

The truth of the matter was that I simply didn't know and I was starting to believe I would never know. I wasn't sure anymore that I would even recognise myself without the fear in my eyes. It was the only feature that remained within me that bore any resemblance to who I had been. I didn't recognise the cracked and scarred face, nor my hardened and bitter eyes. Even my voice had turned into a harsh rasping whisper. I would be all but unrecognisable to those who had known me as a child. But the fear, yes that was mine. In that fear I could finally see myself. I had nothing left of myself but my fear. Where had things gone so wrong?

I closed my eyes and moved away from the mirror. My reflection contained no answers, merely condemnation, and I had had enough of that. I had a whole world for that—a broken, desolate and destroyed world. A small tremor shook through my arms and I gripped my hands around the basin until it passed. They were happening more often now. I wasn't sure if the tremors were a product of my injuries or something else, but they were becoming more common.

In my last fight with Victor, he had completely destroyed me, including fracturing my skull, caving in my chest, and breaking almost all the bones in my arms and legs. Three scars ran across the left side of my face where my head had been crushed. The doctors had told me I was lucky to be alive, but I didn't feel lucky. No, I felt that Victor had intentionally left me alive to suffer. He had humbled me intentionally, knowing exactly how far he could hurt me without killing me. There was no other explanation. I don't believe in luck—If Victor had meant to kill me, I would be dead. The only thing I couldn't figure out was why he had left me alive. He normally wasn't one to gloat in the suffering his victims. I didn't understand Why I was still alive and that scared me. It made no sense. He should have killed me. I knew him enough to trust in that. So why hadn't he?

Another tremor shook my hand as the fear set in again. I thought I had the tremors under control, but clearly they weren't. They only came upon me when I relived my battle in Melbourne. My memories of the event were sketchy at best. I mostly just remembered the pain. I had been a fool. I was nothing more than a bug to him then, and he had swatted me with righteous fury. He had shown me just how much more I had to learn. He hadn't just defeated me—he had destroyed me.

I had thought that defeating Marcus meant that Victor, too, would fall beneath me. I should have known better. After all, even Marcus had determined he would need six of our kind to defeat his former master. What arrogance to think I would be sufficient where six had failed? It took several minutes until the fit passed. I turned away and left my reflection of my fears in the mirror. It would be there waiting for me when I returned. I knew this, it always was.

* * *

"Report," I ordered crisply as I stormed into the command centre. Soldiers on either side of me stood to attention as I brushed past them. I could see them glance nervously as they saw my feet glide over the floor without seeming to move. I ignored them. My senior officer glanced up at my entrance without drawing to attention or saluting. That was fine. I never expected such displays from my subordinates. I was no soldier and had no need for such ceremony. They did what I asked them, that was enough.

"Scouts report an increase of activity in sector twelve," he grunted with a wry grin. Marcellus had been my senior officer now for five years. He had served me well and had been promoted when my last senior officer had been killed in action. I hadn't thought much of it at the time, but Marcellus had proved competent and loyal. He did the job well.

"I thought we had previously cleared that area," I rumbled.

"We thought we had," Marcellus commented. "There must have been bunkers or an underground complex we missed."

"How many?" I grunted, indicating the insurgents.

"Preliminary reports indicate only a few," Marcellus responded quickly.

"Any mages?"

"Our scouts returned, didn't they?" Marcellus grinned in way of answer.

I nodded grimly.

We had been chasing this group for approximately six months now. When the mage wars had broken out, small splinter groups of insurgents had seen their chance to grab power. Most allied or were quickly dominated by mages and turned into local muscle. This particular group was working with Killian Voll. He led the largest contingent of enemy mages and was probably just as responsible as I for this whole war. I had been chasing him for six years, and he had managed to elude me completely. He had been one of the more outspoken mages towards the start of the war, but I hadn't heard anything from him in years. It was possible he was already dead. He could have easily been dispatched in any number of mage battles in the last few years, but I didn't think so. Killian was the most probable leader of our enemies, and I doubted that he'd simply disappear into the night. I actually had no idea how many of my kind remained. We didn't exactly claim credit when we killed one of our own. It was merely something that needed to be done.

Eventually the fighting coalesced into two sides as the fighting intensified. Some, like myself and others that worked for allied forces, did so because we were attempting to bring about peace. I knew such concepts as peace was a lie. That we couldn't have peace until our kind were swept from the world, but I couldn't do that alone, at least not yet, so I worked with other mages. Our foes banded together because they had no choice, but there wasn't any real loyalty among them. They would turn on each other if the opportunity arose. It was as if we as a collective species had gone insane. We no longer considered ourselves human and we had turned on each other and torn each other to pieces. It was sickening. I had seen mages in the midst of savage battles with each other only to gang up and turn on me when I arrived, as I was the more powerful threat. We were truly sick and we no longer deserved our place on the planet. This was a fact and it was a goal I was going to realise.

It wouldn't be easy. As we had turned on each other, greater and greater feats of Mana were required to overcome our foes. The victors of each fight became more powerful through contests, and the survivors were very powerful indeed. Each battle led to an increase in power, each victory led to a new threshold of control that could then be turned upon the next target. At first the battles had been fairly containable; however, this had quickly spiralled out of control. The last mage I had fought had been able to bring down buildings with a wave of his fist. When we fought now, countless others paid the price. As most of the fighting took place in cities, our battles were claiming many thousands of casualties each time we met, and yet the fighting continued. It would keep going, until there was only one side left and even then, I suspected we would simply turn on each other. I knew I would.

I had heard no word of my former master in this time, but I assumed he was in hiding. His plans had been smashed to pieces by Marcus Devereaux. The mad man who had started all this, although to be fair I don't think he had envisioned this hell hole of a world as the outcome. He had simply attempted to overthrow the monster that had been Victor and set himself up in his place. He could not have seen that others of our kind would use the conflict as an opportunity for themselves. He had been a fool, and we had all payed the price. Fool though he was, he could have perhaps prevented this; unfortunately I had killed Marcus in the same battle he had attempted to destroy Victor.

With Victor discredited, Marcus and the Primea dead, there was no one able to reign in the more destructive instincts of our kind. I cannot imagine the carnage that had been wrought the first six months of our war. I had been horribly injured in my fight with Victor and had been moved to a safe location. I had been spared the massacre of our kind as the old and weak had been hunted down and destroyed by the strong. I had been protected from the predations of our kind on the world. I had seen video clips of atrocities performed by mages who had lost their humanity. Many claimed to be gods. But when gods fight, it is the common man who suffers.

I was now tearing across what had once been rural United States searching for my kind with the intention of bringing them to justice. This was a fool's errand; I no longer sought to capture them. There was no point—anyone capable of being captured wasn't a problem. The directive of my orders aside, I never captured anything anyway. That wouldn't serve my purposes.

The fighting here was long over, but the damage was done. The land war that preceded us was the first to be fought on American soil since the Civil War and it had torn the country a new one. I didn't much care for the land war and at one point I thought it likely we were going to lose. They had swept us out of Europe, across the Atlantic and across the States. Yes, we were losing, but somehow we didn't. Our enemies must have overstretched their reach because they crumbled about a year ago. We began to push back on all fronts and we reclaimed lost territory. What remained was nothing more than a mop-up job. The enemy soldiers weren't much of a problem. No, the real problem were the mages. Although the war was all but over, my kind didn't exactly follow the rules, and unchecked they could cause chaos. The real problem was finding all of them before they found us.

Marcellus would return with his report once this next den of insurgents was cleaned out. We had perfected this technique through years of practise. The team would go in. I would remain behind. Should a mage be present, I would be brought in to deal with them. Should a mage attempt to flee the site, I would stop them. Marcellus knew his team was nothing more than bait for the wolf, but as bait goes he was very crafty and cunning bait. He wouldn't be caught easily; he knew the risks and knew when the odds weren't in his favour. That was why he had survived for so long. All I had to do was wait and see what quarry my bait caught.

* * *

"It was just a small group this time," Marcellus reported back, "mostly non-combatants."

This was becoming more common every time the team went out. Large portions of society had been displaced during the invasion. Cities seemed to be the preferred sites for mage battles and this made them horribly unsafe for everyone else. As the population was displaced from the urban centres, they swarmed out into rural areas. Farms and small towns were ill-equipped to deal with the influx of people and had quickly fallen prey to chaos. Small communities turned into armed camps as they fought to keep control of their land and property. Riots and even small mundane battles had been fought over control of resources that up until recently would have been worth little. Those who remained in the cities fared no better. Order collapsed pretty quickly as looting and rioting spread throughout the cities and people were pushed out into the suburbs and outskirts of each city.

Marcellus's report was unnecessary. I had used my powers to observe the team in their mission. I knew exactly what they had encountered and how they had progressed, but I didn't want them to know this. They didn't need to know the extent of my powers. Their mission had gone exactly as planned, but I wasn't surprised—this wasn't the first time we had done this. We would send scouts out to stir up any resistance; should we find something, a more prepared team would be sent in to nullify matters. The only people in any serious danger were the scouts; we had about a two to three ratio of fatalities. Unfortunately there was no other way—if I used my powers to search an area there was a very good chance they would be spotted by enemy mages and a direct fight would ensue and people would die anyway.

I trailed my finger along a scar on the left side of my face as I pondered what to do next. I had had high hopes that we would have stirred up mage activity in this mission. We had been following the activities of a mage known as Gregory Tibus, who had been considered a senior compatriot of Voll. I had hoped that finding Tibus would lead us to Voll. But this looked like a another dead end.

Tibus was Greek born. I hadn't heard much of him from before the uprising. I had heard that he had allied himself with Victor, but that had obviously changed. Most mages seemed to be out for themselves now, trying to carve up the world into little kingdoms of power, especially now that the fighting had died down. In some ways the fighting between our kind was more vicious than it had ever been.

"What's next?" Marcellus grunted. "This was obviously a waste."

I inwardly cursed. Marcellus was right. This had been a waste of time. Our scouts had found nothing and I concluded that no mages had been present in the sector. Unfortunately, in this instance I was wrong. I didn't find out about the mistake until several seconds later, until the distinctive sound of a teleportation brought me spinning around in surprise. I hadn't sensed a thread large enough to contain a mage anywhere in the vicinity.

It was unusually bold of someone to teleport in like this. If I had caught the teleportation thread mid-stream, I could have easily scrambled the incoming mage, scattering them across a wide area. My shield sprang around me as I expected a mage to launch an attack directly at me. But it was only a small box that had been teleported into the room. It didn't look dangerous, but I knew it for what it was. It was a bomb.

I cursed inwardly. This gave me two options. I could remove the bomb before it detonated, or I could follow the scry thread that had left it here. I only had a few seconds before the thread would dissipate to the point that I could no longer track it.

I chose the second option.

I closed my eyes and sent out my own scry thread. It was indeed a fortunate day for me. I had been quick enough to see the disappearing scry thread as it arched across the horizon. Scry threads are normally difficult to see, but this one had been constructed by a poorly educated mage. This wasn't to say it wasn't powerful, it was it just wasn't built very well. It was sloppy and that made it all the easier to track.

My own thread trailed along after it, following it back to its owner. I had no idea if the other mage knew he was leading me back to his base. It took several more seconds before a loud explosion of sound and pressure hit me. My shield absorbed the impact easily, and I had become disciplined enough not to let something as trivial as an explosion distract me from my arts. The scry thread led me past sector twelve and my heart sank as I realised where the thread was heading.

New Haven.

New Haven was a settlement that had sprung up after the main war had spread further south. It was mostly made up of refugees who had fled from the intense fighting to the east in cities such as Chicago and New York. They had had a hard journey as they crossed the great American wasteland. Untold thousands would have died on the journey, with enemy forces on their tails. They must have thought that once they reached here they would be safe. They had been told that Seattle was still standing and in our control. While this was true, cities just weren't safe anymore. Dozens of small camps were set up in the national parks on the east coast as people fled the cities.

New Haven had so far managed to elude becoming a target, but it had really only been a matter of time. A lot of people had moved there after their homes and lives had burned down around them. It was usually small groups of insurgents who took control of these camps, trying to scavenge or steal any medical or relief supplies these settlements received. It wasn't usually our enemies though.

I gritted my teeth as I realised these people would probably go through it all again. We would not be able to displace this mage without massive collateral damage. I didn't dare go close enough to the settlement to determine which mage had decided it was time for me to die. Knowing where he was would be enough for further action to be taken. Unlike his thread, my scry thread was well formed and would be difficult to track. They would never know I had followed them. I would send a team of soldiers in later and I would be leading them. This of course assumed that anyone had survived the bombing. I blinked as my thread disappeared across the horizon and back to my body.

I immediately coughed as I glanced around my command centre. It had been completely devastated. Marcellus was attempting to free someone from under a chunk of concrete that had fallen from the roof. I quickly counted at least five dead and numerous wounded. Marcellus didn't seem to be that badly burned, but others hadn't fared so well. With a flick of my wrist I raised the slab of concrete to allow Marcellus to free the fallen soldier. Marcellus glanced at me with a strange look of both thanks and anger. He knew I could have prevented this and had chosen not to. Removing the slab had done little; the solder was already dead, probably killed instantly in the blast.

"Did you find him?" Marcellus breathed out as he let the soldier fall to the ground.

I nodded briefly. "Let's make sure he pays due price for this."

"Teleporting bombs." Marcellus sighed. "That's a new one."

"Maybe, maybe not. Clean up this mess," I ordered curtly.

"Yes, sir."

I didn't wait around to see if he followed my orders. I didn't particularly want to be around for the clean-up either. Four men had died because of my decision to pursue the Mana thread, and there were those amongst my men who knew I could have prevented it. There would be bloody payment required for this. I may have been partly culpable in allowing this to happen, but I wasn't the one responsible.

Marcellus reported that the command centre had been restored several hours later. I ordered him to assemble a team. We would need to move fast if we were to catch this mage before they fled. I hadn't seen any follow up scry threads, but had they attempted to survey the results of their bombing they would have known it was largely unsuccessful. They would either continue to attack or flee. Either way, we needed to move fast. We were running out of time.

Marcellus assembled the team in record time. I had a feeling there had been many volunteers to make this mage suffer for their actions. I marched out into the clearing where the small number of soldiers had assembled.

"All accounted for," Marcellus reported crisply. I nodded briefly as I glanced at the soldiers in front of me.

"Gentlemen, our target is New Haven."

"Civilian settlement?" One of the soldiers cocked his head.

"Civilian settlement hiding a mage," I corrected. "That will be the end of the discussion from this point.

Those of you who have worked with me before, you know the drill. Those of you who haven't, try to stay out of my way."

* * *

New Haven was approximately three hours' drive north from our position. The roads in this area had long been cleared of debris, but I could see the burnt out husks of cars and trucks as they lay upon the roadside. The war hadn't really ever claimed this area of land, although there had been sporadic outbreaks of fighting. This area was supposed to have been cleared of enemy troops. It was infuriating, but understandable. Teleportation gave mages the ability to move far quicker and further than conventional troops. In some ways, small groups of insurgents were far more dangerous than regular corps.

I didn't really understand what I was doing here. Sure, I was taking out a mage far behind our lines, but I would be far more useful elsewhere. I was easily the most powerful mage we had. I should be on the front line where I would be more effective. Why Command had me chasing down small pockets of resistance far within our own borders was beyond me. Conventional combat tactics had already failed us; why the hell were we still trying to use them? Perhaps it would have been better to just deal with the problem myself, but that would make me no better than any of the mages who had joined our enemies. We were fighting this war in the wrong way, but those in a position of power didn't seem to realise it. It had already almost cost us the war. I didn't exactly understand why we hadn't already lost. It looked almost certain two years ago.

I was reminded briefly of General Hanagan. He had been an American general at the beginning of the outbreak, and had thought he could contain the threat with troops. He had been wrong; he had chosen to escalate with the threat of bombing. I sympathised with him a little; he had been completely outmatched by our kind, something that he hadn't understood at the time. I often wonder if he realised how stupid he had been at the end? My sympathy for the man only went so far though. Chicago was now a smouldering nuclear wasteland thanks to him. He had learned from his mistakes eventually, but by then it had been too late. With a good portion of his forces either destroyed or defected, he had been routed and eventually killed before anyone could extricate him. It had taken us a long time to recover from that defeat. He had thought the threat of bombing would keep his enemies in check. He was a fool. Nuclear power wasn't going to win this war—both sides seemed to realise that. In fact, Chicago had proved that our nuclear arsenal would simply become a liability. I didn't know if Hanagan had thought nukes were a good idea or if one of the mages had acquired one somehow. In the end it didn't matter much. A good many people had died who didn't need to, and the fallout from the incident had the military scrambling to destroy or secure its nuclear arsenal.

They were now only a liability that your opponent could use against you.

Most of the Eastern American continent was now a battleground, or had been at one point. The massive invasion of troops led by mages had swept across the country, and the American military was spread too thinly throughout other theatres to do much about it. It looked at one point like they were going to wipe us completely off the continent. That didn't happen, but our forces were pushed further west every day; we simply didn't have the numbers of mages that our opponents seemed to have. As they pushed us back across the landscape, they left nothing but burned cities and towns behind them. We were powerless to stop them. I still don't understand how we managed to resist them, and I don't know why it looks like we are now winning.

The countryside here actually looked relatively intact, if you discounted the odd burnt out vehicle on the side of the road, or ignored the occasional burnt out farm house. I knew this wouldn't last; as we got closer to New Haven the landscape would change. The scars of our battles would become more visible.

I let only my body travel with the convoy, my mind had no need to. I could have been in New Haven in the blink of an eye. I did, however, scout out the path for the vehicles using my powers. It was a good thing that I did too. Someone had anticipated an attack and had laid an ambush. It would probably have worked too. Had I not stopped it.

The ambush was simple enough: a burnt out bus had been pushed across the road to prevent thoroughfare and a small group of soldiers were lying in wait. It was almost like they knew when we were coming. It was possible that they did. I had to assume that my mage counterpart was also scouting ahead.

The enemy soldiers looked more like kids than military; they had either been forced into insurgency or simply had a taste for chaos. Either way it didn't change things. They were in my way. As I scouted about, it didn't take long to notice the rocket launcher they had, along with enough armament and ammo to take out a small army. They were definitely well supplied. I vaguely wondered where they were getting their equipment from. I would have to investigate that later, but for now their armament could be used against them.

A grenade tossed into a box of rockets brought a quick end to their ambush. They hadn't even known anything was wrong until one of their own grenades seemed to jump by its own volition into an ammunition case and pull out its own pin. The explosion rocked from the ammo box like wildfire, consuming the enemy instantly. There were no survivors. With a contemptuous flick I sent the blocked bus sliding out of the way. If it weren't for the small plume of smoke from the explosion, my soldiers never would have known an ambush had been planned here.

I quickly found and dispatched two more groups that had been lying in wait. The last group appeared to be attempting a hasty retreat. Someone knew we were coming and was trying to protect their troops. Their foreknowledge hadn't saved them. It had probably only bought someone some time, but then again that may have been the whole point of the exercise.

When we arrived at New Haven, we found it had been completely locked down. This wasn't unexpected. What had been unexpected was the twelve people tied to stakes at the gates of the settlement. It didn't take too long to figure out their strategy. Hostage negotiation.

I wasn't surprised when a Mana thread snaked out from the settlement and found me. I identified it long before it reached me and concluded its intention. I also wasn't surprised when a soft voice whispered in my ear through the thread. A Whisper thread, rudimentary magic—nothing special.

My opponent wished to discuss terms.

"You see what lies before you. I will execute these people and it will be on your head. Leave now or these people will suffer for your intrusion."

I wasn't sure if my opponent could hear me or not. The whisper thread he had used could be sufficiently augmented to include hearing, but it required skilful manipulation of the technique. Nothing I had seen so far indicated that he had learned sufficient skills for such a feat. His displays so far had all been about raw power. It was probably safer to assume he couldn't hear me. It didn't matter in the long run anyway. I had no intention of negotiating with him. The people tied to the stakes were already dead, I would bet my life on it. Fortunately I didn't have to gamble. My opponent knew that normally I would need to scry to inspect the hostages. I also assumed that should I attempt to scry across the field, I would be met with resistance. He had been counting on it. The moment I attempted to scry, I would probably receive another threat of the hostages' deaths.

Fortunately I had other options. I hadn't been idle with my studies since the war had begun, and I, like my master, had turned my studies into a very dark area. I used my powers to enhance my eyesight tenfold, allowing me to see details clearly from a distance. I could make out the creases on their clothes and the lack of movement that would normally be associated with death. There was no movement. These people were definitely dead. If my observational skills were wrong, then the Mana reinforced my conviction. There was no doubt, these people were already dead. They had most likely been killed through asphyxiation and they had been killed recently—their bodies were still warm. This was more than just a warning to me. They had been killed as both a threat to keep us away and as a warning to those who remained inside. There were people inside who weren't happy about the new inhabitants. This was a bluff and a good one. Unfortunately it would fail. They couldn't possibly have known I would be able to see through it from this distance.

I nodded to Marcellus. I wasn't sure if he had heard our opponent's voice earlier. Our opponent could have simply wished for only me to hear his voice. Marcellus nodded back. He had identified their targets. We had done this dozens of times before. Keep the mages focused on me, keep the soldiers busy while my team took aim. A sniper shot would take out enemy soldiers while I dealt with the real threat.

I began walking towards the gates slowly, as if I had all the time in the world. I let the Mana rise up in me with every step, letting it flow through me in a display of raw power. I amplified it, enhanced it, and let it emanate from me like a lightning storm.

"You're killing them," the voice whispered in my ear. He was referring of course to his 'hostages'. I ignored him. I wondered how long it would take until he realised this wasn't going to work.

I knew that once I had reached a suitable distance, the sharpshooters within my squad would deal with whoever had been foolish enough to remain in sight. This should keep any stray gunfire from me. I wasn't worried about the gunfire. They would have to hit me with something akin of a howitzer to even dent my shield, but keeping the defenders busy would keep them focused on what I was about to do and not my soldiers.

With my enhanced vision I could have torn the gates off the walls at any point, but I wanted to be closer. I could also have teleported into the compound at any point—again I didn't want to. I needed to minimise damage to the facility and any non-combatants inside, and to do that I needed them to keep their focus on me.

"Stop! Now!" the voice demanded in my ear. I could hear the panic in his words. "Don't make me stop you!"

He was bluffing. What could he do? Any attempt to teleport out wouldn't end well, an attack would be clearly seen, and I would have time to prepare an adequate defence. He would attack me eventually and then I would counterattack and he would fall. That was exactly what I wanted. Keep the fight outside of the inhabited areas—less collateral damage.

He let me get further than I had thought he would before he launched his attack. The tell-tale flare of Mana caused me to involuntarily flinch and I waited for the inevitable impact against my shield. It took several seconds before I realised I hadn't been his target. A column of Mana rose from the settlement and into the sky. The power being expended was mindboggling. I gazed in wonder at the sheer forced being expended into the sky. A haze of Mana issued out from the burst as it impacted its target, and tendrils of lightning flashed as the Mana merged with the atmosphere. Clouds heavy with Mana were forming. The display was impressive. I wondered vaguely where he had learned to do this. This required skill, more skill than he had displayed so far. As the clouds expanded across the settlement, they grew darker with Mana each passing moment.

It had all happened within seconds. Impressive though it was, I still didn't see the reason for all this effort. What was the point of all this power? Fear crept into my mind as I pondered the possible ramifications.

From this distance I couldn't exactly study the configuration of frequency of the Mana being used, and that worried me. Anything that I didn't understand could possibly be used against me. An unknown threat was one that could possibly finish me. Perhaps he had lured me into my death? I didn't have to wait long before the threat was made clear. The clouds burst open once they could contain no more Mana. The oxygen in the sky mixed with the Mana heavy-particles and caught fire. My enemy had set the sky on fire.

As the first droplets fell on my shield, I knew that this wasn't normal fire. This was Mana fire. Not quite as powerful as the supercharged Mana that I used to power a Mana Nova thread, but equally dangerous. My shield could probably withstand the downpour, but my surroundings wouldn't and my soldiers definitely couldn't.

As I looked around, I saw the grass had already caught fire and thick black smoke emanated in every direction. This changed things. I ordered my soldiers back. The Mana fire hadn't reached them yet, but it would. It was expanding exponentially. The soldiers needed to leave; they would not be able to survive long under these conditions. I received a terse reply from Marcellus that he would pull his troops back to a safe distance. I vaguely wondered how far a safe distance was as the temperature increased. It didn't take long before I needed to modulate my shield to withstand the heat, but I didn't want to completely reconfigure my shield—I had seen too many fall through that mistake. Fortunately I didn't have to completely change my shield. It wouldn't tax my reserves too much to simply increase the flow of Mana and rein-force my defences. I smiled as the heat immediately disappeared. I was standing in a firestorm completely unharmed and completely safe. Even so, it wouldn't be smart to stay there as eventually I would become unable to power a shield of this strength. I mentally applauded my opponent; it had been some time since I had been forced to actively focus on shielding myself. This put a time limit on events. The smart thing to do would be to teleport out, but I couldn't do that. My opponent would be waiting for such a thing. I really only had one option, and that was to make my way into New Haven and deal with my opponent before my strength gave out.

I moved on. I didn't bother simulating walking—that was a luxury I could no longer afford. I glided across the landscape as a ghost passing easily across this hell scorched earth. Embers and flame were cast in all direc-tions as my movement displaced the air in the inferno. I didn't seek the safe path; I simply took the most direct path through the fires to the settlement.

New Haven hadn't fared any better than the sur-rounding grounds—the fires had struck it as well. This hadn't exactly been a subtle attack. The buildings in the centre of the settlement were already aflame and the walls, largely made out of wood, had almost crumbled into the flames. I imagined that the shanty town that had made up the majority of the settlement was already nothing more than ash and charred wood.

I couldn't see my opponent through the fog of ash and smoke, but I could see his Mana signature. He was doing as I was: waiting it out. I could hear the screams of people within the settlement, but there was nothing I could do to save them. Even If I attempted to disrupt the effect in the sky above, it was too far spread out for me to completely stop it.

The fire storm had been a very effective way of keeping me at a distance. No one in their right mind would have attempted to pass deeper into this hell. But I was too powerful to be cowed by such a display. Maybe three years ago I would have teleported away rather than bear such onslaught, but it was different now. I could endure this punishment easily and would eagerly do so than let my quarry escape. For all the destruction it had caused, the Mana storm had merely delayed the inevitable. We were at a stalemate, neither of us would teleport while the other waited—that would invite a messy death. And so we waited each other out as I crept closer to the blaze.

It must have taken me ten minutes to reach the charred remains of the gates of New Haven, but my eyes never left my opponent's Mana signature. Any change, any rise towards teleportation would result in instant death. His Mana levels never wavered. He knew as I did that escape wasn't an option. As I got closer, I could see his shield through the smog. It wasn't impressive in itself, but it was modulated against fire. This mage wasn't totally without skill.

With a shield like that it would not be taxing himself

too much to maintain his shield despite the hellfire he had created. If I could see him, then he could also see me and I wasn't going to give him the option of first strike. No, this needed to be over, and over quickly. I used my powers to fly into the air, the motion showering fire rain in every direction as I launched myself at him. As I got closer I could see my opponent appeared to a teenage boy, no more than sixteen at most. As a mage he was more dangerous than any adult, and judging from the inferno he had unleashed on New Haven he was definitely not a weak mage, he was simply inexperienced. That would be his undoing.

There was no subtlety in my attack: it was brutal and direct. I impacted his shield as hard as I could and sent him flying into a flaming wall. The building promptly collapsed on him as the impact tore out its weakened supports. This wasn't going to be a challenging fight. His shield had held, but only barely. It hadn't been modulated to cope with physical damage, and he was weak. I had no idea if he had expended most of his power in the firestorm or if he was merely lacking in power. I had to assume the former. He wouldn't have lasted this long during the mage wars if he was actually this weak. My opponent had been right to try to keep me at a distance. He had known that once the true mage fight started, it would be over quickly.

I saw him rise from the ruins of the building and attempt to draw his powers against me, but it was too late. Several threads lashed against him as I attempted to overpower his shield. The secondary impacts whip-lashed against him and he was thrown to his knees again. He tried in vain to again draw his powers to protect himself, but again he was too slow. I was on him in fury as the fire rained down upon us. The heat and fury of my strikes must have played havoc across his shield, and I knew it wouldn't be long before it failed. In vain he tried to counterattack, but I ignored the attack and let it smash against my shield. I didn't even notice the impact as his thread dissipated against my shield.

I turned on him again in fury. His shield held for several strikes more before it cracked. He must have known what was happening as I tore the power from his shield, he must have felt it weakening and known that it would fail. It must have been terrifying as the liquid fire poured across the surface of his shield. He must have felt the heat first creeping through the gaps in his defence, and then terror as it seeped inside. He wouldn't have suffered long, although he deserved to. This settlement had been sufficient to house and maintain over ten thousand refugees. A lot of people had died here. My opponent deserved to be amongst them.

I telekinetically pulled him to his feet by his neck and brought him to me. I needed to know who he was. Was this Tibus? Would he now lead me to Voll? His eyes widened with surprise as I filled in the gaps in his defence and protected him from the doom of his own making. I dragged him before me so I could see his face. I cursed savagely as I let my shield retract. It wasn't Tibus. I didn't know who this was. He was therefore of no use to me, and he was too dangerous to leave alive. I threw him to the ground behind me as I searched for others. I heard the tell-tale crack of a shield collapsing and a strangled scream as it finally failed completely. He got what he deserved. I didn't wait around to see him die. The only thing that would have caused me to turn around to finish him would have been an attempted teleportation, but he was too weak for that. He died in the firestorm he had created. I suppose there was a lesson in that. It was a pity he wasn't the only one who had paid for his lesson.

The fire lasted for three days before subsiding. The inferno caused by the torrential fires ravaged the land for kilometres in every direction. There had been very few survivors, and the land would be scarred by this for a very long time. It was a fitting tribute to the arrogance of our kind: his for causing this conflagration and mine for allowing it.

* * *

The sudden effect of a massive firestorm in a very cold region had played havoc with the weather, and had been felt in kilometres in every direction. The weather would probably be chaotic for weeks to come.

There were pitifully few survivors from the attack. Only those who had managed to hide in stone buildings had survived, and there were not many of those. Had I not removed them from the inferno, they too would have eventually been consumed. I had torn through the settlement with mechanical precision as I located survivors and teleported them into the waiting arms of Marcellus and his men. Most would arrive nauseated by the act of teleportation, but they would arrive alive.

Our team wasn't really equipped to deal with refugees, so we brought in adequate supplies from our base. These people wouldn't be set free yet. Not until I learned what I needed to know. This had been prompted by a deliberate attack upon me and my men. Had the mage who had died in New Haven been responsible, or had he been working with others? Would this lead to me Tibus? Had Tibus been here, or had this been the act of a renegade mage? It had been appropriate to let the young mage die in the flames, but I could extract the necessary information from others just as easily. Once they were well enough to travel we moved the dozen or so people who had survived the fall of New Haven back to our camp. For the moment at least they would be safe, so we could question them.

It was a curious mix of women, children and men who had been extracted from the fire's wrath. I wasn't concerned about another mage being amongst them; my presence in close proximity would have inevitably caused them to reveal themselves as their Mana sought to protect them. No, these were simple men, women and children whose lives had been turned upside down by me and my kind. I owed them a few days of comfort and protection before I sent them back out into the wild.

I questioned each survivor personally, but wasn't surprised to find that most knew nothing. I had almost given up hope when I found the answers I had been looking for. The older man had obviously been through some rough times. He had lost most of one arm and had visible scars on his face and neck. This wasn't the first time he had had his home taken from him.

There was no visible indication that he was any different from the others. He acted much the same as the rest of the survivors. He didn't look me directly in the eyes. No one ever did. The enlarged irises of my kind were intimidating reminders that we were different. Most people didn't even like being in the same room as one of us. This man was no different in that, he too looked uncomfortable in my presence. I would have been suspicious if he had not been nervous. And yet there was something about him that was strange about him, something elusive. I couldn't put my finger on it.

"How long were you at New Haven?" I opened my interrogation with simple questions.

"Six months," he muttered, and I realised what was different about him. He wasn't afraid of me. In spite of myself I was curious.

"When did the mage arrive?" I continued.

"Three weeks ago."

I wondered if I would get anything but two-word answers from him.

"Did you know his name?"

The man shook his head.

"Did you ever see this mage with him?" I gestured towards a dossier photo we had of Gregory Tibus.

The man looked over at the photo and shrugged. "Maybe, don't like to look."

"So there was more than one mage?" I prompted.

He nodded again. This was useful information, but I wasn't sure how I was going to use it just yet. There didn't seem to be any way to trace the other mage now that New Haven was a smoking hole in the ground. As enticing as this was, it was still a dead end for now. This would need to be investigated later. I wondered briefly what quarry a new search would reveal. There was only one more thing that this man could help me with, and for that I needed privacy.

"That will be all," I ordered the guard who had led him in. The man in the seat rose, but I waved him down. "Just a few seconds more." I nodded as we waited for the guard to leave.

If we had been recording this meeting I would have disabled the cameras. If there had been others I would have sent them away with the guard. What was to come next would only be between myself and this man. I waited for several seconds more as I readied myself. This would need to be done carefully. If I pushed too hard I would lose an opportunity I didn't want to lose. The silence was obviously beginning to unnerve him. It was time to act.

"When did you lose your arm?" I opened gently.

"Four years or so," he grunted again. Back to his usual small responses.

"How?"

"Building fell on me in Chicago."

He had been in Chicago and had gotten out before it had fallen. That explained his stoic demeanour to my presence. A lot of mages had fought in Chicago before it had fallen.

"You seem to have recovered well from the injury," I continued.

This line of questioning wasn't making him any less nervous.

"What's your name?" I inquired, quickly switching my tact.

"David," he grunted.

"Well, David. How would you like your arm back?" I whispered.

I don't think he heard me at first. It took several seconds before his face registered that I had spoken. The look on his face said it all. He didn't believe me, that much was sure, but he had also seen what we were capable of and knew I might not be simply lying. I could see him calculating behind his eyes. What did I have to gain by lying? Why would I offer this? Why him? I could almost see a hundred questions buzzing through his head.

"You can do that?" he queried softly. For the first time he looked at me directly. I could see the hope in his eyes. If I could restore his arm—and from everything he knew about mages he had no reason to doubt me—he would be able to fend for himself in this bitch of a world.

"I can try." I didn't tell him that I hadn't been able to successfully perform the technique yet and I certainly didn't tell him what I had had to do to even get the fundamental understandings of what was required to even contemplate such a feat using Mana. He didn't need to know that he wasn't the first I had approached with such an offer, and that others hadn't survived the process.

He also didn't need to know my own interests in the technique. If I could heal him, then I could heal myself. It could be done. I knew it could be done. Victor had done it. He had healed me from a gunshot wound when I had been shot by Marcus. I remembered the feat well enough. It could be done. It had taken me much searching to find the books I had stolen from my old master. It had taken me even longer to build up the courage to use them, to overcome my ethical and moral objections to the learning contained within those tomes.

I had had to do horrible, evil acts to gain the knowledge necessary for this feat. I was determined that the prices I had paid wouldn't be wasted. Using this knowledge I would finally unlock the secrets that have eluded me; I would be able to heal myself and become whole again. But I wasn't going to practise on myself.

All I needed was patients and time. There was a word for what I was about to do to this man: Necromancy.

CHAPTER TWO

It wasn't actually Necromancy if you used the classical term for the word, but the techniques and theories that I had learned definitely delved into a realm that many would call Necromancy. Regenerative growth sounded about as far as you could get from Necromancy, but the skills and understanding I needed were gained from experimenting on corpses. What was about to be performed was as close to Necromancy as you could get without raising a corpse from the ground.

This man wasn't the first I had offered this to, and he probably wouldn't be the last. The last time I had attempted this, it hadn't gone too well. It had taken a lot of time I didn't have to figure out what had gone wrong. I wasn't sure I truly understood even now, but I wouldn't know for certain until I tried again. Fortunately, due to the war I had a plethora of subjects. There were hundreds of people bearing wounds that would allow me to practise my arts.

All I needed to do was get it right this time.

My subject looked nervous, and I didn't blame him. I had teleported him away from his home and people. He didn't know it, but I had sent him to the other side of the globe. I couldn't perform these rites with the possibility of someone interrupting—I needed complete privacy. If nothing else, I didn't think it would be a good idea for others to learn that I was practising unethical medical procedures. I didn't sugar coat it; I didn't seek to validate or defend my actions. This was wrong. There was no doubt in my mind. It was wrong, but it was necessary.

I was using this man to learn the required Mana technique to heal myself. It was selfish and it was evil, but I had already crossed that line some time ago. It was a necessity—I would be whole again. I would no longer be the crippled half-man I had been forced to become. I would stand on my own and I would bring vengeance on those who had wronged me. I didn't dare stand against Victor again like this. I couldn't, I wouldn't stand a chance. He would destroy me.

It was ironic that I was using Victor's own hiding place to perform my experiments. I had stumbled upon this place before the war. It had been Victor's hidden Nazi scientific research station during the Second World War. He had experimented upon people here and had discovered the powers I was attempting to learn. Did that make me as much of a monster as him? The only difference between us was that I asked first. My subjects had no idea what they were being asked. They had no idea of the horrible risk that they would be subjected to. No, I couldn't claim that I was any more right than Victor. There was no good and there was no evil. There was only power, and those capable and willing to wield it. If you were unwilling to wield your power, you would be swept aside by those who would. That wasn't going to happen to me again.

I didn't do much to placate my subject. Let him be nervous, that was a perfectly logical response to this situation. He sat on an examination bench that was easily over fifty years old and not that comfortable. I knew that from experience. I had once been shackled to that very bench.

"Lie back," I intoned. He looked up at me and gulped as he glanced between me and my assistant. He obviously didn't know who to be more afraid of. Again, I didn't blame him. My assistant had been dead for far longer than this man had been alive.

"Randall won't harm you." I smiled softly. He couldn't harm anyone. There was very little of Randall left, and I firmly controlled what remained. Randall was a drone, a dead man brought back to life to serve a mage. I had encountered their like before. I had seen them take bullets to the chest without flinching and perform acts that would have killed the living. Randall would do all these things and more. He would do anything I told him to. He had no more choice in the matter than any other tool in my hand.

Victor had created Randall during the Second World War. I had encountered Randall when I first arrived in this place. It hadn't taken me long to learn how to control the drones; the books I had stolen from Victor had covered their creation in some detail. It took little effort to seize control of them and bring them under my dominion. My assurances of his safety didn't seem to comfort my subject much. Again, I didn't blame him.

"Lie back … please," I repeated. I instructed Randall to hold the man down and bring his damaged arm into the light. The man flinched as Randall's cold fingers gripped into him and held him down on the examination bench.

The damage had been significant. The break to the arm hadn't been clean. It was a miracle he had survived. He had obviously received skilled medical treatment very quickly after the trauma. That didn't tell me anything though, if he hadn't he'd be dead. The wound had been treated as one would normally treat an amputation. The flesh surrounding the wound had been folded over the stump and then stitched together to create a single scar. The tissue surrounding the wound was gnarled and tough from the damage it had received.

This wouldn't do. I need strong healthy flesh to work with. Dead or damage cells weren't going to be sufficient for my needs. My subject flinched again as Randall applied more pressure to hold him down. His eyes glanced at me nervously as I pulled a scalpel from the gurney behind me.

"Be calm," I whispered, sending a burst of Mana into the stump where his arm had once been. I watched with satisfaction as the Mana did its work. The nerves surrounding the stump went dark one by one as they were lulled into a stupor and then died. They would regrow in time, but for now he didn't need to feel what I was about to do.

With a scalpel I gently opened the old wound. I was no doctor and my technique was sloppy. My work was more akin to a butcher than a surgeon; but it didn't matter, this was damaged flesh anyway. It would need to be removed. I worked quietly and quickly. I could see my patient's heart rate and breathing quicken as I worked. I didn't need a machine to monitor my patient, I could see through the Mana just how he was doing. He would survive this, provided I didn't let him bleed out. He had quite rightly gone into shock; I was after all cutting chunks of flesh from his arm. I had placed Randall in the way to prevent him from seeing what I was doing. He might feel pressure from Randall, but he would feel nothing of what I was doing. Randall's fingers around the man's arm acted as a tourniquet and kept blood loss to a minimum; even so, it was messy work.

It took me half an hour to remove enough flesh until I was confident that I had removed enough to begin the real work. My patient passed out halfway through, and I was grateful for the silence. His haggard breaths and startled glances had been distracting. The wound surrounding the arm was now fresh and openly bleeding. I used Randall's hands to bring the wound into the air. This would minimise further bleeding and bring the bloodied stump into the light. Yes, this looked good. I could work with this.

I took a deep breath as I placed the scalpel into the

bloodied mess I had left on the examination table. I flexed my fingers and watched with interest as the Mana played across my fingers. It still fascinated me even today. I watched for several seconds as the Mana built up in my hands. I ignored the slow but steady trails of blood that ran from the wound. I ignored the white flesh pressed tight on his arm by Randall's dead fingers.

I gritted my teeth. I needed to begin. Why couldn't I begin?

My hands shook as I released the first burst of Mana onto the wound. I had to force myself not to stop as I poured more and more Mana into the man's flesh. The Mana looked sick and fey. This was abhorrent to me and send a chill down my spine. I doubted there was more than one other mage alive today who would have recognised the frequency of the Mana I was using. Victor was the only one. He would recognise it for what it was—after all he had discovered it.

At first nothing changed, but I had expected this. The flesh had experienced a lot of trauma and it was natural that things would take a while. It happened so slowly, but that was okay. I knew what would occur next. The cells would regrow and new flesh would form. The problem was stopping what would happen after that. The issue wasn't encouraging cellular regrowth. The trick was getting it to stop. Cancer is a bitch.

I carefully monitored the growth of the Mana as it soaked into the surrounding cells. If I wasn't careful I would lose control of the growth and it would become cancerous. Once that happened there was very little I could do. Fortunately that didn't seem to be the case this time. I was making progress. I took a few moments to congratulate myself before I returned to my work.

It was humbling to see the Mana solidify into bone, muscle and skin as it spread up my subject's arm. Watching the Mana swirl around the intersection of flesh and magically creating bone, sinew and muscle from nothing. The subject would soon have a fully formed arm.

Not subject! I corrected myself sternly. This man's name was David. Now that things were looking positive I could remind myself of this fact. It was easier to keep them nameless if things didn't go well. It kept me from remembering that these people had friends and family. It didn't stop me from the callousness of my experiments, but it made me less likely to give in to baseless emotion and make mistakes. I couldn't afford mistakes. Too many had already paid for my inattention.

Yes, David's arm was reforming at an acceptable rate. The radius and ulna were forming, surrounded by a ring of healthy flesh. His arm would be tender for a time, but soon it would be indistinguishable from his other arm. There didn't appear to be any sign of cancerous cells. This was looking good.

I breathed a sigh of relief. I was getting closer. Soon I would apply the same techniques to myself … but perhaps I was getting ahead of myself. As the delicate bones of the hand began to form I wondered at how all this was possible. How did the body know what bones went where? I wasn't consciously doing this. I was simply encouraging healing at an exponential rate. I hadn't paid much attention during my science lessons in high school and of course I had never done any further studies. It had just never seemed important. My studies in Mana took precedence in all things.

Perhaps if I had sought knowledge outside the sphere of Mana, things might have gone differently.

* * *

I glanced down at the corpse on my table in fury. Things had looked so favourable. The technique had been performed flawlessly. I had read every damned paragraph in Victor's books numerous times and I was sure that I had done nothing wrong. The technique was right! So why hadn't it worked?

As I looked at the subject's necrotic arm I at least consoled myself with the fact that the outcome this time had been different—worse perhaps, but different. I had left the examination room late last night confident that I had finally found success. Things had looked so positive. The cells had formed and looked healthy, his blood pressure seemed stable. Hell, his restored arm had even bled properly and then clotted when I cut it.

Why hadn't this worked?

Last night I had left a healthy functioning man here. When I returned in the morning I found a corpse with a blackened dead arm. It had shrivelled and become necrotic during the night. Unfortunately the necrotic flesh had poisoned the rest of his system, and he had died sometime before day break. I cursed inwardly even as I instructed Randall to dispose of the corpse.

"Another one?" a voice from behind me murmured.

I didn't turn around to look. I knew who it would be—Karl. He had been one of the original test subjects at this facility. He was almost as dead as Randall, with one notable exception. He still had a pulse and a conscious-ness. Victor had turned this man into a living corpse. He had once been a mage, but his powers had burned out sustaining his extended life. I doubted the price had been worth it.

Victor had obviously thought so too. He had left Karl behind as a failure. Victor had perfected the technique and achieved immortality without the cost, but that wasn't what I was interested in. I had no desire to live for a moment longer in this hell cursed world than I needed to.

I had never discussed my experiments with Karl, and for his part he never seemed to venture any sort of judgement. In my quieter moments I sometimes won-dered how this was possible. How could he stand idly by when I performed the same evils that had been perpe-trated upon him?

I didn't bother answering him. There was no need. He hadn't really expected a response anyway. Karl wasn't quite fully there. Sometimes, like today, he would be aware of his surroundings and could interact with me; others he would fall into a torpor-like sleep and remain immobile for days. He had been locked in a cell for over seventy years. It wasn't hard to assume this would have caused some psychological damage.

"You will never succeed in this," Karl murmured with his desiccated voice.

That was new. That sounded like judgement. I turned to glance at the man. Karl's face contained no clues. His muscles had long atrophied and his face couldn't contain expression even if he had wanted to show it.

"What do you mean?" I sought to read the world's most flawless poker face.

"Perhaps this knowledge is not meant to be learned."

"Victor learned it."

"Are you willing to become as he is?" Karl whispered.

I sighed. The truth was that I didn't know. I didn't even know if it was possible today. I hadn't balked at human experimentation or Necromancy. But I didn't think that I could achieve the same level of atrocity that Victor had. The sheer number of people who had died here was staggering. I couldn't possibly achieve the same evil. I simply didn't have the same level of resources or organisation available to me. And I wasn't sure if that was the only thing stopping me.

"What's one more monster in this world?" I grunted towards my undead accuser. Karl didn't answer. I wasn't even sure if he was even there anymore. Ironically, the dead man moved like a ghost. I grunted and made my way from the examination room. As I turned I saw that Karl hadn't left. He was standing there, staring at me.

His unusually blue eyes pierced into me. I didn't know for sure if his eyes even worked or if he managed to navigate through the complex blind.

"What if everyone felt that way?" he murmured as I pushed my way past him.

That was probably the longest conversation I had had with Karl in some time. Perhaps my frequent visits here were starting to bring him back to the real world. He had been loathe at first to even leave his cell. Now he haunted other areas of the complex. I didn't answer him as I left the medical wing of the facility and made my way back to my office.

This structure had once been a Nazi scientific research station and it still looked the part. Third Reich propaganda and paraphernalia hung everywhere. The office I had claimed as my own had once been Victor's, but I doubted he would recognise it now. There were only two things I had kept. The first was the bookcase that held his books on Mana, and the second was a portrait of a woman in a frame that had been on my old master's desk.

The portrait fascinated me. The portrait was of a woman who for all the world looked like Renee, but there were subtle differences. Who was this woman? Was this Renee? If so, what was she doing in this photo? This photo looked like it was taken in the forties. It was faded with age, but due to the undisturbed nature of its location, it had endured better than most photos from that age would have.

If this woman was Renee then it meant that she, like Victor, had attained the same immortality and never told me. The possibility of this deception sent shivers down my spine. She would have told me. I was sure of it. If the woman wasn't Renee, then who was she? Renee's mother? Renee's grandmother? She was obviously someone important to Victor. The woman was wearing a Nazi uniform, and she was smiling. There appeared to be a building in the background, but the photo was cropped to only show the woman's face and shoulders. No other details were easily distinguishable.

If the woman wasn't Renee, then it didn't really matter who she was? She resembled Renee closely enough to give me fleeting comfort and memories of a better time. I could look at this woman's face and dream of the woman that I hoped I would never see again.

That was enough for now.

* * *

The clanking noise reverberated throughout the cellblock as the wrought iron door locked Randall in place. I wasn't prepared to give him free run of the complex when I wasn't there. When I first encountered him, he had been crazed and uncontrollable. Disturbingly enough, it appeared that a portion of his original mind had taken control of the body during the long period since his creation. I had no intention of letting this occur again. Victor had seized control of the body and had reverted his destructive and mindless nature, turning him into a mindless automation.

I hadn't wanted to originally return to this place, I had been hunting Victor and hoped he was holed up here. I was wrong. It didn't look as though Victor had returned since he had defeated me here so many years ago. I found Randall in the examination chamber where Victor had left him. It had taken me quite some time to learn how to control him, but in time I had learned to control the vessel as if he were an extension of my own senses. At first the sensation of being in two places at once sent shivers down my spine. I would send my consciousness into the corpse, issue orders, and then beat a hasty retreat. Over time, however, I found that my distaste for the experience lessened and I could control Randall for large periods of time.

I had no idea how long I could leave Randall in an inert state before his primal nature would take control again, and I had no wish to leave a potential threat in this place. No, it was best to secure him away so he couldn't cause any damage.

"So you're leaving again?" Karl's whispered voice echoed from behind me.

I didn't bother answering him. He knew I never stayed long, especially after a failure. This place wasn't exactly homey—even the military base felt like a warm abode next to the darkness and cold of this place. I had spent several nights here in the past, but I wouldn't do so by choice.

"Do you know when you will return?"

I turned to face Karl. That was new. He had never asked me that before. He was regaining more and more personality with every visit. This was a good thing, I suppose, although he would never be able to completely regain his humanity. He would always be seen as a monster—too much damage had been done to his body for it to ever function normally again—but perhaps his mind could be recovered.

"No," I replied curiously. "Is there something you need?"

He had never made any requests of me before. It would be interested to see what his response would be.

"Yes," he whispered softly. I almost hadn't heard him. His normal talking tone was mostly whisper anyway. His word had been little more than a brief exhalation of breath.

"Oh?"

"You promised me once that you could end this."

He didn't need to elaborate. I had once promised him I would find a solution to his current state. I had hoped that my experiments into cellular regrowth could be used to restore his form. I still held out hope that once I perfected the technique, I could restore normal function to his withered and desiccated body.

"My experiments haven't exactly been successful," I grunted, ensuring Randall's cell was secure.

"No!" Karl hissed angrily. "I don't want you to restore me. I want you to end this. I want you to kill me."

I sighed softly. I had once promised him that too, many years ago, before the war. At the time I had made the promise, unsure if I would be able to fulfil such a request. I still didn't know if it was possible. The Mana kept his form in a kind of forced stasis. In life, Karl hadn't been powerful enough as a mage to do little more than keep his body in a state of zombie-like preservation. Victor had intentionally experimented on mages hoping to achieve immortality for himself. His experiment with Karl had gifted the man with immortality, but at the cost of his powers.

Had Karl not been left unattended in a cell for close to seventy years, it was possible that with regular consumption he would still resemble a healthy, functioning thirty-year-old man. However, his time in the dark and without sustenance forced a kind of ghoul-like existence on the man. Although he couldn't feel pain—his nerve endings had long since died—his existence must have been a cruel form of hell.

I didn't blame him for wanting it to end.

It was possible that by disrupting the Mana flow throughout his body, I could end the process and he could finally achieve death. It was equally possible that would only make matters worse. If I disrupted the Mana within him and then burned his body, would the Mana simply reform his body from the ashes?

I had once thrown a metal pole through Victor's stomach. He had pulled it from his body and I had watched in terror as the flesh surrounding the wound regrew over the injury, forming new, healthy flesh. How much damage would need to be done to the flesh before this was no longer possible?

"There are risks," I explained as Karl followed me from the cell block. "Very well," I murmured. We passed into the former parade ground and headed towards the examination chamber. The ghoul's wordless silence spoke volumes. He was ready and he understood the risks.

"I assume now is acceptable?" I murmured wryly, heading towards the hospital complex.

Karl followed me and climbed onto the examination table without comment. I took his silence for acceptance. I breathed out slowly. Hopefully this would be more successful than my last procedure. I flexed my fingers as I looked down at the skeleton of a man lying before me. I could see the Mana working through his body repairing his failing flesh, keeping him alive, but other than that his body was still, no movement associated with breath. His body relied solely on the Mana now. I had never taken the opportunity to examine Karl properly earlier, and I immediately wished that I had. The process used to keep Karl alive was some kind of twisted genius, flawed yes, but genius nonetheless.

I could see the Mana moving through him in waves, moving through his nerves and across his muscle structure. It was repairing damage as it occurred. This was probably why Victor had left Karl abandoned in a small room under a mountain. The human body is an amazing machine; when it is damaged there are two ways in which it renews itself: regeneration and repair. Regeneration causes creation of new cells to replace the damaged ones, and repair fixes damaged cells, which results in scar tissue. But Karl's body wasn't regenerating, it only continually repairing the existing flesh, but unable to create new. His whole body at this point was nothing more than scar tissue. Had Karl been allowed freedom, it was possible his body wouldn't have lasted this long. He would have eventually encountered catastrophic damage, and while it would not kill him, it would damage his body beyond its ability to repair. Victor hadn't locked him away to be needlessly cruel. There had been a reason. Victor had been attempting to see how long this process could keep someone alive.

Even so, how was Karl still alive? If such a term could be used. His internal organs were probably barely functioning. The body received all its sustenance from the Mana. How? Was this something Victor had done? Or was this something Karl had unconsciously done to himself? I didn't know the answer to this, but I knew where I could find out.

"I will return," I grunted as I teleported into Victor's office.

Victor had been meticulous in his record keeping. There had been hundreds of documents stored against each of his patients and procedures. It took me some time to find what I was looking for in his archives.

Patient 616.

It didn't have a name anywhere on it. I suppose these people had been just numbers to Victor. I quickly perused the info sheet and came across something curious. The document was dated August 15, 1945.

That was interesting: the procedure had occurred after the war. I had assumed the end of the war had brought an end to Victor's experiments—that didn't seem to be the case. That date was certainly after the theatre of war had finished in Europe. Hell, it was even after Berlin had fallen, and, as far as my admittedly primitive high school history informed me, that was the end of the war for the Germans. If the end of the war hadn't stopped Victor, then what had?

I read quickly through the details of the experiment Victor had performed. It was difficult as my abilities with the German language didn't extend too far into its written form. It was made even more difficult due to the clinical and dark nature of the content. I recognised Victor's writing style easily and his journal notes were succinct and to the point. This was the only reason I was able to understand any of the document. Even so, it was mostly just technical information. It wasn't until I got to Victor's summary of the experiment that I found what I was looking for.

The patient exhibits normal signs of life and function, but it is as if his normal dependence upon external sustenance has been removed. The Vis Viva within the subject's body instantly repairs any damage incurred; however, there is no regeneration of new tissue.

This wasn't new information. I had already surmised this. It was interesting to note that Victor had used the term Vis Viva to describe Mana at that time. I briefly wondered at what point he switched to calling it Mana. The first book on Mana I had read had referred to Mana as Vis Viva also.

The extent of the power required to perform this feat has removed the subject's rudimentary Vis Viva abilities. All conscious power is focused upon the repair of his body. This is unacceptable. I refuse to trade my abilities for extended life. While this experiment has exceeded its scope, I must deem it a failure. It is unlikely that this subject will ever regain his abilities and I refuse to subject myself to this. In time perhaps his powers will return, but they will be far weaker than they should be. This is not what I am seeking. I will continue my search. I know what I seek is possible, I have seen it.

He had seen it? What was this? Had he met someone who had already succeeded in this line of experimentation? Or did he mean that he had somehow foreseen his success. I didn't think either option was very likely. Victor had been very dismissive of the art of divination, calling it petty trickery and intuition. I doubted he would have done so had he known it was possible with our powers. As for seeing someone who had already succeeded at extending their life, that was a more interesting concept. I had assumed Victor was the first to discover these dark arts, but what if he wasn't? What if there were others who had come before him? Was it possible? I hadn't even known that mages existed before I had been inducted in their ranks. Was it possible there was another group of immortals who had been secretly hiding amongst us? It wasn't impossible. Someone like Karl had been living amongst us for half a century. He had no need for food, water or even air.It was unlikely, but not impossible. I read on.

Unfortunately this experiment has removed my use for this subject. Without Vis Viva he cannot possibly achieve the end I seek. I will leave him in this facility when I leave. I suspect eventually the constant strain of extended Vis Viva use will burn him out and he will expire. This note concludes this experiment.

Victor had thought Karl's Mana would burn him out and he would die. That very well could have been a possibility; however, it was obvious that Karl's power had been sufficient to maintain the level of repair his body had required. Even when his internal organs had shut down and withered, the Mana had provided the necessary stimulation to keep him alive. It was an impressive feat. I wondered just how much Mana was being consumed each minute. To look at Karl, it didn't seem that he was using that much raw power. The Mana seemed regulated and even, but that didn't really tell me anything. It did give me an idea though. I returned to Karl.

"When was the last time you used your powers?" I queried as I teleported back into the examination chamber.

"They took away my powers," Karl responded immediately.

"Answer the question," I ordered.

"Since before I was taken."

"Try now. Form a telekinesis thread."

"A what?" Karl inquired.

Of course he probably hadn't used that term to describe it. He was, after all, from a time where such terms wouldn't have been commonplace. He had probably been born in the nineteen twenties.

"Lift something," I commanded, gesturing to a scalpel I had left on the gurney on the other side of the room.

Karl's unblinking eyes turned his expressionless face towards me. His lack of expression didn't mean much though as his face wasn't capable of forming expressions anymore. The muscles had atrophied through lack of use.

"Do it now," I urged.

Karl let out a grunt as he reached his hand out to reach the scalpel. I watched with grim satisfaction as the Mana quivered within his body and ever so slowly formed into a thread running down his arm. It moved so very slowly, far slower than even I had managed when I had first learned to use my powers.

I couldn't see any visible evidence of the effort within Karl's body until I looked at his eyes. His irises had always been expanded due to extended and constant Mana use, but now they almost glowed. The Mana reached his palm and slowly began to form a thread. A gasp escaped Karl's lips. This was surprising for two reasons: one, I didn't know Karl was still capable of expelling air—he didn't need it and I had assumed his lungs had shut down—and two, while not very powerful, the thread was complete. If Karl had wanted it to, it would have lifted the scalpel.

"How is this possible?" Karl whispered.

"Your Mana is growing more powerful through use. With practice you can regain and even exceed your previous powers." I smiled.

"This changes nothing," Karl whispered softly. "I still seek death."

I blinked at him. "What?"

"Can I use this power to be as I was before?"

I pondered that for a second. "No, the damage to your body is too great." I shook my head. "But once I complete my studies, I may be able to regenerate you."

"To what end? Everyone I know is dead," Karl murmured. "Except for the one who did this to me, and I do not wish to be reunited with him."

"You don't want revenge?"

"No, and even if I did, I doubt I would be able to achieve it," Karl said firmly. "No, end this. It is better this way."

"No," I whispered. "I don't understand."

How could he want this? After everything he had endured, everything he had done. To end it like this seemed like such a waste. He had just rediscovered his powers. In prompting him to use his powers, I had encouraged his strength to exceed what was required to maintain himself. I vaguely wondered how powerful he could be now he was not using the entirety of his powers to keep himself alive.

"End this," he repeated.

I gritted my teeth. I didn't have to do this—I didn't even really want to. I looked at his dead face and pondered. What would I have wanted if our situation was reversed? I didn't know. I couldn't know. It's almost impossible to place oneself into that mindset. The debate raged back and forth in my mind.

"You know how to," Karl accused as he leaned forward in the bed. "I can see it in your face."

"I do," I confirmed softly.

"Then do it."

I nodded briefly. In the end it didn't much matter what I wanted. The fact that his powers had returned meant nothing. I had promised and I keep my promises. I was going to deliver.

"I will try," I whispered. "I may not succeed."

Karl nodded and sat back down on the bed.

I breathed out quickly as I summoned my powers.

"This may hurt," I warned as I realised it probably wasn't going to. He no longer had nerves with which to feel pain.

I reached out and placed my hand over his centre, several inches from his chest, and let my powers grow. The Disrupt technique required a pulse of Mana to be sent from my fist to the target, but I suspected this would be insufficient for my needs. I would need to experiment with different delivery methods, using a constant flow of power rather than staggered bursts. I'd never tried a Disrupt delivered by thread before;, and thought it would be best to see what happened with the standard pulse first.

I built the power to a crescendo within my fist before I released it. The Disrupt thread tore from my fingers and hit Karl centre mass. His body shuddered as it took hold, tremors echoed across his flesh from the impact and the Mana reacting with his body. Just as quickly as it had begun, the effect stopped and his Mana returned to normal. I hit him again, with much the same effect. It was infuriating: the strength of my pulse didn't seem to make any difference. It was overcome with much the same ease.

I staggered as I released a string of Disrupt pulses at the Mana. I was expending almost my full strength at disrupting the Mana. No other mage I had ever met had been able to simply shrug off a Disrupt like this. True, under such an effect his ability to draw upon his Mana would be seriously dampened, but he wasn't actively drawing upon his powers—it was happening at a subconscious level. He would have been unable to use the Mana to fight back, but it wasn't stopping his regeneration.

As the pulses continued, and the Mana fought between my Disrupt pulses and Karl's Mana fought against them, I finally began to make a break through. I was winning, but the power I was using was mind blowing. I wouldn't be able to keep this up for much longer, let alone use my powers to incinerate the body once the regenerative process had been broken.

As the Mana processing the regeneration finally shutdown, I saw his body shudder and convulse. I immediately looped his hands into the secure leather straps on the gurney as great wracking gasps overcame him—without the Mana as his life source, his body was attempting to breathe. Unfortunately he no longer had that capacity. Karl's mouth gaped as he sought to bring air into his withered lungs. His fingers reached into claws and dug into the bench as primal instincts for survival overtook him. He fought ineffectually against his bonds as his body convulsed into violent spasms.

I poured more Mana into him and noticed with a small degree of satisfaction that I appeared to have stopped all Mana activity within him. I continued with my assault until I was sure he had expired. I had to be sure; I wasn't going to put him through this again if I could help it.

I wasn't sure if Karl felt pain, but I could tell from his eyes staring at me that he was experiencing distress. His body was dying, and he was unable to convince it that this was what he wanted. His iron will was fighting with his instinctive urge to survive. His pleading eyes sought mine as I attempted to bring his life to an end.

The shuddering wracking his frame eventually stilled and his mouth twisted into a small smile, the first I had seen on his face. His eyes softened and closed. A small exhalation of breath was all the evidence I was going to get that I had succeeded. I gripped the sides of the gurney as weariness overtook me. It had almost cost me all my powers. It would be sometime before I would be strong enough to teleport out of here. I leaned back to survey the corpse on the table. A dull aching began to take hold in the back of my head. I knew this signified I had used too much power too quickly. I hadn't felt that in a long time.

I had once torn a building into pieces and thrown it at an enemy without feeling anywhere near the same level of exhaustion. I could tell that I was weakened almost immediately as the frame of Mana keeping me standing upright began to give out.

It almost wasn't enough, but I had done it. Karl was dead.

No, I hadn't done it. My breath caught in my throat as I noticed it. It began so simply, a small spark of Mana in Karl's core. It burned like a sun in my vision, painful to look at. The spark was inevitably joined by others as the pattern of Mana flowed across his body. I could see it burning across his cold flesh as it consumed and regenerated the damage I had just wrought.

I had failed.

* * *

It took Karl six hours to return to his twisted life. When consciousness returned to him, he turned to me questioningly. He didn't say any words, but it was obvious what he was asking.

"I failed," I replied briefly. "I can't do it."

Karl took this with measured grace. He simply nodded and got up from the table.

"You were dead for about six hours," I commented quickly.

"Didn't seem like it," he murmured softly.

"What's the last thing you remember?"

"Pain," he whispered tersely. "I hadn't felt it in so long. It was excruciating. It seemed to last forever, and when I thought I could endure no more, then came the darkness."

"No pearly gates? No white light?" I prompted, partially curious. "No Jesus welcoming you into heaven?"

"I am Jewish," Karl reminded me briskly.

Of course he was Jewish. Religion hadn't exactly been my strong suit, and while I didn't know enough about the Jewish religion to know who was supposed to greet them into heaven, I knew it wasn't going to be Jesus.

"I felt nothing, after the darkness. I simply woke up and found you staring at me," Karl continued. "I wonder what possible sin I could have committed to have been denied salvation."

"We will find a way," I promised softly. I was very aware that I had already made such a promise and had been unable to fulfil it. This promise could prove to be no different.

"I have no wish to go through that again, unless you are certain ..." Karl trailed off.

"I know, I'm sorry," I whispered.

"You should go rest. You seem depleted."

I often forgot that Karl could see Mana. He would have known how much energy I had just expended in this effort. That Karl thought I still looked depleted six hours after the Mana expenditure was a curious note of just how much Mana I had used. It would be some time before I would be able to teleport back to my command in the States.

The more troubling revelation was, though, if I had expended this much energy trying to disrupt the Mana in a dead man, how much Mana would I need to expend to disrupt a similar pattern in Victor? Even once I recovered my strength from this experiment, it would be unlikely that I would be able to summon enough power to overcome Victor. No, while I was using Mana to keep myself mobile, I would continually be underpowered. Which led me back to my original problem: how had Victor achieved complete cellular regeneration? Once I had learned that, I could then unlock the rest of my power and maybe achieve the necessary output to overcome my former master.

Maybe.

That was the gamble though, wasn't it? My entire efforts up to until now had been a risk. I could only hope that it would pay off. I ran my hand across my face as I made my way back into my former master's offices. If I had the strength, I would have scoured the local villages for a bottle of port or spirits to consume while I waited for my strength to return. It would have been nice to dull my thoughts with alcohol. But tonight that was a luxury I couldn't afford. In my current condition, the furthest I would be able to scry would only be a few kilometres, and I knew the closest towns from this location were most likely outside my range. It would probably be for nothing though; the war had all but decimated most of the villages and towns in central Europe.

It seemed wasteful to use my slowly regained energy for such a pitiful use too, no matter how much relief it would bring me. I glanced around the room that had been Victor's office and pulled up a chair. My gaze quickly passed over the small cot set up in an adjoining room, but it didn't linger. No, sleep would bring the dreams, and I was too tired to deal with them right now. I was too tired to sleep. It seemed this had been the status quo for some time now. My sleeping patterns were well and truly garbled. At least while I was awake I could control my consciousness and keep focused on the current task.

I reached for the latest of Victor's spell books and continued reading where I had left off. Normally I would have used my powers to provide the light for my reading, but tonight I didn't want to waste my strength. Reading spell books by candlelight seemed suitably proper, particularly given the subject matter was on Necromancy. Victor's scrawl in ink across the page reflected in the candle light and shined with an eldritch light. When I had first begun my forays into Mana studies, I had done so via an old floppy disk drive. It hadn't seemed right; the harsh glare of a computer screen made the whole thing seem artificial and fake. No, this was the way that Mana should be studied.

Once again the urge to retrieve a bottle of something rose within me, but I again dismissed the idea as an extravagance. There would be alcohol waiting for me once I returned to my command. There was something about soldiers and alcohol—there was never one without the other, but for now I should focus on my reading lest I fall asleep.

The dull headache that always came after extreme Mana use slowly receded in the back of my mind as I continued my studies. I gently massaged the bridge of my nose as I focused on the page before me. Victor had once told me that true power didn't come from raw strength, but from greater understanding. I hadn't believed him at the time, but I had been young and strong. I hadn't discovered the limits of my strength yet. He had been right, but it was only now that I was broken and weak that I had come to understand this fundamental truth. Power is not about sheer strength, it's about applying pressure to a point. The more pressure you can apply won't necessarily work, but find the right place to apply the pressure and your barrier will break every time.

And so I sought the necessary pressure point in my studies to break through my chains and achieve my goals. I had been lazy in my power before; now I had to be disciplined if I hoped to achieve my goals. Before I could overcome my foes with sheer strength, now I had to outsmart them. While I was more powerful than most mages I had encountered, this was because of one simple fact: I had been trained by Victor Whittlesea and they had not. I had access to his spell books and therefore access to knowledge that they either didn't know about or weren't powerful enough to command. I maintained my advantage, but every day I encountered mages who could match my power and sheer strength. It was only a matter of time until I fell to one. I needed to restore myself back to my full strength. I would need every particle of Mana I could summon when I finally confronted my old master again.

I had heard it said that what doesn't kill you makes you stronger. This is a lie. My last encounter with my former master had left me a broken shell. I would need to be prepared for my next encounter to ensure it would not be he who walked away. I continued reading until I felt sufficiently renewed to be able to return to my command. I couldn't say how long I spent in the dark using only candle light to measure my time. I went through at least a dozen candles before I felt strong enough to cross the Atlantic. I didn't bother saying goodbye when I left. Randall wouldn't understand and Karl wouldn't care.

* * *

I teleported directly back to my quarters when I returned. My soldiers wouldn't be surprised by my absence and subsequent return. They were used to it. I'd often disappear for days on end and then return with new orders. This would appear to be no different.

I gently rubbed the bridge of my nose as I gazed at myself within my bathroom mirror. I was looking old. I felt old. The only problem was, I wasn't. I was in my late 20s. A set of fresh clothes and a shower changed my outlook. My clothes had begun to develop a lived-in quality that I'd come to associate with lack of commodities. As secure as Victor's hidden research station had been, it certainly was lacking in some of the fundamental facilities. I hadn't intended on staying there as long as I had and been caught out.

It was staggering now that I thought about it. The amount of Mana I had used attempting to end Karl could have torn this bunker down around my ears and send earthquakes rampaging out for kilometres in each direction. All that sheer energy and still my goal was unfulfilled.

Victor had once told me that there was more to power than just raw strength. He was right. The same amount of energy would allow me to rend Karl down to an elemental level. Tear him into pieces until only a bloody mess remained, if he still had any blood in him. This act would avail me nothing. He would return in time. The Mana would bind his broken flesh and make him whole anew. All this power and I was unable to figure out how to finish a frail old man who had suffered for far too long. Although he had my sympathies, my true goal was defeating Victor. Unless I could nullify this magic, eventually Victor was going to kill me. While this sorcery was renewing him, he was unstoppable.

I was unable to kill Karl, and Karl had been the subject of a failed experiment. Victor had presumably perfected the technique before performing the sorcery on himself. How much more difficult would it be to end Victor?

I needed to find a way to end this sorcery before

Victor finished me off. Marcus had claimed that a disrupt spell was sufficient, but I knew this to be false. Marcus hadn't had time to study Necromancy to the same degree I had. Nothing so simple as a disrupt thread would resolve this sorcery. I was getting closer, I could almost taste it, but something was missing. I was forgetting something—something important.

I made my way from my quarters to the command centre. It was almost empty when I arrived. I had forgotten to take into account the time. It was one of those annoying things about being able to teleport across time zones. You tended to lose track of daylight. I had hoped that Marcellus would be present, but he was obviously off duty.

"Report," I grunted at the on-duty officer who commanded the night shift. I couldn't remember his name. He had been reassigned after I had sustained significant losses in New York. At first I had tried to remember names and faces, but it quickly proved too difficult. Too many faces and too many names—it was impossible.

"Nothing to report," he immediately replied.

"No movement from New Haven?" I queried. I had expected something to come from that battle at least.

"The scouts we left behind reported in as per regulation. No movement."

This was frustrating. I had hoped that a battle would bring more interest and perhaps flush free my quarry. It seemed I would need to up the ante. That could wait for tomorrow though—there was no sense doing anything in the middle of the night. The clock informed me it was well past midnight.

"It seems that we've cleaned them out then," I murmured softly. I hadn't expected the soldier to hear me, but he nodded in agreement.

Wishful thinking. This wasn't how this would work. We were still trying to fight a conventional war. The problem was we were fighting against a very unconventional foe. Command insisted that we sweep through sector by sector, nullifying any resistance before we moved on. Once a section was clear we would move onto the next. They didn't understand what they were doing. Our enemies had no idea of the various sectors or theatres of war. They didn't care. All we were doing was removing the norms that had been swept up in the wake of a mage fight. It was a stupid strategy, but I couldn't think of a better one.

"Inform Command," I ordered as I left the room.

Command would probably reassign us. I hoped our new accommodation was as functional as this bunker. I wouldn't miss this place when I left, but it had been comfortable. I had stayed in worse. I vaguely wondered what had happened to the original contents of this bunker. The signs were all over the compound. This had once been a nuclear silo. I assumed it had been decommissioned before the war. When we had arrived here it had the bolted down look of a structure that hadn't been used in decades.

I made my way back to my quarters and glanced

briefly at the bottle of American whiskey at the table. I didn't really like American whiskey. It was too sweet, but anything was better than trying to sleep. I took a look at my unkempt bed and pulled a chair up. They say you shouldn't drink alone, but I didn't much care for company when I drank. It wasn't that I was trying to drink away my pain or forget my troubles. I didn't drink to remember the past or old friends. No, I simply drank because it was better than sleeping. Passing out in a haze of alcohol fuelled nausea helped me sleep without my subconscious dredging up the past.

A polite cough alerted me to an intruder. I must have been tired—I hadn't noticed anyone. The shock of the noise almost caused me to rise to my feet and ready my defences. The Mana flared in my body in response to the threat, but I quickly realised that a threat wouldn't have coughed to let me know that they were there. Marcellus was at the door.

"I heard you were back," he grunted by way of greeting.

Although I didn't much like drinking with company, I was willing to make the odd exception from time to time. Marcellus was one of the few I would make an exception for. I gestured towards the chair on the other side of the table. Marcellus grabbed a glass and sat, pouring himself a drink.

"There has still been no activity from New Haven," Marcellus grunted, then finished his drink in a single motion. He grimaced as he glanced at the bottle label briefly before scowling.

"It's all I could find," I muttered by way of apology.

"You look like shit," Marcellus said, pouring himself a glass, "like you haven't slept in a week."

I shrugged.

"You should get some sleep," Marcellus said as he polished off another glass. I glanced briefly at the bottle. It was just under half full. I doubted that would be enough, but I wasn't going to complain. I could acquire more.

"So should you," I replied glibly. I reached for the bottle and poured myself another.

Marcellus raised his own in my direction in a mock salute. "To Sanchez," he toasted sombrely, gulping it in one swallow.

"Sanchez is dead?" I murmured, surprised.

Sanchez had been with us since almost the start. There were very few original members remaining.

"Yeah, he was killed in the bombing," Marcellus whispered. "It makes no sense. I don't see why they went on the attack—they must have known what would happen."

I had thought along the same lines. Something had changed and not necessarily for the better. Was this new tactic an indication of new leadership? Or did it mean something else? The bombing attack on me was a sign of desperation—they must have known it wouldn't have worked. They had attempted to kill me, but instead only managed to kill those around me. I took a deep breath. I could have prevented it, but I had chosen otherwise. I wondered if I had made the right choice. I wondered if there was even a right choice to make.

"I didn't know about Sanchez," I sighed. I hadn't touched my drink.

Marcellus's eyes hardened. "I know."

That explained why Marcellus was here. It had become a small tradition between us as members of the old crew died.

"How many of us are left?"

"Four," Marcellus grunted. "You, me, Cameron and Morre."

I nodded sombrely as I sipped my drink. I didn't feel much like drinking anymore. I may not remember the names of the replacements for my team, but I remembered my first command. I remembered as each of them died and how powerless I had been to prevent it. Even with all my power, I couldn't save everyone. This was a war—people die. I had stopped even trying.

"Maybe one day, you'll be toasting me," Marcellus murmured darkly, his façade slipping slightly to reveal the anger simmering underneath.

He blamed me for Sanchez's death and I didn't blame him. After all, I was responsible. I had allowed it to happen. I may as well have been the one to pull the trigger that ended his life.

"You never know," I grunted, "You could outlive me yet."

I didn't finish my drink.

CHAPTER THREE

Our scouts didn't report in the next morning. This could mean a variety of things, but it most likely meant that they had run into a mage. It would have taken an overwhelming force to prevent them from returning home.

My scry threads had been unsuccessful in finding them, but there was a large area of land to cover and it was possible they had simply hunkered down to hide. The firestorm was also playing havoc with my scry thread. There was too much Mana still in the air and it was like trying to see through static. Ironically enough, if someone had wanted to hide a mage in the region, they couldn't have done it any better this side of a Shading spell. A mage uses a Shading spell when they don't want someone seeing what they are doing. It throws up magical noise making it difficult to see Mana. When you try to look, all you see is the static from the Shading spell. This was like that, only not as bad. However, Shading spells throw up so much noise they are impossible to ignore. It's not like some stealth spell that would allow you to work in the dark. I didn't much like them. I didn't like something that interfered with my ability to see Mana.

No, there was nothing for it. We would need to go in with a small team. I wasn't going to risk the whole contingent on this. Obviously I had made a mistake last time, coming in so aggressively, and had missed something. I wasn't going to make the same mistake again. It was time to change tactics.

The plan was simple: we would take a single truck with a small team, no more than twelve soldiers, and go in under the cover of night. Hopefully we could catch our quarry unawares and close the trap before they even knew what was happening. The trick would be that I would need to appear to be human and not a mage.

The techniques for suppressing one's Mana signature were crude but effective—through a scry spell I would appear no different from the rest of the soldiers around me. The drawback was that while I was suppressing my powers I wouldn't be able to use them. This would make mobility a problem—a serious problem. I could move my legs if I needed to, but I doubted I'd be able to walk. I'd never tried since the hospital, but I knew how weak my body was. This wasn't going to be fun, but I would deal with that when the time came.

"I'm going to need you to come with me on this one," I murmured to Marcellus as he and his team finished loading the truck.

I saw from the raised eyebrow that he didn't understand I'd had to select my small team very carefully. I would normally leave Marcellus in command of the contingent when I went into the field; however, this time I selected a more junior officer. I needed someone I could trust explicitly and I trusted Marcellus far more than anyone else in the regiment.

"You're travelling with us?" Marcellus commented as I jumped into the passenger seat.

I didn't bother answering, but simply gestured towards the driver's seat. I could hear from the noises behind me that the rest of the team was getting into place in the back of the truck. A knock on the wall let us know that everyone was ready to go.

I used to love long car rides as a boy, but I detested them now. It seemed like a waste of time. After all with a merest flick of mana I could teleport myself to the destination in the same time that I could have entered the car. There was also the small fact that I was now sitting in a vehicle that was under someone else's control. I'd never been a particularly skilled driver, but I had been an even worse passenger. I was sure that should my feet still work properly I would have been pressing onto the base of the floor in the passenger seat to indicate when I thought the brake should be used. It was also strange being in an American car. I was used to the driver's controls being on this side. The whole feel of the car seemed different, had we not been driving on the centre of the road I was sure that would have irritated me as well. These distractions were good though—it allowed me to focus on something other than the suppression techniques that I was employing to nullify my mana signature and appear human. These techniques were uncomfortable to perform, and if performed for long enough could become downright painful. It began with a small headache in the base of your skull. It wasn't painful as such it was like that moment where you think 'hey I'm getting a headache' and hope that it doesn't get any more severe. I knew that it was going to get worse though, but I didn't want to focus on that. I knew that from experience—focus on the pain and you will find that you won't be able to bear it. No, this was okay. I could deal with this. I focused out the window.

The landscape on the northern American continent is beautiful. We were far from any cities and the land looked almost untouched by our war. Sure, there were signs every now and then of our conflict—burned out cars and crater pocked ground—but these were few and far between. However, we would soon reach the perimeter of the firestorm and then it would look far different.

"Sir, may I ask a question?" Marcellus broke into my distraction.

"Sure," I replied, turning to face him.

He stopped and stared at me for several seconds. I could see his face twisted in shock.

"What is it?" I barked after several seconds of awkward silence.

"Your eyes," he began. "They're normal."

I smiled wryly. "Ask your question."

It took Marcellus several seconds to compose himself before he could talk. My eyes must have really freaked him out. It was odd; normally it was our expanded irises that freaked people out. It wasn't surprising though—due to the Mana construct for my injury, I was always using Mana and therefore would look strange with normal eyes. This was one of the reasons I had selected Marcellus. I didn't want anyone else in the team to see me so weakened. The team needed to trust that I could protect them—they didn't need to see me looking human.

"Nevermind," Marcellus grunted. "I think I just figured out why you wanted me specifically."

I nodded with a grin and placed my sunglasses on. Marcellus was a smart man and I knew I didn't have to explain it any further to him. I had first met him before the war. When Killian and his cronies had swept through Europe, many soldiers had been displaced and fled across the Atlantic. Marcellus was French born, but ended up serving in an American unit, but then again I was Australian and I was de facto leading it—so I guess it wasn't that odd. I didn't much care for his nationality, but he could be trusted to perform his duties well and that was enough for me.

I heard Marcellus's whistle as we approached the edge of the firestorm. It looked like the surface of another planet. Everything was covered in black ash for miles.

"Holy shit," he whispered as he surveyed the destruction around him.

Fortunately the road was cleared of the worst of it and was still traversable. The first teams that had come in after the fight had to spend several hours clearing the road. A snowplough would have been ideal at making a path, but of course, being this far remote from snow fields, such a device was unlikely to be found. In the end they had made a makeshift plough with two pieces of corrugated tin welded to the front of a truck. The same truck we were sitting in now. It worked perfectly. There was nothing more tangible than ash in the debris— everything had been burned thoroughly. There were no shreds of wood or other wreckage in the mess. The Mana fire had done its job well. It would be a long time before the ground recovered.

I ordered Marcellus to continue on to New Haven, although I knew there wasn't much left there. Some of the stone work and concrete structures had survived the conflagration. It hadn't been much but enough to ensure there were some survivors. I didn't particularly want to return to the ruins, and it wasn't until three quarters of the way through the ash field that I realised that I wouldn't have to.

With my powers suppressed I didn't have the full scope of my sensing abilities, but I knew when I was being scryed upon. The tell-tale prickling of the skin on the back of my neck alerted me to the presence of Mana in my direct vicinity. It took everything I had to keep my powers hidden as I expanded my irises. I breathed in and pretended to yawn as I analysed the scry thread inspecting us. Fortunately with my sunglasses on, they wouldn't immediately see my expanded irises, unless they were really interested in me. Without my Mana, I wouldn't look any different to the rest of the soldiers under my command. I had no way of knowing if an attack was imminent or if they were simply doing routine surveillance—either way I was ready. It was fortunate we were in the ash field, with the static Mana noise in the background making it difficult to identify specifics of the scry thread, but it also would make it more difficult to see what was going on around us. The scry thread followed us for some time—they were awfully interested in us.

They must have determined we were heading to the ruins of New Haven; the thread retracted and the Mana returned to its originator. Again I was grateful for the Mana static, which gave me more of a chance to follow the thread without being detected. I didn't need to get close, I just needed to see where they were operating from. As expected, the scry thread trail didn't lead me back to New Haven. There was nothing left there.

Instead it took me to an industrial complex about three kilometres further east. Being mostly concrete buildings, it had survived the inferno better than most. It was possible our target had moved operations here after New Haven fell, but I doubted it because anyone who survived New Haven was now in our custody—and none of them looked like insurgents or enemy troops.

I didn't get close enough to the complex to linger. The thread ended there, our target was there, and that was good enough for me. As I passed over the complex, a strange sense of unease hit me. There was a very strange Mana signature coming from the complex. I hadn't felt anything like this before and that meant it was dangerous.

This was a dilemma. Do I go in now, or do I send in the troops? It was possible that whatever was in there was a trap specifically for me. In the end it didn't matter much, I had to go. I was never going to get a better shot at this.

"I'm going in," I whispered to Marcellus. I gave him directions to the complex, and vaguely heard him give his confirmation. I then raised the necessary power to teleport and felt the familiar pressure from the Mana construct wrap around my lower body. I wasn't going to teleport directly into the complex; the Mana signature I had felt could have interfered with the jump and I deemed it too dangerous to try. With a soft exhale, I teleported.

* * *

My arrival in the complex didn't seem to be noticed; there didn't appear to be any security guards or watch points. This was unusual. I glanced around expecting to hear shouting or rifle fire, but there was nothing. It was unsettling. Now that I was closer, the strange Mana frequency I had sensed through my scry spell was almost overbearing. Not a threat, but it definitely felt dangerous. Kind of like standing next to a live wire; it wasn't a weapon designed to kill you, but if you weren't careful it would achieve the same end.

The complex was made up of three main buildings and what appeared to be a burned-out office structure to the front. The largest building was where I sensed the Mana coming from, of all three buildings it had survived the fire that had passed the most intact. That seemed like the best place to start.

With a shiver I reinforced the shield around myself and sent out a thread that would tear the large loading bay doors from their hinges and send them exploding inwards. I then leapt in through the newly made gap to deal with anyone who was inside. This seemed as good a way as any to introduce myself to the inhabitants.

It seemed to have worked as it took several seconds before gunfire was turned on me. I landed in the centre of what had obviously been a staging ground. I swept the soldiers from their feet with a contemptuous sweep of Mana as I inspected the building. It wasn't what I had expected. On the far side I could make out Russian tanks, but they weren't the most dangerous thing in the room. At the other end was the thing making all the damned Mana noise I had sensed. It was a four-by-four metre vertical plane of energy. It shimmered with a pinkish-red light that pulsated across everything and put out a small crackling noise. I'd never seen anything like it before, but I knew it for what it was. It was a rift.

I'd read about rifts in my studies and knew the fundamentals about how to produce one, but my studies had gone in another direction and I knew without a doubt that this was beyond my knowledge to produce safely. Rifts were used to force two positions in space together. Once the connection had been made, matter could pass from one point to another in seconds. This explained the Russian heavy ordinance we had found—someone was moving troops using rifts. I had long suspected something like this; enemy troops had been vanishing into the wild too quickly and appearing too regularly for regular logistics to account for it.

Only a master mage could have constructed this; they were inherently unstable and a disruption at either end of the rift would cause untold damage to both ends. As I got closer to the rift, my skin prickled with caution as the Mana sought to reinforce my shield.

I glanced down carefully at the construct and saw how it had been built, and which Mana frequency had been linked to the weave. I felt the heat at the edge of the ring as the Mana particles burned the air around them. The sizzling grew louder and flared in response to my presence. A small shiver passed over me as I realised the Mana from my shield was reacting to the rift field. It was a small distortion and easily within the construct's ability to withstand, but any more serious Mana used in its presence could very well prove fatal.

I backed away carefully from the rift; if my shield was going to cause a distortion at this range, I didn't particularly want to see what would happen if I moved any closer. From the state of the equipment in the warehouse it was clear they were being prepped for movement, and I could only assume they were pulling out. The only question was—where were they going?

As I moved around the rift it took me several minutes

until I found the Mana trail that would lead to the other end of the rift. It was so delicate and very faint. It made scry threads positively easy to spot. This left me with an unfortunate choice: if I wanted to find out where the rift went I really only had two options. I could attempt to follow the Mana thread trail and hope I didn't lose it, or I could attempt to pass through the rift, which might be dangerous to someone using Mana. I would have to take my shield down, which would make me vulnerable to whoever was on the other side. I didn't much like that option, but I didn't think it was going to be possible to follow the Mana trail accurately. There was simply too much of a chance that I'd lose it. This wasn't much of a choice.

I glanced around the complex one more time to figure out if I was going to be shot the moment my shield went down. With a shiver I lowered my shield and moved closer to the rift. The Mana I was using to keep myself mobile was far less potent than my shield, but even so I saw slight ripples of distortion, but I was reasonably confident it wouldn't disrupt the rift structure.

The warmth from the rift was almost tangible as I got close enough to touch the structure. The surface was bathed in a yellow/red hue and was highly reflective. I could see myself in the rift, but every couple of seconds my reflection was washed over as a pulse of Mana rippled across the surface. The end effect was like looking at a mirage of water on a road during a hot day. The warmth from the rift was uncomfortable, but hardly painful. If I had a shield around me I would barely have registered it.

I tried to place my hand against the surface of the rift, but that was impossible, like trying to do the same against a waterfall. The surface offered no resistance and my hand simply passed into the rift. I could see the surface of the rift pulsate out in waves as my hand disturbed the surface, but felt nothing. The nausea common with teleportation wasn't present. This was because a teleport spell had broken me down to a molecular level, converted me into Mana, travelled the required distance, and then rebuilt me. However, the rift simply messed with the spatial distance between two points, and as far as the molecules in my body were concerned it was no different than waving my hand in front of my face. I grinned as I watched the Mana flare up in reaction to the foreign object that was my hand within the rift. There wasn't any difference to the Mana trail—it was simply bridging the connection between two points in space. But the Mana field in front of me flared brightly and I could feel the Mana pass through me like a live wire reacting with the construct that was keeping me mobile. Small shivers of distortion swept across me.

It was time to move. Someone on the other side would surely notice the change to the rift indicating someone was passing through it. Or maybe not—I didn't really understand how rifts worked—but this wasn't exactly the best time to conduct experiments. I took a deep breath and entered the rift. I had expected some kind of visual distortion as I passed through, but there was nothing. One minute I was standing in a warehouse complex and the next I was standing somewhere else. It now looked like I was standing in another equally boring warehouse complex. I was making slow progress here.

Actually, judging from the soldiers now pointing their weapons against my unshielded ass, this wasn't likely to be as boring as the previous warehouse. I was still far too close to the rift to contemplate throwing up a shield. This was going to be interesting.

I placed my hands up in the air and called out loudly, "I surrender!"

I don't think they had expected me to say that. It looked for a second as if they were going to simply shoot me and be done with it. They probably should have—they didn't live long enough to regret their decision.

* * *

I waited as the soldiers moved in behind me and cuffed my arms behind my back. They roughly pushed me forward away from the rift, possibly thinking I was some form of advanced scout. I suspect surrendering had convinced them I wasn't a mage. That ploy would obviously fail once they removed the sunglasses from my face and saw my Mana-soaked irises. But I would be long gone before they could do that. If I did nothing, I would have a long and possibly terminal interrogation session ahead as they sought to get troop movements and locations from me. It would almost be amusing to let them try; unfortunately I didn't have the time.

They were shouting at me in Russian. I had no idea what they were saying, but it was obvious they wanted me to kneel on the ground. Had I misjudged them? Was this simply an execution? In any event I wasn't worried—I was now far enough away from the rift that a shield was now an acceptable risk.

I took a step forward as if to kneel and raised my shield. This action must have been recognised because the moment the shield raised, a gunshot went off. But by that stage, of course, it was too late. With a flick of my wrist I tore the handcuffs into small chunks of metal that fell from my wrists. Several more shots bounced from my shield as the soldiers increased their rate of fire, all the while backing away. These soldiers weren't stupid— they knew they weren't able to take me out without seriously heavy weaponry. I watched with amusement as a grenade was lobbed at me. I simply walked through the explosion, absorbing the impact against my shield and killing the soldier who had thrown it.

With a sweep of my hand I dragged several more soldiers down, but most of them had scattered deeper into the complex. I could still feel scattered shots against my shield, but they were few and far between. I had a choice here: I could seek them out one by one and end them, or figure out where I was and where to find the mage who had created the rift. I knew from my studies that rifts required careful maintenance and reconfiguring to keep them locked into place. The mage wouldn't be far away while the rift was still active.

As for me, I assumed I was somewhere in Russia, perhaps Moscow, but my assumption was wrong. My journeys had never taken me that far north before, but from what I had heard it was a cold country, not the balmy temperature it appeared to be here. However if I wasn't in Russia, then where the hell was I? There was a simple way to find out. I sent a scry thread out. It didn't take me too long to determine my location. I'd seen this city a million times on TV shows and in movies. I was in Los Angeles. The distinctive Hollywood sign, which had survived relatively intact from the fall of the city, was a big giveaway. This just raised further questions. Why the hell were Russian troops congregating in Los Angeles? Now that I had seen both sides of the rift, it was obvious they were moving resources into this city. Perhaps they planned on making a final stand here.

I was returning my scry thread when I saw the familiar spark of a mage's Mana signature not far from me. I couldn't tell at this range who it was, but they kept their distance. This was probably wise on their part—a full-fledged Mana fight that close to the rift was probably a bad idea.

I wasn't going to let this opportunity get away from me. I ended the scry thread and launched myself into the air through a window on the far side of the warehouse, sending several threads out ahead of me, tearing holes in the buildings ahead to get to my target. It wasn't the most subtle of attacks, but it was the quickest way to get to the mage before they teleported away. Assuming, of course, that they were going to teleport away. Judging from my opponent's Mana signature, it didn't look like it. They appeared to be waiting for me. I crashed through an apartment block and found out who was waiting for me.

Gregory Tibus.

I grinned as I clenched my hands into fists and launched several threads at him, hoping to take him unawares. With a casual flick of his wrist he deflected my attacks, but he didn't follow up with an attack of his own. That was strange.

"You are who has been killing us?" he called with his strange Greek accent. "You are not what we expected."

I didn't answer him; instead I used the opportunity to draw my powers together into a single spear-like thread. There was a loud thump as the thread impacted against his shield and sent him barrelling into the building behind him.

I followed up immediately with several more strikes. I hadn't heard the tell-tale sound of a shield cracking and knew my opponent was still a threat. My assumption was confirmed as enemy threads lanced out at me. Had I remained standing where I was, I would not have been able to avoid them. I launched myself backwards on top of the building I had crashed through earlier. With a hammer fisted motion, I slammed a thread down onto the top of the building Tibus was hiding in. With a loud cracking noise, concrete dust and debris was thrown up into the air. The brick building fell in upon itself and onto my opponent.

I knew that, like my attack before, this wouldn't seriously inconvenience him, but I was just getting started. Looping a thread around a gas cylinder on the far side of the complex, I ripped it from its mountings and sent it flying into the ruins. With a flex of my fingers I sent a sheet of flame lancing from my hands into the ruins. The resulting explosion tore the remains of the building into shrapnel, but again I knew my opponent had probably survived. I would have been able to survive such an explosion. This had been a mere distraction until I could finish the job. I launched myself into the explosion to finish him off, while he was avoiding all the flying debris and explosions surrounding him.

We had the same idea. Unfortunately for me, he got in the first shot. As I launched myself forward, a thread launched itself from the inferno and caught me mid-leap. The resulting strike smashed against my shield and sent me spiralling into the wall of my building. The shield impacted the wall, destroying it and sending me sliding across the top floor, incidentally falling into the hole I had made on my way in. I didn't have much time to get my bearings as Tibus then brought the building down upon me using a similar strike to the one I had used earlier. I had prepared for just such a move and used an explosion of telekinetic power to send the debris flying away from me. I noted with satisfaction that several large chunks of concrete hit Tibus as he attempted to bring his strength upon me. It was nothing more than a mere distraction, but it was enough for me to go back onto the offensive. I swatted Tibus from the air with a well-placed thread and launched myself after him to continue the fight as our threads collided once again. With a crackling sizzle, our threads squealed in protest as we applied more power in an attempt to over-power the other's thread.

"You will find I will not fall as easily as the others!" Tibus snarled. He was surprisingly strong and if I had continued on with this test of strength I probably would have lost. Due to my injuries I just couldn't compete in displays of raw strength like this. But I had other methods. I allowed Tibus to get the upper hand, slowly looking like he was beating me back as I gathered my strength. I took a deep breath—what I did next would have been the unthinkable in combat. I teleported.

It was a safe enough jump, simply from in front of him to behind him. I didn't need to scry as the land-ing site was well within my vision. I knew Tibus had thrown everything he had into that thread and therefore wouldn't be able to disrupt me as I jumped. My gambit paid off. Tibus's thread decimated the wall behind me as I blinked out of existence.

As soon as I reappeared, I launched everything I had at Tibus's exposed flank. I hadn't even raised a shield yet. I watched with glee as the strike smashed against Tibus's ribs and I heard the tell-tale sound of a shield crumbling. I hadn't broken his shield completely, but I'd certainly managed to break through it. I'd probably broken most of his ribs on his left side too. Tibus howled with anger and pain and turned in fury to face me, but by then it was too late for him. I'd already raised my shield and continued my offensive. Several threads lashed out against him, causing him to stagger backwards. This was over.

Unfortunately my overconfidence had undone me. With strength born of desperation and impending death, Tibus managed to launch a thread back that latched around my waist and brought me into the air. Tremors immediately rocked down my left side, as the breath was sucked from my body through my shield. The last time I had been in this position had been against my old master, and Victor had broken me. He had literally crushed me until my shield had broken and my bones were shattered. With the tremors I couldn't raise a thread to protect myself and I was at risk of losing my shield.

I saw my end coming and the panic almost overcame me. As the tremors took me I felt my shield wavering and I thought it would fall. For a brief few seconds the panic subsided as I began to accept my fate. The calm that came with accepting my death brought clarity back to my focus and I could reinforce my shield before it fell.

Had Tibus been able to sustain his attack, he would have broken through my shield. Fortunately, Tibus wasn't anywhere near as strong as my former master. Either that, or his injuries were preventing him from using his full strength. He wasn't going to be able to break through my shield. He had obviously come to the same conclusion.

"Why won't you die?" he snarled as he hurled me against the wall, sending me barrelling through yet another wall and landing in the warehouse where the rift had been constructed. I ploughed through the wall and slid across the warehouse floor, finishing just metres before the rift. I watched as it flared yellow in response to a high level of Mana being deployed so close. This must have been Tibus's plan—before I could do anything, Tibus struck me again and sent me barrelling into the eye of the rift.

I passed through in fury and landed hard on the concrete floor on the other side. I watched in desperation as the act of a shielded mage passing through the rift caused a cascade in the structure of the Mana construct. The rift flared red with fury as the edges began to decay. It took me several seconds before I realised I needed to do something or I would be ground zero in a very large explosion. I could possibly teleport away in time, but my soldiers who were still en route would possibly be caught in the blast. I wasn't prepared to sacrifice them a second time.

I could see the degradation of the Mana structure of the rift and see the threads that held it together breaking down. I'd never worked with this frequency of Mana before, but none of that really mattered. I could hardly make it any worse—the structure was already in a critical state. The rift collapsed in on itself fairly quickly as the link between the two ends failed. The portal at this end began to expand outwards at an exponential rate. The threads holding it in place collapsed as the power from the thread overwhelmed their integrity and one by one they broke down. If I had known the theory behind the thread, I could probably have replaced the threads and stabilised the rift, but I'd never worked with rift theory before. No, all I could do was attempt to stabilise the structure and hope that it would be enough to contain the rift as it failed.

With shaking fingers I began to work. I closed my eyes as I reached out and poured more strength into each thread. I could feel the pressure the rift was exerting against them as its full brunt was turned against my threads. It was overwhelming, but somehow I managed to sustain one thread that should have failed and then another and then a third. It became a race against time as to which processes would achieve control over the most threads. Already due to my meddling I could see the rift doing some odd things. Its surface twisted in two directions as two conflicting powers vied for control. I let the power flow from my fingers, stabilising the next thread in line until I had completed a full circle around the rift. Once that occurred, the process of degradation lessened noticeably to the point that if I had wanted to I could probably have stabilised the rift and brought it back to functionality. I had no wish to do that; I didn't need the rift. At this point it was more of a liability than an asset. I still wasn't one hundred per cent sure of what

I was doing, only that the rise of Mana within the construct was lessening, which could only be a good thing. I continued working until I felt a strange thing—another thread snaking into the rift. I glanced up and saw Tibus through the rift attempting to do the same thing I was. He looked focused on his Mana, and it would be easy to strike him down. There were two problems with that. One, he appeared to be trying to remove the rift safely; and two. the rift itself was in the way. Neither of us could strike through that field. I shrugged with resignation. Tibus could wait. I had no intention of being at the centre of a rift explosion. As powerful as I was, I knew I would not be able to withstand that. With Tibus working on the other side, we appeared to be making headway on the rift. I could now see how Tibus was controlling the thread, and I altered my tactics to match his.

With a small sigh I began to withdraw the strength of my bonds around it and let the threads fail in a controlled fashion. I watched with satisfaction as the field collapsed and I lost sight of my erstwhile assistant. The threads used to construct the rift were still active, but I could see them slowly fading. In time they would disappear and the area would be safe again. It took about five minutes for the last thread to finally sizzle and fail. The structure of the rift was already long gone by that stage, but that didn't make the final stages any less dangerous.

It took me several more minutes before I was comfortable enough to confirm that the rift had been removed and was no longer a threat. I would like to say that my ability to defuse an exploding rift was made possible by years of skill at manipulating Mana and my understanding of the theory behind basic Mana construction, but to be honest it was probably more dumb luck than anything else. Had Tibus not intervened, the outcome could have been far different.

As much as I wanted to teleport straight to Los Angeles and finish this, it probably wasn't a good idea. It would be more appropriate to report back to command and let them know about this. Our kind didn't usually work too well together in the field and it was possible I might run into another of our operatives. It would be better to see who, if anyone else, had been assigned to LA. As much as it pained me, it would be better to follow protocol on this one. The last thing I needed was to get drawn into a fight with a mage from my own side accidently. It had happened in the past.

* * *

My reflection was unforgiving as I stared at myself in the barracks mirror. I needed to get control of these tremors. They had almost cost me my life during my battle with Tibus. I still wasn't sure where the clarity that had saved my life had come from. I had never experienced such a thing before. My face in the mirror held no answers; in that face I saw what I always saw: my fear.

A polite cough brought my attention to Marcellus standing at my door.

"What is it?"

"You have been instructed to make contact with command."

"Understood," I grunted as I ran my hand through my hair.

The necessity of using a field phone rankled me, especially considering that in the blink of an eye I could have teleported back to command and delivered my message in person. It was lucky that we even had a working satellite phone available, due to the bomb that had gone off in the command centre earlier. I wasn't looking forward to the conversation. It was usually some stiff military command type who had no idea of what they were talking about on the other end. I was pleasantly surprised when a familiar voice greeted me when I picked up the receiver.

"Levenson," I murmured. "I'm surprised you're back in operations."

"It's an unusual situation," Levenson replied tersely. "You mentioned something about rifts in your report."

I spent the next forty minutes explaining my report. Levenson was a burnt-out mage who had lost his powers during his apprenticeship and therefore I didn't need to explain key concepts. I probably wouldn't have been able to explain the necessary information to a regular military general.

"That would explain the erratic troop movements we've been seeing," Levenson commented once I had finished.

"It would seem they plan on using LA as a base of operations." I commented. "I'd like to continue my assault on Tibus. It was only dumb luck that I didn't get him this time. I can be there and back within the hour."

"No," Levenson ordered firmly, "not alone. We will reallocate your division."

"Bring the whole unit? That seems excessive," I said. "Besides, we have refugees from New Haven to think of."

I had only really said that to confuse the issue. I didn't care much for the safety of the civilians, and I didn't particularly want to play nursemaid for them. Levenson would know this wasn't a good use of my abilities anyway, but he could hardly move the whole division. No, sending me in alone was the best solution. I could tell from the silence at the other end of the line that Levenson was considering his options.

"No, this is more important," Levenson eventually replied. "Yours is not the only report of mages within Los Angeles. I do not want you to going in there by yourself."

I sighed wistfully. I'd had this conversation about a dozen times previously with command. I didn't think I'd have to have it with Levenson though. "Soldiers are not going to be sufficient support once the fighting get started."

"I know," Levenson cut me off. "We're going to send in more mages."

We hadn't done that before. It boded badly.

"Do I know everything I need to know?" I whispered down the line.

"Everything you should know," Levenson replied darkly.

Well, that was a politic answer that didn't really answer my question. I wasn't surprised though—I didn't really trust Levenson, even though he had saved my life and been responsible for turning me into what I was today. I wasn't sure if I was grateful or not for his intervention.

CHAPTER FOUR

We received our orders the following morning. We were to make our way to the east coast via Seattle and liaise with our transport. There were more refugee settlements near Seattle where we could offload our civilians. We didn't have enough trucks to move everyone, so we had to do it the old fashioned way. If I thought I hated travelling by car, I hated travelling by foot even more.

And so we made a small column of about a hundred soldiers and less than fifty civilians and marched towards Seattle. The elderly and children were given priority spots within what truck space we did have, but we also needed to move some of the heavier equipment, so there wasn't a lot of space. We would probably reach Seattle in about a week, but I hoped that if we pushed ourselves we could make it in four days. That was unlikely given the circumstances; old people and children aren't exactly fast. I chaffed at the delay and the necessity of remaining with the troops. If the situation were more urgent, I would have contemplated using a rift to move these people. We could have been in Seattle in seconds. But I didn't trust my understanding enough to attempt it, and the last thing I needed was a wild rift setting off more explosions across the landscape. It was an intriguing option though, and even though I had already discounted it, my mind kept returning to the necessary threads required to summon such a feat. This was probably a good thing; there was precious little else to distract me on the road.

I was quietly surprised that we didn't encounter any more resistance as we moved our column—our enemy had moved their troops to Los Angeles and given up on this section. That was probably a good thing; I doubted our abilities to defend the column properly in the face of a serious attack. If there was a mage operating in this area, the column would have made a very tempting target.

In the end it took us five days to reach Seattle. The city was mostly untouched by the war, but you could see the signs. The streets were empty, as most of the civilians had fled into the wild. Heavy calibre guns had been placed on the rooftops of the buildings near the main highway into the city. It was like walking into an armed camp.

We were to rendezvous with the USS *Abraham Lincoln* to ferry us to our new destination. The *Lincoln* was one of the few remaining aircraft carriers still in service. Something as large as a military aircraft carrier tended to be a target too delicious for most mages to resist. Punching a hole through what is essentially a large metal boat floating in water isn't exactly rocket science for most of my kind, and the temptation to take out a carrier would have been more than most of my kind could resist. The temptation would have been too much for the old me had my enemies presented such a target.

The only reason this ship had survived was that it had a protector. The daunting figure of Master Glave greeted us as we made our way onto the carrier. He acted as watchman for the battle group. His stern eyes glanced across the soldiers until they rested on me. I grinned mirthlessly as the Mana in his body rose in response to the threat of another mage in close proximity. I knew without a doubt that my own Mana would be reacting to him in a similar fashion. I had first met Master Glave about two years ago. He was a dour and humourless man without much to recommend him other than his power. He was powerful, not quite as powerful as I had been in my prime, but I was forced to account him as probably my better in my weakened state. The concession rankled against my soul, but I could not deny the truth. Aside from the reminder of my loss, I didn't much care for the man personally. Anyone who demanded to be called 'master' had some serious issues going on, and Glave couldn't possibly be his real name. This kind of macho name was taken by people who had been given birth names like Clyde or Clarence and felt they needed to compensate for this in their adulthood.

"Master Glave," I whispered, adding slight sarcasm to the title.

"Master Wills," he replied curtly. I could literally see the disdain in his eyes as he spoke to me.

"Not, Master," I replied with a grin. "Just call me Devon."

I knew this would annoy him more than any insult. He was the sort who found too much pride in rank and accolades, and by refusing my own I was also cheapening his. This wasn't my only reason for disliking that title though: Master Wills was the name my former teacher had used for me. For that reason alone I would never be comfortable. I was no one's master and I hadn't achieved anything that could justify taking the title.

"The Admiral has requested your presence on the bridge," Glave grunted as I walked past him.

"Understood."

The aircraft carrier had seen better days. There were obvious signs of recent battle everywhere I looked. The crew looked beaten and in several cases bloody, but still operated with the military precision I had come to expect from the US Navy. The bridge was no exception. The Admiral had his back to me when I entered the bridge, but the rest of the crew was immediately aware of my entrance and saluted accordingly.

"You wanted to see me?" I called over the chatter.

"Master Wills." He nodded by way of greeting as he waved me over. "I thought you would like to know that we received reports that Gregory Tibus was killed in a battle over Los Angeles yesterday."

I grunted softly; this wasn't good news. I had been chasing that bastard for about a year now and I'd missed my shot by only a couple of days? I should have finished him off when I'd had the chance. I regretted not immediately returning to Los Angeles despite my orders. The fact that I hadn't been the one to bring him down set my teeth on edge. He had been my link to Killian Voll, and I had been so close.

"And Voll?" I prompted.

"No confirmed sightings," the Admiral replied. "Sightings are getting fewer every day. It's possible he has already been killed. He has been up to until now the most visible of our targets."

I nodded grimly. There were as many mage deaths between our own kind from infighting than deaths that could be associated to our foes. It was entirely possible that Voll had been taken down in a petty squabble with some renegade mage, but I didn't believe it. There were still too many unaccounted for; for one, my former master Victor was still out there and I refused to believe he would have fallen to some piddling mage. No, there was no one out there capable of taking him down. No one yet, I amended silently.

"In short, it looks like this war may soon be over," the Admiral concluded.

"This is good news." I commented, not believing a word of it.

"Yes, it means that things can return to normal without further intervention from your kind."

I nodded uncomfortably. I had no idea what my place in the new world was going to be. I was a product of the old world—our kind had no place in the coming world and we knew it. That was okay by me though; I could deal with that provided I'd taken out my former master before I fell. I often wondered how others of my kind had planned on dealing with this new world. They must have plans. Or were they simply living day to day like everyone else? When this war started it seemed those who had made plans were the ones who suffered most for it.

"How reliable is the report of Tibus's death?"

Our reports of mage death weren't always reliable. A mage battle wasn't a good place for witnesses and what looked like the end of the battle from afar may simply just have been teleportation.

"Reliable," the Admiral continued. "It's been verified by your kind."

"Who?"

"Stanley Kristoff."

That was good, I liked him. I hadn't known of him before the war at all and had only met him briefly during the battle of New York. He had been a good mage though, and it seemed he hadn't been allied with either Marcus or Victor. This was unusual for a mage of any power, as both sides had openly courted those with power. This indicated that he wasn't amongst the most powerful of our kind, but he was trustworthy, which was more than you could say about most mages.

"We received confirmation of Tibus's death and then nothing. Kristoff's team failed to check in."

Well, that sucked. There was only one reason he would fail to check in. He would be missed. Still, perhaps some good could come out of this. Kristoff wasn't the most powerful mage, but he wasn't weak either—only someone truly competent could have taken him out.

"Voll?"

"It's possible," the Admiral confirmed, "but unlikely. Our last reports have him somewhere in central China."

I didn't need to tell him that his movement reports were never going to be accurate. I shouldn't have to. He should have known. Our kind's activities weren't exactly unknown, especially teleportation. I'd often told command that any survey data on our movements were next to useless, but still most commanders seemed to fall back to the old ways. This was fine when it came down to troop movements and the like, but when you were hunting mages, the last report of their location was a rough guide at best. I was sure that the Admiral was a good sailor and had served his country well, but this was just another example of old-school thinking. The military just couldn't grasp that they weren't fighting enemy soldiers. They were fighting enemy mages who didn't respect or even understand the traditional rules of combat. My opinion of this Admiral immediately lowered.

"How long until we're in Los Angeles?"

* * *

My meeting with the Admiral hadn't exactly gone as I had hoped. I stormed through the corridors of the ship, trying to find where I had been quartered. I hated these ships as I could never find anything. The confined spaces of the corridors and smaller rooms almost begged to illicit claustrophobia. I vaguely thought about using a scry to find Marcellus, but rejected the idea as this would probably have alerted Glave, who was so tightly wound he would assume it was an attack. I had no wish to encounter him again if I could possibly avoid it. I must have circumnavigated the ship three times and I still didn't seem any closer to finding my quarters.

"Master Wills?" a voice called out from across the corridor.

I turned to see a small woman chasing after me down the crowded hall, colliding with other members of the ship as she struggled to catch me. She seemed to be having as much trouble navigating through the busy corridors as I did. The difference was that crew members actively moved out of my way. They offered her no such courtesy.

"I thought it was you!" she huffed breathlessly when she finally managed to catch me. "I couldn't believe my eyes when I saw you walk past."

"Have we met?" I inquired softly. I didn't remember ever meeting this woman before.

"No, but I've seen you from the news clips."

I had hardly been an active figure publically. I preferred to be more of an 'operate from behind the scenes' kind of guy. I had left the political stuff to people like Levenson and those better able to portray the kind of bravura required for public office. This woman must have spent quite some time going through old news feeds if she had acquired more than five minutes footage of me.

"You must have done your research well then," I replied crisply as I turned to go.

"Wait!" she said, reaching out to stop me.

"What is it?" I shook her hand from my shoulder.

"Would you allow me to interview you?"

"Who are you?" I laughed, amazed at her request. "And why on earth would you want to interview me?"

This seemed to throw her into confusion for a second. It was clear that she had thought the answer would be obvious as to why someone would want to interview me. It wasn't; I was genuinely curious.

"My name is Emily Perry and I am, or used to be, a reporter. I'm writing a book on this war and I'd love to get a take on your experiences."

"You don't want my experiences," I murmured bitterly. The last thing I wanted to do was be interviewed by this girl, but it didn't look like she was going to be swayed easily. She even had her notebook out to record anything I said. There was going to be no easy way out of this. She would pursue this with the tenacity of a bulldog seeking food. She had that look about her.

"You were the first, you were right there at the start!" she continued, undaunted by the unimpressed expression on my face.

There was nothing for it. I had hoped I would never need to do this again. I had come across the technique accidently. I quickly glanced around, but no one was paying us any attention in this section of the corridor. I breathed out as I summoned the power into my hands, sickened by the feel of the corrupted Mana slowing down my arm. The frequency of this power wasn't enjoyable. I endured the discomfort as I let the power flow to my fingers. It was similar to the necromantic thread I had used a few days ago, but it was different—this was far more insidious.

Emily was still talking and seemed unaware that I wasn't answering her questions. She faltered slightly when I reached my hands out as if to flick a lock of hair from her face. Her face took on a quizzical expression at my imposition, I saw a flash of anger in her features, then she seemed to have reached a conclusion and allowed it. That had been a mistake on her part.

Her face immediately went blank as my palm slowly pressed against her forehead. Her features slackened as the Mana lanced into her head. She shuddered involuntarily as the Mana began its work. I knew there was some pain to this process, but she wouldn't suffer for long and the pain would soon be forgotten after the process had completed.

Her eyes lost focus as I leaned in, my palm now pressing hard against her face. If I hadn't used the Mana to completely override her senses, she probably would have screamed, but as it was she was helpless.

"You will forget you ever wanted to interview me," I whispered in her ear. "You will not remember this meeting and you will not seek me out again."

The Mana in her body was making her compliant and my words became a compulsion that would make my words an order. In time her psyche would support the compulsion I had implanted in her and would actively produce the necessary reasoning to support the idea. I shuddered as I removed my hand from the poor girl's forehead. I felt sick, but this was the most direct way. She would leave me alone now. She blinked twice as she staggered back. Her eyes attempted to snap into focus on me, but by that stage I was already walking past her.

I had accidently come across the technique in Victor's writings. It had been one of his early discoveries. At first I had rejected the idea of using it. I had been on the receiving end of several compulsions and the experience had soured me on the effect. However, in time, curiosity had gotten the better of me and I grudgingly studied the passage. It had eventually proved to be a dead end, but by then I had already mastered the rudimentary skills necessary for functional use of the compel sorcery.

As I watched the reporter dazedly make her way back up the corridor, I shuddered and let the rising feeling of nausea pass. How quickly I had chosen to use that technique. I had once vowed that I would never become as Victor had, that I would never impose my will on others. That had turned out to be an empty promise. I had quickly discarded my principles when the opportunity presented. The fact that it was for the best was irrelevant. She would be safer if she didn't pursue me. I had seen it in her eyes; she would have followed me when I left this ship for Los Angeles and she would have been exposed to unnecessary danger. No, it was better that she remain behind, her mission unfulfilled. She could acquire the knowledge she needed another way. God, I'm such a liar sometimes.

A hand on my shoulder spun me round, immediately sending the Mana in my body on the defensive. There was a loud crackling noise as the shield that sprang up around me caused the offending hand to be thrown back. The angry face of Master Glave glowered at me through the shield as he nursed his injured hand.

"What did you just do? A few minutes ago. You did something? What was it?" he snarled at me.

Shit. He had sensed the sorcery I had used on Miss Perry. He obviously hadn't known what it had been. I would have been very surprised if he had—that secret was restricted to those with access to Victor's spell books, and that certainly didn't include Glave. I grimaced in the face of Glave's wrath, but wasn't overly concerned. There was nothing he was going to do here. As annoyed as I was, I was kind of impressed. He had been nowhere near me when I had discharged the small amount of Mana required, yet he had somehow sensed it. His sensing skills were impressive to say the least. They were far better than mine. This was worth noting.

"What did you do?" Glave repeated. "I didn't recognise that Mana signature. I don't like unidentified Mana going off on my ship!"

I didn't bother answering him. It was none of his

business and I certainly wasn't going to take the time to explain myself. I could see him getting angrier and angrier. I could almost see the intensity of the Mana rising in his chest as his anger began to overpower him.

"You should calm yourself," I whispered softly. "We wouldn't want an incident."

I left my threat unsaid, but the message was clear. I would protect myself and if necessary kill him. Our alliance was out of necessity only. Although I wasn't sure of who would actually come out the superior between us, I was positive he didn't know either.

"You should watch yourself," he retorted lamely as he finally managed to get his anger under control. "You make enough damned noise with that construct of yours."

He was of course referring to the Mana frame I used to keep myself mobile. That might have explained how he had sensed me so quickly. I was already making enough noise and all he had sensed was the change in frequency. Maybe that explained the speed of his reaction. Or maybe he was just keeping an eye on me. Either way there was nothing I could do about it now.

"You should get that tended to," I grunted, gesturing towards his burnt hand. "And as for the Mana, I will use when and where I like, as is my right."

I could almost feel him glowering at me as I turned the corner in search of my quarters. Since I had already had a run in with Glave, I decided to scry. It made my search so much quicker.

* * *

I was invited to the captain's table that evening. I've never really understood the courtesy of being asked to dine with the captain. I assume the tradition had something to do with colonial times where the fare at the captain's table was of a higher quality. It didn't really make much sense on a modern military vessel where the food was pretty much the same during war time. I had vaguely considered sending my apologies, but didn't want to draw too much further unwanted attention to myself by refusing. No, it would be better to attend, keep quiet, and hope it would be over quickly. I'd had to attend these functions before and they were always painful. The invitation had come with a clean pressed formal uniform. It had been some time since I'd worn a formal uniform and I assumed it would also require that I shave. It had been an equally long time since a razor had touched my face. A tremor overtook me as I raised the razor to my face. I immediately pulsed it away, but it had taken its toll. A small nick in my cheek slowly appeared in the mirror as a small trail of blood oozed from the wound. I had cut myself with the razor, foolish. Stupid. I gritted my fists around the small plastic razor.

What was one more cut on this already broken face? Let it bleed. I've never been squeamish about the sight of my own blood, but watching the blood mix with the water in the sink I couldn't help but feel that perhaps it was prophetic. It was such a simple thing—three small droplets of blood in the water. The blood mixed so easily with the purity of the water, muddying it, defiling it. You can't even see the blood any longer if there is enough water, but the impurity is still there. There was a metaphor in there somewhere. I washed the rest of the blood from my face with a grimace as I ignored my reflection in the mirror.

"Unusual to see you in full uniform," Marcellus commented as I emerged bathroom.

I just grunted at him as I made my way back to our cabin. Due to the cramped nature of the battleship, even I had been paired with a roommate. It wasn't ideal, but I could deal with Marcellus for a short period of time far better than I could anyone else.

"Better you than me." He grinned as he watched me assess the stark white uniform. He could tell that I was less than impressed at being forced to wear white. I wasn't by any means a vain man, but white really wasn't my colour.

"Didn't I tell you?" I smiled. "I'm allowed to bring a guest."

Marcellus's face immediately dropped. "You wouldn't …"

"You're my next in command," I reminded him. "It comes with the rank."

Aside from his continual grumbling, he managed to get ready quicker than I did.

I wasn't sure what I was walking into here. I hadn't been invited to any formal military dinners on an aircraft carrier before. This wasn't exactly dinner with the commander in chief, but I expected it to be formal, boring, and a complete waste of time.

"Have you ever been to one of these things before?" Marcellus hissed as we were presented into the formal dining room.

"No," I replied curtly. "But I've gone to similar dinners. I know what to expect."

"What's the plan then?"

"I'm going to keep my mouth shut and try not to be drawn into conversation," I said, cutting him off before he could ask any more questions.

"What am I supposed to do then?"

"You're there to ensure that I don't have to talk to anyone." I chuckled as I walked into the room. I didn't stop to look, but I could easily visualise the exasperated expression on Marcellus's face.

I had expected a room filled with military grey and functional and stark fittings. Instead it was like I had walked into a dining room in an old southern manor. Due to my lengthy preparation time I was amongst the last of the guests to arrive. Glave's bulky figure could easily be seen towering over the rest of the guests. I also recognised the Admiral and his executive officer from my short time on the bridge. I noticed with some relief that I was seated on the opposite side of the table from Glave and the Admiral.

My relief caught in my throat as I recognised one of the other guests—Emily Perry. I hadn't expected that, but I suppose it wasn't surprising that she had been invited. I took a deep breath and did my best to ignore her. Unfortunately, this was going to prove difficult as she was seated opposite me. Fortunately the compulsion I had placed on her would prevent her from attempting to lure me into conversation. If I didn't want to answer her questions in private, I certainly didn't want to answer them publicly. I had had some doubts about a compulsion being overkill earlier, but with this new development it seemed entirely appropriate.

Sitting next to Emily was a colonel I'd never met before. He kept to himself and didn't appear to be making much in the way of small talk which was impressive considering that there were only about eight people invited to the meal. For the most part he was nondescript and would easily be forgotten if you met him on the street. The only reason he drew my attention was that he appeared to be scowling in my direction. Marcellus and I took our seats as the Admiral waved to the wait staff to begin serving the first course.

It didn't take long until a small bowl of cold soup was placed in front of me. I knew from a certain English comedy series that the soup was supposed to be served cold and I didn't make comment. I dutifully tasted the soup. I wasn't planning on eating much. For one my appetite wasn't what it used to be and two I wasn't a huge fan of tomatoes. I couldn't recall the last time I had eaten a full meal properly. They served a light wine with the meal. I wasn't a wine drinker, but anything that would help me get through meal was a good thing. I quickly finished off my glass and gestured for a refill.

"Tell me, Master Glave," the colonel's voice boomed out from across the table, "if you are here, then who is protecting the ship? I thought you were here to keep us all safe."

The colonel had a snide, piercing voice that immediately set my nerves on edge. It had obviously had the same effect on other people, as the conversation immediately ceased to await Glave's answer. Glave shook his head slowly and glanced in my direction before answering. That was strange, it was almost like he was seeking my confirmation of how much he should tell the colonel.

"I'm aware of everything that is going on," Glave muttered as he placed his napkin over his bowl. "You are perfectly safe."

Glave had intended his statement to end the conversation line, but the colonel wasn't so easily put off.

"So you *people*," he continued, "can truly see through metal walls?"

Glave again looked at me for help. He needn't have bothered; I wasn't going to help him. I had no wish to draw this colonel's attention onto myself.

"You'll have to excuse Colonel Brandon," the Admiral interjected, giving the colonel a warning look and a placating look to Glave.

"Yes, please excuse my curiosity," the colonel said smoothly. "I have so many questions about you people and this is the first time I've met one of you."

"Perhaps we can discuss it another time," Glave said,

his tone indicating that if the two of them did resume this conversation, Colonel Brandon would be unlikely to walk away from it in one piece.

"Perhaps." The colonel smiled, ignoring or not recognising the threat. "What about you, Master Wills? Would you care to elaborate on your remarkable powers?"

Crap. Remaining silent hadn't worked. I hadn't really expected that to work anyway. It had been a long shot at best. I took a deep gulp from my glass before I turned to answer him.

"No," I replied darkly. Unlike Glave, I wasn't going to give the colonel the illusion of good grace about this.

"Then perhaps you could answer some other questions I have," the colonel said unabated. He had either missed the small social clues or was completely ignoring them. "Why do you kill others of your kind? Surely your motivations would lie with them? From a genetic stand point at least."

"What do genetics have to do with anything?" Glave thundered from the other end of the table.

"I kill them because they have become dangerous," I whispered softly.

"And you ..." the colonel prompted. "Are you dangerous?"

I chose not to answer that question, but that didn't seem to faze him because he quickly followed up with another.

"What will happen once you run out of enemies, I wonder?" the colonel mused. "There are very few names left on the wanted lists. Your people are running out of time."

His threat wasn't a subtle one. You had to admire that kind of stupidity and dedication to duty. I could kill this man where he stood and here he was threatening me. Before I could answer, Emily Perry interupted.

"I'm not sure I like the tone of your accusation," she adamantly interjected, cutting the colonel off. "Do you question every soldier's motivations during times of war?"

I could see the Admiral getting more and more agitated at the colonel's behaviour. You could see the old man bristling from behind his stiff military façade. He was far too proud to say anything directly in such a public event, but anyone with half a brain could see what was going on behind the soldiers eyes.

"Yes," the colonel answered, glancing at the Admiral defiantly. "We are on the verge of complete global collapse and these ... 'things' are the ones who brought us here," he hissed. "I think it's necessary to investigate their motives, don't you?"

"The commander has proved his loyalties one hundred times over!" Marcellus snarled, almost rising to his feet. I raised a hand to indicate that Marcellus should remain seated.

"Commander?" the colonel queried curiously. "I wasn't aware you held rank."

"I don't," I grunted. My rank was honorary. Technically I wasn't in command of the division, but the actual commander had been killed in combat about four years ago and had never been replaced.

"Then why do honest American soldiers follow you?"

"Because I keep them alive," I replied curtly as I finished my third glass of wine.

"And yet your casualty rates are amongst the highest in the field."

Okay, that settled it. He'd done his research; no ordinary colonel would have thought to check casualty rate data. He wasn't some two-bit colonel on an aircraft carrier. He was probably on special assignment or something. I wasn't going to play this game. He could hide behind his rank and his privilege all he liked. He was right on one thing though: I wasn't military and therefore I didn't have to answer his questions.

"This is not the place to discuss it," I murmured softly, "and now you will excuse yourself and leave."

"Excuse me?" the colonel blathered. My eyes hardened as I stared down the man.

"Leave the table," I repeated as I let the Mana rise in me. Glave twitched in surprise as the power built within me. The colonel wouldn't have been able to see any difference in me as my irises were already full from the sorcery used to keep me mobile, but the air around me crackled with power. I knew from the way his face immediately went white that he understood the threat I was making. He could leave voluntarily or I would force him to. I would physically eject him from the room as an adult would throw a temper-struck child. Who could stop me? Except for Glave, there was no one who could and I doubted that Glave would be inclined to.

"You wouldn't dare!" The colonel chortled, his face reddening with rage.

"Colonel Brandon, you are dismissed. Please leave the table." The Admiral's harsh voice cracked from across the table, immediately disrupting the disturbing staring contest between me and the colonel.

An immediate wave of relief fell across the room as the tension drained. The colonel twisted to stare at his superior, turning his snide glance at the older man.

"Colonel," the Admiral warned, letting his voice rise.

The colonel shoved his chair back in disgust and threw his napkin on the table in front of him. The Admiral flashed me a warning look as the colonel rose from the table. There would be consequences for this.

"As you order, sir." He roughly saluted and stormed from the room. Glave and I exchanged glances as he left. This perhaps hadn't been the most diplomatic way of resolving this situation, but it had worked. And I found myself in an odd position of camaraderie with Glave. It took some time for the conversation to resume after the colonel's departure. The wait staff took the opportunity to refill my wine glass.

"You'll have to excuse the colonel, he is very dedicated to his duties," the Admiral apologised as the next course was served. Fortunately, after the commotion the colonel had caused, no one seemed interested in conversation with me. I kept one eye on the clock while I used my cutlery to chase food around my plate with little interest in consuming it.

"Are you not eating?" a soft voice cut into my reverie.

I looked up from my plate. Emily Perry. I thought the compulsion wouldn't have allowed her to address me directly.

"No, ma'am," I replied, placing my napkin on the plate. "My appetite isn't what it used to be."

"I can imagine." Emily grimaced as she took a quick glance at the colonel's now empty seat.

I nodded briefly and hoped she would take the hint and not pursue further conversation. I should have just refused the invitation for this damned dinner. I gestured towards the wait staff to replenish my wine glass once again.

"So you've just returned from active fighting?" Emily continued, oblivious to my surprise.

Something must have gone wrong with the compulsion effect. No one should have been able to shake off the compulsion that quickly. Was she a mage? She didn't appear to be. Unless her skills at suppressing her powers were far better than anyone I had ever seen. Surely either Glave or I would have spotted a suppressed Mana user no matter how good their skills in concealment.

So, if she wasn't a mage then perhaps I failed at the compulsion spell. But she had definitely been under when I had completed the spell in the corridor. She had seemed befuddled and it certainly didn't look like she remembered our previous encounter. I remembered clearly the expression on her face as she had wandered off after the compulsion had ended. No, the effect had been completed successfully, of that I was sure.

"Uhh, excuse me ..." Emily trailed off. I quickly realised I had been staring at her for some time. From her nervous expression it was obvious I had made her uncomfortable.

"Your eyes are quite distracting," she stammered, blood rushing to her cheeks. "Do they ever contract?"

"No." I coughed as I brought myself back under control. "Not while I'm using Mana."

Her eyes widened. "You're using Mana right now?"

I nodded. "I have spinal damage. I use the Mana to keep myself mobile."

"How horrid," she murmured sympathetically.

"It could be worse." I shrugged.

"How were you injured?" Emily continued.

"An enemy mage used a telekinetic grip to crush me. It broke my back in three places, shattered my ribs and shoulders, fractured my skull, and caused massive damage to my internal organs."

Emily sucked her breath in as I listed my injuries. "You're lucky to have survived."

"Luck had nothing to do with it," I grunted, keeping my fists clenched to avoid a tremor. "This mage knew what he was doing. I can only conclude that he intended for me to survive."

"Why?"

"I have no idea," I replied honestly. I unclenched my fists. The tremor had passed. The last thing I needed now was a panic attack at the Admiral's table.

"Did you know this mage before the war? The one who hurt you?"

"This happened before the war," I corrected her, "and he was my former master."

Emily's eyes widened in shock. "Your master?"

I nodded. "One of them at least." It seemed strange to acknowledge Renee as a master, but in a way she was more of a teacher to me than Victor had ever been. She had begun my training. She had overseen my initial introduction into the world of Mana. She had taught me, because she thought it best that I learn, not because she wanted something from me.

"Why were you fighting your former master?" Emily pressed.

"I was trying to avenge my sister's death."

"Your master killed her?"

"No," I was forced to admit.

Victor hadn't been responsible for her death, but he had been responsible for putting her on the path to death. If I was really honest with myself, the man most responsible for her death was me. I hadn't pulled the trigger that had ended her life, but I had certainly made it possible for a common gun to end her life—I was the one who had nullified her powers to allow it happen. Any way you looked at it, the responsibility was mine.

"It's complicated."

The arrival of the main course disrupted our conversation. I found myself curiously disappointed by this, despite not wanting to engage in conversation in the first place. I glanced over at the reporter with curiosity. She was pretty enough, though not particularly attractive in a conventional sense. It was obvious from the way she had dressed and held herself that she had no interest in being attractive. Despite this being a formal dinner, she had opted to attend in military fatigues rather than something dressier.

Her long blond hair trailed down her slender neck and hung across her shoulders like a cloak. She seemed so small and vulnerable until you looked at her eyes— they betrayed her true nature. They glittered with deter- mination and strength of character. She wasn't the small vulnerable woman she appeared to be. I had to remind myself that there was a reason she was aboard this ship. She was probably a war correspondent or something and had seen things that would have destroyed those of a tender disposition. She had strength of character that you could see; it was almost a tangible element as obvi- ous as the nose on her face.

"Tell me about yourself," I ordered as I finished off my glass once again. The waiter didn't even need to wait for me to nod before refilling it.

"There's not much to say really," Emily replied. "I was a journalist before the war. I was stationed in the Middle East during the last conflict."

My assessment had been correct.

"That seems like a dangerous place to be stationed," I commented.

"Yeah," Emily said, smiling, "it was one hell of an experience. It was dangerous and I was involved in several fire fights, but I wouldn't have been anywhere else for any amount of money."

"Fire fights?"

"Small skirmishes or police actions mostly," Emily clarified. "The whole region was unstable. It wasn't uncommon for fights to break out between various factions."

"You were stationed with the military?"

"For the most part," Emily confirmed. "though occasionally not. I had a security detachment responsible for my safety. We didn't take chances. We knew where the hotspots were and where there was acceptable risk."

Her mouth twitched slightly at the phrase 'acceptable risk'.

"It's not like that anymore, though We have no way of predicting where the fighting will be."

"Not true," I disagreed. "It's usually fairly predictable where insurgent action is likely to occur."

Emily's mouth twisted in distaste. "Insurgent action? I'm referring to the real war that's going on—the one between your kind."

I nodded noncommittally.

"I've seen the video clips and security footage," Emily continued. "But I've never seen it in real life."

"Perhaps you should ask Master Glave for a demonstration?" I grinned, gesturing towards the intractable man at the other end of the table.

A small snort escaped Emily's lips before she contained

herself. "I don't see much chance of that happening."

"No, me either," I replied with a shared covert glance in Glave's direction.

"I was actually hoping to interview you if you give me the chance," Emily said. "I'm writing a book."

Well, that settled it—the compulsion hadn't worked. The only question was to what degree it had failed. My eyes narrowed as I considered the possibilities. Was she playing with me? She shouldn't have been able to even talk to me, let alone directly ask me about an interview. I was intrigued, I couldn't help but be. What had just happened was supposed to be impossible.

"You know, it's funny," she murmured. "You ever get déjà vu? I feel like I've asked you this before."

My jaw gritted as I glanced at the young woman before me. Had she somehow subverted the compulsion without breaking it? I knew it was possible—I had done it the last time Victor had used a compulsion on me. But I had assumed it was because I was a mage and my powers had assisted me. Emily appeared to have no such assistance. She seemed to be nothing more than a normal human woman. Had my sorcery failed, or had I seriously underestimated her?

"Interview?" she queried, prompting me to realise that I had again been staring at her without speaking for some time.

"No," I announced finally. "No, I don't think that's a good idea."

"Why not?" Emily snapped. "I'd love to get the

perspective of a mage in all this."

"I am sure you would," I replied, attempting to finish the conversation. "Unfortunately I don't think anyone would find my story very entertaining."

"I'm sure that's not the case," Emily shot back. "I'm sure it would make a thrilling story—perhaps in a four-book series?"

She was obviously being sarcastic, but her words sent a shiver down my spine. A four-book series suggested there wouldn't be a fifth book. I've never believed in psychics or fortune tellers, but I knew with certainty that my time was running out. I didn't know how I knew, but I could feel it over me like a dark cloud.

"There are so many questions we have about your kind," Emily continued.

"What makes you think that I can answer them?"

"I'm sure you have more answers than we know now," Emily said curtly.

"Let me rephrase." I sighed. "What makes you think I want to answer them?"

"You don't feel the need to explain yourself?" Emily asked softly. "There has been so much death and destruction."

"I make no apologies for my actions," I replied darkly.

"And what about your people?" Emily pressed.

"My people will be held accountable for their own actions, as will everyone else."

"But surely, you must realise that history won't view your kind well."

"I know," I whispered. "History is written by the winners."

Fortunately dessert was served before she could continue her questioning. I managed to engage myself in a conversation with Marcellus and an officer to the left of me that allowed me to ignore Emily's further attempts at engaging me. It wasn't long before the Admiral thanked us for attending his dinner and excused himself. The junior officers were now allowed to leave the dining room, many of whom immediately took the opportunity to do so.

As I rose, I could see Emily eyeing me off speculatively, but she too was embroiled in a conversation that she couldn't extricate herself from. I nodded to her as I left the room with Marcellus in tow. I had thought that was it, but she caught up to me in the hallway outside the dining room.

"Master Wills?" she called out down the corridor. I thought briefly about just ignoring her, but she would only persist. I nodded to Marcellus to indicate that he should continue on without me, then turned to face the reporter.

"Miss Perry," I greeted as she caught up with me.

"Miss? That's very formal," she commented, placing her hand on my shoulder.

"No more so than Master Wills," I quipped.

"I thought that was your title?" Emily replied quickly. She still hadn't removed her hand.

"I don't care much for it, to be honest. Simply call me Devon."

"Devon?" she repeated as if trying the name on for

size. "It seems like such a normal name."

"Normal? How do you figure?"

"I don't know," she continued. "The only other mages I've heard of are Master Glave and Master Kristoff."

"Assumed names." I nodded. "The only mage other than me to use his real name is Bator."

"Bator?" Emily murmured, confused. "I've never heard of a Master Ba …"

"I wouldn't finish that sentence if I were you," I replied with a grin, turning to leave.

Emily rolled her eyes as she realised what she had almost just said. "Wait! Devon, Why do mages use assumed names?"

I shrugged. "I guess that most mages don't want people snooping into their backgrounds."

"And you don't care about that?"

"Nothing to find really." I chuckled. "My most visible achievement would have been finishing high school—hardly newsworthy. I discovered that I was a mage in my final year, and that would be about all you'd find."

"How old were you?"

"I had just turned eighteen."

"Is that normal?" Emily asked tentatively. I could almost see her taking notes in her head.

"No, not as such. I'm a late bloomer for my kind." I laughed.

"I'm sorry," Emily interjected. "Discovered you were a mage? Weren't you always aware that you were different?"

"No," I mused. "Well, yes, but not in the way you're

talking about. I didn't become a mage until I met Renee."

I involuntarily flinched as I said her name, but fortunately Emily didn't seem to pick up on it. She was too busy taking mental notes in her head.

"She began my training."

"I thought you said that your master was a he?"

"Victor finished my training," I corrected her. "Renee started it. This isn't the place to be discussing such things anyway. Would you care to join me for a drink?"

If I was honest with myself, I would have to admit that I invited her because, despite all my concerns and her aggressive interview techniques, I enjoyed her company and that was a something I hadn't been able to do in a very long time. There was another reason I had done so, too. There was something about her that didn't fit and it was like a thorn in my side. It would drive me nuts if I didn't figure it out.

"I'd love to," Emily said. "But I think the mess hall is closed."

"That's not a problem." I grinned. "I know a place."

My head spun slightly as I swung around, sending out a teleportation thread to collect two bottles of champagne. Emily jumped slightly at the noise the teleporting alcohol made.

"Where did you get those?" Emily inquired as she glanced about, thinking that I had procured them from a nearly shelf or something.

"The kitchens." I grinned. "It's the same stuff we were drinking at dinner."

"Oh, okay," she murmured, a little unsure of herself now.

"Do we need glasses?" I had heard it was considered uncouth to drink straight from the bottle.

"I don't if you don't," Emily returned with a smile.

"We certainly are classy people." I chuckled as I passed her one of the bottles.

"Where are we headed?"

"Topside."

"Is that allowed?" Emily gasped.

"Who's going to stop us?" I replied with a smirk.

The view from the deck of an aircraft carrier in the Pacific Ocean is amazing. The stars seemed to shine so much brighter once you got away from the lights of the control tower. It reminded me of the evenings I used to spend in Omeo when I was younger. The stars seemed so much more real when you removed yourself from the city and its bright lights. It was possible in those moments to realise you are standing on a ball of rock spinning in an infinite galaxy of stars. You can see the curvature of the horizon in all directions and you know yourself for what you truly are—insignificant. All my power, all my strength, and I was nothing next to the grandeur of the night sky. I wasn't too far gone to admit that, but there were those amongst my kind who would dispute it. I was no longer among that number, but had I not been humbled and broken I probably would have been first amongst them. I had been an arrogant child.

"What are you looking at when you stare into the horizon like that?" Emily murmured, her voice only slightly slurred by the alcohol. I hadn't realised she'd drunk so much, but she had consumed quite a bit at the dinner also.

"I dunno," I lied. "Maybe a life after this—after my kind are gone."

"Is that what you're fighting for?"

I nodded. "I guess. I don't really know why I'm fighting anymore."

"Surely you're fighting to make the world a safer place?" Emily interjected. I could tell from her tone she didn't believe what she was saying.

"Heh." I chuckled. "Even you don't believe the propaganda. There is no safer place after this. At its cor,e this is a war much like any other. The only difference is that the people in power didn't initiate this one and that's why everyone is screaming foul."

"But the mages … the destruction …" Emily said.

"It's no more than could be achieved with conventional weapons."

"No," Emily disagreed. "Fourteen cities left in ruins, untold destruction, the complete loss of infrastructure. The world will not recover from this."

"You Americans," I scoffed derisively. "Fourteen American cities have been destroyed. Mankind will recover. How many cities were left in ruins after the Second World War? How many after the First? You just see this as different because it's on your home soil."

That stopped her for a second as she pondered this new idea.

"There are places untouched by this war," I continued.

It pains me now to admit how naive I had been. Civilisation would not recover from this in its current form. The problem was that everything was now interconnected. Globalisation had happened on a massive scale and linked everyone together. Each country still thought itself independent, all the while wilfully ignoring the ties that bound them to their neighbours. It only takes a catalyst to begin the line of destruction, and sadly my kind had been that catalyst.

I hadn't intended or planned it, but my actions had begun the chain of events that had led to this uprising. First was the discovery of my powers—powers that were unchecked and restrained. I hadn't grown up in the mage community and my only guidance towards my powers was another recluse—someone actively hiding from the community. I embraced my role as outcast and actively ignored the edicts of those in positions who should have known better. The Primea should have killed me when I had first stood before her. She had talked to me of just such a thing, and at the time I had foolishly ignored her. She had warned me of what results my actions might lead to. Yes, she should have killed me.

I was over confident and arrogant. I was so sure of my ability to overcome anything that stood against me. I threw myself against stupid odds and somehow survived. I had proudly assumed I knew better when I sought to save my now dead sister. Had I listened to those around me, she probably wouldn't be dead now. Marcus's coup would have failed or never been launched—I had been his spark to turn against his former master. The emergence of our kind perhaps would not have happened at all, or would have taken a far less catastrophic turn. I had often wondered if perhaps I should have submitted to the little evil to save myself from the greater. Had I chosen to submit to Victor and become what he had wanted, none of this would have come to pass. It was so real to me I could almost taste it. Victor would have turned me into the weapon he had planned: a weapon aimed at his own kind. I would have been powerful, maybe even more so than I am now. Inevitably Victor would have set me loose on Marcus and I would have destroyed him and set Victor on the path to Primea. Our kind would be damned under the heel of an immortal tyrant, but millions of people would have been spared this fate. Was that better in the long run? Would Primea have been enough for Victor? He had always claimed to advocate for an exclusionist policy where our kind was concerned. Would that have been enough, or would his Nazi history lead us to a much worse fate? I gritted my teeth as I contemplated the scenario. It pained me to admit it, but that future may very well have been preferable. But that path was no longer available.

"What do you see when you stare at the night sky?" Emily pressed again. "Your expression is so strange."

"I see an end," I repeated, this time answering honestly.

"To the war?"

"No," I whispered. "Mine."

"You want to die?" Emily murmured softly. She seemed surprised.

"No," I shook my head, "but I see it in the stars—it's all I see in the stars. I do not stargaze often."

"And yet you brought me here?" Emily replied. "Why?"

"You wanted to understand me. Now you do."

Emily was silent for a long time as we gazed at the stars. It was as if we were thieves in the night, drinking our stolen wine on borrowed time. If I were more of a romantic it could have been a magical night, but those urges had long since passed in me. Honestly, this was nothing more a crude attempt to manipulate the woman into revealing her secrets to me. I hadn't known it at the time but I wasn't the only one playing games.

"I'm going with you, to Los Angeles," Emily stated unexpectedly.

"No." I cut her off immediately. "It would not be safe."

"Unfortunately, that's not your call," Emily replied firmly. "I've already put in the request and it's been approved by command. It's done."

I sighed. "I make no guarantee for your safety."

"Don't treat me like a child," Emily snapped. "I've been to war zones before."

"Not like this, you haven't."

Emily's face twisted at the insult, but she let it pass. We waited in silence for several seconds before she eventually reached into her pocket. She rummaged around until she found what she was looking for. It was a simple electronic device about the size of a chocolate bar. She passed it to me.

"I know that you said you didn't want me to interview you, but this is a voice recorder," she explained quickly. "If you won't talk to me, then maybe you'll be able to talk to it."

"Are we still on that?"

"No—hear me out," Emily continued. "I think it's important. Your name in particular is going to be remembered after all this, and I think it's only proper that it at least be remembered correctly."

I didn't answer. I had no wish to be remembered after all this. I've had to do things that no amount of explanation can justify. There was no good light I could be cast in. In my anger and in my loss I had indeed turned into the very monster I was trying to fight. I had turned to Necromancy so quickly to restore my powers. I had executed and callously let people die without thought or remorse. No—no good could come from having my story told.

"No," I repeated firmly. "I'm a murderer and a war criminal."

"I know," Emily replied softly. She had no illusions about who or what I was. "That's not what this is about. Don't you want to pass something on to future generations?"

Emily's words cut through me like a knife: future

generations. I would have no future generations and I certainly had no wisdom that I wanted to pass down to them. The only gift I could hope to pass onto the next generation would be a chance to choose their own future. A future without me or Victor—that was the only gift I could hope to give anyone. I only hoped that I could accomplish such a feat. It didn't look likely right now, but I was hopeful for a future in which the sins of our kind could be swept clean.

"I will think on what you say," I whispered as I ran my fingers across the device in my hands. I brought it to my mouth and pressed the record button.

"My name … is Devon Wills and I am … a mage."

I pressed stop and then rewind. I pushed the device into my pocket. Now was not the time.

* * *

I had the nightmare again that night. I had found Renee amongst the ruins of Los Angeles. We had fought and once again I had killed her. I had gazed into her eyes as she fell before me, only this time I wasn't sure whose face it was. Had the face been Renee's or had it been Emily's? In my dream I wasn't so sure. I needed to stop sleeping altogether.

I hadn't intended to sleep anyway, but the wine must have gone to my head, and I woke to find myself on the bunk, still in my uniform. I didn't remember much from the end of last night, but I did remember bidding Emily goodnight and walking her to her quarters. I wasn't sure how I had returned to my own.

I ran my hand across my face as I realised the implications of the dream. I needed to stop seeing Emily. She would merely be a distraction and I didn't need any further distractions when I came against Voll. There was a very high probability that he would be in Los Angeles. Someone had killed Kristoff's team, and Kristoff himself had been a very powerful mage. There were very few of the known mages we were hunting who would have been able to accomplish such a feat. In my present diminished state, even I would have been hard pressed to take out Kristoff. My fight with Voll would be difficult, should he be in Los Angeles. No, Voll was here. I could feel it. All that remained was to find him.

CHAPTER FIVE

We had expected our arrival into Los Angeles to have been noticed. It would have been folly to assume otherwise. What was surprising, though, was the complete lack of response to our arrival. You don't just sail an aircraft carrier into a harbour without being noticed. There should have been hordes of refugees and those caught up the conflict seeking asylum, but there was no one. The docks and even the bayside area of LA was a silent wasteland. It may have just been a consequence of the recent mage fights between Kristoff and Tibus, but I somehow doubted it. This smelled like a trap, and I'd been caught in enough traps to recognise one when I saw it.

The bridge of the aircraft carrier was overbearing with all the command staff present. Glave's foreboding figure lurked at the forefront of the bridge, staring out into the city, but I could see that his eyes weren't focused on the glass before him. His scry threads were out across the docks and the ship, seeking possible danger. He obviously hadn't found anything yet, but it was a large area to scan.

The Admiral and Colonel Brandon were standing to

my right as I prepared to bid my leave. I would be glad to be done with them. I glanced quickly at Glave, but the mage remained silent. He still hadn't found anything.

"I don't like this." The Admiral broke the silence first.

"Nor I," I agreed. "But at least it will allow us to deploy. I will go ahead first to ensure the path is clear."

"You unnecessarily risk yourself," Glave rumbled unexpectedly. This was further proof that the big man was actually worried.

"A sound plan," the colonel's voice interjected quickly, cutting Glave off. "I will begin preparations to deploy."

I turned to face the man.

"I have received orders to take over command of your division," the colonel replied crisply. "Central command was unaware of your division's status regarding a commander."

That was a lie, his death had been reported. I should have expected this. But, the presence of the colonel wouldn't affect things in the long run. My men would obey me; if he became a problem then it was a problem that could very easily be resolved once the shooting started.

"I need thirty minutes to begin loading *my* troops into the choppers," the colonel continued.

My mouth twisted wryly.

"I will instruct you when you may begin your reconnaissance."

I had been dismissed.

I glanced briefly at the Admiral, who looked just as

surprised as I had. This confirmed my suspicions. The colonel obviously had never been part of the aircraft carrier's crew and was on special assignment. The colonel taking control of my division was an unexpected development and one that I wasn't happy with, but this wasn't the time to fight it. That time would come later.

"As you wish." I chuckled as I left the bridge.

I found Marcellus on the deck helping load supplies into one of the four helicopters that would ferry us across the bay onto the docks.

"I don't like this," Marcellus grunted in way of greeting, unwittingly repeating the Admiral's sentiments.

"Want something else you're not going to like?"

"Brandon?" Marcellus spat. "Yeah, we've been notified. He showed me the orders himself—looks very official. What are we going to do about it?"

"Nothing," I replied with a smile, "for the moment."

Marcellus chuckled briefly. "Oh, that reporter wanted to see you too. Apparently she's coming with us."

I nodded sourly. "More wonderful decisions from command."

"Hard to see what use a reporter is going to be when the fighting starts," Marcellus agreed.

It didn't take long to locate Miss Perry in her quarters preparing her kit. I was impressed. She had packed her equipment tightly and appeared to only have the necessities. She was a professional after all.

"You wanted to see me?" I called out in way of greeting.

"Yes," Emily replied quickly, failing to hide her slight start at my voice. "I want to assure you—before things start—I won't get in your way. I won't be a burden. I'll accept your lead. If you say it's too dangerous, I'll take your word for it, but I'm going with you."

"I'm sure you won't be a problem."

Her expression turned quizzical at my odd response. She hadn't expected me to agree so readily. I suspect she had been planning this argument for some time in her head.

"It's not a problem as you're going to remain here," I continued softly.

Her eyes immediately went flinty as she realised what I was saying. "That's not your orders," she reminded me primly.

"And I cannot convince you otherwise?" I said.

Emily looked at me like I was crazy for asking such a question. "No, of course not," she snapped. "Why would you ask?"

I could use a compulsion thread to try to change her mind, but she had already proven a degree of resilience to the effect. It was possible she would just shrug off the effect and come anyway. I didn't want to have to worry about her safety once we landed in LA. She would be far safer on this ship and I could then concentrate on keeping everyone else alive.

"Tell me, do you have ration packs in your kit?" I asked conversationally.

Emily nodded, a little confused. I had figured she

would have been prepared. It was standard course for a field pack after all.

"Good."

"I will let someone know you're here, but it might take some time before they're able to release you," I whispered.

"What?" Emily shrieked.

I took a step back and pulled the door shut behind me. The sturdy metal door closed with a resounding clang. I pressed my fingers against the groove of the door frame and summoned Mana Nova. The super-heated Mana thread welded the door shut in seconds. I could hear her pounding on the door from the other side but I ignored her efforts. It only took a minute until the door was securely welded shut. She might be able to shrug off a compulsion to remain behind, but she would find this barrier much more difficult to overcome. I would notify someone of her predicament after the ship had left port. They should have little difficulty using a cutting torch or something to free her.

The rest of the preparations were finished by the time I returned. Brandon had come down from the bridge to oversee things. He nodded briefly at me as I approached one of the helicopters and directed me towards a head-set piece.

"I may need to give you further instructions," he stated primly. "You may begin your landing now."

It irked me to be issued commands in such a way, but I held my tongue. Words would be had with this colonel once things had settled down. He would soon learn that I was not some piece of ordinance to be checked and then sent into battle.

I flexed my shoulders slightly as I let the teleportation field overcome me. With a slight step forward I was now standing on the docks. I quickly turned to look behind me: the carrier was an awesome sight in the bay. There was no way that anyone could have failed to notice our arrival. I shivered slightly as I let my shield cover me. I was a sitting duck out there on the dock. The bright light and sound of my teleportation wouldn't have been missed. If they were hoping to kill a mage, here was their chance—they wouldn't get a better one.

Nothing happened.

What were they waiting for? They were here. I could almost smell them. Why weren't they attacking? Surely they must see their opportunity. That isn't to say that I was entirely defenceless. All of my strength was being poured into the shield surrounding me, except for the small amount maintaining my mobility. They could probably hit me with a tactical missile and I would survive unscathed, but that wasn't what I was worried about. If this was a trap, they would have other mages ready in waiting. They wouldn't hit me with anything as mundane as a missile.

I could see the Mana, too, was worried. It ebbed across my flesh in hurried pulses. It sensed as I did others of my kind. They were here. They had somehow hidden themselves from Glave's scrying. They were hiding and there were literally thousands of places for them to do so. This area was part of the civilian docks used for commercial shipping, and as such there were shipping containers and crates everywhere. Any one of them could contain enemy troops. It was the perfect place for hiding.

Siphoning power from my shield, I held my hand before me as I let the power grow. It wouldn't take much. I let the power pour into a sphere of Mana before me. The vortex grew to about half a metre but contained precious little Mana. I didn't need that much Mana to generate this type of vortex any longer. I watched the power flow across the vortex with a smile. This was one of the first spells I had learned and I had long since mastered its effects. I waited until the vortex reached its required size and then waited until the right moment to release. An Awareness blast detonation rocketed over the docks and into the city, soaking everything it touched in Mana residue. I had once used this effect to locate Renee in my home city of Melbourne, but today I was using it to hunt enemies. This time I wasn't the hunter, though, I was the prey.

I don't know if they were waiting for me to set off an Awareness blast, but I only had several seconds of sight before I realised I had fallen into their trap. There were hundreds of people in the surrounding area. They looked like they had taken defensive positions behind shipping crates, as if to repel an assault. This was no group of refugees or gangs. This was organised. The largest contingent seemed to be holding up in what appeared to be an office block used by a shipping company. I wasn't sure how they had hidden themselves from Glave, but clearly they had done so.

Maybe they had expected I would land troops? That had been the plan, after all. How had they known exactly where we would land? Were there also troops in other areas of the docks? I glanced briefly to the military docks to my left—that would have been the logical place to make landfall. I couldn't see anything over there. No, it looked like the concentration of troops was here— waiting for me.

I wasn't worried about the enemy soldiers. The five mage auras that appeared to be in the loading docks to my right were the problem. Mages were easy to spot, as their auras shine like beacons through the Mana soaked residue of the Awareness blast. I only had a few precious seconds before a second detonation tore through the city and eradicated my Mana sight.

I had seen this effect before, A Shading detonation. Scrying and any kind of vision enhancement was impossible; hell, I would barely be able to make out a Mana thread right before my eyes. It didn't affect my normal vision as such—other than the distraction that the static made, but it was weakening nonetheless. I had come to rely on my magical sight to enhance my normal vision— without it I would be compromised.

I had never seen Shading used over such a wide area before. As the spell tore across the horizon, my vision retracted and the soldiers disappeared, and more dangerously, the mages also disappeared from my vision. Several shots immediately rang out and pinged off my shield. They hadn't forgotten I was here. I ignored the gunfire as I set myself into a run. If I couldn't see what they were doing, then they couldn't see what I was doing either. I launched myself into flight as I threw myself at the last location where I had seen the mages.

I tore a hole through the roof and onto the ground floor of the loading bay where I was immediately greeted by three figures. I couldn't tell if they were mages or not with all the noise around, but I assumed they were at least some of the ones I had been sent to find.

My assumption was confirmed as a thread launched itself at me and impacted against my shield. I hadn't even seen it through the noise. The magical static caused by the Shading spell meant we couldn't even see our own threads. This made fighting with them far more interesting.

I launched an attack of my own, relying on my intuition and experience, and was greeted by the sight of one of the mages being swept savagely from the loading bay area and deeper into the warehouse—direct hit! I wasn't sure if he was out for the count or not though. It was logical to assume that he had raised a shield, in which case he may have survived. It had been awfully easy though—maybe their gambit with the shading had worked against them?

His companions hadn't been idle; several more

threads were launched in my direction but missed due to my speed. I saw out of the corner of my eye a concrete column explode into shrapnel behind me as one of their threads went wide. I launched a response of my own, but my skill failed me as the thread missed and tore out a section of crates, sending splintered wood flying everywhere. This was pointless. Fighting with threads in this environment was like fighting with needles in a haystack. I could use Mana Nova, but I might just as easily end up hitting myself. No, this required something more primal. I balled up all the energy I had into a single point of detonation, similar to the Awareness blast from before, but much more dangerous.

I was almost prepared to detonate it and set a blast loose that would probably destroy most of the warehouse and hopefully my foes along with it when I began to hear screams coming from my headset. Several more threads hit my shield, but again they were nowhere near powerful enough to even make my shield bend. That cinched it—they couldn't possibly have missed again. These were apprentices. They were a diversion. So where had the masters gone? I had little time to contemplate that, as the apprentices launched another attack against me. It was time to deal with them and then find their masters. I released my blast and saw my foes smack through the concrete walls and fly out as my telekinetic explosion tore through the building. The blast had absolutely wrecked it—there was very little left of the structure. The building had been mostly a shell for the loading bay, but I left it in ruins. I couldn't see my foes amongst the rubble, but I had no doubt that without the ability to teleport they would have been caught up in the blast and killed.

Now all I needed to do was find the other two, who had mysteriously vanished. Where the hell had they gone? I turned back to the clear bay behind me when my question was answered—not because I could see their Mana signatures since everything magical was static, but I could see their effect. Slowly and with titanic strength, the giant aircraft carrier was being lifted from the bay. With all the static I had no idea where the effect was being summoned from.

I was too far away from the carrier to see the stress marks that I knew I would find on the reinforced metal, but I could hear the fury of its rise. Water cascaded into the bay as the carrier was lifted around twenty metres into the air.

I launched myself back into the air from the ruins and landed with accustomed skill on the docks. If it weren't for this damned noise I could teleport back onto the ship to attempt to do something about it, but I couldn't see well enough to teleport. Who knew where I'd even end up? It was too dangerous. Besides, I was too late. I could hear it from here. The twisting and grinding screech of metal on metal was overpowering. I watched with grim detachment as the ship tore itself in two. Even if I was on board there was nothing I could have done to stop that.

The rear half of the carrier tore off and fell back into the water, its descent announced by a massive tidal wave caused by the behemoth's fall. The front half of the ship was held in the air a little longer before it too plummeted back into the depths. The central tower and command structure had been crushed under the pressure of lifting the ship into the air. I could only assume that everyone on the bridge was now dead. I had no idea if this included Glave. For all I knew he could be fighting on the deck, but with all this static I'd have no chance of seeing him.

I could only hope that if anyone had survived the drop that they were able to get to rescue craft before the end. I could just make out through the Mana static the shapes of three choppers. Some of my troops at least had gotten off the ship before it had plummeted. I could hear assorted gunfire coming from the bay as they attempted their landing. Someone at least would make it off that wreck. My breath caught in my throat as I realised the situation of another I had left on the now doomed craft—Emily Perry. She would have no way of making her way to the escape craft. She was sealed within her cabin. Securely sealed—I had seen to that. There was no way she had gotten out of her quarters yet. She was trapped.

Someone had to save her, and I was the only one capable of that now. I glanced towards my soldiers involved in the gunfire exchange with the soldiers on the docks and then out towards the downed ship. In the end, the choice was simple: I had to save Emily.

The sinking ship seemed to be very far out in the harbour and I'd never tried to leap that far before, but I knew that it could be done. Under normal circumstances I would teleport, but this was not an option since I couldn't scry ahead. I would be unable to see through the magical static clearly to register a target site. No, there was only one way that I was getting over there. I readied myself and used my powers to launch myself into the air. The old me would have taken a run up, but I now understood that physical strength meant nothing where the Mana was concerned. I could barely stand without assistance, let alone run, but I could make this jump. Distance was irrelevant too.

I flexed my shoulders as I summoned the power. Usually when making a jump like this, I would tether a thread to the target and use it to guide myself to my intended landing spot. I couldn't do that here as the Shading spell obscured my thread. No, this was going to have to be done the hard way. I could feel the power reverberating through my bones as I built it to a crescendo. With a simple grunt I let myself soar. Without a guiding thread it was pretty much akin to strapping a rocket to my ass and launching myself face first into the horizon.

The remains of the carrier was several kilometres or so out in the harbour bay and I wasn't going to be able to make that jump in one leap. But I only needed to get closer so I could see the target more clearly. As I reached the apex of my leap, I could make out the deck from the forward aft of the carrier. That was enough to attach a thread to.

I felt a slight tremor as the thread connected with something. This was a new experience for me without the ability to guide my threads. I had to go on instinct. As it turned out, my instincts were very good.

As I began to descend my trajectory, I used my tether thread to pull me down towards the carrier. There was only a subtle thump as my feet landed upon the downed carrier's surface.

The carrier was listing at an awful angle to the side as water filled the interior corridors. Smoke from electrical fires rose into the air like a funeral plume for the downed vessel. I did some quick estimates but was unable to tell which half Emily's quarters would have been in. When in doubt—search the larger half, which was the rear half of the carrier. I could see it about fifty metres away. It had landed at a much steeper angle and was almost vertical in the water.

I leapt across the void between the wrecks and clambered into the interior. It's much harder to assess which corridor you need to be in when you're looking at them from a vertical cross-section. I took a guess and dropped down into one of the corridors.

Smoke and flames were pushed aside by my shield as I clambered down, using door frames and hand holds to make my way further into the bowels of the downed ship. The smoke and flames were merely a hindrance than an obstacle, as they only obscured my vision. At the rate the ship was sinking, I was more concerned with the water, which would prove much more troublesome.

I navigated my way for about twenty metres before I realised I was on the wrong floor. I quickly punched a hole into the floor to clamber up to the next level. Another hole in the ship was unlikely to make much difference at this point, and I couldn't easily find any stairs.

This corridor looked a little more familiar, but I was still unsure of where exactly on the downed ship I was. I wished that damned Shading spell would expire already so I could just teleport and get Emily and myself off this wreck. The screeching noises of distressed metal and fizzling was overwhelming. I had no wish to be consumed within this wreck when it finally hit the bay floor—even with my powers I doubted I'd be able to withstand the pressures involved once the sea finally claimed its prize.

I dropped down into a T-intersection and finally realised where I was. If I was correct, Emily's quarters were just to the left corridor and then down the hall. I slid to my left and walked along the walls to the intersection.

The corridor was filled with water. It was rising fast. There was nothing for it. I hoped that the internal doors would be watertight and that Emily would be okay—at least until she ran out of air. This is, of course, assuming she wasn't crushed when the ship sunk. In all likelihood I was about to rescue her corpse, but I wasn't prepared to give up yet. I wasn't sure how long I could hold my breath for. If I tightened the field on my shield structure,

I could make it airtight. This would give me more time; however, it could potentially lead to asphyxiation from the trapped carbon dioxide. Theoretically it would work, but I'd never attempted this before—I had never had the need. I flexed the field around me and felt it tighten around my skin. It would be next to useless should anything serious hit it, but it was watertight. Configured like this, the shield would crack and fail under very little pressure. I also couldn't go too deep under the water, as the shield could burst from the pressure.

I took a deep breath and jumped into the corridor. The freezing water immediately sent my body into a state of shock as the breath was forced from my lungs by the coldness. I peered into that cold dark sea, but was unable to see anything.

I blindly lashed out with a Mana thread, hoping to secure it to the far corridor to pull myself deeper into the murky water. If my memory was correct, then Emily's quarters were about halfway down this corridor. My vision was obscured to the point I could barely see more than a metre in front of me. It didn't take me long to locate Emily's quarters, though—her door was the only one welded shut. The seal around the door looked secure. The vents along the roof were another matter. There would be water in the room. I could only hope that Emily hadn't already drowned.

I briefly considered my options. If I blew the door in with force, the pressure would blow out the rest of the seal and water would crash into the room—probably killing her. I needed to do this intelligently—I needed to cut the door open.

I had used Mana Nova to seal the door shut. Was it possible that I could also use Mana Nova to cut through the door under water? I held my hand out and summoned the power to bring forth a Mana Nova thread. At first nothing happened. Then a thin tendril of Mana shot from my hand and ignited. It was painfully weak, but it was stable.

It would need to be stronger. I pushed more and more power into the thread until it was strong enough to cut steel. Bubbles formed around the thread as the water surrounding it was brought to boil. Even through my shield I could feel the heat.

My first incision into the door gouged out a three-centimetre gash—not deep enough. My second strike tore through the door. Water immediately poured through the gap and into room beyond. If the room hadn't completely flooded before, it would now. Great—I now had a ticking clock. Could I cut through the door before the room completely flooded?

It turns out I couldn't, but by the time I made it through the door there was still a half metre gap of oxygen below the 'roof' of the room.

"Emily!"

"Devon?" she gasped as water washed over her. I breathed a sigh of relief. Emily was clinging to the top of a cabinet. She had a nasty cut down the left side of her face and her left arm looked broken, but she was otherwise okay.

"I've come to get you out!" I said, swimming over to her.

"You locked me in here!" Emily snarled. Her good hand snaked out and slapped my cheek.

"Time and place!" I called back as I considered my options. "Can you swim?"

"I … don't think so," Emily replied. Her anger still hadn't left her face.

If only that damned Shading field would drop already. I could simply teleport both of us out of there. It didn't look like that was going to happen anytime soon, though, so I would need to do this the hard way.

"Do you think you can hold your breath?"

"Yeah, I think so," Emily murmured.

"Okay." I held out an arm around her and pulled her hard against me. She shuddered as she wrapped her arms around my torso and clung to me. I amended my assessment of her injuries; her arm probably wasn't broken, but she had a bad dislocation. It would need to be dealt with, but we didn't have the time to do it then.

"Hold tight," I ordered. "We will be moving quickly."

I extended my shield to encompass us both and headed back under the water. I had just reached the door when I realised my mistake. On my entrance I hadn't made the hole big enough for two people to fit through.

Shit. I hadn't considered how we were going to get out on my way in. With a flick of my wrist I sent a telekinetic thread to tear the door from its hinges and send it floating into the corridor. Emily and I weren't far behind it. Once we were in the corridor, it wasn't too hard to find the surface. All we had to do was keeping heading up. We crested the surface at the top of the corridor, but the water had risen to waist height there. The ship was very quickly sinking, and I had no wish to join it.

"Are you okay?"

Emily still hadn't let go of me. "I think so."

She was awfully pale and I could tell she was in pain, but there was nothing I could immediately do about that. We needed to get off this sinking ship before it took us down with it.

It didn't take long for me to blow a hole in the side of the ship. Seeing as how it was sinking anyway I doubted anyone would mind some additional holes in an already doomed ship. Once we were topside, however, our options were far slimmer.

The impact caused by leaping across the bay would antagonise Emily's already dislocated arm, and I had no wish to cause her further injury. I had no idea how much longer this part of the carrier was going to remain on the surface, but the wreckage of the forward decks looked much more stable. We would be safe there—at least for a few hours. Long enough perhaps for the Shading spell to expire.

I wrapped an arm around Emily again as we leapt from the rear section of the ship to the more stable front end. Emily winced as our feet found purchase on the runway deck. Emily panted for a few seconds, hunched over holding her side. It was possible she had internal injuries; moving her like that again wouldn't be a good idea. My next plan had been to jump onto the docks with her in tow. I would need a new idea.

"We can't stay here," Emily said, as she glanced around the remains of the ship.

"Only for an hour or two," I replied as I attempted to see what was going on dockside. I wasn't going to leave Emily here unprotected, but I really needed an update on how the battle was progressing. Had my team survived their landing? Was Glave still alive? Through this damned Shading I couldn't see a thing.

"You're not listening!" Emily thundered. My attention was brought back to her. "We're not safe here!"

"Huh? What?"

"This is a nuclear vessel!" Emily said angrily.

"What?"

"Boom!" Emily snapped, making a small explosion gesture with the fingers on her good hand.

I sighed. This was the last thing I needed. "Are you sure?"

"There are fail safes, but I'm not sure how much I'd trust them," Emily continued, especially considering how quickly the vessel was downed."

"How quickly will a reaction start?"

"I don't know," Emily said. "I don't even know if an explosion would be likely, but I doubt the designers ever considered the ship being torn in two like this."

She had a point. Whatever fail safes had been put in place wouldn't have taken into account the ship being lifted from the water, twisted until it broke in two and then sent plummeting back into the depths.

"How big an explosion?"

Emily shrugged. "It's a reactor, not a bomb—but if it's going to go, it'd still be a nuclear explosion—so pretty big."

"So you're saying we need to get off this boat?" I replied.

"I don't know!" Emily repeated. "We might be safe, we might not."

I glanced around for a lifeboat or anything that might float; unfortunately this section of the ship was devoid of anything that could be utilised as a raft. The sound of gunfire rocketed across the bay as soldiers met resistance from the beachfront. I needed to get back to them.

"I'll be back," I murmured as I geared myself up for the jump.

"Wait! No! Don't leave me!" Emily immediately shouted.

"I'll send back a chopper to collect you," I replied briskly. Before Emily could comment further, I leapt from the deck. I landed with a grunt on the dock behind one of the choppers a few seconds later. She had called out something, but I couldn't hear it over the rush of wind from the jump.

"Get a chopper back onto the carrier, there are survivors!" I ordered. The main troops moved forward toward the beach. There was precious little cover; the only reason they hadn't already been wiped off the bay was that the other two choppers were providing overhead support.

But I could tell from the fire being returned that they wouldn't be able to keep this up for much longer.

"I can't without orders from the colonel," the pilot replied briefly.

"Where is Colonel Brandon?" I replied.

"Unsure, sir," the pilot replied. "I think he went ahead with the troops."

"In which case, he could be dead," I replied savagely. "Get that chopper in the air, or I'll throw it over to the ship myself."

The pilot balked at my threat and for a second I thought he was going to argue, but eventually he nodded and headed toward the cockpit. The heavy gun mounted on the helicopter opened up in fire as the helicopter rose from the ground and headed towards the down carrier. The enemy soldiers scattered as the new avenue of fire opened up. It was time to take advantage of the lapse in enemy fire.

I leapt into the air and landed with a grunt in front of allied soldiers making their way down the docks. I broadened my shield to protect them as well and watched with a degree of satisfaction as a stream of bullets ricocheted off the shield. Quickly realising what had happened, the soldiers emerged from cover and stood behind me, still firing into the bayside area.

It wasn't difficult to modulate my shield so that it only stopped things passing through it one way, which allowed me to increase the strength of my shield into a wide flat plane in front of us. I kept a secondary shield around myself should anything get through the first one. With all the noise still being thrown up by the Shading spell, it was difficult to see what the hell was going on ahead of us and I had to rely on the soldiers whose vision wasn't so impaired.

The part of the docks closest to the beach was a smaller narrow section designed for car traffic. It would have made the perfect choke point to prevent troops from getting onto the land. We simply marched across it, with the soldiers behind me shooting anyone stupid enough to take a shot at us. I was grateful that they weren't hitting us with anything larger than bullets; with my shield stretched it wasn't unbreakable by conventional means, but it was a calculated risk.

As we reached the beachhead, it was obvious that our resistance had all but fled. Some token shots were taken at us, but the majority of the enemy troops appeared to be dissolving further into the city. We could follow them, but it wouldn't be wise to do so now. It would be far better to regroup, establish a beachhead, and then continue into the city once we had a safe base of operations. I glanced back down the dock; there were some casualties, but all in all it didn't look too bad. That is, if you discounted the massive plume of smoke—all that was left of the carrier. A lot of people had died on that boat. I could only hope the damned thing didn't explode before the Shading spell expired. Once the spell had ended, I would be able to scout the ship for survivors and remove them myself.

* * *

Fortunately, by the time the Shading spell expired, there had been no sign of a reactor explosion. We were going to be safe for the moment, at least—if you considered setting up camp next to a possible nuclear explosion in an enemy-held city safe. The ground forces had repelled the assault and sent the survivors scurrying into the city for safety. We could deal with them later. The bigger issue was the two remaining mages who had been present at the battle. We had no idea where they had gone. But I was sure they would return to finish what they had started.

I had secured Emily with a medical officer who survived the wreck, and it looked like she would recover. She only had minor injuries, and as I suspected her arm had been dislocated, not broken. There were those amongst the wounded who had fared worse, but their injuries weren't too serious. Those with serious injuries didn't make it off the ship in time and had died with the wreck. Master Glave had survived, but had been unable to locate the attackers within the shroud of the Shading spell. He had moved in to face them, but with all the noise he couldn't have pursued them. All in all it had been a very well-orchestrated attack and it had cost us dearly.

Our original mission had been to locate a suitable landing site to begin operations within the city; however, we couldn't do that yet as we were still recovering survivors from the downed ship. For an aircraft carrier that could hold upwards of four thousand crewmembers, there were painfully few survivors.

"We cannot wait any longer," Colonel Brandon grunted as he surveyed the skyline. "We need to begin sending scouts into the city."

I nodded briefly. We were too exposed here and vulnerable to another attack. We had recovered the bodies of the three mages from the warehouse. They had indeed been crushed in the telekinetic blast that destroyed the building. I quickly counted about a hundred soldiers who had died with them. A lot of people were determined to keep us out of Los Angeles. Why?

Brandon sent three teams of soldiers out into the city proper to establish a forward base. From the numbers he sent, he obviously expected to encounter resistance. He rolled up the map he had been working from and nodded to his soldiers, indicating that the meeting was over. Most of the soldiers immediately turned to depart, but before Glave and I could join them, Brandon called us over. "Can I trust you two to do your jobs?"

"How do you figure?"

"You were supposed to protect the ship." He gestured to the still-smouldering wreckage. "If you're unable to perform even that simple a task, then you're useless to me."

I turned to look quickly at Glave, but I needn't have bothered. From his expression I already knew what he was thinking.

"Little man," Glave rumbled, wrapping a thread around the colonel's neck. "You speak of things you do not understand."

The colonel's eyes bulged as the thread took hold. His feet scrambled for purchase as he was slowly lifted from the ground. Soldiers behind him immediately jumped into action. I didn't know these soldiers—they weren't from my team. Brandon had obviously brought some of his own men along. The soldiers raised their weapons, but were unwilling to fire with their colonel in such close proximity. Glave ignored the weapons pointed at him—with a shield around him they weren't a threat anyway. I wondered briefly if the big man was going to kill him, but before the colonel passed out, the mage let his victim go. The colonel fell half a metre to the floor and landed on his knees. Glave cast his gaze witheringly across the soldiers before him.

"You should show respect," he announced, both to the soldiers and his fallen victim.

The colonel coughed in response as he staggered to his feet. He quickly backpedalled from the room, keeping his soldiers in front of him as he fled.

"That was less than politic," I murmured as I watched the soldiers leave.

Glave grunted. "It was no more than you would have done."

"I wouldn't have let him go." I smiled.

Glave chuckled at my joke. But I wasn't sure I was joking. It might have been simpler to have just ended him. We were going to have a tough enough time getting out of there with our asses intact without him playing politics. He was going to become a problem eventually. It may have just been easier to deal with him here.

"Wait here." I nodded to Glave as I followed the soldiers.

Brandon had retreated back several rooms and I could see him preparing to rally troops to return. He obviously intended to pursue this and do something stupid, like arrest Glave. As soon as I entered the room, Brandon ordered me to halt and I was greeted by a host of rifles pointed at me. The colonel had brought in some reinforcements, as there were some very confused expressions from those soldiers who had served with me previously. I waved them down before they could raise their own weapons. The last thing we wanted here was a fire fight amongst our own troops.

"Are you trying to get yourself killed, colonel? I called.

"Military orders must be followed!" the colonel called back from behind his row of troops.

"Lower your weapons," I ordered Brandon's soldiers.

Again I was greeted by stern faces of soldiers who were prepared to do their duty. I could tell from their demeanour that they knew what would happen should the colonel give the order to fire, and they were prepared to fire anyway. It is a kind of stubborn stupidity to do one's duty that seems to override common sense.

"Lower them," Brandon ordered grudgingly. The soldiers complied. That was a good sign at least. He didn't want anyone to die either. I walked over to the colonel so that I could discuss the matter quietly.

"If you go back after him, he will kill you."

"He assaulted a superior officer," Brandon snarled. "Military law dictates—"

"You insulted him," I cut him off. "Keep that up and he might just take matters into his own hands again."

Brandon's face took on a mottled shade of red as he realised his position. His eyes darted from side to side as he struggled to think his way out. He needed us, and he knew it. The first mage he encountered could very well wipe out his entire command without raising a sweat.

"It was still assault," he repeated uncertainly. I didn't have time for this. Somewhere near here were two very powerful mages who needed to be dealt with before they returned to finish their job.

"This isn't the time or place for this," I snarled, finally losing my patience with the colonel, "and I don't have time to explain it to you. If you can't see that then you're not smart enough to be left in command."

"You'd dare?" he whispered.

"If you force me to," I replied simply. "You're going to get people killed."

Brandon remained silent—the first intelligent thing he had done since I had met him.

"Now, if you are finished …" I grunted, "Glave and I are going to go find the remaining mages and deal with them. That's what we are here to do. Not babysit you and your men."

I turned my back on the soldiers. There was a stunned silence as I returned to Glave.

The big man was sitting on a fallen chunk of concrete with his eyes closed. His scry threads snaked out, searching the city for his enemies. It was possible that they had fled the city—but I didn't think so. The attack on the docks had all the trademarks of an opening salvo. We also hadn't seen any heavier ordinance when I had followed the rift here—earlier I had seen tanks and cannons. Perhaps my earlier attack had prevented them from being moved in place. When I had closed the rift, much of their heavier equipment had been left behind. I wondered how much worse this ambush would have gone had they brought their full resources. We could have been wiped out.

"Have you found them?" I asked, loath to disturb the man's concentration.

"I think so," the big man rumbled back.

"Let's go then."

Without the Shading spell in effect, there was nothing to stop us teleporting now. Glave went first and I followed his thread.

* * *

Glave's thread took me to a secluded car park outside an inland shopping mall. The shopping centre looked like it had undergone bombing at some point, as many of the external walls were rubble and others bore the tell-tale mark of scorched burns and bullet fire.

"Have I ever told you that I don't like car parks," I murmured softly as I looked around the mess.

Glave looked at me quizzically as we surveyed our surroundings. As an outpost or fortress, a shopping centre made a pretty lousy defensive structure. There were so many ways into the sizeable building that it would be difficult to keep unwanted people out. The only thing going for it would be a large quantity of food goods. Although how long they would last was debatable. Ahead of us were two smashed glass doors that led into one of the lower floors of the complex. I'd always been uncomfortable around abandoned shopping centres, or any public place lacking people in it. The silence was deafening.

"Are you sure about this?" I whispered.

Glave nodded.

"Awareness? Flush them out?" I suggested.

Glave shook his head and gruffly said, "Don't want to give away our position."

I chuckled. "It's unlikely that we haven't been noticed already."

I wasn't going to argue though; my last experience with an Awareness blast hadn't exactly been a resounding success. I briefly considered sending off a Shading blast of my own. This would stop them from escaping. but I wanted to be sure that my quarry was in the building before I did so.

"Scry?"

Glave nodded.

I sent a scry thread in, but by necessity I kept my thread as light as possible. This restricted my vision but would make it much harder for the thread to be detected. An Awareness blast would give away the thread in seconds, but only a skilled mage would be able to detect a thread this faint in the first place.

The interior of the shopping centre had fared no better than the outside. Looting and rioting had occurred on a massive scale. Someone had attempted to barricade the place—they had gone to a lot of effort to make sure people didn't get inside.

My thread leapt easily over several barricades consisting of sandbags and wire fences. A sense of unease overcame me. These barricades should have been manned. If we had arrived with troops, a group of a dozen soldiers could have kept my team out for quite some time. That they weren't manned meant either they no longer had the manpower to defend their outpost, or they were intentionally luring us in. I followed the trail of defences all the way to the base of the centre until I found my prey. I was sure Glave had come to the same conclusion—although I couldn't see his thread, I was confident that he had followed me.

"I've found one," I whispered as the familiar ping of a Mana signature lit up in my senses through the scry. I had seen this Mana signature before, but I couldn't for the life of me think where. It seemed so familiar, like a song you've heard, but can't name the title.

"You teleport down, I will intercept when they flee," Glave ordered gruffly.

Great, once again I was being used as bait. I didn't mind fulfilling this role when I volunteered, but being ordered into it took some of the fun out of it.

"And if they don't flee?" I replied grimly.

"Then I shall assist," Glave promised.

I sighed as I summoned my powers. Teleportation was an exact art; any mistakes could result in death. It had taken me a long time and much practice to become skilled to the point where I no longer had to think about it. This particular jump should be no different from hundreds of others, but I was going to make it different. For one, I wanted it to be loud. I wanted it to look like I was a beginner. I wanted to make it loud enough that they would be spooked into running. Glave could then intercept and deal with them. It would make it look like I was so inexperienced with the technique and therefore easy prey, but that just made the gambit all the more appealing. If they chose to face me, assuming I was weak, then I would finish them then and there. My gambit worked. As soon as I teleported in, I saw the tell-tale sign of someone immediately teleporting out. Strangely enough, they appeared to be teleporting to where I had just been. It was possible that my inelegant casting of the teleport field had alerted them and they had gone to finish me off. Either way, I hoped that Glave was on the ball. I would have returned to assist him, but I now had bigger problems of my own. As soon as I had materialised, I was greeted with several rather serious strikes to my shield, sending me reeling.

Ironically, it must have been my gambit that saved my life. After the initial attack, the further blows to my shield barely registered and I turned to face my attacker. They hadn't expected me to bring my shield up so quickly. I saw the Mana signature of my enemy as he came for me. Again I was struck by the familiarity of the Mana signature but couldn't immediately place it.

Angered that their attack had missed me, they came at me with fury, but were thwarted by several threads of my own raised in defence. I leapt forward to counter their strike and watched with amusement as the tile where my feet had been only seconds earlier exploded into rubble. My counter strike sent my foe flying onto an escalator on the far side of the hall, his shield visibly flexing as my thread impacted it. He rose from the escalator, and I was on him in seconds as he attempted to bring his defences to bear.

"Oh shit, not you," he exclaimed loudly. He must have recognised me from my own Mana signature. It also wouldn't have been too difficult to recognise me from the construct supporting my spine. No other mages used such a contrivance.

His recognition hadn't helped him. With a quick strike I tore through his defences and wrapped a thread around his chest. With a swift jerk I pulled him from his feet and sent him sliding towards me across the broken marble floor. As he slid to a halt before me, I gasped as

I finally recognised him. I was ready and poised to end his life, but the shock of seeing his face gave me pause. A pause that almost cost my life. With a frantic strike upwards he knocked me onto my back. Several inches to the left and he may have taken my head off.

Him? What the hell? Why was he here?

My mind was still reeling from my discovery. What the hell was going on? Why was he fighting me? We were supposed to be on the same side. In fact, he was supposed to be dead.

The man I was fighting was Master Kristoff. I had once thought I would be hard pressed to overcome him, but I had sold myself short. Now that I had engaged in battle with the man, I could see he was clearly no match for me. This could only end one way, and we both knew it.

I regained my footing and again brought my foe to his knees. He had wisely attempted to flee by attempting to leap to the top story of the centre. I caught him about halfway up. Wrapping a thread around his waist, I brought him slamming down into the marble floor with devastating force. I heard his shield collapse at the impact and he cried out in agony. Holding him in place, I launched at him. I expected a counter attack, but I needn't have worried. This fight was over. The fall had all but finished him off. I brought him to his feet and held him before me. He was already mostly dead. His broken ribs protruded from his chest and his limbs dangled uselessly. It was a miracle he had even survived the fall at all.

"Why?" I whispered to the dying man. I had to know

what had prompted him to turn against us.

"I figured it out," he croaked with a shattered smile. He gurgled as his broken neck lolled awkwardly in mid-air. "I was fighting for the wrong side."

With a quick flick of the thread I ended his life. It was as much mercy as the deserter was going to get from me. I let the body fall to the ground. What the hell was he talking about? Joining Voll wasn't the right side at all. Voll was responsible for some of the worst atrocities of the war. I wondered briefly what to do with the body. It wasn't a particularly good idea to leave it for anyone else to find. It would raise questions. It would be prudent to just remove the body—dump it somewhere in the Pacific. Kristoff was reported dead in Los Angeles several weeks ago. It might be best if that remained the official record. Without remorse I disposed of the body.

CHAPTER SIX

What the hell were they defending down there? It looked like the place had been evacuated months, if not years ago. It was a strange building for mages to occupy. We didn't need barriers and blockades to protect ourselves. In fact, those things would merely slow us down. No, there was definitely something else at play.

It didn't take long to discover a civilian population hiding in the remains of a food court behind the main mall foyer. They were a wretched bunch, but I had seen people in far worse predicaments. They didn't comment or even attempt to stop me as I entered their shanty town. I could see some weapons, which they were very careful to keep within reach, but not actively pointing at me. I could tell by their furtive expressions that they simply hoped I would go away.

If my curiosity hadn't been stirred, I probably would have left them very quickly. There had to be a reason that two mages had chosen to protect this encampment, and I was going to find it. I also might find out why Kristoff had chosen to forsake his duty and turn coat. The survivors weren't much to look at—I'd seen their type a hundred times before. They would have fled from battles and been herded together into large refugee camps. The camps would have then fallen and they would have been sent out into the wild in small packs. This lot looked luckier than most, having found somewhere relatively safe and clean to hide. If it hadn't been for the Mana signature of the mages, we probably would never have found them. It was only Glave's exceptional skills with scrying that had allowed him to find his quarry. I wondered how long the civilians' luck would last.

The food court had been canvased into rows of tents and blankets as people had attempted to turn the space into places of privacy. Most of the refugees turned away or starkly ignored me as I passed them. It was only the loud explosion of a teleportation spell that caused them to take notice. Several weapons were hurriedly grasped and pointed in my direction before they realised I wasn't the cause of the disruption.

I turned to face the newcomer but wasn't surprised when it turned out to be Glave. He looked a little worse for wear. Obviously his fight with the other mage hadn't gone well. He held his side tenderly and walked over to me with a slight limp.

"He got away," he announced grimly.

"Was it Voll?

Glave shook his head. "Someone new. Someone not on the wanted lists."

With Tibus dead, I didn't think Voll had anyone left powerful enough to challenge Glave. That is, of course, assuming Tibus was indeed dead. This was a disturbing line of thought considering that the source of our intel on his death had been Kristoff. It was possible, given new information, that Kristoff may have been a less than reliable source. Then again, maybe not—Glave would have recognised Tibus. Who was this newcomer?

"Are you Army?" a tentative voice called out.

Glave and I immediately turned to see an old woman approach us. She was shaking and I could see that she had had to work her way past several other refugees, who didn't look at all pleased that she had engaged us. It was difficult to place her age from her haggard appearance. She could have easily been as young as forty or as old as seventy. She was of Mexican descent, which made picking her age even harder.

"Are you Army?" she repeated in her broken English.

I nodded briefly as I turned to face her.

She shuddered as she noticed my eyes focusing on her. "You ... have medicine?"

"Are you sick?" I asked curiously. She didn't look sick.

"You come?" She gestured towards a secluded part of the camp. Several refugees scowled as she led us deeper into the makeshift camp. The woman wouldn't answer any more of my questions and simply repeated the phrase "you come, you come," over and over as she led us through to her temporary home.

Her home was an area no more than four metres of space crammed against a fast food counter and a stairwell. A cold breeze wafted down from the stairwell with regular frequency.

A younger woman was sitting beside a young boy wrapped up in blankets. The boy was convulsing, sweat poured from his body, and his breath came in shuddering gasps. He couldn't have been more than ten. He looked woefully underfed and haggard. His blond hair was matted to his head from the sweat of his fever and the filth of his surroundings.

Glave and I glanced at each other nervously.

"Is this your son?" I asked the stupid question. The boy was Caucasian. The young woman by his side answered me with a negative. She looked similar enough to the old woman to be related, perhaps her daughter.

"Do you know his parents?"

Her grasp of the English language was much stronger. Again she shook her head. The boy reached up and grasped her by the arm as a particularly nasty convulsion took him. She firmly pushed him down into his bed and placed another cool rag over his forehead.

"How long has he been convulsing?" I asked, dreading the answer.

"About ten minutes," came the reply. "But he was sick before. About three days."

"Shit," I cursed as Glave and I exchanged glances. Ten minutes would place the convulsions at the same time as my fight with Kristoff.

"Will he die?" the old woman asked, mistaking my cursing for a prognosis.

"No," I answered. "His fever will break."

"How do you know?" the young woman asked quickly.

"I've seen it before," I replied as I attempted to converse with Glave via covert glances. The big man wouldn't hold my gaze.

"You know what we need to do," Glave whispered darkly, still refusing to look directly at me.

"I know what I'm supposed to do," I hissed back, "but he's only a kid."

"Doesn't matter," Glave replied. I could tell that his heart wasn't in it. "We could just … leave him. Maybe he'll burn up?"

"And if he doesn't?" I demanded, "and someone like Voll finds him?"

"Then you need to do it," Glave murmured. "It'd be a kindness."

"No," I whispered softly as I reached forward and pulled back the kid's blankets. I needn't have bothered—I already knew what I was going to find. Several small particles of Mana bubbling across the kid's chest. My fight with Kristoff had sparked the Mana within him. This was what the mages were protecting. He'd probably come down with Mana fever several days ago. Kristoff would have recognised it and decided to simply wait it out.

The Mana on the kid's flesh was a death sentence. Glave expected me to simply end the kid's life, but I couldn't do that. It wasn't fair. The kid hadn't done anything wrong. He was simply in the wrong place at the wrong time. But we definitely couldn't leave him. If he was recruited by Voll or some other petty warlord, he could continue this damned war into the next generation. So, if I couldn't kill him and I couldn't leave him, there was only one left.

"I'm going to take him with us," I announced softly. Glave politely chose not to comment.

In his current condition I couldn't simply teleport him—the additional influx of Mana would probably induce a burnout and kill him. I sent soldiers to recover him early the next morning and left him in the temporary infirmary with Emily. My presence would do him little good right now either—the presence of someone who was literally glowing with Mana would only incite the process, and his body needed time to come to terms with the changes that Mana brought to his system.

I had learned this lesson from my sister. When she had come down with Mana fever, I had hovered over her bed and attempted to help. But my mothering had almost brought her to the brink of death. It wasn't until she had been hospitalised and I was unable to attend her that she recovered. In time, the fever would break as the boy's body learned to control the Mana. If it did not, then he would die.

I wasn't sure what outcome I was hoping for. If he died, I could simply say that it was fate and wash my hands of the matter. If he lived, I would have to train him. Without training his powers could still overcome him and kill him. I had never taken an apprentice before and I was loath to do so now. I had begun my sister's training for much the same reason that I would teach this boy, but I hadn't finished and probably done more harm than good. But I had been young then—I knew a lot more now. I wondered if that would make any difference.

The hypocrisy of my actions haunted me. I had sworn that I was going to end our kind and sweep them from the world, and yet here I was about to train up a new one. By all rights I should have simply torched the kid and been done with it, but I couldn't do that. There was a big difference between killing one of our kind in a fight and executing a kid, and it seemed that there were still some lines I wasn't prepared to cross. I was as surprised as anyone. The whole situation was damned inconvenient.

"Who's the kid?" a soft voice whispered. Emily Perry had recovered from her injuries well enough to be mobile, but it was obvious that she was still in some pain.

"A refugee," I replied. I gazed at the kid from across the ward. I dared go no nearer. I had instructed the medic on how to deal with the kid and all I could do now was to wait for the fever to break.

"And you brought him back here?" Emily asked quizzically.

"He would have died where he was," I replied firmly. That at least was mostly true.

Emily nodded and took me for my word. I could see, though, that she knew that I wasn't telling the entire truth.

"Strange for you to take such an interest," Emily murmured.

I didn't answer.

"He's a mage, isn't he?" Emily accused.

Again I didn't answer her, but I didn't need to. My silence was answer enough.

"There's going to be trouble over this, isn't there?"

"I hope not," I sighed, "but probably."

* * *

It took three days for the boy's fever to break and for it to be safe enough for me to come near him again. Fortunately Emily had kept an eye on him during his sickness and ensured that nothing untoward happened to him. I had heard rumours that Colonel Brandon was curious about the boy, but he hadn't directly approached me yet. His encounter with Glave was causing him to keep his distance. This was fine by me.

We hadn't seen or heard from the other mage that Glave had engaged, but it was obvious from Glave's description of the encounter that he was the more powerful of the two. I hadn't revealed the truth of Kristoff's involvement in the encounter and had no intention of doing so. I had no idea how such information would be construed by command.

My initial assessment of the boy looked accurate—he appeared to be no more than ten years old, incredibly undernourished and frail. His life until now hadn't exactly been cheery. He would have been born no more than four years before the war, early enough not to have any memories of what life was like before all this had happened. Now that his body had adapted to the Mana, I could see a faint but regular Mana signature appearing. It was weak, but it would get stronger with time. He was the first of a new generation of mages born into this conflict—if he survived he would be powerful.

"Do you know where your parents are?" I asked firmly, causing the boy to flinch and Emily to give me a stern glance.

The boy shook his head sadly without answering, but I got the message. They were dead.

"Do you have a name?"

"Justin," the boy whispered, seeking confirmation from Emily. He didn't seem too comfortable around me. This was a good thing. He should learn quickly that our kind would bring him only danger.

"Do you know why you are here?"

"The lights?" the boy murmured, which caused Emily to look at me in confusion.

"That's right." I glanced around the room to ensure privacy. "You're a mage."

The boy flinched again. Perhaps a mage had been responsible for the death of his parents.

"I'm going to teach you," I continued, "but you must do everything I ask."

I had no idea what I was going to do with this kid. He couldn't very well follow me where I was going, but

I couldn't leave him behind either. As I pondered the reality of the situation, I realised that the conflict within had now reached new heights of stupidity.

"What do I have to do?" Justin whispered. "Where do I go?"

"For the moment, we're not going to do anything," I replied curtly, "but when it's time I will begin your training."

I could begin instructing the kid on the basics easily enough, but I would need certain documents from my lair in Poland. It could be easier to just transfer the kid there to begin his training. He would be out of the war there, although I doubted he would cope with the nightmares that were Randall and Karl. He would be safe there, unless someone was actively looking for him. Which brought me to my final concern—the other mage, the one who had gotten away from Glave. Would he come looking for Justin? It was possible. The boy would make perfect bait to seal a trap. Was I enough of a bastard to use a ten-year-old boy as bait in a trap that could very well kill him when it was sprung? Yep, it turns out I was exactly that much of a bastard. I would keep the boy with me and see what happened.

I could see Emily studying me as I spoke to the boy. She looked like she didn't trust me—and nor should she. I was doing something very dangerous and very stupid. I was endangering the boy's life and could very well bring an angry mage down upon this camp.

"You didn't even ask him if he wanted to be trained,"

Emily accused as we left the boy to rest.

"That doesn't figure into it," I replied darkly, remembering my own training. "If he doesn't learn how to control his power, it will kill him."

"Still, you could have been kinder. The boy is obviously in shock."

"That doesn't matter either," I hissed angrily at her. "Should he survive the training, worse fates will await him. You want kindness? Shoot him in the head now and end it. He might even come to regret that you didn't in time."

"You're an asshole!" she snarled. "He's not a soldier! He's not even a mage yet—he's a fucking ten-year-old boy."

I didn't bother to correct her. He wasn't just a ten-year-old boy. He was a ten-year-old mage who wasn't in control of his powers, and that was a far more dangerous thing. No, he needed someone to control him during this time—to provide an example. I could only hope my example would be enough. I had no illusions about my qualifications to raise him on ethical or moral matters. If it were possible, I would have turned him over to another mage more suited for training, but there was no one. It was something I had to do myself. I didn't bother to argue this fact with Emily. There was no point. She would never understand.

"Don't walk away from me!" Emily snapped as she struggled to match my pace.

"I am not going to discuss this with you, Miss Perry."

"Then I'll go to Colonel Brandon!" she called. "I'm sure he'll see reason."

It was an empty threat and we both knew it, but it was threat enough that it needed to be addressed. I stopped and turned to face her. It happened so suddenly that she almost collided into me.

"There is a protocol," I whispered, "as to what we should do when we find mages like this."

My tone suggested that the protocol wasn't to simply give them a cup of tea and wish them well in their endeavours. I hoped she could tell how much I hated the protocol even while I understood its purpose. Fortunately this was the first time I had had to ponder it. The only other mages I had encountered had been trying to kill me. We had a protocol for that too.

"Kill him?" Emily guessed.

I nodded. "He's a threat, or he will become one."

Emily chose not to follow me as I walked away this time. I had obviously made my point. How many people had died because of a single one of my kind? I myself was responsible for hundreds of fatalities in the war. I consoled myself with the fact that they were collateral damage, but it didn't change the fact that without my intervention they would probably still be alive. Even as I fought to save them, I knew that not all could be saved. Those I saved with my right hand were counterbalanced by those I sentenced with my left. Yes, my hands were not clean and my conscience was definitely not clear. Should Justin grow into his power, no doubt he would also bear a similar tally of deaths. Should he seek to end the fighting, he would still be forced to make pragmatic decisions that would affect others' lives. Should he turn bad, the deaths would be countless. Was it best to play the safe bet? There was a grim practicality to the maths—one must die so that many others may live. It's an easy philosophy to agree to on paper, but far more difficult when presented with a living breathing human being—and a young boy at that.

Emily avoided me for the remainder of that day, which was a relief. I had no interest in further explaining my actions to her. Glave had gone out hunting our elusive second mage, but I was pretty confident that he wouldn't find anything. Our patrols had returned with minimal losses.

I spent my time on the roof of the warehouse we had commandeered, ensuring that should our friend return he would not be able to recover the boy, nor finish off my soldiers. The smoke from the downed carrier still billowed out into the skyline behind me. That damned boat was taking one hell of a long time to sink. I could only hope it wouldn't explode before it did.

* * *

Glave still hadn't returned when we came back to the camp. I was beginning to get a little worried. It was possible he had fallen into a trap, but I hadn't seen any noticeable increase in magical noise that would indicate a fight. It was equally possible that he was simply ranging further and further out looking for his quarry.

Our forces now controlled a good section of the city; the Russian survivors from the beachhead attack were disorganised and on the run. They were no match for disciplined and well provisioned soldiers. Most had either surrendered or fled deeper into the city. As we took control of more of the city, we discovered numerous refugee populations that had found shelter in Los Angeles. They had probably been in hiding since LA had originally fallen five years ago. They were in poor shape without decent nutrition and access to medical facilities. This led to other problems for us—mainly sourcing provisions for so many refugees. Refugee camps would need to be established and logistics for provisions would need to be set in place. Unfortunately without the carrier group, we didn't have the resources for any of that. We would need to establish that from scratch; fortunately that wasn't my problem. Satisfied that the soldiers were doing their job, I returned back to the camp.

On my return I was informed that Justin was ready to leave the infirmary. This was good and bad news. Good because it signified that he had finally broken free of the Mana fever and was less likely to succumb to his powers. It was bad because I had no idea what to do with the boy in this war zone of a city. I couldn't very well keep him with me at all times. That would be an unnecessary risk to the boy's safety, but at the same point I couldn't leave the boy to his own devices, that could be an unnecessary risk to everyone else's safety.

"You are to stay with me or Miss Perry at all times," I instructed the boy when I collected him.

"Yes, sir," the boy replied. He seemed compliant enough.

What the hell was I going to do with this kid? I couldn't train him in this environment, and I certainly couldn't disappear for long enough to train him without suspicion. How far I could trust Emily in all this? She seemed to be a better option than turning the kid over to the military, unless my suspicions were correct. If they were correct, things were going to go south very quickly.

"What grade were you in at school?" I asked curiously before silently cursing myself. The kid was probably four when the war broke out. He hadn't gone to school.

"Can you read?" I tried again.

"A little," Justin confirmed. "My parents taught me."

His voice quivered slightly at the mention of his parents. Was it possible that his parents were mages too? It was possible, but it was equally likely that they weren't. The magic did follow bloodline, but there was a difference between being a mage and having the potential. There was a chance that his parents had potential that had never eventuated and that Justin's abilities only surfaced because of the vast amounts of Mana being thrown about around him.

"What have you read?"

"Mostly comic books," Justin said.

Great, well that was just perfect. I couldn't simply

load the boy up with spell books and get him to learn on his own. He would need far more guidance than I had needed. I hadn't exactly been the most successful student, but I at least had some experience in reading complicated technical documents before beginning my training. This kid had nothing. This wasn't going to be easy. I really needed to take the kid somewhere and train him properly, but I couldn't do that. Well, I couldn't do that just yet. Not until whoever had been protecting him came back for him. All I had to do was wait. I hate waiting.

I left the kid with Emily and went back to my post. It had been three days and still no word from Glave. It might be time to consider the possibility that he had fallen in battle and wasn't coming back. This would affect my plans; I had hoped to leave him here to protect the troops while I disappeared for a while, but it didn't look like that was going to be an option.

I had been avoiding Colonel Brandon, but I was sure that Marcellus would have mentioned something had any new orders come in. He was no longer acting as second in command, but he was high enough in the command structure to have heard something. Brandon had replaced all my senior officers with his own. I didn't blame him for this—he hadn't exactly made himself popular with the rest of the unit. Still—he wasn't doing a bad job. He seemed relatively competent. He never took unnecessary risks and genuinely seemed to be trying to keep his men alive. My men could do worse.

I wondered how long we would remain here. We had been sent here to deal with a mage, but after almost a week we had achieved very little. Maybe this was all a wild goose chase.

Or maybe not.

Just when I thought it was all clear, the Mana in my body began to tingle. I sent out a scry thread and quickly located the source of my unease. It was on the far side of the city, but still close enough to affect us, should it escalate. I couldn't tell who the combatants were through the scry thread, but I could surmise that one of them was Glave by his Mana signature, and it appeared he wasn't winning. He appeared to be making a rapid retreat across the skyline of the city, headed back here. I could only catch brief glances of his opponent through the scry—they were both moving so fast it was difficult to see anything clearly.

Glave looked like he was almost done for; I could see his threads were formed mostly of desperation than power. It wouldn't take much to break them. Fortunately his opponent appeared only in slightly better condition, but his threads still hummed with power and speed. If I didn't intervene then, the end to this fight wasn't going to be difficult to predict.

I immediately summoned my powers and wrapped a teleportation field around myself. Once the field dissipated, I found myself in the shell of a ruined apartment block. The fight had already brought down the upper floors and created an uneven ground of rock and concrete debris. Through the wall I could hear the sizzle and crackle of Mana threads connecting on the other side of this building. I leapt over the rubble in my way— hopefully I wouldn't be too late to save Glave. I may have cut it a little fine. Glave had been knocked onto his back and the other mage was standing over him, ready to finish him off. It didn't look like this battle had much left in it. Without my interference, the other mage would finish Glave off fairly quickly. I had to act, and I had to act now.

I couldn't tell from behind who this other mage was, but I knew it wasn't Voll. Voll had a smaller build and this other mage was almost as large as Glave. There was something familiar about him, but I couldn't place it and I didn't have time to examine him properly. Summoning my powers, I swept a thread forward and knocked the mage down from behind.

He hadn't even known I was there. My arrival was just another piece of magical noise thrown up by their fight. He had been so focused on finishing his opponent that he had ignored me. He should have sensed my arrival, but from the look of both combatants this battle had been going on for some time—both mages looked absolutely wrecked and depleted. Was it possible that this fight had been going on for three days? It certainly looked possible—their shields were only a bare fraction of what they should have been.

My thread tore through my opponent's shield as if it was paper and sent him flying into a cloud of debris on the far wall. I heard the tell-tale popping noise that indicated his shield had been smashed. My thread had hit flesh and bone. This was over.

Glave clambered wearily to his feet; he was covered in blood and bruises that his shield was unable to prevent. He tried to raise a thread to finish his foe, but failed to summon the necessary strength. The thread fizzled and dissipated. It seemed all he could do to keep his shield around him and he dared not lower that.

"Finish him," he grunted painfully as he attempted to make his way over to our fallen foe. I followed behind the big man curiously.

The other combatant had fallen about ten metres away on the far wall. Glave staggered over a smashed concrete section of flooring to get to the other mage. I wouldn't have thought there were many mages who could humble Glave so thoroughly.

My impact had made a mess of the left side of the mage's body, but he was recognisable. I knew this man. I hadn't seen him in almost seven years, but I knew him! His body was smashed against the concrete wall and several metal brackets had pierced his side on impact, impaling him to the wall. His head hung down, but I could tell there was still life in him. He gurgled and blood dribbled from his lips as he glanced up. I suppose he wanted to spit in the eye of the person who had killed him, but when he saw us his eyes widened in shock.

"Devon?" he whispered. "But … you're … supposed to be dead?"

Gabriel Tychus. I wasn't surprised that he had almost

taken out Glave—he was a master mage in his own right before the war. He had been a former ally, and the last I had seen of him he was attempting to disappear from the world with Renee. He had seen what was coming and wanted nothing of it. He had all but begged me to go with him. I was often sorry I hadn't taken him up on his offer. With herculean effort, Gabriel pulled himself from the metal brackets sliding down the wall in an effort to free himself. He left a red trail of gore behind him—he didn't have long to go.

"Finish him," Glave snarled at me as we watched Gabriel attempt to brace himself against the wall to stand against his foes. I shook my head in disbelief. How was it that Gabriel was here? It was mind boggling. Was he working with Voll? That seemed … unlikely.

Glave growled in fury at my delay and again attempted to summon a thread to finish the fallen mage.

"Wait!" I ordered, but Glave ignored me.

Glave struggled to gather enough power to adequately form the thread. I could see the power building with the big man, but ever so slowly. I couldn't let Glave finish that thread—Gabriel needed to survive so I could question him. He might know where Renee was, and I needed that information desperately. No, Gabriel couldn't die yet. I wouldn't allow it, but it didn't look like Glave was going to listen to reason.

"Wait!" I screamed, but the big man didn't seem to hear me. He left me with no choice. I could see Gabriel struggling to raise a shield, but he was just in too bad a shape to defend himself. I would need to interfere. I raised a thread of my own and struck my ally down before he could raise his thread.

My thread tore through Glave's shield and took the big man's head off. His defences had been so completely worn down that his shield hadn't even slowed my thread. Gabriel gazed at me in disbelief as Glave's headless body hit the ground.

"Thought … you … were dead …" Gabriel repeated as he slid down the wall to the ground. His wounds were severe. He had probably broken most of his ribs on the left and also likely he had internal organ damage. Not to mention the puncture wounds from the metal brackets on the wall. It didn't look good. I had survived worse when I had fallen to Victor, but I had been rescued by a fully qualified medical team and taken straight to a state of the art hospital. Neither of those things existed any longer.

I could see his dark skin fading as he succumbed to blood loss and went into shock. He was going to be no good to me like this? I could teleport him to the medic at the base, but I doubted he'd survive being moved. I could bring the medic here, but It was unlikely that he would be able to do much good here.

"You're dead … He said … that you were dead." Gabriel grasped my arm before passing out. I had no idea who "he" was, or why it was so important, but hopefully I would find out later. So, I couldn't move him and I couldn't bring someone here. That really left only one option, and it wasn't a good one. I sighed as I knelt down over my fallen friend to begin my work.

I ripped his shirt to expose his stomach and chest, and winced as I realised the full extent of the damage. It was amazing he was even still breathing. The whole left side of his chest was caved in and he was bleeding freely down his side. He should have died instantly. Freed from the constraints of his clothes the blood was now pooling at my knees. I could see his Mana force ebbing as it faded from his body. If I did nothing he would soon be dead, but that wasn't the plan. I placed my hand on his shattered chest and let the Mana flow down my arm. The frequency of the Mana left a bitter and fey taste in my mouth as it always did when I attempted this. The last time I had tried was on the poor amputee who I had eventually killed in Poland. I had no reason to expect that today's efforts would be any different, but I had no choice. I needed him conscious. I needed information and I couldn't retrieve it from his corpse.

I watched as the Mana seeped out across his chest like a web of lines insidiously spreading across his body. I could see the Mana doing its work, causing cellular regeneration and creation. It worked at a microscopic level, but already I could see its effect. The skin around the wound turned white and then pink as the rent in his flesh was made whole. Slowly but surely the flesh was being netted together to promote regeneration. I would need to pour almost all my power into the effect to keep it going—it would require a vast expenditure of Mana. If there were any other mages in this region, they were in for a show. Fortunately for me, I was alone. It would not do for another to see this art being worked. I was about fifteen minutes into the technique when I realised something was different. The power being drawn was dwindling. Had I failed? No, the broken flesh seemed to still be undergoing mitosis and repairing his damaged organs. His breath was coming more easily and less in haggard gasps. The process appeared to be working properly. So what was different? Had I had an epiphany after my last attempt and suddenly mastered the technique? If so, how would I determine what was different? What the hell was going on? And then it hit me like a brick as I realised—Gabriel was a mage, whereas none of my other patients had been.

Once I realised this simple fact, I could see the effect for myself. It wasn't my power that was being consumed—it was Gabriel's own. The Mana in his body was actively fighting to preserve the flesh and duplicate the effect. Once I had started the process, his Mana had rushed in to provide the necessary power. Was it merely a question of the Mana though? No, there had to be something else. If it was only about the Mana, Victor would not have been able to perform this technique on others. I knew he had used this sorcery at least once on a non-mage. He had used the technique on Winters when I had sent him to hospital during a fight. Winters had claimed as much when he tracked me down afterwards. I had left him in a fairly bad shape—regeneration was really the only plausible explanation for how quickly he had recovered. This procedure couldn't be used on non-mages or, rather, it wouldn't be effective. It wasn't what Victor had used, but it might be close enough for what I needed right now.

Colour returned to the Gabriel's face and his breathing became regular and deep. The wound on his side had already closed up and I could see the Mana inside his chest repairing the damage to his organs. It seemed to be working. What I was afraid of was what would happen next. As I had expected, the newly regrown cells quickly turned necrotic, their brief life burned up like wildfire. The only difference now was that the regeneration effect was still at work. I watched with satisfaction as the Mana within Gabriel turned on the necrotic flesh and repaired as it, went leaving a trail of newly repaired cells behind it, which would in turn fall prey to necrosis and require repair. It was a vicious cycle, and there was no way to end it.

I watched with curiosity as every ounce of magical effort was thrown into the repair of the cells as the Mana worked furiously throughout the body. But eventually the Mana would exhaust itself and fail, and the body would die. I had only bought Gabriel minutes of life at best. It was now time to make use of them.

Gabriel coughed as I brought him around. His eyes were wide and glassed and he seemed disorientated. "I feel … strange," he murmured, "numb."

"You're dying," I replied firmly. There was no sense in sugar coating it.

He seemed to take this with a degree of calmness. His

eyes widened as he glanced down at the noise the Mana in his body was making as his flesh repaired itself over and over again.

"What have you done to me?" Gabriel whispered. His words were slurred and weak, and his eyes were unfocused. It was possible that he didn't know where he was or even who he was. I would need to hurry.

"I've extended your life," I replied quickly, "but only by a few minutes at best."

"Devon?" It was almost as if he had finally realised who he was talking to. "How are you still alive? Victor said he killed you."

"He tried," I said. "He failed."

Gabriel coughed as he tried to sit up straight. I helped him up as moving him now would make no difference in the long run. His battle was being fought at a cellular level now and not in a mundane.

"Renee thought you … lived …" Gabriel whispered. "But … you never came back. You never …"

Gabriel trailed off as his attention waned and his breathing quickened. He wouldn't last much longer. I needed to get more from him before he passed. I needed to know where Renee was. Was she safe? Had she managed to escape all this? It was important.

"Gabriel," I said, grasping his chin to face me. "Where is Renee? Where has she been hiding during this war?"

"With Victor …" Gabriel murmured.

"Where?" I demanded as I sought to get back the man's attention.

His eyes lolled back in his head. "And your son," he finished.

A son? What the hell? I didn't have a son. Even as I denied the knowledge, I remembered the look in Renee's eyes when I had last left her. She had been trying to get me to stay, saying she couldn't do it alone. I had thought at the time that she was talking about standing against her grandfather, but now I wondered if she had meant something else.

Had she been trying to tell me that she was pregnant? It seemed impossible, and yet I knew it for truth. We had only spent one night together before I had gone off to kill her grandfather, but I had had a strange sense of fear when I looked at her that night. No, it was more than possible. Suddenly it all made sense and everything clicked into place. She had been trying to get me to stay with her, but I had refused because I hadn't known why. I had been so obsessed with rescuing my sister that I hadn't listened. I wondered if I had taken the time to listen if anything would have changed. Would I have still raced off to rescue my sister? Or would I have gone with Renee?

Now she was with Victor. How had that happened? He must have come for her in the early days of the war. We hadn't heard anything about Victor in military reports—he had all but disappeared off the planet. At the time I was grateful for this fact as it meant we wouldn't have to deal with him just yet and I would have time to recover my strength before the showdown.

Gabriel was almost spent, but I needed more

information from him. Where? When? How? I poured more power into Gabriel's body, which his Mana greedily devoured, increasing the pattern of sickness tenfold. The Mana literally raced through his veins doing its deadly work, but with more power the process of eventual decay would be delayed.

"Where is Renee, Gabriel?" I hissed. "Where?"

"I don't … know," Gabriel whispered. "We … escaped …"

Escaped?

"Victor was … hiding us," Gabriel gasped. "Kept us safe from the war. He collected those worthy to continue his new order."

So that was it. He was rebuilding the order in secret. Selecting only the mages he thought were worthy of being included, and he had done so right under our very noses. The pattern would repeat. The world at large would think our kind exterminated—dead and buried. And all the while we would be among them. Give it ten, maybe twenty, maybe even a hundred years. We would arise again—some fool idiot would attempt to overthrow Victor, and this war would repeat. It needed to be stopped before the cycle could continue.

"Renee wanted to keep her son away from Victor," Gabriel continued. "I helped. We fled and saw what the world had become after Victor had sheltered us."

"Where is she now, Gabriel?"

"I don't know," Gabriel coughed. "And … I don't think I'd tell you if I did. You're just like him."

"Where is Renee?" I repeated, ignoring his insult and throwing a compulsion behind my words.

Gabriel's eyes widened as the Mana entered into his mind to make him compliant. The effect must have only lasted for seconds, but it was enough. Gabriel grasped at his pocket and pulled out a very badly beaten mobile phone. His hands were shaking so much he had trouble forcing it into my hand. The mobile network was still functional in parts of the world. He was giving me a way of contacting Renee. I was sure that should I open this phone I would find a contact card for Renee in this small electronic device. I grunted and placed the phone into my pocket. I couldn't focus on that right then. I wasn't sure if I wanted to speak to Renee; I simply wanted to ensure that she was all right. My hand trailed down to the phone in my pocket as the urge to use it almost overcame me. It wasn't until I glanced down at Gabriel and realised that the Mana I had used for the compulsion thread had been absorbed and reassigned to keep the pattern of mitosis going.

Wait … What? I glanced again. The Mana in Gabriel's body had absorbed my Mana as a new source of power. His own system had subverted the external Mana and made it its own. Could it do that with all types of Mana? I raised my hand and summoned Mana Nova. Sure enough, as I brought the deadly fire towards Gabriel's body, the flame spluttered and halted as its power source was consumed. What had I discovered? I didn't need anyone to answer that for me. I already knew damned well what I had discovered. I had discovered a way to bring Victor down. I could use his own strength against him. Infect him with this sorcery and his own powers would be consumed by the effect to keep him alive. The spells granting him longevity and regeneration would be consumed by my sorcery and he would be finally vulnerable. I could kill him. I could end this. It was ironic—all I needed to do to kill Victor was to attempt to heal him.

A hundred variables went through my mind. This looked possible, but I needed to test it and for that I would need to return to Poland. If this was right, then I could finally end Karl's existence as he had wanted. That would be my test—if it worked on Karl, then it would work on Victor. Gabriel glared balefully at me as I began to plan my experiments in my head.

"Rest easy, old friend," I murmured. "You've just given me the final piece I need to destroy Victor."

Gabriel coughed and attempted to grasp my shoulder, but he was too weak. All his energy was being consumed by the spell effect.

"Don't … hurt her …" he gasped as the light left his eyes.

I could bring him back with another infusion of power, but there didn't seem to be much point. It would only prolong the inevitable. Let the poor man's suffering end. I watched with fascination as his body quickly succumbed to necrosis and his very matter was consumed by the spell.

"Goodbye old friend," I whispered to the pile of ash that was all that remained of his body.

CHAPTER SEVEN

A cloud of dust and ash washed over me as the bullets buzzed past my head like mosquitos. With a grunt I pushed myself forward, feeling the tell-tale pinpricks of discomfort that indicated that I'd been hit. I shrugged it off as I pushed forward. Loud explosions rocketed behind me as my last position turned into a large crater.

It didn't take me long to see the cause of the attack: a large tank rolled into view. A painful concussion of force and blinding light took me and I was propelled backwards as the tank's next shot hit me squarely in the chest. The impact sent me sprawling and I hit the building behind me with the force of a tank blast. My body slammed through the concrete wall as if it were made of polystyrene, sending chunks of metal and shrapnel flying in all directions. It only took me several seconds to recover as I used my powers to right myself and send the tank sprawling. A burst of equally concussive force burst from my fingers directed it cascading down the road like a paper cup caught in the wind.

A shiver of excitement crept over me; there was something here, something that was a danger. I could feel it with senses honed from years of battle. It wasn't the tank—that barely even registered as a threat to me. My premonition served me well as I leapt out of the way seconds before the façade of the building was brought smashing down. I didn't see who had done it, but I had felt the rise of their power and I caught a glimpse of a Mana thread from above. I looked upwards into the city-scape of buildings surrounding me. They were nothing more than empty husks now—the lives that once gave them meaning were long gone and I could already see signs of nature beginning to reclaim what was hers. It was subtle: a crack of broken concrete with a small sprout of grass growing through it. The grass seemed out of place in this concrete wasteland—the colour was all wrong against the grey of this war-torn world. The vibrancy of it hurt my eyes. I gritted my fists as I thought about lashing out; I could destroy that blade of grass just as easily as I had destroyed the tank, but I knew that in the end it didn't matter, another would simply rise in its place. No matter how I struggled I would not be able to overcome this basic rule of nature. I was foolish to even try.

I saw my enemy at once, in the reflection in the glass of the building in front of me. I could see them silhou-etted in shadow as they leapt from the building above me and onto the one in front. They were powerful, but I wasn't afraid. After all, it didn't matter if I fell either, another would rise to take my place. I propelled myself up the side of the building, my Mana gouging into the sheer glass as if it were no stronger than butter, as I rose to face this threat in fury.

I launched into the air, high above my foe. I looked down at the city below me: the damage didn't seem as bad from up here. The city looked almost vibrant once again—there were signs of life everywhere. Unable to see the individual blades of grass, I simply saw the green of the many blades and it wasn't as painful as before. I now understood their place as part of the system, and it was a system that would survive long after I fell. It would continue no matter my small efforts to thwart it.

I spun in a lazy arc and landed behind my foe, who hadn't turned to face me yet. I could see the power radiating from them like waves of the ocean against the rocks. Their shield was blurring their shape, making it impossible for me to see who it was. With a shout, the figure turned and swept a host of threads at me, seeking to knock me from the rooftop. I leapt again into the air, my hands darting to block the threads that sought to entangle me. As I launched my threads in defence, I watched with grim satisfaction as they blocked those of my opponents. But I couldn't get the advantage. More and more threads were brought against me—too many for me to dodge. I wrenched my arm away as a thread wrapped itself around my forearm and pulled me towards the ground. The sizzling noise of the thread snapping against my shield was all I could hear as I tumbled down. Several more threads latched onto me, pulling me down, faster and faster. I could see the rooftop rising to meet me with grim certainty, but there was nothing I could do to stop it. I threw everything I had into my shield in an attempt to survive the fall, but it was too late. I hit the rooftop and fell through it as if it were nothing. The threads disengaged into a haze of pain and darkness as I was hurled down into the central core of the building.

I felt each concrete floor as I consecutively broke through each level. My foe was on me as we broke through the centre of the building, their threads lashing at my shield seeking to bring it down. In the dust and debris I couldn't see my foe clearly, but I could see their eyes. The stranger's eyes were alien on their face. Pale blue eyes pierced into me accusingly as they sought to end my life. Although I could see nothing more than two pin points of blue in a sea of Mana, I could see the rage and the anger behind those eyes and I knew with certainty that I was responsible for that anger.

Concrete slabs and piles of debris followed us down as we broke through the building. I wasn't fighting anymore, there wasn't much point—I knew when my end was near. I was outclassed—my foe was more powerful than me and it was right that they should take me. With an explosion of pain, my shield shattered around me and I landed on the final floor with a crater of debris and destruction spread out around me. How I had survived I didn't know, but I wasn't going to survive for long. With the clinical precision that comes with study of Necromancy, I could see the damage to my body was irrecoverable—I was dying. Death doesn't always come as an enemy and I had long made my peace with my defeat.

My enemy landed over me, the haze of their shield burning as they leaned in to face me. I could see the blue of their eyes with burning intensity as they peered down at me. As my eyes adjusted to the light of the mana field, I could finally make out the details of the face behind the shield.

I smiled in silence as I saw my own face in my defeat. There was no doubt I was the one who had defeated me. My opponent lowered their shield, and I saw with stark clarity the lines of power that kept me standing on my foe. It was me. It was what I had become. I saw the arrogance on my broken face, the power of lust, and just how far I had fallen. I saw myself as the thing I had always feared I would become.

The figure took two steps forward and its face took on a cruel expression. I wondered briefly how many of my kind had seen this face as their final seconds ticked by? I saw the fury and enjoyment rise on the figure's face as he summoned his power to end my life. I knew that joy. I knew what he was experiencing as he completed his dominion over me.

Unwilling to watch his face, my head lolled to the side and I stared in horror at a shard of mirrored glass that had fallen from the ceiling during our descent. The reflection in the mirror was as I had remembered myself—young, carefree. Who I should have been. It was torture that this had been taken from me. Especially now that I should be reminded of it in my final moments.

I opened my mouth to scream, but before I could

make a sound, the sudden noise of a Mana thread brought my head snapping around. My foe was spinning backwards as a thread launched at them from behind me. The threads overpowered my foe with such a display of power that it was blinding. Thread impacted with thread and eventually with shield as the newcomer overpowered my foe and forced them to flee. I didn't see where he went and my eyes were growing dark. In the distance I heard a staggered shriek and an explosion of Mana that sounded like a shield breaking. And then there was nothing; my vision was fading fast as the darkness set in and I thought I would be forever lost in that darkness. It was terrifying—I gazed into the abyss and saw that all I had been, all that I ever would be was nothing. In that one terrible moment I knew what I had been and all my works for what they were. If I could have, I would have wept, but I was too far gone for even that. Just when I thought the darkness would consume me, a face burst into my vision like a blinding light. Blue eyes pierced into me as a face as familiar as my own stared down at me. In that face I could see the stern gaze of my father and the compassion of my mother. A single tear rolled down the face and I would have done anything to halt its path. They pushed the hair from my face and stared down at me in love. I knew that face. It wasn't my face, but it was of me. I had never met him but I knew him. He was my son.

My son lifted me gently and brought me to a place where it was safe. He hadn't saved me from death—no I was too far gone for that, but he had taken me somewhere

where I could die in peace—a place where there was no shame in defeat and no stigma of weakness. As I looked into my son's eyes, it suddenly wasn't scary any longer. Everything would be all right. I was finally safe.

"You need to let it all go." Ghostly words whispered throughout my mind as I let myself drift off into that darkness.

I awoke with a start.

It took me a few seconds to realise where I was. I hadn't meant to fall asleep, but I was too tired to immediately teleport back to the camp. I couldn't have slept for more than a few hours at most. I glanced briefly at Gabriel's remains and Glave's body, which still lay in the corner. With a shaking hand I brushed my hair from my face and immediately stopped as I glanced at my hand. The details of my dream had seemed so clear at the time, but with each precious second that passed I was losing them. Already I could see the image of my son's face blurring and fading from my memory.

I am not a believer in a higher power. I can fathom no greater power than mine—but in that instant I understood. There were a million explanations for my dream, rational explanations that would explain away the mystery of what I had just seen. I don't believe in a god, but I know a system when I see one. I can see a higher power in the design of evolution and I can see the divine in the passing of strength from father to son. In the end, I hadn't experienced the divine. I merely had a dream, but I knew it was more than that. It was a sign of things to come and what I would need to do.

I don't understand how I knew this, but I knew it as surely as if I had been spoken to from on high. I needed to change—what I was doing was wrong. The killing of my kind needed to stop. We weren't an aberrant of the human race, we were part of it and to think of ourselves as separate was foolish. Were we the next stage of evolution? Who knows? Was our kind the future of our species? I didn't know. I didn't care. The anger and the pain I had felt had gone and it felt as if an iron collar had been removed from around my throat. All the deaths I had used as justification were immediately revealed for what they were. It was nothing more than an attempt by a weak man to justify the violence he needed to appease the ghosts of his past. But it wasn't like that anymore. In that one moment I was free and unshackled. I was able to see myself for what I truly was, and I smiled. I wasn't as broken as I had once thought. There was a path back, I knew it. I just had to find it. It was possible to come back from this. It was possible that I could reclaim what I had lost. At first, I had sought it for selfish reasons, for me, for my glory. That wasn't the path. That wasn't my destiny. I would recover myself, because I had no choice. I had a son. It wasn't about me any longer.

* * *

I returned to the camp alone. I had much to think about. The camp was quiet when I returned, but I hadn't expected that my encounter with Gabriel would have changed much. We had fought on the other side of the city—far outside the range of their scouts and sentry posts. They would have had no idea what had just happened.

Now that Glave was gone, I guess it fell to me to solely protect the camp, but the idea left a sour taste in my mouth. For the first time in a long time I began to make plans that didn't involve combat—perhaps it was time to cash out. Simply run away and find somewhere safe to hide this whole thing out as Renee had originally wanted me to.

A shiver went through my body as I immediately rejected the idea. I had a son. I couldn't leave the world in this state for him. No, there was still more I needed to do. Victor couldn't be allowed dominion of this world—his new order would need to be destroyed before it could become a threat. My son would be powerful. The mixture of bloodlines between my own and his own would be highly prized by Victor. He would not allow such a prize freedom. He would attempt to do to my son what he had tried to do to me, and what he had done to my sister. He would turn him into a weapon. My son deserved better. Familiar urges rose from within my chest as my thoughts turned to the protection of another. I had felt this way before and it hadn't exactly worked out way I had planned. I resolved that this time would be different.

"Devon?" A voice cut into my reverie from behind

me. I turned my head to see Emily Perry cautiously approaching from behind. "Is Glave with you?"

"He's dead," I replied curtly.

"When?" She didn't seem surprised.

"A few hours ago."

"Are we in any danger?" Emily breathed softly as she scanned the skyline.

"Where is the boy?"

"He's safe," Emily replied, obviously a little annoyed at my tone. "Devon," she whispered, drawing my attention behind me. "I wanted to apologise for our argument earlier. I shouldn't have said those things."

"It's okay." I kept my eyes focused on the city. She was lying to me. I could see it on her face. Normally I couldn't get much from her expression, but now her expression was literally screaming distrust and deception. Something had changed.

"No, it's not," Emily replied firmly. "I misjudged you and I immediately assumed the worst."

"You probably weren't far from wrong," I grunted, hoping to end the conversation quickly.

"No," Emily said, "I don't think so—Glave or any of the other mages wouldn't have saved the boy. They would have simply ended his life and been done with it."

"Maybe, maybe not," I conceded. "I'm still not sure I'm doing the right thing."

"Why did you do it?" Emily pressed.

"I'm not sure," I answered. I was surprised by just how honest I was being with this woman. Especially considering she wasn't exactly being honest with me. "It just doesn't seem right to kill the boy. It's not his fault."

"So what is your plan then?" Emily continued. I could see she trying to keep it light.

"I really don't know," I grunted, as I sat down. "But I think my time with the army is just about done."

Emily raised an eyebrow. "I didn't expect you to say that."

That cinched it. I could see it in her eyes. She definitely had a plan here, and it depended upon me remaining with the army. If my suspicions were correct, she would now attempt to keep me talking for as long as possible.

"No?" I smiled. "Perhaps you don't know me as well you think you do."

"Where would you go?"

"Does it really matter? One place is pretty much the same as another to me."

"I suppose." Emily smiled. "Will you take me with you when you go?"

"Why would I do that?

"Do I mean so little to you?"

"Lady," I sighed, "I barely know you. Why would I take you with me? Why would you even want to come with me?"

"I thought we had something ..." Emily seemed unsure of herself. That reaction seemed genuine. She really did think she'd made some kind of impact on me. She was probably right. I wouldn't like to see harm come to the girl, but I was hardly going to bring her with me.

Especially now that I was coming to suspect a horrible truth about her. All that remained was to see what she would do once I rejected her.

"No," I declared firmly.

I wasn't surprised when the deception that she'd been holding in place dropped from her face and I could see the cunning desperation behind her eyes. I had thought that my mask was still firmly in place too, but she must have read my reaction from my own features. With a snarl she pulled a gun from her side holster and placed it against my face.

"I don't know if you've got a shield up or not," she hissed, "but this isn't loaded with ordinary bullets. You're tired from battle; you won't be able to stand against it. It'll plough straight through your shield and into your head in seconds."

She was right about my abilities. I was tired, I was weak. I hadn't slept in god knows how long. I had often wondered about my ability to shrug off the need to sleep—I certainly hadn't had that skill as a child. In my teenage years if I didn't get a solid eight hours sleep I would fall apart the next day. Now, it seemed I could go for weeks. Was this a by-product of Mana?

I knew Victor had studied it; he had claimed he survived on Mana alone, without the need to sleep, eat or consume water. I had found no mention of this in the spell books I had recovered, but the technique may have been stored in newer spell books I hadn't found. As I thought about my time with him in Singapore, it seemed to confirm my suspicions. I had never seen him eat or drink. His housekeeper cooked meals only for me and his other student, Aaron Chen. Perhaps he had used the Mana to sustain himself. It was strange that he had never taught me the technique. He had always been very careful to keep his studies into Necromancy from me.

"Then shoot me," I whispered.

"You're baiting me to shoot you?" Emily exclaimed as she lowered her gun in surprise. "I would say it was arrogance, but I think you genuinely want to die."

"Raise your side arm," I ordered.

"No … I don't want to."

"Raise it," I snapped harshly. "Point it at me."

Emily did as she was ordered and pointed her gun back at me. I could see the indecision in her eyes.

"Do as you have been ordered," I murmured.

The gun shook in her hands. If she wasn't careful she was going to drop it.

"Do it!" I hissed.

"Why couldn't you have been like Glave? Or any of the others? It would have been so easy, but you—you're different." Emily sighed uncertainly. She lowered her gun. "What are you going to do now?" Emily whispered, her eyes wide with fear.

"Nothing," I stated. "I'm going to do nothing."

I reached out and took the gun from her fingers and threw it on the ground. Her eyes never left mine.

"The next time you're in this position," I advised, "fire and keep firing, then run. Others of my kind won't be so courteous, but you already know that, don't you? You've killed my kind before."

I didn't need to see the evidence in her eyes to know I had spoken truth. I didn't need to see the slumping of her shoulders to know just what she was. She killed my kind when they lay sleeping, when they were defence-less. She killed them after forcing them to trust her. I turned from her and began to walk away.

"So that's it?" Emily exclaimed, her eyes narrowing in anger. "You're not going to ask me who sent me or why?"

"No," I replied simply without turning around. "I know why, and I already know who. You were sent by Levenson. He is trying to clean up all the loose ends in this mess he helped create."

Emily didn't seem to register what I was saying. She hadn't known Levenson had been involved in starting this whole mess. It had been his collusion with Marcus that had led to the stand-off with Victor, which had sparked off this war. It was Levenson who had recruited me, and it was he who had recovered my broken and shattered body after my battle with Victor and encour-aged me to turn myself into a weapon against my kind. I don't think he had expected the war to escalate to the point it had, and it wasn't surprising that he was trying to clean up his mess. In some ways he was right—I was a liability that would need to be dealt with, and it would be cleaner to deal with me quietly before the war ended. It was all guess work at this point, but it seemed to fit the facts. I didn't begrudge him this betrayal. In his place I might have done the same. No, that's not true, I reflected. I would have succeeded.

"You knew I was sent here to kill you," Emily mused. "What would have happened had I fired?"

"I would have killed you," I answered. "I can withstand cannon fire. Your *special* bullet wouldn't have made any difference. I was never in any danger."

Emily blanched slightly at my reply. It was obvious that her decision not to fire had been a close thing.

"There is one question you could answer," I continued. "Why now? Why not six months ago? What has changed?"

"I don't know," Emily whispered. "I was told something about missing civilians. We thought you were colluding with the enemy. I didn't think you were rescuing children."

Missing civilians. I sighed wistfully. So Levenson knew about my experiments, or at least he knew that I was taking civilians who were never returned. It was perhaps lucky that we had found Justin when we had. It was logical that Emily would jump to the wrong conclusion. I had thought I had been more careful in covering my tracks about my test subjects, but obviously I hadn't. This meant two things: one, someone within my division was independently reporting back to Levenson; and two, my time serving with the allied forces was indeed finished. It was about time.

It was a good thing that I didn't bother to register my return to the camp with command. If Emily's orders had changed, then I could only assume the good colonel's had too. If that was the case, I could very well be walking into an armed confrontation when I went to recover the boy.

As much as I feared it, I didn't have much choice. I quickly collected some private effects, placed them in a backpack and threw it over my shoulder.

"You're taking the voice recorder?" Emily interjected.

I hadn't bothered to notice that she'd followed me. What else was she going to do now? She'd had orders to kill me. She'd failed.

"Yes," I replied gruffly. "Perhaps I'll do as you asked me and record my memoirs."

Emily didn't react at my harsh tone. "You should. You really should. I think it's important for people to know why you did all this."

There was a hint of reproach in her voice, but I let her have her little retort.

"You should be gone when I leave," I advised.

"I will be," Emily promised. "I think it's about to get very exciting here in a few minutes and I have no interest in being involved."

"Smart girl." I chuckled. "Do you know if they've moved Justin?"

"No."

"It doesn't matter."

"Devon." Emily sighed. "Be careful."

"I'll be all right."

"I wasn't worried about you," Emily called as I turned and left her.

CHAPTER EIGHT

Brandon had moved Justin from the infirmary. There was only one reason he would have done that. I had hoped Brandon wouldn't get in my way, but I was wrong and now a large number of soldiers were going to pay for that mistake. There weren't too many places secure enough to hold his prisoner—locating Justin would not be difficult.

Unfortunately, though, my arrival at the infirmary had been noticed and I was intercepted before I could reach my destination. A contingent of soldiers barred my entry from the makeshift brig; at their head was Colonel Brandon himself.

Looking behind me I saw a second contingent approaching from behind.

"Where have you been?" Brandon grunted by way of greeting. He wanted to play it like we were all one big family? Fine, I'd play along.

"Destroying enemies of the state," I answered lightly as I glanced around.

"Where is the other mage?" Brandon continued in his gruff tone.

"Dead. He fell yesterday."

"You didn't think to report this?" Brandon snarled. This was the first time he had shown any sign of anger. He usually seemed calm—too calm.

"No," I replied softly in the face of his rage. "I thought it more important to avenge him."

If Brandon had any intuition or skill at reading people, he would have seen my words for the lies they were. He gave no indication that he had sensed my deception though. As I stared into his eyes, I saw nothing but relief. Brandon was a far worse liar than Emily. So, Glave had been on the kill list too. Once I would have accepted the necessity of the big man's death. Now it seemed like a waste. It was ironic considering I had been the one to kill him.

I glanced briefly around at the soldiers arrayed before and behind me. They were prepped for combat; they knew what this was and I could see from the grimaces on their faces they also knew the odds. I had no wish to kill these men, but I would do so if forced to.

"Where is the boy?" I whispered.

"Why do you want him?" Brandon's eyes were firm. He wasn't going to back down.

I saw the brief nod that was the order issued. Brandon tensed as he awaited the response to his command. I felt the impact of the gunshot spread across my shield, rocking my head forward. The sound of the bullet impacting my shield rang out across the compound. It actually stung a little. This must have been one of those fancy bullets Emily had spoken of. I didn't turn around to see who had fired on me. Colonel Brandon's eyes flared in triumph and immediately faded as he realised I was untouched.

"That was a nice try," I murmured softly. "Take me by surprise. Keep me focused on you, while you shoot me from behind. It might have worked. But I lost a friend that way."

I turned around to see Marcellus's grimacing face. He was looking at me in horror, a smoking gun still held in his hands.

"I told them it would do no good," he whispered with a resigned look on his face.

This betrayal hurt far more than the bullet had. I had trusted him. I hadn't quite realised just how much I had relied on him. To see him standing before me, having tried to kill me, was almost more than I could bear.

"Why?" I gasped.

"You were killing us," Marcellus accused, a single tear rolling from his eyes. "You could have saved us, but one by one you let us die. There's only you and me left."

The accusation hit home. I didn't know the rest of my original squad had died. I suppose I should have checked in with Marcellus, but there wasn't time.

"When?"

"Camerons was killed on the beachhead and Morre never made it off the carrier," Marcellus muttered. "And now, there will only be you."

Marcellus fired again, point blank into my chest. He knew, as I did, that the bullet wouldn't pierce my shield. He knew I would immediately kill him. I probably should have, but I just couldn't bring myself to do it. He had betrayed me, sure, but although he was the one to pull the trigger, he wasn't the one to give the order. I clenched my teeth as I stared into the face of my friend, who was prepared for me to kill him. For the sake of what we had once had, I would fail him in this.

Unfortunately I hadn't expected the others to take action. I suppose I should have. These were trained soldiers and their instincts were those of honed killers. If the first shot doesn't down your prey, then you fire more. With military precision the soldiers formed firing lines around me and opened fire. It didn't make any difference to me, but unfortunately Marcellus was standing very close to me, and assault rifles aren't known for accuracy. I watched in horror as bullets intended for me hit him. Time seemed to slow down as small bullet holes appeared in my friend. He began to fall so very slowly. I leapt forward and wrapped my arms around him before he could hit the ground. He would be protected by my shield from any further shots, but I could see it was already too late. He was dying. I could have extended his life as I did with Gabriel, but there didn't seem much point.

"Why?" Marcellus whispered as blood trickled from his mouth. "Why did you let us die? We trusted you. We believed in you. I believed in you." His words ended in spluttering coughs.

"Because," I murmured sadly, "there are greater evils than me."

I had once thought that way, that the end result would justify the means. Now I saw the truth for what it was. In my actions I had become as great an evil as anything I had sought to protect people from. This was a truth I couldn't deny.

I could see the same truth reflected in the dying man's eyes as he looked up at me. I could see the accusation. To him there was no greater evil than me. I couldn't fault him.

"Rest easy, my friend," I whispered as I placed him on the ground. I was going to promise him that his death would be avenged, but there didn't seem to be much point. His death had been pointless. A meaningless accident. Even the soldiers firing at me weren't really responsible. Killing them would mean nothing. In fact, killing the soldiers wouldn't bring Marcellus any peace. I closed my friend's eyes and quickly stood up as more bullets bounced off my shield.

With my shield at full strength I could barely feel the impact. There was nothing to stop me from teleporting away, but that wouldn't achieve my goals. I could also kill every soldier within a ten mile radius, but I'd already determined that I wasn't going to do that. No, I needed something more subtle. This was unfortunate, as subtlety wasn't my strong suit.

I reached out with a telekinetic thread and immediately broke that thread into a vortex of smaller threads. I had once thought I had mastered this technique years ago. I had used it to literally tear a car to pieces once and sent its occupants falling down onto the highway. My mastery then was nothing compared to what I could do now.

A nexus of threads spread out across the soldiers. The threads crept into their rifles and triggered the safety catches. Thirty soldiers gasped in unison as they were disarmed and their weapons fell to pieces in front of them. Several soldiers attempted to pull out side arms, only to shout in dismay as those too were disassembled.

By this stage, most of the soldiers had a pretty good idea which way this was going to go and were attempting to beat a hasty retreat, but that wouldn't serve my purposes either. With a flick of my fingers, I sent the threads around thirty necks and pulled them from their feet. Hands clawed at their throats as I kept them floating several metres from the ground. I pulled the unfortunate colonel before me. His eyes bulged as the telekinetic thread cut off his breathing canal. He gasped for breath as I grabbed him by the chin to force him to pay attention to me.

"Is the boy alive?"

He couldn't move his neck freely with the telekinetic thread, but he signalled that the boy was inside the brig.

"This was a waste," I whispered into his ear. "You had no chance."

"Orders," the colonel gasped. "We had orders."

I let the colonel fall to his knees. He immediately rubbed his neck as he gazed up at me. "Killian Voll has been reported dead this morning," he croaked. "We had orders."

I nodded. With Killian dead, this war was as good as over. I would be considered nothing more than a liability to the new order when it rose. They weren't going to allow me to survive. I may very well have done them a favour by killing Glave if they had planned on exterminating all of our kind. In any event, Levenson knew I was a liability no matter what happened. It made sense to order my death the moment Killian was out of the picture. I would deal with Levenson later.

"I'm going to leave you here," I grunted to the colonel. "I'm going to leave your men here, but I'm taking the boy with me and you won't follow me."

My warning was unnecessary. They didn't have the capacity to follow me where I was going anyway. The colonel's baleful eyes softened as he listened to my pronouncement. He'd obviously expected me to simply kill them all. The sound of his soldiers falling to the ground and gasping for breath followed me as I entered the brig and secured Justin. They hadn't harmed him. He looked at me a little confused as he tried to understand the situation. The soldiers who had guarded him were pointing guns at me, but they weren't a worry.

"Justin," I called, "come with me. Quickly."

Justin hurried past the guards. I thought for a second that one of them might try something stupid, but they eventually relaxed and allowed the boy to pass. I breathed a sigh of relief as the boy stood next to me and I lowered my shield to take us away.

I teleported us both out of the country several

seconds later. I was done with this place. I should have teleported the boy out in the first place and never set foot back in the camp.

* * *

Justin threw up on arrival. He had never experienced teleportation before. I should have expected such a result, but my tolerance was spent and this was little more than an unnecessary and unwelcome inconvenience. I waited with impatience as the boy excavated the contents of his stomach onto the ground.

"Are you finished?" I enquired .

Justin wiped his mouth and nodded quietly. He looked a little better, but still looked an awful shade of green. I smiled thinly as I remembered my first forays into teleportation. I'd lost my lunch too. I can't remember when I stopped getting bouts of nausea every time I teleported, but it wasn't missed.

"Where are we?" Justin asked as he glanced around.

"Scotland, I think," I murmured. I hadn't exactly been paying attention to where I was teleporting to. Anywhere east of the States had been sufficient.

"It's cold," Justin continued, wrapping his arms around his chest.

I hadn't noticed. One of the advantages of having a shield is that you don't tend to notice temperature variations that quickly. I could tell from the frost forming on the grass at our feet and the mist rising from the boy's mouth that he had a point. Due to the time zone differ-ence it would be night soon and it would only get colder. We would require some shelter sooner rather than later and I needed to figure out where I was going to offload this kid. I couldn't very well have him tag around with me for the next few years. Not with what I was planning.

Most of Europe and the UK had been heavily affected by the fighting, so it was unlikely we would be disturbed. This place wasn't ideal, but it would do for the next few days or weeks—however long it took for Justin to learn to defend himself. Once he had mastered the basics it would be safe to leave him alone somewhere. Maybe I could set him up in a refugee camp somewhere and visit with new learning material when he was ready. It was strange to be making these kinds of plans. I'd never had to concern myself with this stuff before. I'd always dealt with the immediate threat.

I sent out a scry thread and located a small cottage that seemed abandoned and sturdy a few miles away. It was safe enough to teleport to, but I wanted the boy's stomach to be relatively intact when we arrived so I elected to walk. I don't know if Justin appreciated this or not. He remained quiet the whole trip and meekly followed behind me.

The cottage had obviously been abandoned and there were signs of looting from inside, but other than some damage to the rear of the cottage it seemed structurally sound. Closing the door to the kitchen at the rear of the cottage helped keep the cold out. I quickly lit a fire in the fireplace, noticing that Justin flinched as I summoned the necessary flame to light the brittle wood. With the dimming sun outside, the fireplace provided our only source of illumination. Electricity had long been disconnected from the cottage if the fallen power lines outside were to be believed.

"I'm hungry," Justin mumbled as he warmed his hands before the fire. It was doubtful that there was any food remaining in the kitchen.

I held my hands out before me and send the Mana funnelling down in my palms. The eldritch glow on my hands seemed to fascinate the boy as he watched me convert the Mana particles into proteins, nutrients, sugars and more complex chemicals. I had learned this technique from my old master who had demonstrated it in the creation of a diamond. The atomic structure of a diamond is far easier than what I was doing now. I could have created a diamond with my eyes closed. This would require far more concentration. A small lattice of Mana appeared in my hand as I completed the chemical process of converting Mana into matter. The structure flexed as it began to form and eventually became a solid small block of what could only be described as food. I quickly passed it to the boy, who gazed at me in wonder. It was little more than a hardened biscuit designed to last a long time, be portable, and easy to consume and digest. They had a variety of names, but most of my squad had simply referred to them as D-Rations, after the chocolate rations from the First World War.

His wonder quickly turned to disgust as he tasted the bar. The military ration tasted a little better than a boiled potato, but was a good source of energy, and provided that we didn't try to live exclusively on the damned things they would keep us going.

I'd used this technique rarely over the past few years, but I had improved immeasurably from the first time I had tried it. Things hadn't been going so well at the time: our division had been cut off from supplies and low in numbers. I'd turned to creating food to increase our supplies. It hadn't been overly effective. I hadn't been able to produce anything near the quantities we needed to survive and the process just weakened me too much. I'd experimented with a variety of different food sources before I found that D-Rations were the easiest to duplicate. The men hadn't been overly thrilled at the concept either—they'd somehow managed to remove all the taste, texture and enjoyment from the food bar. The infusion of energy was beneficial, but there was no temptation to eat the damned thing. The boy looked like he was enjoying it as much as the soldiers had. It did have one thing in its favour, though: atomically it was far simpler to produce than other processed foods.

"Don't you need to eat?" he asked as he offered me the remaining half.

"No." I shook my head. "I'll be fine for now."

Truth is I didn't have any appetite any longer. I couldn't even remember the last time I ate something. Maybe some rations at the camp? I definitely remember eating something at the captain's dinner table on the carrier. I should probably have been more concerned about that.

I waited for the kid to finish his meal before I began his training. I had an eerie sense of déjà vu as I contemplated what I was about to do. The last time I had done this had been with my half-sister Allie. Hopefully this would work out better than that time. I shook the memory from my mind—reminiscing about her wouldn't help me or the kid now.

"Hold out your hand," Isaid as I grasped the boy's wrist. I could see the blood pumping in his veins through my tight grip, but I didn't let up. To his credit, he didn't squirm or show any sign of discomfort, although I must have been hurting him.

His hand went a purplish shade of red as the blood pooled from the lack of circulation. Already I could see his body's response as it attempted to send Mana down to free the blockage. Justin glanced at me in a curious mixture of amazement and pain.

"You're making it do that," I informed him as I released his hand.

The Mana in his body immediately went back to its usual swirling pattern. The boy's eyes immediately focused as he tried to make the Mana move back down his arm. It had taken Allie all afternoon just to get the Mana to move—I wasn't expecting much from Justin. The boy flinched as I grabbed his hand again. The Mana flowed to the affected area much quicker this time, and more importantly, I felt the subtle effects of the Mana struggling to repel the assault. It was painfully weak, but I could feel it working its force against me.

I let go. The Mana remained behind in the kid's hand.

"Excellent," I whispered as I watched the Mana slowly return to normal. "Let me know when you can control it."

I lowered myself into a floral recliner in the corner of the room and let the boy get on with his studies. I pulled my coat firmly around me, stoked the fire, and attempted to meditate. I knew that sleep would elude me, but I had no intention of disturbing the boy while he mastered this fundamental skill and he was still too weak to leave him alone.

I took Gabriel's phone from my pocket and held it in my hands. With this device I could talk to Renee. A tremor passed through me, and I almost dropped the phone. I pressed the power button and the display informed me there was over 50% battery power left. I briefly wondered how Gabriel had been keeping the phone charged as I pressed the unlock screen.

I had hoped for a password or something that would keep me from accessing the phone, but there was nothing. There was nothing stopping me from accessing the contact list and getting Renee's number.

The urge to call her almost overcame me, until I tried to imagine just how that conversation would go. What did I have to tell her? Would I tell her that I had become a killer just like her father and her grandfather? Would

I tell of the things I had done? How would she react? How could she possibly accept me? She couldn't. She wouldn't. She would reject me and I couldn't face that.

No, it was far better that I remain dead as far as she was concerned. It was better she think I died in Melbourne, when I had last fought her grandfather. It was a kindness of sorts, yet why couldn't I take my finger from the contacts button?

I steeled myself. I was being weak and I needed to be strong now. I put the phone back in my pocket. I couldn't afford such weakness now. Perhaps afterwards, once Victor was dead, I would contact Renee. It's amazing the lies we're able to tell ourselves. I almost believed myself, I really did.

* * *

It took Justin about four days to gain rudimentary control of the Mana. I had expected about this time frame. Allie and I had been exceptions to the rule. Both Allie and I learned by seeing the Mana and could somehow figure out how it worked; Justin didn't learn that way. He had to do it the hard way.

I had taken the opportunity to retrieve one of the rudimentary spell books I had recovered on my searches and gave it to the boy. His eyes glazed over as he turned the pages. It was dry reading, especially as he was used to reading comic books.

It took him another week before he was able to form

a solid enough Mana thread. It was still painfully weak and would easily disperse. This was taking far too long. I didn't have the patience or the time. It was hard not to compare the boy to my sister. Allie had formed much stronger threads on her first try. But it was unfair to compare the boy to Allie and I knew it. The difference was just so extreme. Allie hadn't pestered me with questions or problems. She had taken what I had shown her and simply duplicated it. I was beginning to understand Victor's interest in her—if Justin was any indication of what the usual training of our kind required.

"It's just not working the way it should," Justin whined after another failure.

I rubbed the bridge of my nose as I contemplated my next move. The problem was the boy was too much in his head. For him it was an intellectual challenge, one that could be analysed, broken down and assessed. Mana didn't work that way. It was instinctual. Trying to focus on summoning the Mana would only hinder you. That's why I was so good at it. I never thought about anything.

We'd have to try something different.

About twenty minutes from the cottage was a small creek and pond, only about ten metres in diameter, but sufficient for my needs. It would be a good source of rounded rocks.

As I had hoped, the shoreline of the pond was covered in small rocks, nestled on the cold black sandy dirt. I picked up one of the rocks and held it firmly between my fingers. I could feel the light weight and its smooth texture. It was perfect. I passed it to the boy as I floated out over the pond.

The water rippled beneath me as the magic I used to keep myself floating worked upon it. Raising both arms, I lifted three heavier rocks from the pond bed and brought them to the surface. With a wave of my fist, I kept them levitating in the air and made them float in lazy circles around me, forming an impromptu shield.

"Take your rock," I called. "Aim it well. The lesson ends when you manage to hit me."

I sped up the rocks floating around me. Justin looked out across the pond. I was only about five metres away, but as far as his skills with the Mana went, I could have been standing kilometres away.

"I can't!" Justin began. This was a lie—he most definitely could. I had been able to lift small objects using the Mana, but that wasn't the point of this exercise.

"Don't use the Mana, just throw it," I cut him off.

"You want me to throw a rock at you?" he queried with a puzzled look on his face.

"Don't miss," I advised softly.

Justin threw the rock up in the air several times before drawing his arm back and taking aim. I could tell from the look on his face that he was conflicted about this. He obviously didn't get the point of what I was trying to do. This was good—if he knew what I was planning it wouldn't have worked.

With a small grunt he let the rock fly. I didn't even have to dodge, the shot was miles off. With a flick of my hand I took control of the rock and sent it flying back towards him. He shouted out in pain as the rock hit him squarely in the hip. I had slowed the momentum of the rock so it would hurt, but not injure.

Pain is a teacher no one will ignore and anger is a motivation that overcomes one's inhibitions. As much as I hated it, Victor had taught me that.

"I warned you not to miss," I replied firmly as the boy angrily glared in my direction. He retrieved the rock from the ground at his feet.

His next shot fared no better. In his anger he hadn't even attempted to take aim, he just hurled the rock with more power than aim. I easily recovered the rock as it flew past my shoulder and sent it hurtling back towards him, catching him in the shoulder.

He didn't say a word as he rubbed his shoulder and picked up the stone. I could see the anger in his eyes like flame in the night. His muscles bunched up as he threw the rock. This time his shot rang true. Had I allowed the missile to hit, it would have impacted squarely against my chest, but with a flick of the wrist I brought one of the rocks orbiting me to obstruct the throw. The loud thunk as the two rocks collided echoed across the pond.

With accustomed ease, I again recovered his stone and sent it back to its owner. This time the boy's shout as it impacted his chest was more in anger than in pain. He recovered the stone and immediately sent it back at me, impacting once again against the rocks.

He didn't even wait for me to return the stone to him.

He scooped up a second rock and launched it at me with a strangled and frustrated shout. His second missile fared the same as the first, impacting squarely against my rock formed shield.

"It's not fair!" he accused, blustering with rage. "You're cheating! You're using Mana!"

I didn't answer; instead I sent the two rocks barrelling back towards him. With a strangled shriek the boy threw up his hands to protect himself, when something curious happened. I watched with a self-satisfied smile as the boy formed a rudimentary thread, which lanced out and caught one of the rocks and sent it plummeting into the pond. The other rock hit him in the side, but he ignored the pain as he stared at the telekinetic thread he'd formed to protect himself.

"There. You see? You can do it," I said.

With a flick of my wrist I lifted several more stones from the shoreline and sent them flying at the boy from different angles. He dodged two as he threw himself backwards and used the summoned thread to block a third.

He howled as he scooped up several more stones and threw them in my direction. I watched with elation as the thread looped around and grasped one of the stones and hurled it with greater speed and accuracy in my direction. The loud thump as it hit one of the stones would have been heard for miles.

I smiled as a small crack appeared in the large stone where the smaller stone struck against it. I watched proudly as the crack widened until the rock broke into two pieces. I wasn't entirely sure how hard Justin had accelerated that rock, but had it hit someone it would have killed them instantly.

The look of astonishment on the boy's face as the rock crumbled into smaller chunks and fell into the water almost caused him to lose focus and drop his Mana thread. I flicked my fingers and sent one of the fragments from my former shield flying at my apprentice. With admirable speed, he telekinetically grabbed the missile directed at him and launched it back at me.

With a smile I drew a Mana shield around myself and let the stone hit me.

"You win," I said as I floated across the water, letting the two other rocks fall into the depths behind me. I had made my point and the boy was on his way to learning what he needed to know.

* * *

When we returned to the cottage, I gave the boy a set of exercises designed to help enhance and improve his abilities to summon the Mana. His success meant we could move onto more complex and advanced techniques. I watched him as he now formed the Mana threads with far more ease.

The look of intense concentration on his face was a good sign. He was taking this seriously. These techniques might very well one day save his life. My ability to summon Mana quicker than my foe had brought an end to my enemies more than once.

I had taken this next particular exercise from a series of spell books I had recovered when I raided Marcus's house. I suppose I wanted to preserve something of our art even as I hunted down and killed its practitioners. I would use these books to train Justin.

Justin sat cross-legged on the floor with his hands outstretched on each side of him. Small threads lanced out in erratic motions to catch the falling items and thrust them back into the air. I could see from the look of intense concentration that he was in a losing battle. I heard a muffled curse and a clanging noise from behind me that indicated a bookend had hit the ground, followed in quick succession with four other crashes as the rest of the items quickly followed suit.

"Try again," I ordered without looking up.

"Sir," Justin's voice murmured. "Something's wrong."

I glanced up at the boy and cursed as I saw the Mana on his arms attempting to form rudimentary protection. His skills weren't advanced enough to form the shield field yet, but if they were he would have been throwing everything he had into a shield around him. That was the problem—he had nothing left for the exercise.

I sighed as I glanced down at the shield surrounding me. The Mana had recognised a threat. I cursed myself. I had let my attention wane and was about to pay the price.

"Stay here," I muttered as I pulled the Mana around

me to rise. Now that I was paying attention I could feel the threat too. Someone had managed to sneak up on me, but who knew that I was here? Whoever it was, they had to be a mage—no one else would illicit such a response.

"Stay hidden." I pondered briefly if I should take the boy with me where he could be protected, but I rejected the idea. It was unlikely the boy was the target. He would be safer in hiding. And I would be stronger if I didn't have to protect him.

I pulled open the door to the cottage and saw the familiar Mana-soaked aura of a mage on the other side of the road. It was too dark to make out who it was at this distance, but the Mana signature looked familiar. That was to be expected though—there weren't that many of us left.

I walked out onto the street. The intruder just watched and waited as I approached. They didn't seem to show any concern, although they held a powerful shield, almost as powerful as mine. They waited patiently as I crept forward, but I could see from the flickers in the pattern of their shield that they weren't as calm as they appeared. Their shield fluctuated as Mana constantly sought to renew itself. They were worried—no, worse: they were scared.

"State your intention," I called out as I fought back the urge to simply strike them down. I wouldn't have even hesitated three days ago. They would already be dead.

"I'm seeking information," a female voice replied. "No more."

The accent was strange and her grasp on English was a little off—like a second language. Her voice was familiar, but I couldn't place where I'd heard it before.

"What information?" I asked as I readied myself for a trap. Perhaps she wasn't the only one here. Perhaps I was being lured into a false sense of security. It was possible. I'd seen battles go sour when one mage assumed they were in control when in fact they weren't.

"I'm looking for Gabriel Tychus," the intruder called back.

A shiver tore through my shield as I suddenly recognised the voice. I immediately threw everything I had into my shield. I *had* met this woman before, and she had almost killed me. She had once sworn that she would kill me. She thought I had killed her husband. She had tried to exact revenge, but failed. Although I had spared her, she was sure to be still seeking my life. I had assumed she had died in the wars. I'd lost contact with her during the war, but clearly she had survived. Her name was May Chen, and I was now sure that this wouldn't end without a fight. I should have struck first—it was too late now.

"I'm not looking for a fight, Devon," May said, although I noticed she'd reinforced her shield, probably in reaction to my shield unconsciously being strengthened too.

"I know that he was with you," May continued. "I followed your Mana signature from LA. I want to know where he is."

"How did you find me?" I asked, trying to buying time some time to think.

"Mana residue," May replied curtly.

I had of course heard of it, but it was awfully difficult to detect. I had never developed the necessary acumen to make much use of it. After more than a few seconds, any residue left behind was next to incomprehensible. It was theoretically possible that May had followed me from the teleport threads I had left behind. I wouldn't have believed it had any other mage made the claim, but May had been the principle enforcer of the Primea. She had tracked down rogue mages and brought them to justice. She might be telling the truth, but I doubted it. It had been a long time in mana terms since Gabriel had died.

"I know you saw him," May called out, "and then I lost him. I followed him here. Where is he?"

Shit. Gabriel's body had burned up, leaving no evidence of his death other than a high Mana residue, which could be mistakenly attributed to the fight that took place at the same site. I could of course lie and say that he simply teleported away, but such deception was beneath me and easy to prove incorrect anyway. May had tracked me from the site of the fight through to the camp in LA and then to here. She wouldn't have missed a second thread from Gabriel teleporting out.

"You're lying," I called out. "You can't track Mana residue after such a long time."

"He's here, I know it!" May hissed.

"He's dead," I said. I expected May to immediately strike me down. At first I thought she hadn't heard me, but then her shoulders slumped in defeat.

"How?"

"Does it matter?"

"You killed him?" May still seemed curiously calm.

"Yes," I admitted, "but not intentionally."

"There was a fight," May prompted. "I found the body of one of our kind. I assumed that Gabriel escaped. I was surprised to find you. I thought you were dead."

"That was Glave that you found," I said. "Had I not intervened, Gabriel would have killed him."

"Where is his body?" May prompted.

"I burned it."

May's eyes narrowed suspiciously. The beautiful thing about people who want to kill is that they seldom bother to hide their emotions. They wear their suspicions plainly on their faces. She didn't trust me and I didn't blame her.

"No, he's here!" May repeated. "You're lying to me!"

"How did you track me?"

"GPS," May finally admitted softly. She didn't look happy at the confession.

Shit, I hadn't even considered that. I had taken Gabriel's phone after he had died. I had all but forgotten about it. Now that May had drawn attention to it, I could feel its weight in my pocket. I pulled out his phone slowly and showed it to May.

"Then he's dead?" May whispered calmly.

This was wrong. Something was definitely out of place here. May wasn't acting as I would have expected from her. That was dangerous. I glanced around again—expecting a trap. I half contemplated sending off an Awareness blast to flush out any others who may be waiting in hiding.

May must have sensed my distraction, because the moment I redirected my power towards an Awareness blast, she attacked. It was brutal, quick and efficient. A thread tore from her small frame and destroyed my shield in seconds, then a trio of disrupt pulses hit me squarely in the chest. I gasped in pain as each disrupt thread tore through my system like a virus. It was over in seconds.

As the Mana in my body was affected, the Mana frame that kept me standing dissipated, and as my support structure was removed I fell to the ground, dropping the phone as the effect passed over me. I gritted my teeth as I sought to bring what little Mana I could still control to bear. With wrought iron control I brought a shield up, but by this stage May was already standing over me. It wouldn't take her long to finish me. I cursed myself as I tried to regain control of my powers. I should have struck first. It was ironic, really: the first mage I met after determining I was going to stop killing my kind was the one who would kill me.

I could see the indecision on her face as she glanced at me, trying to decide if I was finished. She had obviously presumed that three pulses would be enough to completely incapacitate my ability to draw Mana—she was wrong. That isn't to say that I wasn't in pain—the disrupt pulse was doing a wonderful job of messing with my nervous system. The disrupt effect pulsed through my body with reckless abandon, sending jolts of pain across my chest and side where I had been hit. I tried to clamber away, to push myself from her, but without the Mana I was having trouble controlling my legs.

This was over, and she now knew it.

May reached down and grabbed me by the chin, her shielded fingers crackling with power against my shielded face. She sent a pulse through her hand and into my shield, immediately frying it and bringing it down. I could raise it again, but that wouldn't buy me more than a few more seconds.

She leaned in and brought her face next to my ear. "I've dreamed of this moment."

I tried to summon the power to teleport out of there. Unfortunately, that was out of my capabilities right then. The disrupt effect caused the Mana in my body to go haywire, and without control I'd be in serious trouble. If I lost focus mid-teleport, I'd scatter my molecules across a wide space between here and wherever I was trying to go.

"You can't imagine how long I've wanted this. I thought it was something that would never happen. I'd heard you were dead, but you're not. You couldn't be, because I hadn't killed you."

She seemed to be building herself up to something. I

could see the conflict in her eyes. Something wasn't right and it was playing upon her.

"If you're going to do it, May, do it now," I grunted.

"So ready to die?" May taunted as she telekinetically wrapped a thread around my throat and brought me into the air. "In every way I've thought of this, it was never this easy," May snarled. "Defeating you as a broken thing isn't what I wanted. It brings me no pleasure—I wanted to defeat you in your strength."

"This is all you're going to get," I chortled as her thread cut off my airway. I wasn't going to beg for my life. May thought she was avenging the death of her husband, and for all I knew probably Gabriel's too. She wasn't going to listen.

"Do it already!" I gasped as bright lights began flashing in my head.

"Something isn't right," she whispered. "Something's wrong. This was too easy. This is—"

May didn't get a chance to finish. There was a strangled shout from the house as a small figure barrelled out from the doorway. Several highly ineffective threads were launched at May, which cascaded uselessly against her shield.

"Leave him alone!" Justin howled as he rushed forward.

May dropped me to deal with the new threat as several more of Justin's threads harmlessly bounced off her shield without even causing a ripple. I drew myself to my feet. It had been some time since I had relied on muscle alone to hold my weight. I was surprised they were able to accomplish the task. They could—but barely, and it hurt.

"Wait," I called as I threw myself between them, shuddering as my legs protested in agony at this unusual treatment. May could strike him down as easily as she could have finished me off. She didn't seem inclined to do so though; she stared at Justin in amazement and amusement.

"Leave the kid alone," I grunted. "He's not part of this."

"I have no intention of harming the child," May muttered contemptuously. "I'm not a murderer."

She almost spat her accusation at me. Once I would have denied her. I hadn't murdered her husband; I'd been there when he died, but I wasn't the one responsible. Her husband and been betrayed by Winters, who had shot him in cold blood from behind to enact his revenge on me. Given that I had gone on to kill Winters, there really was no one else who could bear the brunt of her vengeance.

"You once spared my life." May murmured quietly, "and so I'm going to do the same."

"Why? What changed?"

"I'm not going to kill you in front of the kid."

"So what happens now?"

"I don't know," May admitted. "But we should go inside and seek shelter. It's not safe to be out in the open."

"Not safe?" I prompted.

May didn't answer. Instead she took several steps backwards, sighed deeply and lowered her shield. She was vulnerable. I could see the Mana on her flesh almost screaming its protest. Her neck and shoulders were rigid as she forced herself to contain her Mana.

"He's hunting us through the Mana," she continued as she took another step forward. I could strike her down now and there would be nothing she could do to stop me.

"Who?"

"You know who." May's lips curled in disdain.

"Bullshit! No one's heard from Victor in six years," I snapped, then immediately stopped as my mind caught up with my mouth. We had received reports that Killian Voll and Gregory Tibus had both been reported dead. Who had killed them? Voll, in particular, was a powerful mage. He wouldn't have fallen to just anyone, but he could easily have been overcome by Victor. So that meant what? Victor was cleaning the table? Taking out anyone who had shown themselves? Had he finally chosen to end the war? It seemed likely. I wondered what had prompted a change in tactics amongst my enemies. It was possible that they were reacting to being hunted down and killed by Victor.

"We should go, we've expended too much power here anyway," May said. "I know a safe place."

"I'm not going to be able to teleport for quite some time," I said as I gestured to my shattered Mana signature.

"Then we'll wait," May finished as she picked up Gabriel's phone.

* * *

It was rather surreal sitting in the cottage lounge room with a woman who had twice tried to kill me. I could tell from the way that Justin's eyes never left her that he didn't trust her either.

She was dressed in much the same way as me, in faded and torn military fatigues. But she looked like she'd been in the field for far longer than I. Her face was criss-crossed with scars and burns.

"You really shouldn't be carrying this with you," May murmured as she turned Gabriel's phone over in her hand.

"I didn't think about it," I replied casually as I rose to my feet. The disrupt effect was still playing havoc with my nervous system and it felt better to stretch it out. It wasn't exactly the kind of thing that you could just walk off, but that didn't mean I wasn't going to try.

"No, most of our kind don't," May responded. "Gabriel wanted a way to keep in contact without any chance of being intercepted or bringing unwanted attention onto us."

"Unwanted attention?"

"We're being hunted."

I never got a chance to ask her about that as a wave from the disrupt effect that had hit me earlier surged again through my body. The effect hit the Mana structure surrounding me and caused it to fail. As my support was knocked out, I staggered and would have fallen, but fortunately my muscles were able to take the strain. I staggered and limped back over to the recliner. It took me several minutes to reapply the Mana and rebuild the construct.

May stared at me silently during the whole process. I could see her trying to assess me; she would be able to easily see what I was doing, but I could see from the look of confusion on her face she was mystified as to why it was necessary.

"You're not what I expected," May murmured finally.

"No?" I replied curiously. "What did you expect?"

"I don't know," May mused. "Something like you used to be—full of surety and fire."

I laughed. "I was never sure of myself."

"You know what I mean," May argued. "You were so full of yourself—you weren't going to let anyone get in your way. Even when you were declared outcast, it didn't stop you. I assumed you were dead simply because you weren't more visible in the world."

"That changed when Victor broke my back," I grunted.

"So that's what happened."

I nodded briefly. "Yeah. I tried to take him down. I failed. I was very lucky to survive."

May raised an eyebrow. "You really are. Victor believes that he killed you."

"You were with Victor?"

May shook her head. "Gabriel was for a time. He told me when he warned me about Victor."

"Warned you?"

"Yeah, I was on Victor's target list—still am I suppose," May reflected sadly. "I was working with Killian Voll. Victor has been killing us off one by one."

I raised an eyebrow. I hadn't expected that. May had been working with the mages that I'd spent the last six years tracking down. It was funny the way things work out.

"How did that happen? Last I heard you were working for the Primea."

May's eyes flared for a second and her jaw set defiantly. "You really don't know how bad it was at first—particularly for those close to the Primea," May said. "Marcus declared himself Primea; he didn't have the support, but we swore him in anyway. Better to have someone in power than a vacuum. Or at least, that's what we figured. We were wrong." May sighed wistfully. "His first order was to declare Victor an outcast for poisoning his mother. This caused chaos."

I had suspected as much. Victor's Nazi ties had prevented him from taking the Primeaship during the last round of elections. The posting was supposed to go to the most powerful among us, which would have been Victor; however, that would have led to a war as no one was comfortable with a Nazi in a position of power. Instead, Victor had opted to retire and throw his support behind another candidate. One that he assumed he could control. At least, I assumed that had been his plan. This had all happened about forty years before my birth so I couldn't be sure of the exact details. When I had first met the Primea, she had been old and sick—from what I had heard she had never been that well to begin with. Perhaps that had been Victor's plan all along—to become the power behind the throne.

"All hell broke loose when Marcus failed to return from bringing Victor to justice."

"I killed him," I whispered. "He killed my sister."

May's eyebrows rose, but she continued with her story. "We had a dozen contenders for the position, and political infighting turned into very real fighting. It was chaos—dozens of us were killed in the first few days. It was a massacre."

I had been fighting for survival in a surgical facility at the time after my brush in with Victor. And since I had already been declared an outcast at that point, I avoided the worst of it by simply not being there.

"Killian Voll seemed like the most obvious contender for the position," May continued. "He seemed the most powerful amongst those who remained—so I signed up with him. At first things seemed to be getting back under control and then it got worse—way worse." May sighed. "It all came to a head when one of our order approached a small European nation, doesn't matter which one, and offered his services with a small border dispute they were having with a much larger power. I think it was an attempt to carve out a little kingdom for himself out of Europe. It didn't exactly go as planned."

"Land war in Europe," I murmured. I'd seen the news footage. Just like in the First World War, the larger powers were brought into play, leading to an escalation of arms and eventually a world war. It was unlikely to have happened a third time—but that was exactly what happened. "Killian was furious at first and immediately ordered the death of the renegade, but by then it was too late. Others of our kind joined him and turned on Killian. He had no choice but to join the Soviets to attempt to establish order, and once that happened he lost control real fast."

"He should never have had it in the first place," I commented wryly.

"There was no one else," May replied angrily. "Everyone else in a position to claim had been killed or discredited."

In one fell swoop we had managed to kill or remove all of our most powerful leaders, leaving a vacuum in the most important positions of power. Our kind isn't exactly well known for our laid back and peaceful nature—of course we turned on each other. I wasn't one to point fingers though—I was the one most responsible for it. I had been responsible for discrediting Victor and I had killed Marcus.

"Killian did the only thing he could—he went public," May whispered. "I advised him against it. He thought he could bring this whole thing to a head—but he couldn't.

It just made it worse. Eventually we found ourselves fighting two wars: one conventional that we didn't want to be in, and the other a political war amongst our kind that we needed to resolve quickly. The problem was, we were winning and in those conditions it's hard to rationalise pulling back.

"Things got worse, once the States got involved," May murmured. "Unlike the last two World Wars, they got involved almost immediately. They thought they could enter the war, clean it up and get out quickly. They just didn't understand what they were dealing with."

"They still don't." I shrugged.

"They must have been surprised when troops invaded their home soil. Killian hadn't wanted to do it, but by that stage it was too far gone. The only other alternative was to turn on his own troops—so he went along with it. At this point everyone thought that the only prize left on the table was world domination and an end to the political instability of the 21st century."

I nodded. "It might have been better had the Second World War continued to its logical conclusion. The States and the Soviet Union weren't allies and everyone knew it. Did you know that Churchill wanted to re-arm the Nazis and launch a war against the Soviet Union immediately after the Second World War? I wonder if he perhaps saw all this coming."

May shook her head. "I don't think anyone saw us coming—they were too secure in their nuclear power to think that this could happen. I can't remember who resorted to nukes first—but it hadn't worked out the way they had hoped for either side."

I snorted. "I'll say."

"I last saw Killian about three weeks ago," May continued. "He knew things were falling apart—he had overextended himself deep into enemy territory and something was killing us. At first he thought it was enemy mages, but it was happening too far behind our lines for it to be the enemy. It was happening too quickly and there was nothing he could do about it. Unfortunately he was being forced to fight a conventional war in unconventional ways."

"I felt the same way."

"Hell, we'd lost the conventional war about a year ago." May shrugged. "And we knew it, but of course it was too late to do anything about it. That's when Victor found me. Gabriel saved me, pulled me straight out of the fight. Victor had cornered me in Philadelphia and there was nothing I could do about it. He was just too strong. Everything I tried, he countered. It was a nightmare. Gabriel got me out of there. I owed him."

A tear formed in the corner of May's eyes as she said his name. I didn't know what to say; the woman's tears were making me uncomfortable. I wasn't used to seeing her like this. In a strange way, her previous complaint about me being broken also applied to her. She had always seemed so strong and self-possessed. It was strange to see her so unsure of herself.

"So, what about you?" May grunted. "What the hell

are you doing out here in this wasteland?"

"I didn't exactly have a long-term plan." I gestured towards Justin. "I needed to get somewhere off the grid. I didn't think anyone would be able to trace me here." I smiled wryly.

"You're lucky it was me and not Victor," May interjected.

I rubbed my bruised throat. "Yeah, I feel real lucky."

"Victor would have killed you," May whispered softly. "The only reason he hasn't come after you yet is that he doesn't know you're alive. Gabriel was trying to get enough of us together to stand against him."

That made sense; Gabriel was obviously working behind the scenes to try to diffuse the war sufficiently so that some of our kind would survive. In hindsight it was obvious that he'd recruited Kristoff, although I had no hard evidence of this fact. Kristoff had claimed he'd joined the wrong side—I'd assumed at the time that he was referring to Voll. But what if he was referring to Gabriel?

"I can deal with Victor," I stated.

"What? Like you did before?" May scoffed.

"No." I smiled. "I can now counter his powers. I've already defeated him once. If it wasn't for his regeneration he'd have already fallen."

"Are you sure?" May seemed hopeful.

"Yes," I replied. I hoped I sounded more confident than I felt.

"You're planning on facing him. When?"

"I don't know." I rubbed the bridge of my nose. My plans hadn't been finalised, and finding Justin had been a huge complication. "I hadn't expected to find the boy. He needed to be taken somewhere safe."

May glanced between me and the boy quickly. "I know somewhere safe. Gabriel's base—there are enough of us there to keep us relatively safe, especially if you take care of Victor."

"Renee?"

May looked uncomfortable and nodded.

"My son?" my words were a faint whisper.

May nodded.

"Don't tell Renee you found me. It's better that I remain dead for now."

I glanced at the small woman in front of me. How far could I trust her? I trusted her enough to think that she wouldn't cause harm to Justin, and that was all that was important at the moment. I had some doubt that she would honour her promise to me about Renee, but she'd make a far better teacher for Justin than I. Without the boy I was free to return to Poland and finish my studies, which would hopefully allow me to unlock the necessary power to finally defeat my former master.

"Take the boy," I grunted.

"You could come with us," May whispered, but I could see in her heart that she didn't believe it any more than I did.

"Strange offer—from someone who has vowed to kill me." I grinned wryly.

May didn't answer. Neither of us liked the reminder that I'd been responsible for her husband's death. He'd been my friend, maybe not at the end, but I still thought of him as such.

"You know I can't," I replied.

"I know."

This disrupt effect would only last a few more hours at most. I would be able to teleport in the morning. I didn't want May to tell me where she was going, and she seemed more comfortable with me not knowing anyway. Although I had tried to sound sure of myself earlier, I think we both knew I was probably going to my death. I didn't bother to say goodbye to the boy.

He and May saw me off when I went to leave the next morning. I saw in Justin's eyes that he knew what was happening and why I was going. He would be better hands with May, in that I was now certain.

"If you're going, you should probably take this." May passed Gabriel's phone back to me.

"No, where I'm going I don't want to be tracked."

"Take the battery out," May advised. "It can still be tracked if it has power."

"No," I replied firmly. I didn't want the damn phone. The temptation to use it would be too much. I placed the phone in her hands and closed her fingers over it.

"Devon," May whispered. "Good luck. I was wrong about you."

I smiled as I turned away. "No. No you weren't."

CHAPTER NINE

With the usual tell-tale explosion of sound I teleported back to the secret compound under the Tatras mountains in Poland. With a flick of my fingers I sent up a Mana flare to provide light to the complex. The generators that had once powered the compound had long since fallen into disrepair, and although I could have salvaged them and brought them back online, I didn't need to. I could provide all the warmth and light I needed with my magic.

As usual, my arrival wasn't greeted with much notice from the compound's inhabitants—both of them were dead. As I stared at Randall's weathered and pale face, I was confirmed in my decision not to bring the boy here. He didn't need to see this. Using my sorcery to take control of Randall, I sent him to prepare the room I would need for what was going to come next. Then I headed down into the cells.

Karl was in his usual place in his cell, staring off into space. It normally took several seconds before he responded to my presence. He seemed to disappear into his mind often. I didn't judge him too harshly though— he had occupied this room for almost seventy years. I knocked courteously on the open cell door and waited. I could be here some time.

"You have returned," Karl responded almost immediately. I jumped; he had responded far too quickly.

I glanced into the cell to see an unusual sight. Karl's withered body was literally swarming with Mana particles. I took a step back. This was curious, I hadn't expected this. When I had realised that the majority of his Mana was being used to maintain his body, I'd asked him to try to use the power for minor telekinesis. This act may have stimulated something and caused his power to increase.

Judging from his Mana aura, he wasn't powerful by any sense of the word, but it had happened so quickly—if he continued gaining in strength he would become formidable.

"You see what you have done?" Karl whispered tonelessly, taking a step towards me. His eyes bored into me with judgment as I took another step back away from the cell.

"Unintended," I gasped as the man bore down on me, but he cut me off before I could finish.

"Fix it!" he hissed. "The hunger is almost overwhelming. I can't focus. I can't think. It dominates me!"

"You need to use the Mana," I began, but was again cut off.

"No!" he snarled. His fingers wrapped around my lapels. His anger had given him strength and I could almost feel him pull me forward. Previously Karl had barely been able to lift his own arms—his regenerative powers had increased tenfold. If given enough time, it might restore his youth and vitality. It would be interesting to see what happened.

"You promised to kill me," Karl whispered into my ear as he brought his fetid face closer to mine. "You have brought no others with you to experiment on, so you must be returning to fulfil your promise."

"I have," I murmured. I attempted to extricate myself from the wight's grasp. He let me go immediately.

"When?" he pressed.

"I have some tests," I replied firmly. Killing Karl would serve me nothing if I didn't understand how the technique could be used to bring down my former master.

Karl sighed. "There are always tests. Perform your tests—then do as you promised. Just be quick."

I took a step back from the man as I attempted to surmise what difference his new state would bring into the equation. Would the fact that his body was actively healing itself affect what I was about to do? I didn't know, and Karl wasn't going to give me the time to test the effect properly.

I nodded briefly at Karl and gestured down the corridor. I'd often wondered if the man had any fears walking down this hall during these moments. He knew he was going to be experimented on, just had he had during his days when the camp had been a Nazi scientific base. Surely there must be some old memories lurking within that dusty mind that this experience triggered? If so, he didn't seem to show it. He walked with his usual small-stepped shuffle down the corridor without any visible signs of distress or alarm.

Randall met us at the door to the operating surgery. As per my instructions, the place had been scrubbed clean. Karl walked straight past Randall and sat on the table with an audible grunt. This was new too. Previously Randall had to assist the man onto the table.

I wished I could see how far Karl's regeneration would take him.

I sighed and moved to the head of the table. I placed my hand upon the man's withered shoulder. It felt like touching distressed leather, wrinkly and desiccated. Under this flesh I could feel the familiar pulse of his Mana signature. It took me several moments of concentration to locate the thread responsible for his regeneration.

I had examined it before, but previously it had been weak and difficult to observe. Now it was strong and I could see how Victor had done it. It was a stroke of genius; I could see how the thread had been built and how it was being maintained. I could also see why Victor had considered it a failure. It was taking far too much power for such a small effect. Karl had never been the most powerful of our kind, and the thread had nullified his powers for over half a century until my own mistake had caused an escalation of the Mana within the man. The thread, now with access to more power, was thriving.

Using a Mana technique I'd found within Victor's spell books, it began working on his body at a cellular level. The technique was flawed in that it only regenerated existing cells rather than create new ones, but given enough power it might be successful in its endeavour. There didn't seem to be a way to disrupt the effect permanently as it renewed itself almost immediately when the thread was broken. The whole process needed to be taken down intact rather than in pieces. But that wasn't possible—the amount of energy required was enormous and I hadn't been able to generate enough power.

True to form—I hadn't considered other options, I had instead sought a way to increase my power. There was a metaphor in that ideal for my kind. We didn't look for other options; we simply attempted to overpower our way through our obstacles.

There was another option that I'd discovered when I had used the effect on Gabriel. I could circumvent this process towards another end—not stopping it, but accelerating it, twisting it and making it my own. It was devilishly simple in its application. If you can't beat it, then change it. All I had to do was to attempt to heal the man on the gurney before me.

I breathed out as I squeezed my fingers into the man's flesh. In another man this would have been uncomfortable, but Karl's nerves had been dead for years—he would feel nothing. Surprisingly, he shivered when I began to summon the Mana.

As I twisted the frequency of the Mana into the fey

abomination I had discovered, the Mana across his flesh rushed to the infected area, only to be consumed into the process that I was creating.

I gritted my teeth as I poured more energy into Karl's shoulder; I could see the disruption spreading across his chest and down his left arm, but I was fighting for every inch of it. This wasn't the same experience as before; Gabriel's Mana signature had embraced the magic, Karl's was actively fighting me. Perhaps this was to be expected; after all, the same Mana had kept him alive for over half a century. With a small exhalation I increased the output of power into the man. I drew upon what reserves I had and threw them into the process. Karl began twitching on the gurney as I continued my work.

The twitches turned into stuttered gasps that grew stronger as the power consumed him. I closed my eyes and concentrated on what I was doing. It was difficult; I was trying to end a spell effect that had existed for far longer than I had been alive. Mana isn't sentient and doesn't have a conscious will, but for all intents and purposes it may as well be.

"Stop!" Karl screamed suddenly, his voice turning hoarse with anguish as the spell effect overtook him.

I ignored him—this was what he wanted. It would soon be over.

"Stop it!" he screamed again.

I immediately opened my eyes to glance down at my patient. My hand pressed against his shoulder was soaked with blood. The flesh under my fist had broken beneath my claw-like grasp. His skin should have been too leathery for that, but now it appeared pink and new. I saw the effect ripple across the man's flesh and the veins in his body began to pulsate as blood pumped through them again. The flesh around the veins took on a slightly blue tinge and then turned from the weathered grey shade of dead skin to a healthy pink hue.

"What have you done?" Karl exclaimed as he sat up from the gurney, his eyes staring accusingly down at his chest. "What have you done to me?"

I took a step back as the process completed its horrid transformation across the man's body, leaving fresh healthy skin behind it. Karl's eyes narrowed in anger as he rose from the gurney. With an audible smack, a telekinetic thread smashed against my shoulder, sending me spinning. If I'd had the energy a shield would have sprung up around me, but most of my strength had been expended in the procedure. My shoulder throbbed from where I'd been hit, but I used my telekinetic framework that kept me standing to send myself flying backwards into the air as another slash from the enraged Karl smashed the ground where I had been lying.

"What have you done to me?" Karl growled again, his voice a deep timbre and strong. Muscle tone and strength formed on his body as he stalked forward to finish me off. He may have gotten in the first strike, but I was far from helpless. My leap hadn't exactly been one of desperation; it had placed me closer to the door and allowed me to keep the gurney between us. With a flick of my wrist I sent the gurney sliding towards him.

I didn't wait around to see what happened. I heard Karl shout and a loud thump as I threw myself through the doorway and braced against the sturdy examination room door behind me. I needed to get out of there while I was still vulnerable.

"You can't run from me!" Karl screamed. Several thumps slammed into the door. He was getting stronger, but that was okay—so was I.

Every second I could feel the Mana regenerating, making me more powerful. With a dry smile I raised a shield around myself and shivered as the familiar sensation wrapped around me like a second skin. There was no danger now. Karl wasn't powerful enough to overcome my shield. The only problem that remained was how to calm him down sufficiently to find out what had gone wrong? I had somehow restored his youth and vitality. That hadn't been the plan, and judging from the smashing against the wooden door, he wasn't that pleased about it either.

How the hell had that happened? I was positive that I had used the same technique I had used on Gabriel. How could it function one way in one instance and the complete opposite in another instance?

With a flick of my wrist I disbarred the door and was immediately assaulted by several threads against my shield. They were painfully weak and barely registered against my defences. Karl threw himself at me, shuddering in pain as his fists smashed against my shield. I was forced to take several steps back under the weight of his assault.

"It hurts!" he howled in fury. "Make it stop!"

It hurts? Was he referring to his shoulder? No, that seemed to have healed itself. At first I was bewildered, but then I realised what was happening. The man had gone for so long without functional nerve endings and had been in state of almost complete isolation. The cold air must have felt like thousands of small stabbing needles into his flesh.

Fortunately creating a shield was beyond his skills, so there was nothing to stop my sorcery from taking effect. At first I contemplated hitting him with a disrupt effect, but I quickly discounted that idea. If the air was agony for him, then I couldn't imagine what the pain of the disrupt effect across his nerves would be.

I grasped him around the forehead and began work. I delved my sorcery deep into his core as I sought out each of his nerve endings and numbed them. Eventually Karl stopped struggling and fighting me as each of his nerve endings were suppressed. He eventually gave a small sigh and sagged into my arms as he lost consciousness.

I gently wrapped a telekinetic thread around him, put the overturned gurney back on its feet, and placed him on it. I didn't know how long he would remain unconscious but I was sure that I would need to have some answers when he revived. If I understood the technique from Victor's spell book, his nerve sensitivity would restore slowly so he wouldn't be bombarded. Hopefully his body would adapt to the unfamiliar sensation and he would be able to cope with the feeling of air on his skin. I couldn't imagine what that must have felt like when you're used to feeling nothing—it was probably like the worst case of pins and needles across your entire body.

I glanced down at Karl's inert form as began my work. This time I took the precaution of looping the straps on the side of the gurney to his wrists. This precaution was most likely a waste of time, however, as the leather on the straps looked aged and probably wouldn't be able to withstand much pressure. It was a miracle that it was even still intact—I guess that's German engineering for you.

As I examined the thread I could see the vast differences caused by my interference. The old thread only regenerated existing cells; however, this new thread appeared to be prompting cellular growth. This would explain the vast differences in Karl's appearance. His whole body was undergoing complete cellular rebirth.

Was this what Victor had been attempting to do? It certainly wasn't what he had achieved. I had restored youth and vigour to Karl. Victor appeared to be locked into a state of perpetual stasis. He didn't seem to be ageing, but he didn't look young and healthy. If I had to place a bet, I'd say that he had remained locked into the age he had been when he had first performed the sorcery on himself.

As I followed the threads through Karl's inert body, I couldn't even begin to fathom where I'd gone wrong, but

I was now in the same position that I had been in originally. There was no nexus point that I could strike to end the process. Any attempt to disrupt the effect would be washed away as the Mana within the man renewed itself. I somehow needed to corrupt the process to achieve a different end, but I had no idea how to do that.

At the core of things, the human body is a very well organised series of processes. Trying to destroy those processes externally wouldn't take effect now that Karl's body was in a state of advanced mitosis.

More in futility than anything else, I attempted to disrupt the effect—I didn't think this would yield any valuable results, but it was worth a try. As expected, the disrupt spread through his body, but was ultimately only responsible for negating the Mana for a short time. The last time I had tried this, Karl's body had been in such an advanced stage of decay that it had almost killed him—the Mana was literally the only thing keeping him alive. This time the effect was minimal as his body was in a much better state now. It was no different from what I would have expected had I used the same effect on myself. On Karl, the effect only caused pain and an increased difficulty to control the Mana.

I applied the numbing effects to his body once again as I considered my options. There was nothing that I could do for the man now and should I wake him I was sure he wouldn't thank me for the experience. This really only left one option. I tied the numbing threads into his own internal Mana processes. His own Mana would now keep him inert and unconscious. This was the only small gift I could give him now while I returned to my books on Necromancy to continue my studies. I owed him that much at least.

After six hours with Victor's damned spell books I'd still come up with nothing. It was infuriating that somehow Victor had broken one of the natural laws of biology and I couldn't figure out a way to undo it. The natural law that everything ends should have been simple to restore, but it was strangely elusive. For all my studies and tampering, it seemed that once immortality had been granted it was impossible to remove.

This whole process hadn't worked out the way I had hoped. I needed more information—information that I didn't have. The spell books that Victor had left behind contained notes and results from his failures. I needed the document that detailed his success, but I didn't think that such a document existed any longer. There was only one way that I was going to get the information I needed. I'd have to face Victor once again.

May had claimed that Victor was hunting people through the Mana, but that didn't explain why he hadn't come after me. He must have known I was still around—true, I wasn't as powerful as I had been in my former glory, but I was still a threat. Especially once he found out that I was following in his footsteps and learning Necromancy. I would be a target too hard to resist. So why hadn't he come for me?

I didn't know and that concerned me. I suppose

I could ask him when I found him, but I had no idea where Victor was. The good news was that I knew someone who did.

I teleported out.

* * *

"Hello, old friend," I murmured as the light flicked on suddenly. I was blinded as I had up until now been sitting in almost complete darkness. That was okay though, I didn't need to see the intruder to be able to tell who it was.

"Devon, I.. uhh wasn't expecting you." Levenon's voice broke as he fought to gain control of himself.

"No, I would imagine not," I replied dryly as I swung around on his office chair. I almost wished I had a white cat sitting on my lap as I spun around. It always looked so classy when the Bond villains did that. It wasn't quite as impressive in real life.

"You're supposed to be dead," he continued. I could see from the look on Levenson's face that he was buying time, contemplating something stupid. His left hand twitched near the side arm at his belt.

"I'm not here to kill you," I murmured, casually helping myself to his private stash of whiskey.

My assurances didn't seem to alleviate Levenson's concerns any. "Then why are you here?"

"Can't I visit an old friend?" I muttered as I rose from the chair. Levenson took a step back.

"Cut the bullshit, Devon," he snarled, his hand trailing down to his holster.

"You know that won't do you any good, even with those fancy bullets of yours," I grunted. I gestured with my glass towards his gun. With a flick of my wrist I telekinetically poured another glass and sent it trailing over to him. "Besides, I'm just here to talk."

"What do we have to talk about?" Levenson asked nervously. He chugged his drink in one gulp, his face twisting as the whiskey burned on the way down.

"I'm looking for Victor Whittlesea."

"I don't know …"

"Don't lie to me!" I cut him off harshly. "I'm not stupid and I can see his hand in recent events."

"How did you know?" Levenson sighed as he made his way to the bar.

"It's the only thing that makes sense," I replied calmly. "You're trying to reset the board—bring everything back to the way it was. For that to happen you need my kind to disappear. You can't kill us and you were losing the conventional war."

Levenson nodded as he made himself another drink.

"But you and I both know that the war never really mattered."

"We were losing," Levenson interrupted. "It was a simple matter of numbers."

"So you approached him?" I pressed. "What? Six months ago? A year? Two years?"

"I didn't find him—he found me. A year ago."

"What did he offer?"

"The old world," Levenson explained as he sipped this drink. "Where your kind were nothing more than a myth."

I scoffed. "You thought you could brush all this away?"

"If your kind were all dead," Levenson murmured, "or at least those who chose to show themselves, things could return to the way they were."

"Including those of us who helped you," I whispered dryly.

"Everyone," Levenson said, his voice little more than a gasp. Kristoff had been right. He had been on the wrong side. One by one, Levenson had turned on us and given our locations to Victor.

"Why you? Why now?"

"Because we were losing. He knew that we would agree to such demands. I guess he simply had to wait until there was a clear winner, and we were desperate enough to agree to it."

It made perfect sense. Victor would preserve those among his kind who he determined deserved it, all the while convincing the rest of the world that those who had started this war had died in it. We would become nothing more than a footnote in history. It was a good plan—the only problem was that it was bullshit. We would never remain hidden; Victor would be forced to kill almost all of us, and even then that would only delay the problem. Eventually we would become numerous enough again that this process would repeat. Returning to the old ways was not a valid solution here. It was a dream—a dream of those who no longer lived in this world, but longed for a world that was no longer possible.

"Where is he?"

"I don't know," Levenson began, until he noticed my expression. "But I know where he's going to be tomorrow night."

"Where?" I said suspiciously.

"There's a dinner party."

I raised an eyebrow. That seemed like an odd place to find him.

"He's masquerading as a general," Levenson explained. "He needs the legitimacy—he'll be there. Most of the senior command will be there. It's to celebrate our victory."

"Are you invited?"

Levenson nodded. This might work out for the better; with so many norms around I could get close enough to Victor to do what I needed to.

"Very well, we'll go together. You can get me in."

"Why would I do that?"

"Because if you don't, I will kill you."

There were several seconds of silence as Levenson acknowledged the threat. "Fine," he sighed resignedly.

"Only one thing remains," I whispered as I rose from Levenson's office chair.

"What?" Levenson took several steps back.

"To ensure your loyalty," I murmured as I flicked a wrist, closing and locking the door behind us.

In one swift motion Levenson brought his gun forward, and to my surprise he actually got off one shot before I destroyed the weapon.

"Someone will have heard the shot," Levenson snarled as he threw the tattered weapon to the ground.

"It doesn't matter," I whispered with a smile as I closed in on the man.

Levenson raised his arms as if to throw a punch—I really had to admire his courage. It was useless, but a good indication of his character: continue fighting way past the point of preferred capitulation. This was why I liked him so much.

With a delicate thread sent straight into his chest, I built a Mana construct that would render him immobile. The Mana would attack his nerves and send him into a state of paralysis. It was similar to the Mana I had used on Karl, except in this instance I wanted him awake and conscious.

"I wonder if you could have possibly have predicted this," I murmured conversationally, "when you pulled my dying body from the ruins of Melbourne."

Levenson couldn't talk, but I could see well enough from his expression what he wanted to say.

"You thought yourself so clever, so able to predict and manipulate the outcome you wanted," I continued in the face of his baleful stare. "Did you see this happening? No, probably not. Self-sacrifice wouldn't have come easy to the likes of you."

I moved closer to the man as I began my work. For all

his comments on "your kind", Levenson had once been one of our kind, but he had burned out at a young age, which had nullified his powers. It happens occasionally to apprentices who push themselves too hard. It had happened to me, but fortunately I had recovered. Levenson had not.

As I followed the trail of electrical signals through his nerves, I could see evidence of the damage: the channels were still there, they were just twisted and scarred as his body had healed the damage. I could see trace elements of the Mana in his body from long ago. Once the process had been damaged his body, he had gone into shock and stopped producing the necessary hormones required for Mana production. The body adapted and life continued.

But it didn't have to be that way.

I could see the fear and pain in the man's eyes as I conducted my examination. I was gentle, but this was an invasive procedure, and I was sure that once I was finished he would be forever changed. He wouldn't thank me for it, but I needed to ensure he was appropriately motivated for what was going to come next.

I couldn't heal the damage to his Mana pathways, but new pathways could be created if the host was stimulated correctly. With surgical precision, I began the process. The production of hormones occurred almost immediately and the body went into shock as a process long forgotten began once again. I smiled with satisfaction as I saw the first small glimmers of Mana particles begin to form within the pathways. The process would intensify until full Mana production ensued within the host.

I watched as the pain intensified behind Levenson's inert eyes, I could have nullified this pain, but I wanted him to experience it. He had tried to kill me and there needed to be a consequence. I had promised I wouldn't kill him, and I was going to keep that promise. What I was going to do could perhaps have been considered a gift. He wouldn't see it as such, but an argument could be made.

Levenson wouldn't have had any idea what was going on. Eventually his eyes widened. I saw the tell-tale iris expansion that came with Mana sight. He was finally seeing me as I truly was.

"You will need to take it easy for the next few hours—the pain will be severe," I muttered harshly as I removed my threads.

Levenson immediately staggered back and I thought he was going to fall, he caught himself on the bench and brought his hands to his head.

"What have you done?" he gasped, his fists clenched.

"You know what I've done," I replied firmly. "I've restored your powers."

"That's not possible!" he shrieked. "I begged my master! He said it wasn't possible!"

"As you can see, it is."

"Why?" he gasped. "Why now?"

"Because with your powers returned, Victor will kill you along with the rest of us," I answered him. "You're

going to have to work very carefully if you want to survive this."

Levenson glanced at me with a curious mixture of
hatred and gratitude. I had just fulfilled a childhood
dream, and yet he knew as well as I did just how dangerous a position this placed him in.

"I won't let you control me!" he hissed.

"I'm not going to control you," I replied with a smile.
"I've simply ensured that we have similar motivations."

Levenson didn't answer.

"I suggest you take another drink, take some pain
killers and try to sleep. You're going to be in for a hell
of a night."

I had no idea how powerful Levenson would be once
his full powers were restored, but it was safe enough to
imagine that he would be as an infant amongst giants
in terms of power levels at first. He would improve and
gain strength though it would be doubtful that he would
achieve any meaningful level of power. That wasn't the
point of the exercise though—I wanted him to become
one of the hunted rather than the hunter.

"I didn't want this," he whispered. I could tell a lie
when I heard it though. His eyes told the truth.

"I know," I replied. "See you tomorrow."

* * *

Levenson didn't look much better the next day. I found
him hunched over his desk; it didn't look like he had

moved much since last night. He barely even registered my entrance into the room, but his Mana-soaked eyes never left me as I walked over to him.

"Get up," I ordered. "I need you cleaned up and ready to go."

Levenson didn't answer with much more than a grunt. As I moved closer to the desk, the scent of fresh vomit overcame me.

"This won't do," I tutted as I placed a hand on the back of his head. He was burning up. With a small infusion of Mana I took his pain away. He immediately shuddered as the Mana went about its work.

"So it's true," he declared, his voice suddenly strong. "I'd heard the reports, but I'd always discounted them."

"To what do you refer?" I enquired as I walked over to his bar. I was to be disappointed though—he had already consumed his stocks.

"You're using fucking Necromancy!" he accused. "I'd heard the stories when I was younger of that dark art, but it was forbidden."

"I would not deny such an accusation," I replied calmly.

"How could you?" He rose from the desk.

"Listen to me," I snarled. "I will do anything I need to do to destroy Victor. Anything!"

"You're no better than he is."

"I never claimed to be," I replied. "Now, get ready. We need to leave."

"I'm not going anywhere," Levenson snapped.

"Yes," I answered patiently. "Yes you are, because if you don't Victor will eventually find out that your powers have returned. You will seem like a threat and he will end you. You need to work with me, at least for now."

I could see the thoughts processing behind his eyes. He wasn't a stupid man and he knew the odds of being able to take down Victor. Perhaps he had a follow-up plan to throw himself on Victor's mercy. Perhaps he thought it safer to disappear into the night and run. Option two would have been safer, but I wasn't going to allow him that.

"You're fucking crazy."

He seemed compliant, and that was enough for now. I waited as he showered and shaved and prepared for the event. Once he was ready, I waited as he ordered a car to be brought round the front and we were escorted by two military aides to the car.

Levenson's guards didn't comment about an additional guest. In fact, they didn't even acknowledge my presence. That was fine with me. They were simply there to get me into the complex without a fight. We weren't accosted as we made our way towards a large manor about an hour's drive from the military complex. Security was just as tight at the manor and our details were scrutinised as we passed the main gates. It seemed that my plan had worked; arriving with Levenson had allowed me to get into the manor without cause for alarm.

As we arrived closer to the main house, the hairs on

my arm rose as the Mana prepared for defence. I knew immediately what this meant—danger. There was a mage in the manor, a powerful one. Only one was powerful enough to register such an effect—my old master. It had been six years since we had last met, and it had been an encounter that hadn't ended well. I shivered in excitement, sending a tremor down my arm to my hand. I gritted my teeth as I attempted to bring myself under control. I wasn't here to confront my old master and correct old wrongs. I wasn't here to get into a fight, although I hoped Victor would assume that's what my motives were. No, I was here for information about the regenerative effects on the only person who had successfully mastered the technique.

Levenson must have felt it too, as his face went ashen as the car pulled up to the main door. He glanced nervously at me as one of his aides opened the door. I smiled thinly and nodded at the man as he exited the car. I don't think I helped him any with his anxiety, but I was more concerned with bringing my own nerves under control. I clenched my hands into fists as I exited the car and took a deep breath before I entered the building.

Victor would probably know that we had arrived; his defences would have alerted him to the arrival of one of our kind, but I had hoped to conceal my presence. I wanted to observe the man without him being aware of it. Misdirection was probably a better ally in this endeavour, but I would use whatever advantage I could.

We had arrived late to the party—things were in full

swing but arrival went mostly unnoticed. I made my way to the central reception hall with Levenson in tow—he didn't seem to want to leave my side. Surrounding us were generals, military aides, politicians and dignitaries from foreign nations. Many of the guests nodded or waved at Levenson as he passed. None chose to engage him in conversation, but that was probably more to do with my stern presence by his side. We progressed through the venue as we searched for my former master. I knew he was there; I could sense his presence and I used this to lead me right to him.

It didn't take too long to find him; he was engaged in a conversation with a group of generals. As Levenson claimed, he was dressed in an American uniform—playing the card of a retired general pressed back into service. He hadn't noticed us yet and from his Mana signature didn't appear to be making much of an effort to be protecting himself.

A tremor tore through my body at the moment I first set eyes upon the man; it was so violent that even Levenson turned to stare at me as I attempted to bring force the shaking to stop.

"This was a bad idea," he whispered firmly. "We should leave."

"No," I rumbled. It only took a few seconds to get myself back under control. I needed to do better than this. I couldn't let Victor see me like this. I needed to appear calm, confident and in control. I needed to be powerful.

Victor hadn't changed much since our last encounter; his powers had kept him locked at the same age for over half a century. I would have been very surprised had be changed.

At this distance I wouldn't be able to get the information I needed from his Mana signature. Victor's Mana signature had always seemed strange to me, but I had always assumed that every signature was different. This to a degree was true: everyone's Mana signature was slightly different, but Victor's was very different. Tonight I would find out why.

"Introduce me," I grunted to Levenson as I pushed him towards my former master.

I intentionally approached Victor from behind and as such other members of his entourage noticed us first and made way to allow Levenson to join the conversation.

"General Pattinson," Levenson began addressing one of the other members of the entourage, "May I introduce Devon Wills?" Levenson's voice broke slightly at the end of that sentence, but otherwise he played his part perfectly.

"Is that so?" General Pattinson raised an eyebrow. "I had heard that he was dead."

"Fortunately the rumours of his death were premature," Levenson continued.

Victor still hadn't turned around, but I could tell from the tenseness in his shoulders that he was biding his time.

"Pleased to meet you," Pattinson said, reaching out for a handshake. "What brings you here?" he continued awkwardly when I ignored his handshake.

"Same as the rest of you," I answered. "I'm here to celebrate the end of the war."

I took a small pride in watching Victor shudder as he heard my voice. It was such a small twitch and would have been easily missed had I not been looking for it. I revelled in it. I had finally broken through the iron mask that the man had placed over himself. It was true then— he really did think he had killed me during our last confrontation, and judging from his reaction he wasn't pleased to discover his mistake. I watched in glee as Victor slowly turned around to face us, his face impassive as he stared at me. I caught another twitch when he saw Levenson; that he had flinched a second time indicated just how unnerved the old man had become.

"I don't believe we've met," Victor said in his crisp German accent. It was so out of place amongst the American accents. "I am General Charles Hurstbridge."

The other generals nodded along in agreement. I could recognise a compel effect when I saw one.

"I don't believe we've had the pleasure," Victor continued in his authoritarian tone. "I, too, was under the impression that you had died."

"I'm difficult to kill."

"So it would seem," Victor replied dismissively.

"I didn't mean to interrupt." I smiled. "I'll let you get back to your conversation."

That was enough for now. Let him know that I was here, let him begin to worry. It would eat at him and hopefully crack through that damned impassive exterior. I didn't hang around to listen to the conversation and I beat a hasty retreat. It was time to get to work. Now that Victor was aware of my presence, the Mana would be heightened by the anticipated threat of an attack. This would make it easier for me to examine the way his Mana signature interpreted the Necromancy thread sustaining him.

I grasped Levenson firmly by the arm and pushed him towards the door. He had served his purpose. I had Victor where I needed him. Victor would rightly assume that Levenson was going to be central to my plans.

"You'd best make your excuses to leave," I murmured softly to Levenson. "You probably don't want to be around for what's going to happen next." I could see from the fearful expression on his face that Levenson wanted nothing more than to leave. Levenson scurried towards the door like it led the way to salvation. If he was lucky, Victor wouldn't pursue him. I didn't care much for his chances.

It didn't take long before a Mana thread snaked itself towards me and Victor's voice boomed in my ear. "Why have you intruded into my affairs once again?"

I glanced over at Victor to see that he was still deep in conversation with the generals. The thread itself was an impressive piece of Mana work, but I'd have expected nothing less from the man. It was an advanced variant on the Whisper thread, except rather than forming the words focally, he had literally constructed the sound waves necessary to project sound. It was beyond my level to synthesise, but I didn't need to hide the fact that I was talking. A normal Whisper thread would be sufficient for my needs.

"Is that anyway to greet an old friend?" I smirked. "There are so few of us left."

"I don't know how you survived Melbourne," Victor's thread rumbled back, "but I will kill you again if necessary."

"Ah, but you won't," I mocked. "Not here—you can't. You're a just regular general here. I'm perfectly safe here."

"This party will end," the thread promised, "and you are only alive still because I was unaware of your continued existence. I will seek you out now."

"I'm looking forward to it," I replied as I began my examination of his Mana signature. It was complex and contained hundreds of intricacies. Many were easy to interpret and isolate, others were more intricate. It was like trying to listen to three pieces of music all laid atop one another—at first it seemed like a cacophony, but eventually with patience you can isolate the individual pieces. I could see evidence of the Necromantic thread; it was close enough to what I had seen in Karl, yet so vastly different that it was hard to draw a comparison.

In the Wight the thread had dominated him, consumed him. To continue the music metaphor, it was like the lead singer screaming out the lyrics. In Victor it was

294

more like the percussion, the heartbeat of the music—easy to miss the delicacies of the piece, but once you find it you realise that the lyrics wouldn't be possible without it.

"I am surprised to see that you have returned," Victor's voice burst into my dissection. "The injuries you sustained appear to be significant. You should have remained dead."

I gritted my teeth as another tremor threatened to overcome me. With iron forced willpower I brought myself under control. This wasn't the time.

"Your use of a Mana construct to keep yourself mobile is inventive. Tell me, Devon, are you paralysed?" Victor asked.

I didn't give him the satisfaction of an answer. Instead I delved deeper as I found the regenerative thread and began to inspect it. I never would have thought of doing it this way—it was genius, twisted yes, evil yes, but genius nonetheless.

"I could heal you," Victor broke in. "Restore the use of your legs, and make you whole again."

"I can do that myself," I quipped back. I was glad that the offer had come after I had already learned what I needed, as it was impossible to focus on anything other than Victor.

I saw Victor shudder as my Whisper thread delivered my message.

"Is that so?" His voice sounded calm, but I could tell from his stance that he was worried. From his point of view, the only way I could have figured out how to heal myself was via the study of Necromancy, and if I had successfully learned cellular regrowth, then it was possible I could overcome his regeneration. I watched with mirth as Victor excused himself from the conversation and made his way across to the bar. His eyes were focused on me like daggers as he moved through the crowd.

"You must then be responsible for the revival of Mana in Levenson?" Victor queried. He was trying to sound strong and sure, but that was because of the soundwave he had formed. Had Victor been using his real voice, I was sure that his words wouldn't seem so confident. His bid to heal me would allow him the upper hand, but I no longer needed such deals.

"Indeed," I replied as I made my way to the bar too.

"That was unwise in this present climate," Victor continued as I slid onto the barstool next to him.

I nodded briefly as I ordered a drink from the bartender. "Perhaps, but he tried to have me killed. A lesson must be learned."

I could see Victor nodding in agreement out of the corner of my eye, but I daren't turn my head to look directly at him.

"You were always my most disappointing student. It is ironic that you could perhaps have been my greatest."

"I had no wish to follow in your footsteps," I replied darkly, and I found that for the first time in my conversation with the man I had told the truth. It was strange because it had taken me a long time to realise that I of everyone he had trained had followed most closely in his footsteps. Marcus's forays into Necromancy paled in comparison to my own.

"And yet you are," Victor prompted.

"Yes."

"I will find killing you again disappointing." Victor cut off the last word as if it were distasteful. "Yes, it is sad that it has come to this," Victor murmured softly.

"It is too late for regrets, Master," I whispered.

The sound of an incoming rocket caused us to look questioningly at each other. I could see the confusion evident on Victor's face as both our shields sprang into effect instantaneously. I took grim pride in knowing that my shield sprung around me just as fast as the old man's. Time seemed to slow down as we leapt backwards, each expecting an attack from the other as the rocket hit the exterior of the building and the room turned into an inferno of splintered, smouldering wood and flame.

Both of our shields buckled as the concussive force tore across us, though both held up against the onslaught. I realised that I would never get a better chance to strike him down. Before I could act, a second shockwave of embers and debris hit us as the building collapsed in on itself. A small concussive force of Mana swept out from Victor as he forced the worst of the wreckage away.

I had missed my chance. But I wasn't ready for that yet, and I could tell from the look of outrage on Victor's face that he hadn't planned this either. I could see him attempting to draw his powers to the fore to bring against me.

I prepared my shield as we circled around each other in the ruins of the manor. I cursed inwardly—this wasn't the plan. Had Levenson planned this? If so, he was in for a surprise. A helicopter circled around and harsh lights focused on us.

"Victor Whittlesea!" a voice called from above. "It's time to die! You tried to kill me once and failed! Now I'm going to return the favour!"

We glanced up to see a figure descend gracefully into the ruins of the ballroom. I had never met the man personally, but knew him from the news clips—Killian Voll. He and several other mages descended from the helicopter. I grinned mirthlessly. These mages represented the last of the known mages we were seeking. Killian had thrown all in an attempt to end Victor. It was perhaps ironic that he had chosen the party thrown to celebrate his death to announce his survival.

I glanced quickly at the mages as they arrayed themselves against Victor. Perhaps this would be enough; I vaguely recalled another attempt on the old man's life that had begun in a very similar fashion. It hadn't ended well. No, something wasn't right—this wasn't the right time. Killian would fail and with his death this war would be over, but that wouldn't be enough. Victor must die before all this could end.

True, with one rocket Killian had probably wiped out most of the senior command, but others would rise to take their place. This war had never been about conventional troops and leadership, it had always been about who had had more mages, and until Victor had chosen to show himself that had been Voll. Once Voll died, it would be Victor who would continue things.

I watched with amusement as Killian and his cronies fanned out to attempt to overpower the master Mage standing before me. Victor looked in my direction to see if I was going to intervene or if perhaps I had been behind this attempt. I didn't give the him anything, keeping my face impassive in the face of Victor's fury.

"Voll," he murmured, "I should have killed you when I had the chance. You will not escape me again."

CHAPTER TEN

It appeared like everything seemed to happen all at once. Victor spun into action as a dozen threads sought out his foes, including myself. Fortunately I had expected such an act and had already moved to defend myself as the threads smashed into the ground where I had been standing.

Several of the other mages hadn't been so lucky and their shields buckled as Victor sent them barrelling into the wreckage. I couldn't see Voll, but I knew that he had managed to dodge the attack intended to kill him.

Several counter-attacks were levelled against Victor, who dispatched several threads that could level mountains with threads that contained far less energy. There was a reason this man was an undisputed master.

I vaguely pondered throwing my hat into the ring. I could influence the outcome of this fight, but if I committed myself I needed to ensure that Victor would fall, and that was by no means a surety now.

I had only one chance, and this wasn't going to be it.

Victor must have realised by now that I was not going to be a threat, as he had focused his attention solely upon Killian and his men. Marcus had once thought that six master mages would be enough to take down Victor, but the dozen that Killian had brought were getting in each other's way. The simple fact was that our kind don't work well together.

Two of these idiots' threads collided with each other in an attempt to finish the old man. The loud clash echoed across the ruined room. Victor's single thread took them both down and sent them sliding across the ruined floor. Only one of the two rose again.

Watching Victor fight was a lesson unto itself. He didn't appear to move during combat, certainly not to the same degree that I would. Even paralysed, I still launched myself into the air and tried to fight acrobatically. In my weakened state, I couldn't compete like that any longer. I didn't have the flexibility or the stamina and I weakening my potential power in trying to do so. Victor relied on his magic to protect himself. I had seen him only step once to the side in this whole battle, and even that looked grudgingly taken.

I needed to leave and I needed to leave now, but I couldn't bring myself to do it. The experience from watching Victor's Mana signature in battle was invaluable and had confirmed my earlier suspicions. I was glad I had chosen not to intervene—it would have failed.

"Wills!" Killian called out in fury. "Help us! You can end this!"

Killian was trying to force one of the old man's threads back to lay an attack directly against him. I could only see a couple of his allies still standing. I had to assume that in asking for my help he had already come to the conclusion that he was outmatched.

I didn't bother to reply; instead I watched as Victor slowly but surely overpowered him. Killian's thread wavered and cracked. Victor was merciless and pressed his attack viciously, sending a dozen snake-like hits against Voll's shield. Killian's shield amazingly held, despite the abuse it endured.

With a shout of anger and pain, Killian launched himself into the air to avoid the inevitable death awaiting him. It would seem that Victor had been waiting for such a moment; as soon as Killian's feet left the ground a second thread appeared from nowhere and swatted the man as if he were no more a threat than a fly. Killian's shield was smashed into pieces as Victor's thread knocked him from the sky.

Had Victor been able to follow up the attack, he would have finished him, but another of Killian's allies intervened and took Victor's attention away from finishing off his stricken foe. The ally didn't fare too well as he was quickly overpowered and killed, but it allowed Killian to regain his feet and raise his defences once again. Blood was flowing freely from his mouth and he appeared to be favouring his right side. He glanced around in fury and despair as he now took stock. He had come to the conclusion that this simply wasn't going to work.

He backed away warily and gestured to his remaining men that it was time to leave. I wasn't certain that Victor would allow them to leave, until I heard the tell-tale sound of a rocket bearing down on our position again. I glanced up in rage as I saw a missile launched from the helicopter flying above.

Victor smiled contemptuously and with a flick of his fingers sent the missile back to its originator. The helicopter exploded in a haze of yellow mist and shrapnel rained from the sky. Killian appeared to have been waiting for such a moment. At first I thought he was going to attack, but I was wrong. Instead he chose to retreat. He wasn't as stupid as I had first thought—he knew when he was beaten.

He formed the Mana necessary for teleportation but I could tell it wouldn't work. Victor brought his powers to bear and sent a wave of Mana disruption at the disappearing figures. Two were immediately fragged—they were foolish and had sent scry threads out first. Killian appeared to disappear just seconds before the disruption wave hit where he had been standing. He had chosen a small burst of teleportation—somewhere within sight. I didn't know where he had gone, but it was time to go. I had no wish to remain behind to face Victor alone.

Like Killian, I wasn't going to muck around with a scry thread. I picked an area on the far side of the compound and teleported there. Once I landed, I jumped again in three small jumps before I took stock and contemplated a longer jump. Now that I knew what I needed, things were going to move very quickly, but I had to be careful how I proceeded. I wasn't going to simply return to Poland and possibly lead Victor back to my work. Now that he was aware of me, I would need to be cautious. He would be looking for me, possibly even hunting me. But I knew that wouldn't happen for a few days at least. He would need to come up with a believable story for how he had survived the attack on the manor, and that would require him to be found by rescue teams. I had some time before he put his plans in motion.

In the meantime I had to get out of there. I scryed in a random direction and teleported away. To my surprise, someone waiting there for me when I arrived. I heard the sound of teleportation as I materialised and knew I had two choices: teleport away immediately, or double down and raise a shield. Then I cursed. May had already told me that Victor was tracking us through our scry threads. It was possible that he had followed me here with an intention to finish me. That's what I would have done.

I had a third option, which was to throw everything I had into an attack before my assailant could materialise, but I didn't think that was a good solution. No, best to protect myself first. I threw a shield around myself and prepared for the worst. In the end it didn't matter much anyway, as the teleportee wasn't Victor. It was a very ragged and seriously injured looking Killian Voll.

"Why didn't you help us?" Killian snarled. "You know what he's planning! He's going to kill all of us!"

"You wouldn't have won," I informed him, "Even with my help. I've already tried and failed."

"Better to die like that, than wait to be picked off one by one," Killian replied.

"Then go back," I replied simply, "and die."

Killian looked at me with a strange mixture of anger, exhaustion and grief. "There's nothing left," he sighed as he moved closer.

At first I thought he was coming for me, and I readied myself for an attack, but he was moving over to a log to sit down. I had no intention to sitting next to him. This wasn't a camping trip and we weren't friends.

"We're not safe here," I grunted as I glanced back behind us. However it was clear that we had some time. If Victor was going to pursue us he would have already done so.

"Nowhere is safe," Killian sighed wearily. "Trust me, I know. He'll find us no matter where we go."

"What do you want from me?"

"From you? Nothing." Killian shrugged. "The moment where you could have helped has passed."

"Then be on your way," I murmured, "I have work to do."

Killian shifted uncomfortably and winced as he inadvertently jostled his injured side. "I don't think I'm going anywhere,"

Now that I had a chance to look at him properly. Killian was probably right. He was horribly injured. Most likely dying.

"You've got at least three broken ribs on your left side," I informed him.

He nodded. "You're probably right. Feels like it."

"You could possibly bleed out."

"Why didn't you help us? You hate Victor as much as any of us. Before I die, I need to know."

"Until you can overcome the sorcery that keeps Victor alive, there is no point in killing him. When I first fought him, I broke his shield and threw a metal pole through his stomach. He pulled the pole from his body and healed himself."

"Then he's unbeatable."

"Pretty much," I agreed.

"He's killed so many of us. It's over." Killian held his head in his hands.

I didn't answer immediately. "Perhaps he was right to do so."

Killian sighed and leaned back on the tree behind him. "I was just trying to save our kind."

"You started a war. You killed innocent people." I accused.

"No!" Killian's voice rose. "I sought to stop a war! I was trying to prevent it."

"You did a wonderful job," I replied wryly.

"I made mistakes," Killian grunted. "Who hasn't? I'll own them, but those who followed me didn't deserve this."

"Then perhaps you should be more careful where you lead."

"Devon," Killian whispered, suddenly serious, "I'm dying, aren't I?"

"Yes," I whispered as gently as I could muster.

"Good. I don't think I want to live in the world that's coming."

"I know exactly what you mean."

"Please, don't leave," Killian murmured as his voice trailed off. "I don't want to die alo—"

He never finished that sentence. It took Killian an hour to die, and as I promised I remained with him until the last moment. He wasn't conscious for most of it. I don't know if my presence made a difference, but he seemed peaceful when he passed.

Once he was dead I burned his body until there was nothing left but ashes. It was strange doing so, but it seemed a fitting end to a worthy foe. I'd never understood the whole "honour your fallen foe" thing before this moment. It seemed alien. He was dead. What did he care? But then I understood—it wasn't for him. It was for me. I'd spent the best part of the last six years trying to kill this man. I'd done so for a variety of reasons that didn't much matter now. He was dead—the war was over. That was all that was important.

I vaguely wondered why Victor hadn't pursued me; I was only a few kilometres from the site of the attack. I had heard in the distance emergency vehicles and support teams arriving on the scene. It would have been simple for Victor to find me, and yet he didn't.

Perhaps he was trying to establish an alibi for his survival, or maybe he was scared of me. He would see my studies into Necromancy as the first very real threat he had faced in a very long time. It would be easy to imagine that he might find fear in such a scenario, but perhaps I flatter myself. In any event, it was time to go. I had what I came for, and if I was very lucky Victor would take my bait and pursue a very motivated Levenson.

It was all coming into place.

* * *

Or so I had thought. I had taken special care in retuning to Poland. I had no intention of letting Victor follow me. Using a variety of teleportation and shading detonations, I made my path all but untraceable. When I arrived at the station, it was as I had left it. Karl was still in his induced torpor and Randall was still locked away.

It took me some time before everything was in readiness; the room still bore the signs of Karl's Mana assisted rage. Karl was pretty much in the same state that he had been when I left him. I had expected further regeneration. I could see a slight darkening that would indicate hair around the base of his skull and his skin had an abnormally pink hue, but it didn't look like the sorcery had accelerated his regeneration any further. If things went well, he would never awake from his sleep.

I placed a palm over the man's chest as I attempted to figure out just what the hell had caused my previous attempt to go so horribly wrong. Now that I had seen the successful thread employed in Victor, I had hoped my examination of Karl would be easy. I wasn't wholly wrong. I could now see the fey lines of Mana that were responsible for the regeneration and they were similar to the bands of Mana that flowed through my former master, but they weren't identical. The differences were minor, but distinct. It was now simply a matter of finding out exactly how to undo the process.

My earlier theory was correct: fighting the process would only result in an increased level of regenerative effects. My theory at this was to try to subvert the process to cause the correct end result. But there were hundreds of variables and I had no way of testing them all—even if I had the time. It was guesswork at best.

The trick to the procedure would be to isolate the thread responsible for the regeneration. Once I had done that I could begin work. But the damn thing moved throughout the body in pulses, and when I found the thread it would dissipate. It took me about ten minutes before I determined that I'd found the right thread.

Now I had to make a choice. Did I really want to end Karl's life? Was it the right thing to do? I didn't blame him for seeking death when he was but a twisted wight of a man, but now he seemed healthy and his quality of life would be comparable to anyone else on this god forsaken planet right now. The fact that he was almost a hundred years old was irrelevant. Still, I had made a promise that I would do this thing.

If there was one thing I did, it was keep my promises. I was only moments away from starting the sorcery that would end the man's life when the hairs on the back of my neck shot upright. In seconds a shield sprang up around me and for the second time I had been discovered somewhere I wasn't supposed to be.

Victor was here.

I took a deep breath and steadied myself. The time had finally come. I wasn't one hundred per cent ready, but that didn't matter. It would be just as effective to test my theory on Victor as it would on Karl. In many ways it was more fitting that he died here. So many people had died here because of him; there was a sense of justice that he now join them. With a calming hand on the wight's body, I promised to return. I hoped I'd be able to fulfil this promise, but the odds weren't in my favour. Like the last time, Victor was waiting for me in the compound above, but unlike last time I knew exactly what I was walking into and was more prepared.

Victor was still clad in his military uniform, although it was slightly scorched from the fire. He had an shield around him, but not that impressive: it could be broken. Perhaps a year ago I would have been impressed by such sorcery, but my own skills had progressed far since I had last faced him.

"I thought I would never have to return here," Victor called out as I emerged from the stairwell. "Damn you for making me return a second time."

"I can imagine this place would bring back some old ghosts," I replied grimly as I approached my former teacher. Victor didn't reply, but stood his ground.

I was about to suggest that he was lucky that he could return to this place, that there were many who could not. But I was not on solid ethical ground there either—there were graves I had filled littering the outside of this compound that made me just as complicit as him.

"It is strange that it has come to this. With Master Voll's death, you are the last one who could stand against me," Victor said.

"Let's not fool ourselves," I grunted as I began to circle around him. "Voll was never a threat to you."

"Perhaps not," Victor conceded. He didn't turn to face me as my arc brought me behind him.

"I never understood why you left this place standing," I called. "It must have been well within your powers to destroy it, even then."

"I could have, I suppose," Victor agreed.

"It would have been wise," I prompted. "It contained everything I needed to bring you down."

Victor's Mana arched across his body at the threat. "Did it now? Perhaps it's time to test that. One last lesson, master to student."

"I'm not going to play your games, Victor," I snarled as I prepared an attack. The Mana rushed to my hands as the desire to strike him down almost overcame me. Victor seemed impassive in the face of my aggression, but I could see the tell on this face and the subtle flow of power into his shield. He was a lot more worried than he wanted me to see, and he was right to be worried. He knew as well as I did that it didn't matter how powerful our shields were, this battle wasn't about sheer strength—the use of Mana Nova balanced out that particular variable.

I leapt back as Victor released a thread that I assumed was directed at me. It lanced under the ground into the medical complex. I didn't have time to contemplate what he was doing as I had launched an attack of my own. Victor sidestepped as the Mana Nova thread I'd prepared speared towards him. A thread of his own lanced out in defence and deflected my follow-up attack.

I back-peddled out of the way as Victor turned on me. I had no intention of jumping into the air; I'd seen all too well how Victor dealt with those whose feet left the ground. Victor's attack was precise. He wasted no effort in posturing and useless gestures. He had had decades to perfect his use of the Mana Nova thread; I'd only had years. There was no doubt that he deserved the title of master, but in the face of his attack I was holding my own. It wasn't clear how I was doing this; in comparison to my former master my threads were sloppy and ill formed. I'd never seen it before, but with the direct comparison between the two the differences were obvious. With a grunt and a grim smile I adjusted my threads to match his.

The change in my thread was noticeable immediately. I was now using far less power than I had previously and it felt no more straining than the telekinesis threads I was using to keep myself mobile.

The shock on Victor's face was visible even through his shield. "Impressive."

I didn't have to time to pat myself on the back as Victor launched a vicious series of attacks at me and I was forced to give more ground.

The sound of the door to the medical wing opening

was almost my downfall as Victor's thread lanced through my shield and hit my right shoulder, burning off the sleeve from my jacket. I only just barely managed to avoid losing my arm. Pain burst through my arm as the thread passed close enough to the skin to burn. I used the pain and immediately went on the offensive, and was amazed as I began to force the old man into retreat. It wasn't going to last, but it was gratifying to see that I was making some headway. In the face of my pain-filled fury, Victor was no match for this level of power and that could have been the end of it if I had maintained that level of attack. Unfortunately, I couldn't.

The noise that had distracted me was Randall emerging from the medical wing. He had been securely locked up. I could only assume that this had been the purpose of Victor's earlier thread. Randall did appear to be under Victor's control. This was confusing. I didn't quite see how Randall was going to affect the outcome of this battle. Why go to the effort?

That was a problem. Anything I didn't understand could possibly kill me. I also realised that this might explain why I had been doing so well against Victor. He had been dividing his power between controlling Randall and fighting me.

I immediately ceased my attack and backed off, which was lucky because a second Mana Nova thread lanced out and gouged a large hole in the concrete where I had been standing only seconds before. Had I continued my assault, it would have taken my head from my shoulders.

What the hell? That Mana Nova thread came from Randall! Victor was using Mana through the undead vessel. How was that even possible? This changed things.

There was no way I was going to be able to defend against two Mana Nova threads from two sources. I glanced to see the dead man and the master circle around, attempting to keep me between them.

"And so it ends, Devon," Victor intoned. "There is no escape."

I was forced to agree with him; with things the way they were, there was only one outcome to this scenario. However, when the situation is unfavourable—change the situation. I immediately went on the attack again, focusing everything I had on Victor. If I could keep Victor focused on defending himself when the killing stroke came from Randall, I would be ready for it. It was only a matter of timing, and I had survived a hundred battles in similar circumstances. I was ready.

As I had predicted, the old man staggered backwards under the assault of my attack and Randall moved in for the kill. It must have looked like I was attempting to finish off Victor before Randall could kill me—that was exactly what I wanted my former master to think.

I sensed Randall move into position and summon the Mana Nova thread that would end my life. It wasn't of course Randall that was doing this, he was nothing more than a marionette to the puppet master that was Victor. It didn't matter much as in the end the result would be the same. I waited until the very last moment before I let my body go slack and fall to the ground. I had timed it perfectly—the thread was only inches from my face and descending fast. If I cocked this up now it would be over. I immediately threw every ounce of strength that remained in my body into a seize thread in an attempt to wrest control of Randall away from Victor.

It worked! With a quick blink I saw the change in Randall's eyes. I immediately redirected Randall's thread towards my former master. Had I been able to control the dead man's face, I would have shouted with triumph as the thread struck through Victor's shield and slashed a large gouge across his chest. On a normal human that would have been the end of the game, but on Victor it wasn't a mortal wound.

It must have hurt though, as Victor cried out in pain and staggered back and in seconds I was forced from Randall's vision as the old man attempted regain control, but I wasn't going to be so easily dominated. I fought back for control of Randall and the next stage of our fight began.

"Impressive, Master Wills," I heard Victor gasp as our minds contested for dominion over the dead man. A series of Mana nodes animated the wretch, which acted in the same fashion as the nervous system would in a human body. Randall staggered and jerked like someone having a seizure as the two of us vied for control. His limbs flailed as control was exerted and then thwarted. It was a strange sensation sharing someone else's head with Victor—I could feel him in there.

The pressure mounted as the old man increased the power of his attack. and for a second I was almost forcibly rejected from what remained of Randall's mind. Somewhere deep inside of me I found a source of strength I didn't even know I had. I fought back with everything I could muster. This was something I understood, this was something I could do. Both of us had expended so much of our strength in this contest that the outcome of the battle now relied upon it. Once rejected from Randall, it would take some time to bring our defences back to strength, during which time one could simply finish off the other.

I railed against my former master with fury born of revenge, loss and pain. I was fighting to avenge the death of my sister, of my father, of most likely everyone who had ever known me. It was likely that everyone I had grown up with was dead, and it was this man's fault. The rage rose within and made me strong. I turned that anger into power and I turned that power against Victor. It was hard to judge the scope of our battlefield within the dead man's mind, but I could see Victor faltering. Being linked as we were I could see into his mind and I sensed the doubts and fear. Was this the time he would fail? He had been living in fear of this day for so very long. Everything he had ever done was to forestall this very event and it had all been for nought.

His fear had done far more damage than I ever could. He had all but defeated himself, and I revelled in it. I grinned as I forced Randall from the old man's control and snapped the last threads of Victor's hold over his victim. I heard Victor cry out as his consciousness was sent back into his body and I watched in triumph as his shield fell. I immediately jumped back into my own mind and launched a thread at my defenceless opponent. It sliced through his side, causing him to fall to his knees. Blood was pooling at Victor's knees as he held his side, his other hand keeping him upright.

The Mana pooled towards his damaged side; it had already healed the gash on his chest, but I doubted that Victor would remain conscious long enough to fend me off. If he passed out, it was over. With a flick of my wrist I sent a blast of power that shattered Randall into a million pieces. His body immediately exploded into ash and dust. He deserved his peace. He had finally achieved something that he and others like him would have yearned for. He had finally achieved revenge for his death and the death of countless others who had died in this facility.

I drew myself in on Victor like an executioner coming to finish the job. He stared up at me with naked hatred in his eyes. The mask born of his iron will had been shattered and I could finally see the man behind it. I saw the fear and madness that lurked in the recesses of his mind. I had long sensed it was there, but to finally see it was a revelation. This was not some paragon of our art that could not be defeated; he was a mere flesh and blood man and he was at my mercy. He would find no mercy in me.

"You have defeated me," Victor croaked. "But you cannot kill me. I cannot be killed."

"Yes you can," I replied grimly, "and I know how."

The old man gaped at me as I wrenched his head back and placed my hand on his forehead. His eyes went wild as I began the work. When I had used the same technique on Karl, I had tried to be careful and gentle. Now I was just a butcher, cold, efficient, quick and brutal, with no care for the damage being done to his mind.

I watched impassively as the power rose within him and I saw it fighting me still, even as I broke through his defences and isolated the threads responsible for his regeneration. He could not stop me now; he was too weak and it was too late for any kind of defence to ultimately succeed. I revelled as the healing of the wound at his side began to falter and then fail as the magic was drawn elsewhere. I watched the man's eyes as he saw what I was doing, and I saw the moment of clarity when he finally understood the danger. He hadn't realised that this was possible, he had truly thought himself immortal. Nothing is immortal—everything ends. Victor would learn that today. The fear that had plagued him all those years would finally be realised today. I would take that fear and use it against him, but with great fear comes great strength and Victor had been using that fear all his life to make him powerful. He wasn't going to go easy into the great unknown, and with the rising force of a hurricane the old man rallied his defences and worked against me. With a flick of his wrist he sent out a thread, but I sneered at his foolishness. Randall was gone. The drone wouldn't be able help him now. It was only a matter of time.

But I was wrong to discount the thread—it hadn't been to seek out Randall. There was one other in this facility who hated us both equally. One who had I had left in a state of torpor and who Victor had just awakened. I heard the bellow of rage and pain clearly and I knew immediately what had happened. Karl would find his way up here and he would attempt to strike both of us down. Victor might survive if I hadn't completely nullified his sorcery by the time Karl arrived, but I wouldn't be able to defend myself. Weak though Karl was, in sorcery it wouldn't matter.

This left me with a choice: could I finish off the old man before the Wight arrived, or I could draw back to defend myself? Victor had to die and I doubted I would get a better chance than now. He was defeated and lying almost defenceless beneath me. I just had to finish him off. Yes, there was only one option here, and though it might cost me my life, I would gladly pay that price to finish off my former master.

I redoubled my efforts to break through the old man's defences and if I had more time, I might have won, but I felt the sharp rise of the Mana within me screaming for defence, and I had no strength left to give. Everything I had was used to suppress Victor's regeneration powers. With a snarl and a primal scream Karl threw himself at us. He hit me more solidly than Victor and the impact sent me onto my back.

Karl's eyes bored into me and I could see the depths of his madness. There was no humanity left within him. Karl had been right to seek death—there was no coming back from what he had endured. My last doubts about the ethical dilemma of ending his life faded as Karl gave another animal shriek. A second followed shortly afterwards as Karl finally got a clear view of Victor. At first I thought that it might shock him sufficiently to bring him back, but Karl charged at his former tormentor with Mana flaring along his fists. Victor pushed himself away, using his magic to put distance between us, sliding along the ground like a snake escaping its prey. Karl bellowed and pursued after his prey as I attempted to get to my feet. The Mana within me was unreliable and the braces around my legs were shaky. My muscles screamed in protest, but I wasn't going to let this moment get away. I leapt into the air to pursue my quarry, but it was too late. I recognised the signs of a teleport spell emanating from Victor and had I been fresh I might have been able to do something about it. As it was, I was too weak and too slow.

The disruption pulse hit the ground where Victor had been lying just seconds after he had vacated. He was gone. I could follow him, but I didn't have the necessary strength to follow very far, and once I found him it would again be luck of the draw to see who came out triumphant. Besides, I now had more pressing problems.

With one enemy escaped, Karl turned back to face me. The Wight raised his power in an attempt to throw himself at me. There was no technique to his attack. It was a simple primal burst of power. It was nothing that my shield couldn't withstand, but that didn't mean I was going to let him attack me. With a telekinetic swipe, I immobilised Karl until I could send him back to sleep while I contemplated my options. As much as I hated to admit it, I had missed my chance. I could only hope that I would get another. In the meantime I had more serious matters to concern myself with. I had a promise to fulfil. I used the Mana once again to send Karl into a state of torpor.

It was lucky that Karl had never learned the necessary skills to raise a shield; that would have made my ability to render him unconscious much more difficult. I gently lifted him from the ground and brought him back to the examination room. This would be the last time I would do this. I laid him down on the gurney, which was now starting to look its age. Karl hadn't exactly been careful when he had stormed from this room to hunt me down earlier.

I was fatigued and close to complete mental exhaustion, but I wasn't going to put this off anymore. I placed my palm on Karl's forehead and began to work. It was strange that the threads responsible for Victor's regeneration were so much easier to locate, though I suppose it had something to do with the spell Victor had had perfected. By comparison, Karl was a complete mess of tangled threads and charred Mana nodes. It took me a long time before I was able to locate the right series of threads.

My work began slowly, one thread at a time. I had to be so very careful that I didn't cause the thread to fizzle before the work was done, and yet I had a distinct time limit before the thread would reach the required Mana node and then renew itself. It took me three tries before I was successful. Nothing happened at first and the effects were so subtle, but I knew success when I saw it. I didn't start to notice any physical changes until I had done about a dozen more. The pinkish hue of Karl's skin began to turn a slightly whitish-grey colour and his breathing slowed from the steady rhythm into a haggard gasp. Still, I had to do more; wave after wave of threads needed to be converted, and I felt the steady rise of the headache that indicated overuse of Mana. I ignored it as I poured more power into the construct below me.

I wished I could wake the man to say goodbye, but there was no point. If he was still in there he was buried under the massive psychosis that had caused him to revert to the primal state I had seen earlier. No, there was nothing to be gained from waking him. I quietly said my goodbyes and was greeted by silence.

The blood in my veins pulsated throughout my body as I kept the pressure upon the delicate structure of Mana through the man's body. Any failure on my part would result in a continuance of the previous state and healing would begin anew.

I worked in silence as the Mana did its gruesome work. I took no pride in my work as the veins in the man's body bulged into a dark brownish shape as the Mana passed across them. I watched as his skin shrivelled against his muscles and his muscles withered. It took a full ten minutes before he had reverted to the state he was in when I had first met him, and I was pretty sure that brain death had occurred long before he reached his previous undead state. With the Mana subverted and now feasting on his power rather than renewing, it was only a matter of time.

I watched with a strange sense of regret and satisfaction as the body turned grey and dark and eventually faded away into ash as the Mana consumed him. Like Glave before him, nothing was left of the body but an outline of ash on the gurney surface.

I had fulfilled my promise. Karl was gone.

I turned my hands over to notice with distaste the purplish blotch of broken blood vessels in the veins on my wrist. I had overdone it. The last time I had overused, the veins in my wrist ruptured. I had burned myself out and temporarily lost my ability to draw Mana.

It had taken everything I had to end the process within the Wight. True, I had already been tired and battle weary when I started, but the Wight wasn't fighting me the way that Victor would. The battle would be a lot harder with Victor, and his body hadn't undergone the same amount of trauma that Karl's had. After everything was said and done, I didn't know if I was powerful enough to overpower Victor and then the regenerative process without help and therein lay the problem.

* * *

I rested for three days in that hell hole before I was ready to move. It wasn't exactly a restful sleep, but I knew Victor would be unlikely to return after his defeat. Now that Karl and Randall had gone, the loneliness of the place was starting to get to me. Not that they had ever been good company, but at least they were something. Now that I was on my own, it seemed that the ghosts of this facility had finally taken over and they were angry at my intrusion.

I'd never believed in ghosts or an afterlife. Nothing in my studies had ever caused me to believe in such a thing. It was difficult to tell night from day here as the only light that ever reached this place was the light from the glow spell I routinely let off to provide illumination.

On the third day of my stay I had had enough, it was time to go. The ghosts of this tomb deserved their privacy and I wouldn't return. In fact, I would ensure no one did. I stood in the middle of the parade ground, not too from the blood stains Victor had left on its concrete surface, or from the pile of dust and bones that was all that remained of Randall, and I glanced around.

This would be the last time I would see these grounds, which had been the closest thing I could have called home for the past six years. I wouldn't miss it, but it was important I remember it for what it was. It was a dark place filled with the memories of people long past; I was nothing more than a passing footnote in the history of this facility, but I would be an important footnote because I would be the one who ended it. I could have simply barred up the gates to prevent access to the facility and hope that its remoteness would protect it, but I wasn't going to take that chance.

If another mage found this place they could follow the same footsteps I had. No, this facility must be destroyed completely. There must be nothing left. I took a deep breath and reached out with the power. My threads passed across metal girders, which bore lights that had long since stopped working, and into the concrete foundations of the building below me. They exploded out from me in a wave that spread in all directions. With careful precision, I launched fireballs into the main administration complex and watched with approval as the fire tore through the building, consuming everything in its path. As it reached the generators that would have provided power and light over the grounds, an explosion rumbled throughout the complex as long since forgotten fuel exploded when the inferno over took it.

I let my mind pass through the inferno as the scry thread I was using passed through Victor's office. It was already mostly consumed by flame and I noted with satisfaction that the books on Necromancy had already succumbed to the fire. No one would be learning from them now. Before I left the room, I glanced one last time at the picture of the woman on Victor's desk. The resemblance to Renee was staggering and I watched the photo curl and bubble in the frame as the fire took it. I could have saved the photo, but I wanted no reminders. Let it burn with the rest of the relics in this place.

I brought the sturdy metal beams supporting the roof down. With a vicious motion I pulled the parade ground concrete up in sheets to reveal the hospital and cell blocks below. With careful precision I directed the fire below to burn clean the evil that had been perpetrated there. My shield crackled red with the power expended to keep the fire from me as the heat and smoke rose in the complex, but I wasn't done yet.

With telekinetic bands stronger than steel, I tore the foundations from the roof and from the ground beneath me. The rumbling sound reverberated throughout the cavern as the mountain began to reclaim its own. It happened slowly at first; as the supports were removed, dust, dirt and debris fell from the ceiling like rain, scattering with sparks across the surface of my shield. Larger rocks and then huge shelves of mountain began to slide down into the cavern. I should leave this place now, but I wanted to be sure that nothing would survive. I sent a massive shockwave of Mana upwards into the mountain ceiling to dislodge any remaining support beams embedded into the ceiling. The explosion of rock and dirt as the Mana wiped away the structure was staggering, and the noise swept across me like a wave washing through a sand castle. On all sides the walls of the cavern collapsed as the mountain came crashing down upon me.

The last sight before I teleported out was of a huge sheet of rock sliding down on my position. It would have complete decimated the examination room and cellblocks. The landslides and avalanches caused by my destruction of the Nazi complex went on for some time. The tunnel leading into the complex was forever buried under the rock and snow from the mountain above. The outside of the mountain didn't look that much different from the way it had before, but the complex was gone. Its evil was now buried under hundreds of tonnes of rock, dirt and snow.

I waited for four hours on the snow topped peak of a neighbouring mountain to see if any evidence of the complex remained on the surface, and then conceded victory. It was gone. I could think of no better final gift to Karl, Randall and the others who had died there, including my own victims, than ensuring their final resting place was undisturbed.

I didn't really know what my next step was going to be. I knew it would be unlikely that Victor would attack me again for some time, if at all. He had just come face to face with his own mortality for the first time in a century. He would be running scared. He would be hiding and waiting. I needed to draw him out so I could finish him, but I didn't know where to start.

Where had Victor been hiding all these years? If I could find his new hiding hole I could possibly finish him, but I was in uncharted territory. Victor was afraid of me. He wouldn't face me directly again if he could help it. He could have other agents to send against me in the hope that one of them might get lucky.

I wasn't going to let this opportunity pass. Victor was

hurt and he was afraid and for the first time ever he was vulnerable. I had once thought I would have only one chance to destroy Victor, but it seems that the fates had conspired to give me a second. I wouldn't let this one go to waste. The next time I faced Victor, either he or I would die. There was no alternative any longer. We didn't live in a world where one could survive while the other lived. Like in the western movies I used to watch as a child, this town simply wasn't big enough for the two of us.

* * *

I had no idea where Victor had fled to after his defeat in Poland, but knew someone who might. Levenson had already indicated he didn't know where Victor was hiding outside of his role as an American general. I doubted Victor was going to go back to playing an allied general. That would make him too easy to find, but it was a risk I wasn't going to take. Every lead needed to be followed up. Levenson looked less than pleased to find me sitting in his office chair when he returned back to his office.

"I knew you weren't dead," he muttered as he made his way over to his drinks cabinet. I didn't have the heart to tell him that'd already cleaned him out.

"Has Victor returned?" I inquired, sipping on the last of his scotch.

"No," Levenson grunted as he realised his predicament. "Will he?"

"I doubt it," Levenson replied sourly. "General Charles

Hurstbridge was pronounced dead on arrival after the attack on command."

"Without a body? I nodded, impressed. "Your doing?"

"Of course," Levenson muttered. "I think it's safe to say that our previous alliance is over."

"Glad to hear it."

"Don't look so smug," Levenson snapped. "I still think we're all dead. I was in the process of putting my affairs in order to disappear before you arrived."

"It's a pity you weren't quicker." I smiled. "You might have avoided this conversation."

Levenson scowled at me as he moved to the cabinet on the far side of the office and retrieved another bottle of scotch. It was nice to know he had a spare.

"Why are you here?"

"You know why I'm here," I replied firmly. "I'm looking for Victor."

"I already told you I have no idea where he is."

"You must have some idea," I asked. "You were never curious? You must have known, as I did, the threat he represented."

"I looked for him at the start of the war." Levenson nodded. "But it's a large world and he is, after all, just one man."

"I told you how dangerous he was."

"Yes," Levenson allowed, "but your memory of the battle of Melbourne was sketchy at best. To be honest, at the time I assumed that you had killed him and were wounded in the battle."

"No," I replied firmly, "That's not it."

"Obviously not, "Levenson amended, "but at the time, considering no one saw nor heard from him, it made sense that he was dead."

It did make sense; it was wrong, but I couldn't fault his logic. Victor had always been amongst the most powerful of our kind and one of the most active. It didn't make any sense for him to remove himself from the world the way he had.

No, actually, that wasn't right at all. It all made perfect sense. Victor didn't understand this world. He was a product of a forgotten generation. He had no place in this world and the culture today didn't make sense to him. That perhaps explained why he had pursued such an isolationist policy in relation to our kind. When our kind had chosen to reveal themselves and start a fucking world war, of course Victor would hide. He had seen this all before, he had already been involved in a world war. To him we would have been nothing more than children squabbling in the dark.

The real question was, why had he chosen to come back? What had changed?

I didn't know, but I knew who might. I had hoped it wouldn't come to this. I wasn't sure I had the strength, but I had no choice. I would have to find May Chen. She had known where Victor was hiding Renee and my son. My feelings on this matter were divided; I really wanted to see Renee again and I feared it with all my dread. It was time to pay for my sins.

CHAPTER ELEVEN

Finding May Chen would prove easier than I had thought;—I used the same trick that she had used to find me. I had held onto that damned phone for long enough to remember the phone number attached to it, my memory skills had been enhanced by Victors teachings. And of course, once I had the number I could use GPS coordinates to locate them. Levenson was able to provide the coordinates easily.

According to the data provided, they were in South Africa. The southern continent of Africa hadn't been involved in the war. It had swept across Europe and over to the Americas but it hadn't moved too far south. South Africa would have remained largely untouched by our kind. May had indicated that Renee and Gabriel had escaped from Victor, so I was pretty sure he wasn't going to be there.

I took a phone from Levenson before I left the base and programmed in May's number. It would be polite to send notification of my arrival before simply teleporting into the base. It would be unfortunate to be dragged into a fight simply because I hadn't announced myself. I teleported to a location five kilometres from where the GPS signal from May's phone had last been registered and waited. The fact that we were able to get a GPS signal at all showed that the phone was on, or as May had told me at least indicated that the battery was in.

I held the phone before me, but I just couldn't seem to press the dial button. I stared at the screen until the numbers made no sense, but I just couldn't click on that little phone icon on the screen. My stomach made me feel like I was going to be sick and my hand was shaking.

Why couldn't I ring the damn number? I had gone into battle with less angst than this.

It took me a full ten minutes before I was finally able to steel myself sufficiently to press the dial button. It seemed to take forever before it was answered.

"Hello?" May's voice finally answered. "Who is this?"

"May," I gasped, more of a whisper than a word, "its Devon."

There was a few seconds of silence on the other end of the phone.

"Why are you calling?" May murmured down the line.

"I need your help," I said. "Can I teleport to you?"

"You know where I am?"

"You're not the only one who can track GPS."

I could almost hear the indecision in the silence between her words. She still didn't trust me, she'd made that pretty clear from our last meeting, but she also knew how loath I was to see Renee again.

"Renee is here." she finally grunted. "I kept your promise, she doesn't know you're alive."

"Thank you," I mumbled, "but this is more important."

"Your son is here."

"I know."

"Should I tell her you're coming?" May left the question hanging.

That was the million dollar question. Was it better for her to know that I was alive and that May had kept it from her? Or would it be better to simply see me alive for the first time. I had no idea. The old Renee might very well have clocked me out at first sight, but I didn't know if she had changed. She must have changed. Hell, I had been changed by all this.

"I don't know," I finally admitted.

"Then you're a fuckload of help," May sneered down the line. "I tell you what, I'll let you tell her yourself. I'd like to stay out of it."

"I'll be there in a few minutes," I replied.

It took me more than a few minutes to get the nerve together to teleport. When I finally did muster the courage, May was waiting for me outside. It was a small farmstead on the outskirts of a small town, about as remote as you could get and still have access to modern amenities. The building looked old, and had a decidedly colonial English feel. The house had been remodelled several times since its construction, but retained its original style. It looked comfortable and safe. This seemed like a good place to wait out the war.

"Devon," May greeted coldly. "I trust that nothing is following you."

"No." I nodded. "I'm not bringing danger with me."

"Last time we spoke you were going to kill Victor," May continued. "Is he dead?"

"No," I admitted. "I wasn't able to kill him."

"Then we are in danger," May concluded.

"No, I may not have killed him," I said, "but I didn't lose. He fled."

May sucked in her breath at the statement. "Then he can be defeated."

I nodded my head. "And he now knows it."

"That makes him more dangerous than before," May warned.

"It only makes him more scared than before," I corrected.

"Why are you here?"

"I need to know where he's hiding."

"I don't know," May blurted out.

"I know." I smiled sadly. "I'm not here to ask you."

"They're inside," May whispered, "and she's probably aware of you."

"I know." She would have felt me teleport in. It was an inelegant way of announcing myself to someone who thought you were dead, but I had no better way.

"I'll give you some space," May called as I headed towards the door of the homestead.

The inside of the building looked nothing like the outside; inside was modern, sleek and stylish. The doorway led into a large lounge room that looked over a large section of land to the south of the building. The homestead was built onto the side of a large hill, so the view of the African savannah was pretty impressive, but I didn't notice the view at first. I didn't notice anything around me at all. I only noticed the woman in front of me. Renee was looking out the windows. She hadn't acknowledged me, but she knew I was there. I could tell by the taut strain of her neck and her hands clasped into fists behind her that she knew I was there.

"Hello Renee," I murmured. My voice sounded oddly discordant as the soft words echoed throughout the room.

"Devon," Renee replied. Her voice broke a little as she said my name. She still hadn't turned to look at me. My name sounded strange coming from her lips, as if she was speaking a stranger's name. I was so used to her calling me 'Twitch' that my real name sounded wrong.

I didn't know what to say. In all my most fevered dreams I'd never imagined it like this. My subconscious had dreamed of meeting Renee in a hundred different ways and tortured me of her death in a thousand more, but none of that was worse than the reality.

"I knew you weren't dead," she whispered. "Somehow I knew. I don't know how. I guess I thought I would have felt it if you'd died."

"Renee," I began, but my voice cracked. How do you respond to that? Do I try to explain myself? Do I beg for forgiveness? I deserved the opportunity for neither.

"Why have you come? Now of all times?" Renee asked quietly.

"You know why I'm here," I replied.

"You're going to kill my grandfather," Renee said sadly.

"Yes."

"Oh," Renee replied casually. "I thought you might have wanted to have seen your son."

Her words pierced through me like a dagger and ripped out my heart with all the viciousness of a tiger devouring its prey. I couldn't deny them though, she was right. I should have wanted to see my son, but that thought scared me more than any battle I had ever faced.

"I don't know what kind of father I would have made," I replied, but Renee cut me off with a small sigh. Her stance suggested that she was readying herself. The Mana was flaring up and down the length of her arm like wildfire and yet it didn't appear to be trying to protect itself. There was no readiness to conjure a shield, nothing that would indicate an attack. I cursed myself for the maniac I was. This was the woman I had once loved, the woman who still loved me in a strange, twisted way, and my psyche was analysing her, looking for weakness, waiting for an attack. What was wrong with me?

Renee took a deep breath and turned to face me. Her face was hard and cruel and there was nothing but ice in her eyes. Her features faltered when she saw me though. Her eyes widened as she looked upon me and it was like ice breaking. The hard shell crumbled and I could see the woman within.

"What has happened to you?" Renee whispered. Her

eyes cast over the construct that I used to keep myself mobile and I saw only pity. I'd never seen that look from her before. Pity? I didn't want her pity! I didn't deserve it.

"I have become the monster your grandfather intended me to be," I whispered as I allowed Renee to complete her inspection. Every glance, every flinch was like a knife wound to my heart. I bore it with stoic duty though. I deserved this. I owed her this.

"He thought he had killed you. He told me he killed you," Renee murmured, "I didn't believe it, but you never came back."

"He did all but kill me," I replied softly as I took a step closer.

"Don't!" Renee snapped. "Just … stay there … Just, give me a few minutes."

I let Renee continue her inspection. Every second of it was torture as her eyes passed across each scar on my face. How much did her eyes see? Did she see the evil that I had perpetrated in the name of my cause? Could she see the marks that it had left in me? Surely she must have; I wasn't the same stupid kid she had once known. That kid was as foreign to me as a stranger on the street.

"There is nothing of you left that I recognise," Renee whispered. "You're a different man. I now understand why you didn't come back to me. You were dead."

I didn't argue the point.

"I will not help you." Renee stated so softly I could barely hear her, despite the strange acoustics of the room. "You should go."

"And what of our son?" I replied darkly, feeling like a bastard for using our child as an argument against her. I knew it was wrong and I knew it was unfair, but I did it anyway. "What will happen when Victor comes for him? And you know he will."

"Victor will not come for Ethan," Renee snapped, her eyes flaring in rage. I flinched as I heard my son's name for the first time. "Ethan is not a mage."

"Not yet," I interjected, but I was cut off.

"Not ever!" Renee snarled.

"You can't control that," I replied firmly. "You know it will happen. It is simply a matter of time, given his parentage."

"Then I will take him and I will run!" Renee hissed. "I will run as far and for as long as I have to. No one is going to take my son."

"So that's your answer," I muttered with distaste. "You will raise him to live in fear, scared of who he is."

"Better that than to become like his father," Renee hissed.

"I don't want that either." I sighed. "I never wanted that."

"I wish you had never come back," Renee snarled with tears in her eyes. "I wish you had stayed dead."

She fled the room. I let her go.

* * *

"Well, that didn't go very well," I murmured softly as I walked back out into the courtyard.

"What did you expect?" May snapped. She hadn't made a point of it, but I knew that she had been listening. "Did you just think you could waltz in here like nothing had happened?"

"No." I sighed. "I don't think I knew what I was expecting."

May looked at me for a long time as she pondered her next words. I could see it in her eyes, the recrimination, and the accusation. She had spent a lifetime hating me, and for the first time ever she was struggling with sympathy for me. I didn't care for her sympathy either, but at least, unlike Renee, May was better at hiding it.

"Come on." May exhaled. "I'll get you some food."

May led me around the side of the building and in through what was obviously a kitchen door. Like the lounge room, the kitchen was modern and fully stocked.

"We do our own farming here mostly," May informed me. "Although we do trade for goods with the town from time to time. The war hasn't reached here yet."

"I doubt that it will," I murmured. "Both sides seem pretty devastated."

"Since when has that ever mattered?" May said. "An American counter-attack is coming, you know it, I know it. They will spread back through Europe in an attempt to end the war. New alliances will be formed and the war will continue."

I couldn't argue with her, it was inevitable. "At least the involvement of our kind is over."

May almost scoffed. "The damage is already done."

"So what are you saying? That it's game over? Human race done for?"

"No," May replied. "It'll take more than that to wipe out the human race, but I think maybe we're looking at another dark age."

"Maybe that's a good thing." I chuckled. "A fresh start."

May looked at me with a strange expression. "You might be right."

May offered me a soup, made from vegetables from their garden. I hadn't eaten anything in days and it smelled delicious. She directed me towards a small table on the far side of the kitchen that overlooked the same view I had seen from the lounge room.

"Are you safe here?" I asked between mouthfuls. "I mean, from our kind."

"There are five mages here," May replied. "We're as safe as we can be."

"Does Victor know of this place?"

"Yes." May sighed softly. "He leaves us alone."

"He's waiting."

"I know."

"When the child's power awakens ..."

"I know," May repeated angrily. "Renee knows it too."

"Then what?" Again May cut me off. "What would you have us do? I've fought Victor, I almost died fighting Victor. I know what he's like, he's simply too powerful. He knows I'm here and leaves me alone. He won't kill me, he had the opportunity and didn't take it. What would you have me do? What can we do? If I were to try something, I'd get us all killed."

I didn't have an answer to that. In their shoes I didn't blame them. They must assumed that while they remained hidden and not participate in the war they were safe from Victor, and they were probably right. Victor was only actively hunting down combatants, but that wasn't the only danger here.

Once my son became a mage, Victor would return for him. He wouldn't be able to help himself. My son had the potential to be amongst the most powerful mages alive today, and Victor wouldn't allow a threat like that to survive. He would either twist him and subvert him or he would kill him if he couldn't control him. If my son was anything like Renee or myself, I doubted that he would be easily controlled. That thought sent chills down my spine.

"I've arranged a room for you," May stated when we had finished eating.

"Why?"

"Renee asked me to."

"You said you didn't tell her I was alive after we met in Scotland?"

"I didn't have to," May replied softly. "She already knew. She's had a room prepared for you for years."

It was similar the rest of the house, modern and functional. I didn't know where Renee was within the house, but I could feel her presence and with that feeling came a warning to leave her alone.

I glanced around the room; for all its nicety it had the feeling of a jail cell. Functional bed, side table, no furnishings, no artwork or pictures—this wasn't someone's room. It was a room used for strangers. It was perfectly pleasant, but after my living conditions for the past six years it was simply unpleasant. Fortunately there was a doorway on the far side of the room that led out onto a shared balcony. There was a table and chairs set up on the balcony that looked over the savannah. The stars were particularly bright tonight. A polite cough brought my attention away from the stars and back down to earth.

"Master Wills," a male voice interjected, "Someone wanted to say hello."

With my heart in my throat, I turned around to face the newcomers. There were two of them: a tall man and a small boy. At first a shot of terror overtook me until I realised I recognised the boy. Justin.

"Won't you join me?" I offered as I gestured towards the other end of the table. Justin immediately leapt forward and pulled up a seat, but his companion remained standing. I smiled grimly as I recognised a defensive pattern in the man's shoulders. The Mana was warning him to be careful, sensing a threat. His Mana was wise to consider me a threat.

"Master Devon!" Justin interjected. "May said you wouldn't be coming back, but I knew she was wrong!"

Great, it seemed that everyone could predict my actions, even a twelve-year-old boy. That wasn't going to bode well for my ability to outwit my enemies.

"Aren't you clever?" I smirked back at the boy with a smile. The guard immediately relaxed as the boy beamed back at me. There was no threat here, no matter what the Mana was telling him.

"How are your studies going?" I enquired as the boy's guard finally took a seat.

"They're going very well, sir!" Justin said. "Master Lehrer is a very good teacher."

Really? He could hardly be a worse teacher than me. Justin continued on about his studies and how his new master was teaching him to read properly. The boy was talking so much that Lehrer and I had to talk in between his breaths.

"How did you come to take on his training?" I interjected between the boy's sentences.

"Mistress Chen asked me to. She felt she would be distracted from security in case any others of our kind should happen upon us."

"Has that ever happened?"

"Once or twice," Lehrer said non-committedly. "Mistress Chen is quite formidable."

I nodded. Justin was still talking, heatedly describing basic Mana principles that I had mastered years ago.

"The boy is actually quite talented," Lehrer stated, changing the topic. "Naturally adept. He will be quite powerful one day."

"Well, that's just great." I smiled dryly. "If there's one thing this world needs, it's more master mages."

"I must say, it is a pleasure to finally meet you again,"

Lehrer continued, ignoring my sarcasm.

"I'm sorry, I don't believe we've met," I murmured as my mind went into overdrive, attempting to remember where I had met this man. He didn't seem familiar. He was young, looked to be in his early twenties or so.

"It was a long time ago," Lehrer continued. "I don't blame you for forgetting, it was from before the war. We were presented together at the Occursus in Singapore. I was Master Morrigan's apprentice."

The Occursus in Singapore—that seemed like a lifetime ago, but it was only about eight or so years ago. It seemed like much more, it seemed like a lifetime, someone else's life. I had thought I had understood everything there was to know about being damaged and death and destruction, but I was just a boy. I had no idea of the horrors yet to come. I remembered that day well, I often dwelt upon it. I had taken vows that bound myself to the order of mages. I'd broken those vows. I'd cast them aside and blatantly ignored them. I thought I had known better. I was wrong. If I could do it all again, hell, I'd probably have done the same thing. I remember that night well: I was preoccupied at the time, but I did vaguely remember a small boy, about the same age as Justin was now, being presented to the Primea at the same time. This man could have been that boy.

"My apologies," I waved him off. "I should have remembered."

"That's quite all right." Lehrer smiled. "My master said he was quite impressed with you at the time."

"Impressed with me? How?" I prompted, curious.

"To be chosen by Master Whittlesea as an apprentice was quite the honour, and then to stand up against him in public even more so. He thought you a rare breed."

I smirked. "Looks can be deceiving."

"Indeed," Lehrer continued. "I doubt my master would have said such things if he had have known what was coming."

"No," I agreed readily. Where the hell was he going with this? Was he trying to stir up trouble? If so I wasn't going to bite.

"My master never much cared for Master Whittlesea," Lehrer continued, unaware of my internal concerns.

"Then he must have followed Master Devereaux."

"Actually, no." Lehrer smiled. "He cared for neither. He chose to exile himself when Devereaux took the Primeaship. An action that probably resulted in my survival."

"And your master?"

Lehrir shook his head. "Sadly not with us. He chose to exile us to Oslo."

I nodded sympathetically. Oslo wasn't far enough from the fighting in central Europe. It would have been consumed in the fighting, or at least a mage would have attracted the attentions of enemy mages early in the war when it was a free for all.

"He died saving me. I escaped from the fighting and fled further south. I was still running when Master Tychus found me. He brought me here."

"Then you have been fortunate," I grunted.

"Really? I don't feel fortunate," Lehrer stated.

"More fortunate than some," I muttered, unwilling to discuss this further and turning to face the boy, "So tell me, Justin, how powerful have you become?"

Justin smiled beatifically as if he had been waiting for just such a question. With a slight flex of his fingers he summoned a Mana thread and held it before him. He had improved noticeably. His construction was a little off, but I recognised enough of my own style in his work to see my influence. It was a well-constructed thread, but it wasn't a masterfully built one. He still had much more to learn. However he had something that the rest of us probably didn't. He had time.

* * *

I slept soundly that night for what seemed like the first time in over half a decade. My slumber wasn't interrupted by nightmares or dreams and lasted a full eight hours. I awoke with a start in the morning. I hadn't meant to fall asleep. Someone had placed a blanket over me in the night. Someone had been in my room and I hadn't awoken.

The presence of someone in my room should have triggered a threat warning in the Mana and woken me up. That was disconcerting; for a moment I lay in readiness in case a trap had been planted. But it wasn't a trap, it was only a blanket—a red tartan blanket of all things. I didn't belong in this place.

I ran my hand through my hair and stood up. The door was slightly open, but I had left it that way when I arrived. I slid out into the hall feeling better than I had in months and made my way carefully over to the kitchen.

May was in the kitchen preparing breakfast. She glanced over at me, her nose wrinkling in distaste.

"You should shower," May called out.

Lehrer and Justin were eating something from a bowl. I quickly glanced around the kitchen but couldn't see anyone else. Even though the place didn't remind me of my own childhood in anyway shape or form it felt familiar enough. This was a family eating breakfast. I hadn't experienced anything like this in so long. It almost hurt.

"She and Ethan are eating in her quarters," May answered my unspoken question. "Congee?" May offered me a bowl.

"Yes, please," I replied as I gripped the bowl. The scent of the food washed over me and I was immediately drawn back into the world before the war. Victor's housemaid had made congee during my apprenticeship. I had eaten this dish often. It was nothing more than a salty porridge, but it was everything I needed right now. It was delicious.

"You've had it before?" May queried, noting my obvious enjoyment.

"Oh yes." I eagerly passed my bowl back for more.

"Great." May grinned as she ladled a second portion into my bowl. "I was serious about that shower—you smell like death. You're stinking up my kitchen."

That wiped the smile from my face. "Do you have a change of clothes?" I asked. It would be good to get out of my military uniform and into some regular clothes.

"In your size, probably not," May murmured.

"Never mind, I'll make some." I smiled as I headed back to the door. "By the way, thanks for the blanket."

"It wasn't me," May replied softly.

I made my way back upstairs. There was a bathroom with a shower unit across from my bedroom. A shower sounded like good idea right about now. I couldn't remember the last time I'd had a hot shower, maybe the aircraft carrier.

My uniform had seen better days; the Mana Nova Victor had hit me with in Poland had pretty much shredded the right hand side of my shirt, and there was enough collective stains and grime on the fabric to make a new uniform. I peeled my clothes off and rested them on the clean porcelain bench by the taps. They left a grimy mark on the pristine surface. On the far wall next to the door was a full length mirror. I let my gaze pass across my war-torn body, across the numerous scars and burns that marked my journey. I looked wrong, like I didn't belong here. I was a creature of this war and I had been shaped by it. I inspected each mark on my body as if they were something foreign, from the burns on my ankle from Vin the night I had killed him, to the multitude of scars and burns that crisscrossed my body. I had become a weapon of war. I didn't belong in this normal looking bathroom, with these normal looking towels hanging from the wall. This wasn't my world and I had no right to intrude. I gazed at myself for a long while before I could shake the feeling that I was somewhere that I didn't belong. The shower didn't bring me much pleasure.

When I finished I put my old uniform back on. I could have easily created new garments, forming them from the Mana, but that didn't seem right. They would have covered me like a lie and I would have smothered in the deception. No matter what else I was, I was a soldier. I should act like it.

When I emerged from the bathroom, May was waiting for me.

"Renee would like to see you," she murmured as she gestured back towards the main lounge room.

Renee was standing in much the same position as she had been the last time we had met, with her back to me staring out over the savannah.

"I'm sorry I reacted so strongly yesterday."

"It's all right, I don't blame you." I shrugged.

"You are just so different than I remember you," Renee said.

"I have become the thing you always feared I would become," I prompted—her unspoken words.

Renee nodded quickly and wiped her eyes.

"I feel that way too," I whispered softly.

"It's my fault," Renee said. "I should have explained, been more patient, done more. Maybe things could have been different."

"No," I gasped. All these years I had struggled with the recrimination that Renee would cast at me. I had never in a million years occurred to me that she would blame herself. Why would she? It wasn't her fault. It was mine. I had made my choices. I had to live with them. However, in all my years I had never considered that other people had to live with my decisions too.

"I don't think this could have turned out any differently," I muttered. "I think it was fate."

For a moment she looked at me and I saw the old Renee in her face. Her mouth twisted into a mocking grin that usually indicated I had said or done something stupid. It was only there for a flash before she covered her emotions, but I saw it and she knew I had seen it.

"I don't believe in fate," Renee murmured.

"I have lived through too many things that should have killed me to believe otherwise."

"Devon," Renee began hesitantly, "don't you want to see your son?"

I looked at the woman as if she had asked me if I wanted to jump into a pit of snakes. The fear must have been apparent on my face because Renee almost physically flinched. Did I want to meet my son? Of course I wanted to see my son. How could I not? That wasn't the question. The question was: should I meet him? What damage would be done? Would the pain and misery that I seemed to wear like a shroud be passed down the bloodline to my son? He should be protected. He could be the one honestly good part to survive me of this world. He didn't need to be tainted by association with me. In the end I convinced myself of a thousand reasons why I should have said no. A hundred thousand logical, practical reasons, but in the end I found my lips saying four simple words. I couldn't help myself. They just came out.

"Of course, I do."

Renee looked at me strangely as if trying to reconcile the information she was seeing on my face with the words I had said. It took her what seemed like an eternity before she responded.

"He's through there." She pointed towards a door to my left.

I had faced down armoured tanks with less fear than that simple wooden door. It took everything I had to walk calmly over to the door and open it. Renee's eyes never left me. The expression on her face was difficult to discern; she was obviously concerned for her son, but she needn't have worried. I wasn't going to hurt the boy. But there was something else behind her eyes too, something elusive. I couldn't figure it out.

Beyond the door was a smaller room that had been converted into a TV room. A large TV dominated the far wall and a series of small couches surrounded the rest of the room. The TV was showing early morning superhero cartoons. I vaguely remembered watching the same kinds of shows when I was his age. My son was sitting with his back to me, facing the TV, engrossed in the show. I could probably have burst through the door with an explosion behind me and the kid wouldn't have budged an inch. I smiled thinly. I had been the same.

I couldn't see much of my son from this angle, other than the back of his head. He had dark hair like mine. I moved around to one of the couches, careful not to disturb the boy. I slowly sat down, noting that boy still hadn't acknowledged my presence. From this angle I could see more of my son and my breath caught in my chest as I finally saw his face.

There was no doubt about it; in the profile of my son I could clearly see my father's face. The curve of his nose and the weird expression on his face when he was concentrating was the spitting image of my father. I could see Renee in there too: the twisting curl of his lips was his mothers', but the real evidence was in the eyes. He had the Wills' eyes, deep blue irises that seemed like they were made from ice. He had my father's eyes—he had my eyes. He was my son. Not that I had any doubts, but now I knew it to be true. I had expected to see some similarities between myself and the boy, but I hadn't expected to see my father. I curled my hands into fists as I sought to get my emotions back under control. I couldn't afford to break down into tears now.

The sound of laser gun fire from the TV rose to a crescendo. The heroes appeared to be involved in a massive fire fight with an overwhelming army of aliens.

"They'll all survive you know," my son commented to me. "They always do."

He seemed disappointed by this fact. He wasn't

expecting an answer from me, merely informing me of the story. He'd obviously seen this before—the TV was hooked up to a DVD player. This made sense; I doubted that any of the major television networks were still active, even this far from the war.

"I'm Ethan Wills," my son continued, never taking his eyes from the TV. "What's your name?"

My heart caught in my throat again; I hadn't expected he would have my surname. I also didn't know how to respond to his question. Should I lie, should I tell the truth? I had no idea. Before I could respond, the boy had moved onto a different question.

"Have you seen this show?" Ethan continued. "It's not very good, but it's my favourite. We can watch something else though, if you want."

He gestured towards a pile of DVDs stacked up next to the TV. All the while his eyes never left the TV. The fire fight was almost over and Ethan had been right—it looked like the heroes would all survive.

"I think I've seen this before," I murmured. "But we can watch whatever you want."

Ethan finally took his first look at me. It took everything I had not to flinch as his small features turned their gaze upon me. He inspected me for a few seconds before an explosion happened on the TV, drawing his attention back to the screen.

"Are you an army man?" he asked curiously, noting my uniform.

"Not anymore," I replied, trying to keep my tone light.

"You're wearing the costume," he accused.

"I used to be," I amended quickly. The boy didn't miss a beat.

"Oh?" Ethan murmured as if this was only mildly interesting. "Did you fight in any battles?"

"Yes," I whispered, hoping like hell he would change the topic.

"Is it like it is on TV?" He gestured towards the screen.

"No," I murmured.

"I didn't think so." Ethan smiled to himself as if he'd just figured out something very clever.

"What's your name anyway?" Ethan asked suddenly. "You never answered before."

"Devon," I murmured. "My name is Devon."

This seemed to stop the boy in his tracks. He turned from the TV to stare at me, his small face twisted as I could see the suspicion forming in his mind. I immediately cursed myself. Why had I given him my real name?

"My daddy's name was Devon too," Ethan began. "But he's dead. He died in the war."

"I know," I gasped. Those two words were all that I could force from my lips. Every fibre of my being wanted me to proclaim myself as the kid's father. I wanted it so much it hurt. It hurt more than anything else I'd ever experienced, but it wasn't about me. What would it do to this kid if his father returned, only to run off again? It could destroy him, and I wasn't going to risk that.

"Oh?" Ethan smiled sadly. "Did you know him?"

"I knew of him," I lied quickly.

"What was he like?" Ethan paused the TV. "Mummy said that he was a great man."

Did she now? I knew that Renee would be listening in on this conversation from behind the door. I could almost make out her shadow through the gap between the door and the floor. She remained silent, but I could tell that she was there.

"He was," I began, "and he loved your mummy very much. I think he would have very much liked to have met you."

"I wish I could have met him too." Ethan mused. "Mum talks about him sometimes."

"Does she? What does she say?"

"Just that I'm a lot like him," Ethan explained. "Though she usually only says that when I've been naughty."

I smiled as I imagined the boy's childhood. It didn't seem so bad; he looked almost normal and that wouldn't have been easy to achieve during these times. It wouldn't have been easy on Renee to raise a kid during a war. It wouldn't have been easy to keep him safe from the war raging around them, yet somehow she had done it.

"How did he die?" Ethan's small voice cut into my reverie.

"He went to war." I sighed. I didn't know what else to say. In way I had died.

"Oh."

"Yeah," I agreed as I rose to my feet. I wanted to

spend all day with the kid, watching stupid cartoons, but I knew that if I did I would come clean and that wasn't right. The boy deserved the illusion of a loving father who had died during the war, not the truth. I needed time alone to think, to reassess my plans. For the first time in my life I began to make plans, not around what I wanted, but what would be best for another. It had been a long time since I had thought this way.

"Are you going?" Ethan said. "We could put on a different video."

"Yeah, I've got to go Kiddo," I murmured, "but I'll be back."

"Oh, okay." Ethan smiled. "I'll be here."

"Sure." I smiled.

"Devon? You knew my father right?" Ethan called out as I moved to go. "Am I like my father?"

I tousled his hair as I moved to the door. "You are what is best of him. You remind me of him a lot. He'd be proud of you I'm sure."

"That can't have been easy," Renee murmured softly as I closed the door. "He's only just started asking about his father."

"He's a good kid," I replied for want for anything better to say.

"He's like his dad," Renee said with a twisted smile. "He drives me crazy at times."

"And no sign of the Mana?"

Renee shook her head. "No, and I had definitely manifested by his age."

"I didn't manifest until I was eighteen," I reminded her.

"Yes, but you weren't surrounded by mages," Renee retorted with a smile. "It wasn't until you met me. You should have manifested long before you did. You were a time bomb waiting to happen."

"Yeah," I replied with a grin. "I've often wondered about that. Are you saying that you sparked me?"

"Who knows?" Renee replied. "Not intentionally anyway, but what's to say that we didn't meet on a tram in Melbourne all those years ago, before that night in the nightclub, and that I didn't rub off on you?"

"Makes as much sense as anything else," I agreed, not particularly liking our detour down memory lane.

"What are you going to do now?" Renee whispered. She had sensed the change in my mood.

"I don't know," I said softly. "This changes everything."

"Kids have a way of doing that," Renee replied dryly.

"You're sure he won't manifest?"

"No way to know for certain," Renee shrugged, "but it's not uncommon for mages to produce non-mage kids."

"Uncommon?" I prompted. The Mana was passed down through bloodlines. I knew as well as Renee did that it was incredibly unusual to find mages who didn't have mages for parents. My own father had the potential to become a mage, but had burnt out during childhood and never manifested the power. Maybe Ethan would be the same.

"It's been known to happen," Renee amended.

And that was the crux of it. Was I prepared to bet my son's life on that gamble? Ethan was the progeny of three of the most powerful mage families known. It was probably arrogance to include my own family within that list, but both my sister and I had become powerful enough to challenge the old masters. Ethan's grandfather was Marcus Devereaux, son of the Primea, and his great grandfather was Victor Whittlesea. No, this boy could not possibly be anything but a mage. I knew it. I knew it with every fibre of my being. It was inevitable. But we still had time, the boy hadn't manifested. Victor would have no interest Ethan until he did. We still had time. I could wait. For the sake of my son, I would wait.

I didn't have to wait long.

*　*　*

Seven hours and forty-three minutes. It wasn't fair how little time I had had, but I deserved no less. It's funny how things work out. I had made the decision to stay with Renee and Ethan, to help them as best I could until the time came, but I thought I might have years. I certainly hadn't expected it to happen the second night I was there. I hadn't told Renee of my plans. I hadn't even really formulated them myself. We had just begun dinner. It had again been a small meal of vegetables from the garden. Perhaps meat was hard to come by.

"Do you grow all this yourself?" I murmured, before placing a piece of broccoli into my mouth.

Renee nodded. "We grow all our own food. There is farmland for miles in each direction."

"Do you often eat out here?" I continued. I knew that I was asking stupid questions, but I was desperate to keep talking.

"Normally we eat as a family." Renee smiled. "But tonight, for some strange reason, everyone else has found something else to do."

"Strange," I commented.

"Isn't it?" Renee agreed.

"Renee …" I began, but she cut me off.

"Don't," Renee snapped.

I stopped in my tracks. For a single second we stared at each other and our defences were down. I could see through her anger, through her pride, and I could see the woman I remembered—the woman who had loved me. I was sure she could see past my shields. She could see the things I had done. They must have been reflected in my eyes. She must have seen the evil I had become. And yet, as I looked at her, I could see that it didn't matter. She knew me, she didn't care what I had done. She loved me anyway. She still damned loved me.

"Say whatever it is you were going to say," Renee finished lamely.

"I was going to say thank you," I murmured softly.

I don't think she had expected that. Her eyes flashed, and in a second her defences were back in place. I could see nothing through the stone wall that she had erected across her face.

"Do you think …" I began.

"No," Renee stated. I hadn't managed to get out what I had been going to say, but I didn't need to. Renee had never needed me to say what I was thinking. She had always known.

"I don't think it could have worked out any differently," Renee whispered sadly. "As much as I once thought it could have."

"No," I agreed. "I was too young and too obsessed with my own power to listen to anything anyone said. Had you told me you were going to have my child, I probably still would have left. I would have promised to return, but we both know how empty a promise that would turn out to be."

"I should have gone with you," Renee murmured. "But I was angry and you seemed determined to kill yourself."

"I was," I muttered. The truth of it seemed plain to me now. There was no denying it. "You were right. Had you come with me, you would have been swept up in this, and our son …" I couldn't finish that thought.

We stopped and stared in silence at each other for the next few minutes, but it wasn't the same. Our walls were up. Nothing was getting through. I desperately wanted to lower my walls, but I couldn't. I didn't know how.

"Do you still love me?" Renee whispered. With those five words she found a way to break through my defences. She shattered them. Before I could answer, Renee continued. "I hated you. I hated you for so long. I hated you for being weak, for leaving me, for a hundred reasons. I hated you right up until I saw you talking with our son. You didn't tell him who you were. You did what was best for him."

"It's not about what I want," I murmured. "It's never been about me."

Renee's eyes were hard. "And because it's not about you, you will leave him again. I can see it in your eyes. You're not here for your son. I don't know why you're here. The war has brought you here and the war will take you again. Don't you understand? It's always been about you. You and your decisions. It's never not been about you."

"What kind of father could I be?" I said, discarding my previous plans of staying in that moment.

"His." Renee's words were cold.

She was right, of course she was right, and unfortunately I never got to reply. I never got to tell Renee how much I longed to stay with her and my son.

"Renee, come quick!" May burst onto the balcony. Mana flared in both Renee and me as if preparing for an attack. At first I had assumed it was an attack, as May was responsible for the defence of the estate—but it was worse than that. May led us back into the house and towards one of the bedrooms. She flung open the door to a child's bedroom. Renee pushed past me to go to her son, who was thrashing under his covers.

"He's got a fever," May gasped. "And ..."

She let that sentence go unsaid. Upon the boy's chest

were small particles of Mana. It had begun. The boy was wracked with feverish spasms and his sheets had almost been pushed onto the floor. Renee wiped sweat from the boy's forehead and tried to keep his spasms from sending him falling from the bed.

"Renee, we can't be here," I murmured, but she ignored me.

The particles were forming in the centre of his chest and slowly moving outwards. They were faint but clearly visible. It was a testament to Ethan's future power that the particles could be seen so clearly so early in the process. Judging by the way the Mana was forming, he was going to be powerful indeed. I wasn't sure if this was a good thing or not.

Renee was desperately trying to follow the path of the Mana on the boy's chest almost as if she thought she could eradicate the process before it began. She wouldn't be able to stop it without causing Ethan harm. She murmured the words "No, no, no, no" like a mantra as a new particle formed. I doubted she was thinking rationally right now. She knew as I did that her grandfather would now take an interest in our son.

"Renee!" I snapped. "We must leave. It's dangerous!"

"I know!" Renee snarled as she tore herself away from her son. "Don't you think I know that?"

While he was in this state, any exposure to Mana could possibly be fatal for the boy. When my sister had manifested, I hadn't known what was happening and I remained close. It had almost killed her; it was only when she was taken to hospital and I had been unable to tend her that she recovered. I hadn't known any of this at the time of course, but I wasn't going to make the same mistake with my son.

"We will need a nurse," May whispered from the doorway. "Someone who can care for him while he's feverish."

"Where's the closest hospital?"

"There's a medical facility in town …" May began, but she didn't have time to finish her sentence—I'd already teleported out.

It didn't take me long to find the hospital, although the word "hospital" was pushing the term. I teleported into the alley at the side of the building and made my way around to the main entrance. It wasn't a large building, but it had the Red Cross sign displayed on the front door. It would have to do. I burst through the doors and into the foyer in fury, the door almost exploding with force as I passed into the waiting room.

"I need a doctor!" I snarled at the confused-looking receptionist and several other support staff. At first I wasn't sure they could understand me until the receptionist pulled out a pistol from under the counter. She wasn't pointing it directly at me, but her message was clear.

"No, no doctors here, no drugs either. You go away. There is nothing for you here."

"Nurse then!" I demanded. "Is there a nurse, someone skilled with medicine?"

"Mage!" one of the other support staff screamed as they finally noticed my eyes.

This seemed to have a drastic effect on the receptionist, who immediately dropped the gun. She was smart. In fact, the more I looked at her, the more I suspected she wasn't just the receptionist. She was wearing scrubs, but then so was everyone there. The difference was her scrubs were dirty. There was blood on them.

"You're a nurse?" I guessed.

"You have injuries?" Her accent was strange, but her English was understandable.

"No," I grunted. "You will come with me."

"I will not," she replied forcefully.

"You will," I stated, "or I will kill everyone here."

Her eyes widened in shock. She glanced quickly at my face to determine if I was telling the truth. It must have only been several seconds before she answered me, but it felt like eons.

"No, I will not go with you," she repeated, staring me down. She was now holding the gun under the counter.

"It's my son," I begged. "He's sick. You were right, I won't hurt anyone, but I need your help."

"Bring him here." Her gaze was iron.

"No," I snapped. "It's not safe! You need to come with me. I promise I will return you unharmed. I promise!"

It was a strange reversal of situation. I had come in here full of fire and fury, and now I was literally begging this woman to help me.

"Boy is injured?"

I shook my head. "Fever, sickness."

I didn't know how to explain Mana sickness to her, but I knew that if something wasn't done about the fever, his life would be in danger. We needed someone who wasn't a mage to tend him while he was sick. Once the fever broke it would be safe for us to be in his presence again. It was only for the next twenty-four, maybe forty-eight hours that we needed her.

"I will get my bag," she eventually conceded. "But you will pay."

"Lady, if my son survives, money is no object."

I didn't say what would happen if he died, but I could tell from the steely gaze in her eyes that she was well aware of what was going through my head. She disappeared for several seconds before returning with a small black carry bag. She headed for the door and I followed quickly. It was when we got to the car park that I realised my next problem.

My original plan was to immediately teleport her back to the estate; unfortunately that wouldn't be any good. If I teleported the woman, she would most likely arrive nauseated and in no condition to help my son. Any magical transport option this side of a rift was going to result in the nurse being unable to do her job, and I wasn't going to risk a rift for this. No, this would have to be handled the old-fashioned way.

"Do you have a car?" I asked, cursing my own stupidity. I should have foreseen this, but I had rushed in without thinking.

The nurse looked at me like I was crazy, but eventually nodded towards the rear of the building where there were several cars. She headed towards a small, soft-top Jeep and hopped into the driver's seat. This led me to my next problem: I had no idea where the estate was in relation to the surgery by road. There's a big difference between a scry vision and the street directory.

"What's your name?" I called over to her. It was difficult to talk with the wind rushing between us through tears in the vinyl canvas.

"Carla," she yelled back, as we tore out of the car park and onto the road. It only took us several minutes before we were on the main highway out of the settlement.

"Thank you, Carla," I yelled over the howling wind— now that we were on the highway the noise was almost overwhelming.

"I do not do this for you." It was strange the way her voice cut through the noise from the road.

"I know, but thank you all the same." I smiled as I launched a scry thread in an attempt to locate the estate.

Launching the scry thread straight up into the air allowed me to get a bird's eye view of the highway and surrounding lands. It looked completely unfamiliar in the dark, but eventually I found a few landmarks I recognised and directed Carla towards them.

The drive took the best part of an hour, and I was beside myself with worry with each second that passed. May was waiting for us in the driveway as we made our way up to the front door. She ushered us inside with a minimum of greeting and directed Carla towards Ethan's bedroom.

"Where is Renee?" I hissed as the nurse rushed to my son.

"She's outside."

"Give her whatever she needs," I ordered, gesturing towards Carla as I headed for the door.

"Where are you going?"

"To stop Renee from doing something stupid," I called back.

Renee was standing out on the second-storey balcony looking at the sky. She had her back to me and seemed totally engrossed in the view.

"He'll know," Renee murmured as I emerged from the doorway behind her. "I don't know how, but he'll know and he'll come for him."

I nodded silently.

"I can fight him," Renee hissed. "I can stop him."

"Getting yourself killed won't help our son."

"He won't kill me!" Renee snarled back. "He can't bring himself to do it!"

"No, maybe not," I reflected, "but you won't be able to defeat him and won't accomplish anything."

"I need to do something!" Renee said. "I can't just wait."

"He won't come here," I murmured as I wrapped my arms around her. "Not while I'm here."

I hoped to God that this was true, but I had no way of knowing for sure. This was an unusual situation. I'd never been in a position where Victor was scared, and that made him more dangerous than ever in some ways, but more predicable in others. No, I doubted he would come for the boy while I was present. He would have to deal with me first. Winner takes all.

"Why are you so special?" Renee hissed as she pulled back from me. "Why does he fear you?"

"Because I know how to kill him," I said, letting her slip from my arms. "I almost did kill him."

Renee stared at me in disbelief. "He can't be killed, Marcus proved that."

"I don't know what Marcus had planned," I cut her off. "He never got a chance to complete his plans when I killed him."

"You killed him?" Renee whispered darkly.

"You didn't know?"

Renee shook her head as the news sunk in that I was responsible for her father's death. "Why?"

"He was responsible for my sister's death," I said.

Renee was operating under no illusions; she knew who her father was and what he was capable of. She had known just how unscrupulous he could be. He had used me for his own ends in his fight with Victor. Renee knew just what kind of man her father had been.

"I mean, I knew he was dead," Renee murmured. "I just assumed that Victor had done it."

"No," I said sadly. "I killed him, and then in my anger, in my stupidity, I thought I could take on Victor. I thought I could end it all in one fell swoop. I was wrong. Victor broke me and left me for dead, but he couldn't kill me. I was stronger than that. I waited. I planned for this day and nothing will stand in my way. I have to be the one to stand against him."

"He'll kill you," Renee whispered.

"Maybe," I nodded, "but there is no one else."

"Why does it have to be you?" Renee murmured as she threw herself back into my arms. "I don't think I could bear to lose you again."

I held this woman in my arms as if the very act of holding her could change the fates, but she knew as I did that there was no escaping this. I would have to face Victor again, I knew it, and as much as Renee might rail against it, she knew it too.

"Renee," I whispered. "Where is Victor hiding?"

"Melbourne," she replied. "He's hiding in Melbourne."

Of course it was Melbourne; how could it have been anywhere else but Melbourne? Victor had assumed he had killed me. He hadn't known that Levenson had pulled my wrecked body from the ruins of Melbourne. Melbourne was far enough away from the fighting that it would be unlikely he would be disturbed. He had used Melbourne for such a purpose in the past; he had originally chosen Melbourne to hide Renee from others of our kind.

It made perfect sense that he would hide from me in Melbourne. It had been destroyed in the fight between Marcus and Victor; it had been the place where my sister had died and where I had been broken. I had no desire to return home. But I was going to.

I held Renee tighter as I worked my way up to saying goodbye for the last time. My chances of beating Victor were by no means in my favour, and it was incredibly unlikely that I would return.

"Devon," Renee murmured into my shoulder. "Goodbye."

"I love you," I whispered back. "I've always loved you."

Renee didn't reply. With a final kiss on her forehead I turned to leave. She didn't watch me go, her eyes were firmly placed on a small door that led into our son's bedroom. I would have liked to have said goodbye to my son as well, but due to the Mana fever I couldn't be near him. I said a soft goodbye from his doorway, which was as close as I dared before retreating.

* * *

I stood on the edge of the estate, trying to gain the courage to leave. It was harder than I had thought it would be. The magic within me just didn't seem to want to leave my son.

"You're going then?" a voice from behind me cut in.

"Yes," I said without looking around. May's voice was easily recognisable.

"Good," May murmured with satisfaction. "Because I'm going with you."

"I've just had the same argument with Renee," I said firmly. "Must I have it with you too?"

"No," May replied. "No argument; if you go alone you will die. We are amongst the most powerful mages left amongst our kind, if not the only two who could claim the title master. Everyone else are just apprentices or learners."

"No," I repeated once again.

"You don't have a say in the matter," May replied forcefully with a smile. "I am going with you."

I sighed inwardly. "Why?"

"Because I want revenge," May whispered, "and I doubt I will ever get a better chance."

At least she was honest.

"You might not return," I said, hoping to dissuade her.

"I've come to terms with that." May sighed. "There is very little for me here."

I smiled darkly at that. The exact opposite for me was true: there was a whole life here for me. I could almost see it. It was so close I could touch it. I would become a different man here, the man I had meant to be. I would cast off the filth of the Necromancer and even leave the temptations of being a mage behind. Here, I could become what I was always meant to be—a man.

"Come if you must," I grunted bitterly.

We left the estate the same night. I didn't really have time to waste; like Renee, I knew that Victor would somehow be aware that Ethan had gone into Mana fever, so we had a few days before he would come for the boy. I planned to get to Victor first, but before that happened I needed some things.

I turned on the mobile phone Levenson had issued me with and dialled his number. Levenson's grumpy voice answered.

"Aren't you in hiding yet?" I said, smiling down the phone. "I'm surprised you're still there."

Levenson grunted, "What can I do for you?"

Levenson didn't talk while I explained what I needed from him. He knew as well as I did what I was asking for. I needed something that Victor wouldn't expect coming. I needed some assurances.

"Are you sure?" he whispered finally.

"Yes."

CHAPTER TWELVE

It was strange to return to the city of my birth. I had gone to great lengths to avoid going back during the war. There were too many memories here, too much pain. My city hadn't fared well in my absence; it had become little more than abandoned ruins, controlled by roving bands of thugs and people looking simply to survive. Melbourne had had six years to recover from the battle Marcus had launched in an attempt to take down his former master, but it seemed any attempt to repair the damage or take control of the city had been repelled. It didn't take much guesswork to determine by whom. Victor would value his privacy.

The moment that May and I teleported within sight of the city, I felt my former master's presence. I didn't teleport directly into the city—I wasn't ready for that yet. I needed to see my home for one last time before I did battle in it, plus it would be too dangerous to teleport directly into the battle zone. I teleported to the Dandenong ranges, where there was a lookout spot that gave a beautiful panoramic view of the city. I had been there as a boy on several occasions; seeing it as an adult was a vastly different experience. As a child everything seemed so large—now it all looked so small. I had seen too much of the world. I had travelled too far. The world was far larger than my small piece of it. My home looked small and insignificant, but it wasn't. Well, it wasn't to me. It was my home and I had lost it. It was time to take back my home from my former master.

I glanced across the suburbs that I had grown up in and I thought about my childhood friends and wondered if they were okay. I could have visited them, but there would be time for that afterwards. I had ensured that they had gotten out of Melbourne before the real war had started, though I had done so through agents rather than directly. My mother and friends were now securely tucked away in Omeo, with my sister's parents. It was remote enough and far enough away from the war that they would be safe. Early in the war I had scryed on them from time to time, but it quickly became too painful. I never once thought to visit them, better to let them think that I was dead. It would be a kindness. I wondered if I would get the chance after all this to return to them, to let them know that I was still alive. I didn't think so, the boy they had known was gone, and I doubted that the man that I had become would bring them any comfort. No, they were safe and that was enough for me.

"Why are we here?" May grunted as she looked out across my home.

"Because Victor will not be alone," I murmured softly. "He has collected others—he will send them against us first."

"How do you know?"

"Because he is scared."

May looked at me like I was crazy, and I didn't blame her. I was having trouble coming to terms with the concept as well, but I could feel it. I knew my former master because in many ways I had become just like him. Victor was terrified. I wasn't going to underestimate him.

"Are you ready?" I whispered softly.

May nodded in agreement.

"Good," I replied softly, "because I'm not."

I didn't teleport directly into the city. It was still too risky for that. Instead May and I flew across the suburbs, heading towards the city with all the speed that two master mages could attain. The landscape below us blurred into a haze as we passed over it. I didn't look at my home as I sailed across it save for the scant moments it took to determine where my next Mana thread was going to latch to propel me forward. We travelled as spiders across a web would travel, thread after thread pushing us forward as we crossed suburbs in mere seconds.

It didn't take long to get to the city proper where, as I had expected, Victor had prepared a suitable welcome for us. We could see them long before we got there— they had been waiting for us and had been for some time. Three distinct Mana signatures were standing on top of a toppled building, and I saw numerous soldiers on the ground waiting for us.

Victor had known we were coming. It confirmed that he was aware my son had become a mage and he had taken suitable action against just this event. Against my better judgment, I continued. I should have turned back, I should have tried another angle, but time was running out. Should I delay, Victor would slip through my fingers.

The sky seemed to open up with fire as the soldiers on the ground began shooting at us. I watched with amusement as the heavy cannon ordinance exploded around us and bullets whizzed past. They couldn't harm us, but they weren't the threat. There was no more than a passing interestd as two of the mages launched themselves into the air in an attempt to intercept us. They seemed determined to keep us out of the city. The third mage remained behind; perhaps he was supposed to stop us if we got past the first two.

"They're only apprentices!" May called with glee as she narrowed into an attack path. I could only hope she was right, but something didn't feel right here. The threads that the two mages had executed were well formed, but they weren't very powerful. Victor had done his best, but the apprentices weren't anywhere near as powerful as we were. That might have explained the lightshow of military fireworks. It was a distraction that would allow his apprentices to get the better of us. If that was the plan, it was a poor one.

I gestured towards May as I selected my target. She nodded and eagerly swooped in to deal with the other. I lost sight of them in a haze of gunfire and smoke, but knew May was far more powerful than her opponent.

The end result of this skirmish was all but assured.

I waited until my own target was almost on me before I let the thread holding me in place fall and I dropped to the ground like a rock. I could see the shock on his face as I disappeared beneath him and he soared uselessly over me. He had forgotten one of Victor's most prized tenets: true strength only comes when your feet are firmly on the ground. It took him several seconds to gain control of his momentum and he swung around in fury and launched himself at me, barrelling down in triumph—he thought he had an easy victory. I waited until mere seconds before his thread was to collide with my shield before I let out a primal blast of telekinetic power. It wasn't well formed, but it was powerful. The blast radiated out from me in all directions, destroying the road and sweeping his pitiful thread away as if it were nothing more than a child's toy. It took several more seconds before the shockwave hit him directly with the fury of a hurricane, and by then of course it was too late.

He survived the initial blast, but the impact had knocked him off his path and sent him flying off course. His shield had protected him from the blast, but it didn't protect him from what came next. I sent out a Mana Nova thread that easily sliced through his shield and ended the poor man's life. As his body landed in two pieces beside me, I corrected myself—poor boy's life. My enemy looked like only about seventeen or eighteen. If he had been a member of Victor's new order of mages, then he had paid the full price for his membership.

I launched back into the air and took a contemptuous swipe at the soldiers on the ground, sending several cannons barrelling into the soldiers below as they were telekinetically torn apart. I could hear the shouts and screams from the soldiers below as their own ordinance was turned against them.

I pondered my next move. This was too easy, not what I had expected at all. Had I truly expended Victor's resources? Was this really the best defence he could muster after all this time? I didn't think so. I watched with satisfaction as May easily dispatched her foe, crushing him and sending him falling into the Yarra River.

A mounted machine-gun on the top of Flinders Street Station opened up and sent a stream of bullets flying at me and with a flick of my wrist I tore the machine-gun from its place and sent it tumbling down into the street below. It seemed like a sacrilege that they should be standing on that exact spot. I had once stood on that rooftop when I first sought out Renee to teach me the magic—I had set off an awareness blast that had rocketed through the city. It seemed like so long ago now, it seemed like a lifetime. I took my time and removed every solder from that rooftop.

I could see the third and last remaining mage lurking within the boundaries of the city proper as he contemplated how to repel us. Even from here I could see the worry on his face; he had been told they would be able to defeat us, he had been told that the soldiers below would distract us enough so his friends could dispatch us. He had been told he was special and that the training Victor had given him would allow him to overcome us. He had been lied to; he had been nothing more than a distraction. No, it was worse than that. He and his friends had been a trap. There was no other reason for this.

I immediately pulled back and shouted as May swooped in to finish him off. I don't know if she heard me or not, but she tore the poor mage from the building he had been standing on and shredded through his shield in seconds. She landed on the rooftop next to him and it was obvious that he was completely outclassed. This fight could only end in one way and I wasn't surprised when our opponent fell to the ground. Then the trap closed.

* * *

Time seemed to slow down as May rose from the rooftop in triumph. Two dozen or so Mana Nova threads were unexpectedly launched from the tops of the buildings surrounding her. I gasped in surprise as dozens of Mana signatures surged into life as the threads took flight. How the hell had he hidden so many mages? Where had he even found them all? Had he covered the whole city in an illusion to hide them? Then I realised, it all made sense. They weren't mages. They were drones. That was why I hadn't noticed them earlier—they had been inactive. It was similar to what he had done in Poland. Victor was using drones to send his own powers out into the city, except he was doing it on a far greater scale. He had created an army of drones to destroy us. I gulped as the realisation overtook me; with that amount of firepower he could very well achieve my death long before I had the opportunity to get close enough to return fire.

May saw her danger as quickly as I did and launched into the air in an attempt to escape it. I watched in futility as two or three dozen threads took off after her. The building she had been standing upon was shredded as a dozen threads gouged out a large chunk of rooftop as they sought to finish her. Three, four, then a dozen more lines of Mana Nova threads chased her down. It was almost beautiful to behold as the deadly lines wove their way through the cityscape seeking their enemy. I would have appreciated their beauty a lot more if they didn't spell instant death to anything that touched them.

I sprang into action and immediately turned several of the drones into a fine red mist as I leapt into the fray, but it was too late. There were simply too many threads and it wasn't possible to keep track of them all. I quickly lost sight of May as she used the buildings to provide cover, but she was out of options and they'd inevitably block her in. Her only recourse would be to propel herself upwards with the force of a tornado, and once that happened her remaining cover would be gone. I wouldn't have wanted to make that decision, but I saw with despair that she had to make that exact choice. She launched upwards to the sky like a rocket and I watched in impotence as a dozen or more threads followed her up. It was like they were caught in the wake of her passing, but they were in fact gaining on her. Every second closing the gap between them, and to make matters worse, May was slowing down.

I'd taken out about a dozen of the drones, but the number of threads chasing May didn't seem to decrease any. I watched with satisfaction as the thread they were controlling fizzled and faded, but there were still too many, and unfortunately, as the number of threads decreased the control that the others seemed to gain increased. At first the Mana Nova threads had appeared clunky and uncoordinated, often causing as much damage to their surroundings as their intended target, but as their numbers dwindled they were becoming more controlled and more accurate.

Each of the drones was being controlled by Victor himself, and as the vessel was destroyed he would be able to allocate his attention towards a lesser number of threads. It was an impressive display of might. Victor had once told me that true power doesn't come from sheer strength, but from control. He was wrong: it came from the application of both. He had proved that point today.

It was kind of beautiful seeing the threads swirling into a tight column as they pursued May further into the night sky. They twisted along an axis as they gained speed towards their diminutive target. I struggled to get to her in time, but I didn't see May's last moments. I couldn't see her through the mass of Mana threads that brought about her doom, but I could hear them. A large explosion took her life as the threads collapsed into a sphere of Mana-powered pyrotechnics that trapped her inside. The resulting conflagration of power tore across the Melbourne skyline, indicating that May was gone.

The light of the explosion flared out in all directions, and for a few seconds it was if a new star had been born. The explosion's light illuminating the twilight sky made it seem like midday. May wouldn't have suffered; she would have been destroyed almost instantly. There was no way her shield would have even slowed their passage as they converged upon her. She would have been disintegrated in seconds as the Mana Nova consumed her flesh. It would have been painless. I could only hope for the same when my turn came.

I didn't have much time to mourn the loss of my companion, as the threads turned upon me in fury as the drones selected their new target. I wondered briefly why Victor hadn't send threads after me initially and had instead relentlessly pursued May. Had he chosen to deal with us one at a time? Was he unable to divide his attention any further? It made a strange sense, but something wasn't right. I had made more than a nuisance of myself in dispatching a dozen or so of his vessels while his focus had been on May. He should have easily been able to use some of his power to at least slow me down.

Then I realised why he hadn't been able to do that; although there were numerous threads they were being centrally controlled by Victor. He had split his mind into several dozen undead vessels, but he was still only one person acting in concert. It was like when we learn to form a shield thread; instinctively we try to focus on each individual threads. But that's impossible—we simply can't focus on that many separate elements. Instead, we form a pattern of threads and in the act of the pattern the field is formed. Victor wasn't controlling each vessel individually, he was controlling them as one would a mindless automation: each operating from a single set of instructions. That changed things immensely; it meant that each thread couldn't make its own decisions in my pursuit, but followed the same set of orders as each other. Understanding how Victor had done this didn't lessen the impressiveness of the act, though it did perhaps give me a glimpse as to how I might survive this.

I had just destroyed another vessel when I saw a wave of threads tearing through the street, consuming everything in their path. With a grim smile, I threw myself into the air and my Mana threads tore gouges into the skyscraper walls surrounding me as I made good my escape. If I sought to escape in the same way May had, my fate would be the same. But I couldn't think of a better solution. It was difficult to think with two dozen threads actively chasing after me.

I glanced behind me as the surging multitude of threads pursued me down the street. I somehow needed to follow them back to their source, but I knew that should I attempt to turn and change direction, my speed would fail and they would take me. I needed to go faster, but I'd pretty much already used most of my strength to keep me going at this speed. It was a simply matter of physics—I wasn't as fast the Mana threads. They weren't as good at manoeuvring as I was though, and I used that to my advantage. If I avoided travelling in straight lines, they couldn't attain their full speed. I used the city like a playground, playing the world's most dangerous game of hide and go seek, but I knew it would end in the same way as it had for May. It was inevitable. There were simply too many.

I rounded a corner, my magic tearing chunks off a corner of the building and sending them tumbling down into the city below. A dozen or more threads rounded the corner, impacting the sides of the buildings and letting their power burn through glass, concrete and stone.

I pulled myself round into a tight arc, throwing myself into the next block as the threads pursued me. I tore through the city with a dozen or more threads in close pursuit and rounded the corner without attempting to slow down. My thread tore loose from its connection as the stone wall I had latched on to collapsed into rubble. I careened down the street sideways and would have hit the ground had I not pulled myself into a around, literally throwing myself into the next block and gaining control again, only seconds before the pursing threads would have had me. I tore through the ruined city like a tornado being chased by a hurricane that was powered by a volcanic blast, but it still wasn't enough. In an attempt to elude my prey, I even strengthened my shield and threw myself directly through the centre of a building, tearing through the office block as if it were made of paper and emerging on the other side unharmed. This trick bought me nothing more than a few minutes, but it did reveal two more drones standing on the building tops on the other side. Small lines of power arched from their outstretched hands as they added their power to the Mana Nova threads trailing behind me. My earlier guess had proved correct: had they the power of independent thought, they could have easily altered the angle of their threads and finished me. Instead they made no attempt to change the direction of their attack. I only had a few seconds of sight before I was off, but that was enough. They were unshielded drones. Victor hadn't worried about protecting them. I sent two volleys of flame in their direction as I passed by, narrowly ducking under their Mana Nova threads, and that was enough. I watched with satisfaction as several of the threads pursuing me fizzled and failed.

I didn't have time to congratulate myself though; there were still at least a dozen more pursuing me. I tore past the burning bodies of the drones as I worked my way deeper into the city. Perhaps I could use that trick of throwing myself through the building again to buy myself more time. If I could figure out where the drones were standing, I could find a better position from which to strike at them, but that would mean leaving the safety of the city. The knowledge of where my enemy was a luxury I couldn't afford.

I barely recognised most the city as I flew through it; a building or street triggered my memory and gave me a brief idea of where I was, but the ruined city was so different than the one I had known as a child. I saw faces briefly as I passed across the streets—there were still people here, but they had wisely decided to stay out of this. They looked like they had their own problems, with the soldiers from the river pulling back into the city in pursuit of me. The original occupants of the city were rioting and turning on the soldiers.

The distraction of the battle below had almost proved my undoing, as the threads arched out from a city corner and blocked my escape. If I continued in that same direction, I'd barrel straight into a mess of three or four threads. In desperation I glanced around the city, seeking an escape, but there was none. Like May, I vaguely contemplated going up, but then I realised where I was. Up wasn't the only option I had. I braced myself as I looped a thread around a street lamp and curled into a tight spin. I barrelled straight down and into a flight of stairs positioned in a nearby footpath.

The stairs led into the underground shopping district of Melbourne Central. Had I not been shielded, my descent through the stairwell would have killed me—I didn't exactly descend gracefully. I fell down the flight of stairs like a rag doll, emerging battered and bruised but intact on the other side. It was pitch black, but I could see a dim light ahead.

Unfortunately my lighting problems resolved itself

as several Mana Nova threads sailed down the stairwell after me, casting an eldritch glow across the walls and abandoned storefronts of the centre. With a new source of light I was now able to recognise where I was. Launching into the air again, I tore through the small corridor into the shopping centre main lobby and glanced up at the cone-shaped ceiling. I watched with dismay as threads smashed through the windows as they sought me out. I launched down into the levels below, hearing the familiar sizzle of the threads behind me. They sounded so very close now, and there were just too many obstructions in the complex for me to get my speed up. It wasn't a problem for the threads as they would simply tear through any obstruction without a loss of momentum, but every time I bounced off a cart or shop sign I slowed down.

With a small grin, I sent a disrupt pulse arching down the corridor. I made the pulse wide enough to encompass the whole corridor and there was nowhere for the threads to go. I watched with glee as the disrupt thread did its work and the Mana Nova thread immediately failed and fizzled to nothing. This caused an unexpected problem as they had been the only source of light in this cramped corridor. I emerged only seconds later into a side street and out into the city again. New threads were on me in moments and I pushed deeper into the city to elude my eventual death. Disrupting the threads had been a neat trick, but until I could deal with the drones, they would simply create new threads.

Most of the city was an unrecognisable mess, but the familiar sight of Flinders Street Station meant I was running out of city, and that meant danger. I tore across Flinders Street, passing so low across the ground that dust and garbage was picked up in my passing and thrown down the street, only to be consumed by the Mana powered death that followed me. I raced down Elizabeth Street and passed the apartment block that had once been my father's home. I didn't have time to meander in memory, but the sight of it as it was now tore through my heart. I didn't have any time to experience my melancholy, though, as a string of threads had emerged from ahead. I immediately ripped a chunk of marble from a building that had probably stood unmolested for over two hundred years. I pulled myself into a tight arc and threw myself down a side street to emerge in what I thought was a refuge on the other side. I was wrong.

In horror I glanced around and realised that the details of this place were etched in my mind. A tremor rippled through my body and for a second I thought that the Mana sustaining my shield was going to fail. It took everything I had to gain control of myself. I had been here before—I had almost died here.

I was standing in the very same place where Victor had brought the building down upon me. It had to be here. I had known that this place was here, of course. I watched in dismay as the threads arced around both corners of the building as they sought me out. There was no escape. I could maybe punch my way through the building, but that would take too long. I watched as the threads arced out as they prepared to finally hone in on their end target. It wasn't possible to see any kind of emotion in the Mana thread, but they looked almost triumphant as they arced towards me.

I took a deep breath as I accepted my fate. I would die here for a second time. At least this time it would be quick. I would be consumed in a single burst of light and there would be nothing.

Like last time, my thoughts were on those who I had failed: my sister, my father, my lover and my son. Like last time, I apologised for letting them down and failing to protect them. I thought it would be over quickly, but I was wrong. The threads came to embrace me and it seemed like I had all the time in the world.

No! This was not going to be the last time. A strange sense of calm overcame me and I knew in seconds what I needed to do. I had been foolish. I had played the game the way Victor had wanted it to be played, but I was a mage and I had options other than running.

I teleported mere seconds before the threads took out the building. The impact of so many threads at the mid-level of the building tore out the remaining sup-ports and sent the building collapsing in on itself as the floors below could no longer support the weight of the ones above.

No further threads appeared. Victor must have assumed I had been consumed in the blast. He would probably send in a scry thread in a few seconds to assure that the deed was done. I had only gained moments at most, but I was going to make the best use of them.

As a wave of dust and debris passed across my shield, I propelled upwards into the night sky. I watched with satisfaction as little pinpricks of Mana flared up across the cityscape. Victor had realised his mistake. He had just given away the position of his drones. There were only about fourteen left.

I sent several volleys of flame down into the city, as I slowed down. I watched with pleasure as several Mana Nova threads fizzled and failed as their owners were consumed in fire. Only a dozen left. I waited until they were almost on me as my body succumbed to gravity, and then teleported directly down,. Unable to turn at the speed they had been travelling, they were unable to stop me. I travelled across the city as would a vengeful god, tearing each vessel from its post like a rag doll in my grasp. I tore them to pieces until there were only three left. They were starting to respond quicker in the face of their destruction. The last one I destroyed had almost managed to elude me by throwing itself from the building. That manoeuvre hadn't saved it. I had pulled him from his descent and destroyed him, leaving his body to finish its fall. I could almost see the look on Victor's face as he felt his connection to each of his vessels fail and go black. I couldn't imagine what that must have felt like. Dear god, I hoped it hurt.

Without the drones powering the Mana Nova threads, the conflagration of death that had followed me had lessened. Without the sheer number of drones Victor had before, they weren't going to be a threat to the same degree. My guess was confirmed when I saw the remaining drones slowly rise in unison from behind a building as Victor changed tactics.

Each drone was now protected by an impressive shield. I threw myself to the side as three threads arced from the drones and sought me out. They smashed the rooftop where I had been standing. It wasn't Mana Nova, but it was still dangerous. I soon realised why they weren't using Mana Nova; through his connection to the vessels, Victor couldn't exert the same level of control as a normal mage could over his own body. We unconsciously used spatial awareness to know where the shield should finish and the Mana Nova thread should start, otherwise we'd be constantly tearing our own shields to pieces. Victor had no such awareness from wherever he was hiding and thus had to make allowances. I would make these allowances cost him.

I teleported behind one of the drones and sliced through his shield in seconds. Just because they weren't going to use Mana Nova didn't mean that I couldn't. My thread tore through its shield as if it was made of butter and the drone's head fell cleanly from its shoulders. With an arc of my wrist I sent my thread tearing through the centre drone and would have taken out the third had it not suddenly launched a Mana Nova thread of its own to protect itself, destroying its own shield in the process. It all happened so quickly that I surmised Victor must have withdrawn from the middle drone in an attempt to protect the third. It seemed that its body was already falling before I had killed it, and the third drone was reacting with a speed that was almost human.

Almost human, but not quite.

I circled around, keeping a Mana Nova thread between us. The drone's eyes held no emotion as they gazed upon me. I vaguely wondered who they had been. Had they been corpses that Victor had pulled from the street, or had he known them? Reanimation took some time; Victor had been preparing for this for a long time, since he had known I would be coming for him. He had known ever since our battle in Poland?

I instinctively deflected the Mana Nova strike levelled at me. It was child's play; the thing before me was so very, very slow—nowhere near the level of a master mage.

I threw myself at the thing in fury, and it couldn't react anywhere near quickly enough. Its Mana Nova thread tore into the floor and gouged a large chunk of masonry from the rooftop. The impact of me hitting the drone sent us both tumbling down from the rooftop and onto one of the buildings below.

I grasped the thing's face with my fists through two shields and brought my face towards it.

"This won't work, Victor!" I snarled as we fell. "You're going to have to face me. You can't hide behind your minions! You're going to have to come and finish the job yourself!"

The building below us was a car park, I could make out the shapes of three or four cars on its rooftop as we tumbled down towards it. The impact of our bodies hitting the roof caused a large explosion of dust and debris. The concrete beneath us cracked and crumbled, and I felt the shield protecting the thing beneath me fail. A large shelf of concrete broke off as the roof gave way and fell down onto the level below. Two cars fell into the gap created by our landing, the second shrieking as the car alarm went off. The drone's body was probably liquefied inside from the impact, but what would kill a normal human won't necessarily kill a drone. I knew that Victor was still in there.

"You are going to have to face me," I whispered one last time at the drone before I sent a Mana Nova thread through its head to ensure the connection was severed. With a casual flick of my wrist I sent the thread lancing into the car behind me and ending the infernal alarm.

NOW

Victor hasn't responded yet, but a team of soldiers has just stormed onto the roof. I'm going to send them back down the hard way. Victor is grasping at straws. He's now counting on humans to kill me. Foolish. Let him send his soldiers; with every second I am recovering more of my strength for this, my last battle. I am ready.

I reach down and caress the mobile phone in my pocket. It's my ace in the hole, my insurance in case everything goes badly. It's still intact. From my other pocket I withdraw the voice recorder Emily Perry had given me. This seems like the last chance I'll have to use it.

"I'm not sure when I became the villain of my story," I whisper, tearing a soldier from the rooftop and sending him tumbling below. "But I'm now quite certain that this is exactly what I've become."

The sound of gunfire interrupts me as another soldier rushes onto the roof. I sweep the gun from his hand and break his neck. I can hear the fighting below intensifying as more soldiers converge on this position.

A loud explosion rocks the rooftop I'm standing, from a tank shell hitting the side of the building. A cocktail of shrapnel, concrete and dust is raining down on me. I casually reach out and crush the tank into a twisted wreck. Crushing the reinforced steel on the armoured tank doesn't take much effort.

The dying sounds of the downed weapon of war echoes throughout the city. It's a fitting warning to those who might still be in the area—stay away, keep away! Nothing awaits them here but death. The warning had probably come a little too late, in a few minutes it would be too late anyway.

I glance at my watch again and for a second time contemplate turning my phone on. No, it's still too early for that. I bring the voice recorder back to my lips.

"My name is Devon Wills," I whisper, feeling the weight behind the words, "and I am a mage."

I continue pouring my words into this small device, which may not even survive the upcoming battle. I should perhaps send it away to ensure its survival—it will contain my last words and my only reasons for what I have done. Or perhaps it's better to leave it to fate: if it is meant to be found—it will be.

"Understand I don't say these things to defend my actions, nor to extol what virtues I do possess," I murmur. "I did what I did simply because I had no choice and will not try to justify my actions to you. It is not for you to judge me—that is for my peers alone to do and I no longer have peers amongst the likes of you and your kind."

I bite off the last words—the air around me is turning into flame. They used a grenade. I emerge unscathed and finish the foolish soldier who had attempted to thwart my words. They've just paid for their crime—dearly.

My words pour from me like a river as I explain my reasons and my past into the small electronic device. I'm doing everything Emily Perry had begged me to do. I explain why this war happened. I don't shirk my responsibility or attempt to defend my reasons. I take the blame. This future is my fault. All my actions attempting to prevent it have brought me to this single point. I can only hope things aren't too far gone to come back.

A small trail of blood runs across my eyes from a cut on my forehead. I don't remember feeling it happen, but it was probably from when my shield had been weakened as I fell down the stairs in the shopping centre. I ignore the wound and keep talking. I'm not sure who I imagine will recover this device. It's possible I'm not talking to anyone in particular, but screaming my story into the twilight night for only the wind and the gods to hear. I tell the machine everything, every mistake, every hope that was never realised, every failed goal and every depravity I had succumbed to.

"And so we come to the end. It is fitting that my ending takes place where I began," I whisper finally. It's been some time since the last batch of soldiers. Have they finally given up? I caress the phone in my pocket for the fourth time since I began my story. How long have I been up here, talking into this damned box? Ten minutes? Twenty? All I know is that Victor should have come for me by now. He's late.

"Victor!" I call out, using the Mana to amplify my voice. "Come out and finish this. It is time!"

My voice will have been heard across every inch of this city. He will have heard me, but more so, he will have felt the Mana surge across the city. A shockwave caused by my Mana passes over familiar buildings, now smouldering rubble, and across the beloved landmarks of my childhood now falling into ruins.

A loud explosion preceding a teleport spell brings me spinning around to face my old master. He is here. I steady my nerves and grip my fingers into fists. I casually clip the loose battery on my mobile phone into place and close the lid. I flick the phone on, never once taking my eyes from my adversary. The familiar electronic jingle notifies me that it has finished loading. I drop it into the rubble beneath me as I step forward and look at my upcoming death squarely in the eyes. I will not flinch in the face of it, I am ready.

Victor physically looks much different to how he had when I last saw him. He has been using the Mana to sustain him after all. He looks smaller, weaker, somehow diminished. Is it because I'm finally seeing him as he was, rather than the man he has become? Is it only now that I am standing face to face with him on this blasted rooftop that I recognise his humanity?

I turn to face him with a small gesture of welcome. I will obey the courtesies in this. After all, there's no need to be rude. One of us will not be walking away from this confrontation, and I'm still not sure it will be me.

"You have come far, my apprentice," Victor said sadly. "Of all my students, you are the one of whom I am most proud."

"I don't want your admiration," I scoff savagely, but I'm lying. I do want it. I crave it with every word that leaves the man's lips. He's a murderer and a monster and still I crave his respect. I have done everything I can to destroy him and still I want his endorsement. I hate myself right now. I hate myself for wanting it so badly. I won't let such a desire show on my face, but it is clear between us. There can be no lies between us. Not here, not now.

"Victor," I murmur, my voice breaking, "you know what must happen now."

Victor nods as if we are chatting of things far removed from the battlefield. I imagine we are still master and student, and he is explaining some concept of Mana I had somehow missed.

"Your son could have been truly great with my guidance," he murmurs. My heart turns to stone. Victor smiles, I know he sees his words taking their effect across my face. Any humanity left in me has surely dissipated now. Did he say those words on purpose? Victor has known me like no other teacher; he has seen inside my mind and he know what buttons to press. A smile escapes his lips. In this place I will not be manipulated. I will not be coerced. This has happened because I willed it. Everyone who died because of me demanded it. I will not allow his games to distract me.

"Are you ready then?" Victor whispers. "Do you wish to learn your final lesson?"

I grit my teeth and let the power rise within me. Victor has kept his shield powered while speaking. He respects me that much at least. He's not going to underestimate me.

"There is only one problem," the old man continues. "I have no more lessons to give."

"I have a lesson for you," I reply darkly, my voice cracking.

"What lesson is that?" His voice is harsh.

"I'm going to show you how to die!" I state. It's not a threat, I didn't say it in anger. It's a simple promise. a foretelling of things to come.

"Come then," he intones, drawing forth his Mana Nova to defend himself.

In this battle there will be no tricks, no subtle distractions, and no other sources of attack. We have exhausted all such options. We've come to what it was always going to be: two men standing on a rooftop who could not live in the same world as each other any longer.

Victor is no faster than me, and no more powerful. I have finally caught up with him in sheer strength and control. Victor is older and has more experience with Mana, but I'm younger and have more vitality. I also have resources that the old man lacks. Our relative strengths had made us equals. It was possible that I could win this fight on my own merits, but I would no longer allow my arrogance to affect the outcome of this battle. Should he overpower me and take me, my son will suffer for it and that is a price too great for me to pay.

Fighting Victor is hard; he's a foe I have never defeated. I loop a thread around Victor's and send his attack swinging wide. I move in close; Victor doesn't cope when his opponents are too close. But we're in a small car park and there isn't much room. Anyway, Victor thinks that the outcome of this fight isn't going to be determined by space but by power.

Victor is wrong.

I smile as I dart in closer, letting Victor's thread go wide. He raises his arm in fury as I spin towards him, almost colliding with him. His shield immediately strengthens, but he needn't worry. My thread dissolves as I ready my powers for another, more insidious purpose. He could bring his thread back at any moment. His eyes narrow as he sees his opportunity.

Time seems to be slowing down; I have to act! I create a small particle in the palm of my hand and approach my enemy. Victor's face is turning from fear to concern then amazement as he sees the thread that will end his life. He knows what I'm doing, and now that I've completed the final thread and ignited the construct, I can see he also understands why.

He responds with a Mana Nova thread arcing round towards my head. It will shear through my shield in seconds and remove my head in another. I stagger as my shield and mobility constructs collapse, and mere seconds later Victor's thread strikes me.

Victor surveys the work I've completed on myself. I had discovered this techniques by accident and although I hadn't known it at the time, it would be my salvation. I had used to it keep my friend at death's door while I interrogated him. The process had consumed him, leaving nothing but ash in its wake. It was a death sentence, and I have delivered it onto myself. I shudder as the Mana within me burns. It feels like fire coursing through my veins. Before my eyes, the damage to my legs heals as the magic pulses through me like wildfire.

Staggering forward, I latch onto Victor's shielded form, my Mana-soaked fists passing easily through his shield as its power is converted to sustain my regeneration. I smile brokenly as the old man's strength is added to my own. The spells that power the old man's regeneration are consumed by the fey sickness I cast upon myself. My limbs don't seem to work properly and I have pulsating waves of heat and cold passing across me. My whole body seems numb and vital at the same time. There is no pain, but I know it will come soon enough.

A bout of nausea takes me as the wave of magic passes through me. Quicker and quicker the magic surges until I feel nothing but the Mana. My head rolls back as the world spins in my vision. My fists on Victor's shoulders are the only thing keeping me standing.

With a gasp I fall to my knees, taking Victor down with me. I can see from the Mana signature on the old man's chest that he is experiencing the same as me. His powers are being drained as the parasitic Mana construct within me consumes everything available, including the old man's regenerative construct.

"You have killed us both!" Victor gasps as the realisation overtakes him. He struggles, but as his regenerative powers fail him so does his stolen youth. I can see him aging before my eyes, the years he has lived finally taking their toll on his face.

I pull the old man close, and my construct passes from me to Victor like a virus, spilling into his own chest as it recognises damaged flesh that needs repair. I have done it! I've destroyed the magic sustaining him and replaced it with my own.

Infecting him has only started the process. I now need to inflict catastrophic damage to his body—enough damage to overpower the healing process beyond its ability to repair. There is still a possibility that we could survive this, but I have already assured our destruction. It is already done, but in this moment of weakness I will do anything to take it back. I might survive this, just as Victor might. It is a faint hope, the dying wish of a weak and desperate man. It is fortunate that the decision isn't in my hands.

I glance down at the mobile phone half buried in the rubble. It is such a small object, with a single blue blinking light on its screen. It is such an insignificant thing, and I had been sure that Victor wouldn't have realised its importance. At first it had been nothing more than a backup plan. But looking into the blinking light, I now know it could never have been any other way. There was rightness to this.

Far above, so far above where I can't see it, a fighter jet is homing in on the GPS signal provided by my phone. It's going to deliver a payload that will destroy the block. I can't see it, not yet, but I know it's coming.

I tighten my grip on Victor, and smile when I finally hear a jet passing overhead and the screaming of a rocket. I don't turn to face it. Victor cries out—he can see his forthcoming death and how I had achieved it.

I wonder if it will hurt. There is no chance of survival; with our bodies incinerated the magic will increase its fury in regenerating us. Over and over our cells will die and regrow.

The explosion is about to take effect. With such catastrophic damage our bodies will absorb all available Mana in an attempt to renew our damaged cells. It will require too much power and it will consume everything in its path. As our power fails, so will the healing that is keeping us alive. Necrosis will follow as the flesh fails us and we will finally be allowed to die.

Will it hurt? I close my eyes as the inferno engulfs us. My last sight before my eyes are forever consumed in flame is of Victor. He has grasped my head and pulled me to face him.

"Why?" he howls in agony.

"Because I'm a villain, but I'm not …"

I never got the chance to finish that sentence.

The End.

ABOUT THE AUTHOR

As an avid science fiction and fantasy reader Christopher George has been immersing himself in books from a young age. In 2004 Christopher completed his Bachelor of Multimedia at Monash University and has been working as an IT professional ever since. He currently lives in Melbourne with his partner, her daughter and three cats.

For more information about the book and the series
go to
www.christophergeorgenovels.com
or like him on Facebook